The Twelve

The Twelve

A S Washington & De'Quan Foster

New Jersey
2012

De'Quan Foster dedicates this book:

In Loving Memory

of

Joe Kubert & Lazaro Quesada

Thank you for your inspiration. . .

A.S. Washington dedicates this book:

To all the lovers and writers of fantasy, superheroes and science fiction

Especially Joe Abercrombie. . .

The Coming

Aeon, The Creator and Lord of the Universe looked into the wide expanse of the cosmos remembering the exact moment when what he was exploded during a moment of intense contemplation. Twelve million millennia had passed since that moment. He spent the time naming the galaxies, planets, and stars while maintaining the mathematical balance necessary to sustain the universe. The complexity and labor of the task gave him very little time to focus on anything else; as the universe continued to expand with a constant increase of galaxies, planets, black holes, pocket dimensions, and the Parallel Universe that was the result of the energies and images that resonated from Aeon's mind.

Aeon realized that the universe might never cease expanding while he was actively using his own power, as he was tied to all the energies of the cosmos. With the creation of each new celestial body his work grew and taxed his powers, and then the universe exploded again. This second explosion was far different from the first that had given him physical form and the coming of the universe. It was a physical explosion emerging from his core. That day was the first day that the gases comingled with one another, creating small explosions of their own. Comets and asteroids burst open into the black void of the universe. Stars erupted with flame and light. Suns and moons glowed with radiance, and the universe became a moving entity, controlled only by the precise mathematics of Aeon's power.

The Creator smiled at that moment, falling more deeply in love with what his mind and body had birthed. But it came at a cost. The vast energies that gave life to the celestial bodies constantly fed off of Aeon's vastness as the universe continued to expand as he thought pass what was already there. He realized by looking into a future without his intervention; that once all of his energy was taken by the universe, it would explode again, returning him to his original form, thus destroying the beauty of the universe that he now gained pleasure from seeing and loved immensely.

With the knowledge of the future now impressed upon him, he decided that in order to preserve the universe, he would have to remove himself from the physical plane by submerging himself into a stasis sleep. The sleep would rapidly slow the growth of the universe and allow the energies to sustain themselves, rather than feed from him directly. And so he slept.

Aeon's first stasis lasted for twenty four million millennia. Aeon determined that it would be necessary for him to recharge himself for twice the amount of time that it took him to allow the universe to expand to its current depth. His plan was to create for himself a companion, who would aid him in the creation of complex life, as well as maintaining the balance of the universe while he was in stasis sleep.

Emerging from this stasis, Aeon could feel the immediate pull on his power from the universe, but it was not as violent as it had been when he drew nearer to his stasis. Though as weak as it was to him, it created a massive sonic boom of energy that returned the universal expansion to its previous speed. He knew that his long sleep had allowed him to amass enough energy to do the necessary work in creating his companion.

Aeon would call him Thutmos, which means Charm of the Sacred. Aeon spent ten million millennia molding Thutmos from the universe's energies and his own power. Aeon began to have a conversation about Thutmos's tasks and the coming of life through Aeon's hand.

"Where should we begin?" asked Aeon, his voice akin to the sound of a trillion raging storms. The sound waves that emanated from his voice cracked the surfaces of the celestial bodies, giving them their original shapes.

"We should begin at the center, where the circle passes through the celestial poles," replied Thutmos, his voice akin to a billion raging storms.

"A wise choice my son," said Aeon.

"Will you set the creation in motion?" asked Thutmos eager to see it.

"Yes," replied Aeon, waving his hand in a circular motion at the planet at the exact center of the universe. "This planet is at the core of the universe. It has no sister planet in another dimension or parallel in another universe. Merridia stands alone and will forever be known as the first planet, where the original lower beings sprang from the hand of the true and only Lord of the Universe. With your eyes being the only others to have seen the Spring of Creation, you will also be known to the ages as The Divine Witness." Thutmos looked as Aeon took the planet in one hand and pulled it out of orbit. The Creator glanced over the planet and smiled and then set his gaze upon Thutmos. "Can you see it?" asked Aeon in a soft voice.

"I do," said Thutmos and smiled. The instant he set his eyes on the planet, he could see it erupting with movement. Oceans sprang up; waterfalls surged into deep chasms of liquid, earthquakes rumbled across the entire planet; volcanoes blasted and storms raged in every corner. The violent moment gave the planet even more defined shape and separated the lands from one another as Aeon felt they should be.

"Now that you have seen the Spring of Creation, become part of it. Join in the bringing of life," said Aeon, touching his other hand to Thutmos's shoulder. "Be not afraid," he uttered hearing Thutmos's unspoken fear.

Thutmos set his hand upon the planet, and a wild scream echoed from the core of the planet. The planet shook with a wicked ferocity and then another explosion ripped from within the planet. From the center of the explosion, a being emerged about the size of Thutmos's small finger, standing seven feet tall with a mass of eight hundred pounds. His eyes glowed a startling gold and his hair matched, streaming down his back in perfect strands. He was naked, and a golden field of energy radiated around his body. Despite being recently born, he was fully grown, with striking features.

Screaming at the top of his lungs, the naked man let out a blast of energy from his mouth powerful enough to level a dozen mountains. The energy bounced off of Thutmos like a pebble against the stalk of a tree.

"A lively little god," said Aeon smiling as he looked at the feisty creature that he had just birthed within the planet Merridia. "What shall you call him?"

"I Lord?" asked Thutmos surprised that Aeon would offer him such a gift as to name the first being created on a living celestial body.

"Of course my son, it shall be your task to name all the living things that shall spring forth upon the planets throughout the universe. That shall be your task as I slumber and contemplate the purpose of life for my greatest creation to come," said Aeon motioning for him to begin.

"Then I shall call him Corvus, for he is of the core of his planet and at the very core of the universe and shall forever be tied to the fate of Merridia. There shall be no one more powerful than he who steps on Merridia save for those who are endowed by The One Who Eclipses All," said Thutmos.

"You give him great gifts my son," said Aeon smiling.

"And more my Lord if it pleases thee," said Thutmos, seeking approval before carrying on.

"Yes, my son, Prince of the Universe, let your word be as one with my own. What pleases thy heart pleases mine own," said Aeon.

"Corvus, you shall rule Merridia as its chief god. Your word shall be law and you shall raise among you a great and magnificent family of gods who shall be offered praise by Merridia's inhabitants. The people of Merridia shall be made to your liking by your hand, and by the hands of those you grant power to, as Our Father has granted power to me and I unto you with his blessing. Merridia shall serve as the seat of knowledge and a stronghold of power throughout the universe and its history shall help to shape the history of so many others. You shall wear the black and gold garb, a symbol of the deep depths of space and time and the radiant power of the everlasting stars that shall be the Suns of Merridia. Does this please you my child?" asked Thutmos.

"My lord," said Corvus bowing his head as his godly garb covered his nakedness, immediately learning and understanding the cosmos and the hierarchy therein as Thutmos spoke the truth of his existence, and the existence of all things to come.

"Go now then and continue what we have started child," said Aeon.

Corvus shot like a rocket back to Merridia and dove into the planet's surface, going through to the other side, creating a shock-wave that would set creation further into motion on the planet.

"I have faith in you that you shall see my vision through our everlasting connection and make the universe the wondrous place that it shall be where all may live in utter happiness," said Aeon without receiving a word from Thutmos and disappeared into stasis.

Thutmos knew that he was alone to govern the universe's mathematical balance in Aeon's absence. But his task now also included maintaining the balance of life throughout the universe. Thutmos knew that the Merridians had already begun to multiply on their planet, but what had escaped him was that Aeon set off over a billion other births of life across the universe. The Spring of Creation was so vast that as he marveled at Corvus's birth, he didn't notice the forces pulling at Aeon's, nor his own power for life giving energy. Part of his dilemma, was that he alone before Corvus did not understand how to give life, as it was something that only Aeon was capable of until he received the gift. Now it was squarely upon him to see that it was done to the satisfaction of his Lord.

Thousands upon thousands of years passed as life began to grow and Thutmos could only watch and marvel at its growth. Thinking of the way things sprung up so neatly in their own perfection, he thought that his own creation must have been similar in some fashion.

Thutmos kept a close watch on and even developed a friendship with Corvus. He treated him as a son and even asked his opinion upon matters that could affect the entire universe. Today however, was something that Corvus surprisingly had more first-hand knowledge on, though Thutmos should have known by his position in the universe.

"Do you find it wise to have others among you who can call themselves gods?" asked Thutmos of Corvus's brothers, consorts, and children.

"They give me comfort and a family," replied Corvus.

"Our great Lord is all the comfort I require," said Thutmos.

"Then that should be enough," said Corvus happily.

"True enough my son. Though I am most powerful among all others with the exception of one, I do not know what it is like to rule. Free will is abound for all to be just or corrupt and I simply keep the balance, setting things into motion from afar, yet no one answers to me," said Thutmos, almost melancholy.

"Then you will consult the Father?" asked Corvus curiously.

"It is only his guidance that shall give me insight," said Thutmos, vanishing abruptly from Corvus's sight.

Thutmos stretched his power across the universe to maintain its systematic movement and sat in contemplation for seven million millennia. He heard the voice of Aeon on a great many occasions, offering advice and comfort in order for him to find peace with his status as Chieftain of The Ripples of Time and Space, a new name that he had been given by The Architect of Life.

Thutmos was afraid of having all the knowledge and all the power that he possessed, he feared making companions of his own. He felt that it was Aeon's plan to do so, but he had watched planets, gods, stars, galaxies and even universal systems destroyed by feuds and wars by those closest among one another.

It will not be you my son. Thutmos heard Aeon's voice clearly in his mind and felt a tide of relief wash over him.

Thutmos had peered into the future a dozen-million times and had seen the pain that his sons and daughters would wreak about the universe. But he knew that an assurance from Aeon was unlike any assurance that he could offer to himself.

Five million more millennia passed and Aeon spoke to Thutmos from his stasis.

"You shall set in motion the coming of the governing body of the universe. Grant them the knowledge and understanding forward so that they may serve their Lord fully in giving life to the generations to come. Hold no secret from them, give them the will to act freely, teach them so that they may live as one with Me in Our Union," said Aeon with calm authority.

"It shall be as you see fit Lordship," said Thutmos.

"Have no mind to it. You are first among all my children. While there will be the coming of more, they shall have not your place in all the days of life before or after Me, and that shall be the Law of Power," said Aeon and Thutmos could feel Aeon's smile melt into his own.

"Then I shall do as instructed. I am overjoyed to be forever The Most Favored of my Lord Aeon," said Thutmos.

Twenty billions suns imploded. A trillion stars sprinkled the illuminated dust of their destruction, black holes joined together and the entire expanse of space shook violently, changing life upon many planets. Ice ages sprang up, planets once full of life became consumed with fire, baron wastelands sparkled with fresh water, and new species of life swam out of the waters and onto the land, and insects crawled from under rocks, and in some places the lowliest became gods and even some gods fell to their deaths.

From the center of the universe out from the darkest matter a few meters from Merridia, a being emerged bathed in an array of colors, which were great energies flowing through him.

Thutmos watched him grow rapidly, becoming as he was, a son of Aeon, and a brother.

"I know you," he said to Thutmos. "But who am I?" His face begged for the answer.

"You are my brother, Primsec, the First of the Second, a son of The Bringer of All," said Thutmos. Thutmos smiled having felt the happiness in Primsec's mind. Primsec wailed in jubilation and the colors that flowed through and around him burst out into the universe. Comets rippled from his energies and collided with a dozen planets, melting them to extinction.

"It is done," said Thutmos and the kaleidoscope of colors left Primsec and he was as Thutmos was.

"We must destroy in order to be?" asked Primsec.

"We do not destroy; we seek to maintain a balance. For your energies to reside in the universe it must be returned from whence it came. As you emerge from the Void of Power, others must return to it. As you are you may do no wrong. Only what must be done in the name of The Creator. Our Father," said Thutmos instructing him upon the way of things.

"Is our purpose the same?" begged Primsec.

"It is. Our purpose is to serve Aeon and the universe until that which comes after our Lord," said Thutmos.

"What came before our Lord?" Primsec begged again, his face like unto a child fresh to the world.

Thutmos smiled.

"No thing," said Thutmos as he opened his arms wide. Primsec was drawn to Thutmos. There was a pull on his being that he could not withstand. Gravity was a small needle compared to what drew him to Thutmos. When Primsec was close enough, Thutmos embraced him. Primsec folded into Thutmos and Thutmos into Primsec.

Once joined, Primsec could see everything that preceded him. He even saw Aeon teaching Thutmos about the Universe, when he was as curious as he was. Thutmos's knowledge folded into Primsec's psyche and greater power flowed to him through Thutmos. He felt filled with glory and righteousness. Primsec saw what was to come in all that existed except the coming of Aeon's greatest creation.

After two million millennia, Primsec folded from Thutmos in greater glory.

"We've done all this in that time," said Primsec as he stared into the expanse of the universe.

"As I said, as you now know. Nothing is truly destroyed in the coming of Our Union. The power of Aeon endures where all else fails," said Thutmos. "Now go and see that the Spring of Creation continues."

Primsec rocketed into the blackness of space, zipping through the centers of stars and suns, all the while catching comets in flight and throwing them in another direction. In all the years with Thutmos he had not grown up. His spirit was one of adventure and intrigue. All that existed awed him to no end, and he loved everything more than himself. From afar Thutmos gave him another name, speaking it to him like a whisper.

"You are The Everlasting Grace and The Smile of Our Union," said Thutmos pleased.

Time stretched on and Thutmos became absorbed in his duties while Primsec kept him company from afar, ever interrupting him with new ideas, throwing planets to him and asking his council on where they might go. Thutmos would smile like a parent mostly, but often he would role his eyes at him like an annoyed superior, not wanting to be troubled with trifle things.

"He is more like you than you know," said Aeon, his voice rising into space and Thutmos shuddered at his power, the force of Aeon's might overwhelming him like a great weight.

"My Lord!" said Thutmos elated to see his father. "You have been gone from my sight for too long. Quite rested you are?" said Thutmos still in awe having not felt power greater than his own for so long.

"You called for me. You should not be surprised," said Aeon looking at Thutmos inquisitively.

"Did I?" said Thutmos confused.

"If not, then who are they?" said Aeon opening his hands, revealing two stars in his hands, two nearly identical beings asleep within them.

"Surely I could not have sent them," said Thutmos, he spoke as if questioning Aeon's assertion.

Aeon smiled, "They manifested with me out of your longing." Still smiling Aeon placed the stars in the dark expanse of space. From his eyes fiery projectiles flew into the stars, igniting them, making them brighter. With a rumbling roar, the two beings sprang to life and darted from the stars.

The sound of their movement reverberated across space and time as they rocketed around with no purpose or sense of direction. In flight they grew to nearly the size of Thutmos and Primsec. Thutmos followed them with his eyes, marveling at their rapid growth and carefree nature. They were like Primsec in that regard.

"Come," said Aeon and the two darting creatures met his gaze, only a few feet from him.

"Chasm, Everdon. I know you," said Thutmos as he spoke their names.

Chasm and Everdon bowed to Thutmos.

"You are The Most Favored. Like unto a brother to us," said Chasm, her eyes narrowed investigating Thutmos. He was unfamiliar, but she knew him well.

"Yes," Everdon added.

"Will you stay with us Father?" begged Thutmos.

"You know well the answer," said Aeon gravely.

"It is your burden to shoulder as The Most Favored," said Chasm fully knowledgeable of everything in Thutmos's mind.

"Yes," said Everdon, solidifying Chasm's assertion.

Thutmos shed a tear as he looked upon Aeon.

"The Chain of Balance will come. You have sped the process along by interrupting my stasis. The others have been called by you in your longing for me. Chasm will guide you in all your contemplation and Everdon shall solidify your notions. Their bond to you is like our own. They will reside forever with you in the first quadrant. The others shall take their places as Primsec has already done. Everything is as it should be. You shall see me again during The Laying of Fire in the Home of the Souls," said Aeon.

"I know not what these things are," said Thutmos.

"You need not know. You need only do, and maintain the balance," said Aeon, "all things will be revealed as they must."

True Power

Every step could be heard booming through the massive throne room as his anger boiled over. Grinding his sword against the transparent floor hadn't produced the faintest scratch upon the surface as he had intended. Just below him, he could see the clouds over the center of Merridia turning grey. Thunder had rolled at least four times as he waited, hoping to mar the nearly indestructible surface as he paced in front of the dais that a wondrous golden throne, adorned with black and red diamonds sat upon. Looking at the throne he rolled his golden eyes and huffed in annoyance. A gust of air bounced off of the golden walls howling like the wind.

A whistling sound began as the howl of his breath dissipated and a flash of light brightened the already sunlit throne room. From within the light materialized a being adorned in white robes and a silver crown. His beard was black as night and his eyes were gold, nearly identical to the being pacing back and forth. He stood two feet taller, well over eight feet and held a white scepter in his left hand with a violet orb set at its top. The whistling began again and the orb began to glow. Without warning, a beam of energy shot toward the angry man, screaming as if in pain.

With little care and a roll of his bright eyes, he caught the beam of energy on the blade his sword and directed it back toward his black bearded attacker. The defender's red cape flapped and whipped around his legs from the force of the impact as he turned his back.

"The great Black Dawn," said the white-robed attacker, his voice deep and melodic.

"Gorgon Ray," said Black Dawn his shoulders rising slow and falling, "uncle do you seek to anger me?" Black Dawn turned slowly to the side looking over his shoulder at his uncle, twirling his sword.

"You're not nearly as good a warrior as your father, but you've improved much," said Gorgon Ray.

"At least I am punctual," said Black Dawn his voice soft as he tried to reign in his anger.

Sheathing his sword within the scabbard on his back, Black Dawn approached Gorgon Ray at a deliberate pace, anticipating another attack. Ever since he was born, his uncle had tested his combat skill without warning. The assaults were never the same. One day Gorgon Ray would attack with a sword, another day with beams of energy, and then others with his mind.

"That you are," said Gorgon Ray pulling Black Dawn into a tight embrace. "But you are not King; therefore you are accountable to he who is. His behavior is not yours to command."

Gorgon Ray smiled without parting his lips and took a step back. With his hands still on Black Dawn's shoulders he examined him from head to toe. Looking at his black armor Gorgon Ray could see a red phoenix with its wings spread from Black Dawn's waste to the front of his shoulders. His hands trailed down his black cloth covered arms down to the gold and red gauntlets covering his hands and forearms.

"These are among the most powerful weapons in all the universe," said Gorgon Ray, the expression on his face glowing with elation. "I crafted them hundreds of years before you were born, for me; when I sought to supplant my brother, your father. In those days he was arrogant and full of pride." Gorgon Ray's mind strayed as he looked off remembering the time.

"Then you met with the same fate as all those who challenge him," said Black Dawn assured.

"Not quite," said Gorgon Ray chuckling deep in his belly.

"What do you mean?" said Black Dawn interested.

"While your father is a great deal older than us all, he had not the wisdom of his age," said Gorgon Ray.

"Merridia is of his doing-," said Black Dawn.

"Yes, but not all things are as you may think," said Gorgon Ray cutting him off. "The Mother Merridia is only slave to your father's power when he is here; for as much as your Father is chieftain of all the gods and all the men and women of Merridia, he is child of The Mother." Gorgon Ray trailed off and stepped around Black Dawn toward the dais. "I too was born of The Mother Merridia, thus my power is the same as his own, but I am not able to draw from her power as he is. Thus your father has the true power of all things here. Our harmony with the mother and the gauntlets' ability to drain energy on contact is why I was able to subdue him, more or less, but only for a moment," said Gorgon Ray finishing as he began to look around and admire the beauty of the throne room.

Atop the dais on either side of the throne were two golden statues of women with intense stares clad in armor, spears in their hands thrusting at invisible enemies. Upon their heads were jeweled crowns. Hard golden locks flowed down their backs below their shoulder blades. Tunics rose just above the knee; greaves protected their shins, and on their feet they wore jeweled sandals. As ferocious as they appeared, they were as pretty as any maiden fit for a king.

Behind the throne stood a golden statue in far more glory than the warrior women and nearly three times their size. The statue wore a golden crown adorned with green and black jewels. In his right hand was a golden spear; its bladed tip wrapped around a jewel radiating a black energy that hummed as it reverberated in and out of itself. The statue's right palm was facing toward the ceiling. In its hand sat a book open at its center, the pages flapping in the wind of the humming dark mass of energy. Gorgon Ray stared into the face of gold, fixating his stark golden eyes on the emptiness of the black jeweled eyes set into the head of the statue. A smirk lined Gorgon Ray's face as he turned and surveyed the rest of the room.

Circling, he saw at least six statues, and between their feet were thrones of varying colors adorned with an array of jewels. Gorgon Ray stared at the likeness of himself and scoffed at it. Looking over his shoulder at Black Dawn he spoke.

"You'd think that with all of your father's power, he'd at least be able to nail down a proper representation of me," said Gorgon Ray nearly incredulous.

"Former glories are the hardest to forget," said Black Dawn bored.

"You are still young," said Gorgon Ray laughing as he spoke, "I can see why you have little care of things that once were. They are the very things that make us what we are."

"And what exactly is that?" said Black Dawn wondering.

"Gods," said Gorgon Ray flatly.

"Please spare me another lecture, I am fully aware of what I am," said Black Dawn, his anger again at a near boiling point.

"Then why are you always so swift to action," said Gorgon Ray as he strode toward him in a flash. Grabbing Black Dawn's breast plate, he pulled him in closer to him. "Know this then boy," began Gorgon Ray sharply, "time is of no consequence to you," shaking him and releasing him at once he said, "come to know patience."

"Heed the words of your uncle my son, for he speaks the truth," said a booming voice.

Black Dawn and Gorgon Ray turned toward the statue behind the throne, the black eyes glowing. After a few seconds a flash of golden lightning crackled from every direction and Corvus appeared as if he were being drawn into existence.

"My king," said Gorgon Ray and Black Dawn together, falling to one knee and bowing their heads. The two rose quickly and Black Dawn approached Corvus and embraced him with love, his head nestled into his father's broad chest. Corvus studied Black Dawn for a moment but not as long as Gorgon Ray had. Tilting his head, his eyes gave away that he had a thought burning in his mind, but he did not speak. He turned slowly and strolled atop the dais and took his seat upon the throne.

"Sci-," said Black Dawn beginning to speak, swiftly cut off.

"I am fully aware of her actions," said Corvus dismissively.

"Then you plan to punish her," said Black Dawn eager to know.

"No," said Corvus flatly.

Gorgon Ray could see Black Dawn's fist tightening in an intense fit of anger. He was sure his teeth were clinched, eyes narrowed in anger with his father. He came to stand at Black Dawn's side, resting a hand on his shoulder.

"Brother. Your son's concerns are well warranted," said Gorgon Ray.

"Be that as it may, Scicremeon is a fine warrior and I'll not have her put to death for killing another warrior-," said Corvus with an air of finality in his voice that usually went unchallenged.

"You would have her bring war?" said Black Dawn cutting Corvus off, his tone rising. When Corvus did not answer he said, "It wouldn't be the first time."

"That war was very short lived," said Corvus dismissively.

"Indeed," said Gorgon Ray chuckling.

"Will there be no punishment levied at all for her deeds?" asked Black Dawn with a wanting look.

"He accepted her challenge," said Corvus rising from the throne and taking the book from the hand of the great statue behind him. "Do you know what this is my dear boy?" Corvus inclined his head toward Black Dawn lifting the book slightly.

"Of course I do," said Black Dawn.

"You may want to give it greater attention one day than simply knowing what it is," said Corvus, lifting his hand over the book as he sat back down. The pages began to turn quickly, a soft flapping noise entering the room as each page landed against another. When the pages finally stopped turning Corvus said, "Ah hah," and then smiled a great big smile, pearly white teeth showing. "This short passage reads," said Corvus and the voice of a woman filled the room.

Like his father Hishron Blackbeard before him, Aygron Stormblade was a fierce warrior and sought to prove himself against other skilled warriors. With the teachings and guidance of his father he mastered the shield, sword, the mace, and the hammer. Along with his mastery of weapons, Aygron studied well fighting without weapons. While still a boy he would challenge men twice his size in contests of strength besting them at every turn.

By his sixteenth birthday, Aygron enlisted in the Merridian Brigade, serving his father who was captain. Tales of Aygron's might spread throughout all of Merridia. Before others could come to challenge him, he would stop in every village and every city challenging the greatest warriors among them. By his twenty-first birthday no one in all the lands of Merridia would even seek to challenge Aygron and most would cower before him, long before a blade was ever drawn.

Aygron became captain thirty years later when his father fell in battle. He led the brigade on twenty successful campaigns against the invading Chalendorans and their powerful magicians. While the power of the Chalendorans were great, Aygron was able to overcome them with the Black Moon Gems that he had found after falling from the great mountain Zar'dos, the highest peak in all of Merridia. Soon after his final victory over the Chalendorans, the Black Moon Gems returned to the place from whence they came.

Black Dawn looked at the statue behind him and stared into its black jeweled eyes. Looking down, he saw his father studying him with a smirk being forced back by pursed lips. Black Dawn narrowed his eyes and turned to Gorgon Ray who had already been staring deep into the side of his face as if he wanted to eat him, but Gorgon Ray said nothing. The voice continued to speak.

Ten years had passed since the Chalendorans were pushed back and Aygron eventually settled down in his home village, taking for himself a beautiful wife, Lapinia. The two lived in happiness for sixty years and had together three children, all who were great men that fell in glorious battles to a new Chalendoran army. With the death of all his children Aygron took up the sword to avenge the death of his children and quell the invasion of his enemies once again. However, before he departed he was finally challenged for the first time by a hooded warrior. Still young and spritely, Aygron took the challenge; confident in his ability to prevail victorious as he had done hundreds of times. While Aygron fought his shrouded adversary he was cut down from behind by a Chalendoran magician who appeared from nowhere. The killer's name is unknown, but has since been known as the Slayer of the Stormblade.

A great many saw the treachery of the hooded warrior and tried desperately to slay him for his deception. With the aid of the magician, the hooded challenger was able to escape unharmed.

The funeral that was held for Aygron Stormblade was wondrous indeed. It was attended by every member of the Merridian Brigade, and all across Merridia who had ever heard the name Aygron; that was able to make the journey. Even King Chale of Chalendor attended the funeral, paying his final respects to the one Merridian who saw that his conquest of Merridia never came to fruition. With the death of Aygron, Chale made a pact with Lapinia. The agreement was that for as long as he lived no Chalendoran would ever set foot on Merridia and the tribes of the Old Planet would live in peace with Chalendor as a friend.

Not long after Aygron was laid to rest in the center of Zar'dos, Lapinia gave birth to a daughter, Scicremeon. Scicremeon grew up happy even without knowing her father. For many years she found comfort in her mother and the members of her village. But when she turned eleven, she found that a void had opened in her heart and she wanted to know of her father. Lapinia sought for as long as she could to shield Scicremeon from the knowledge of her father's death, though eventually she relented. With the knowledge embedded in her mind Scicremeon sought revenge and sought to master every weapon known in Merridia, so that one day her father's killer would fall upon her blade. Since then, she has been driven only by blood, challenging all she meets in fair combat to test her metal so that she might know she is ready, or fall in weakness, unfulfilled. When King Chale finally sees the grave, she will venture on to Chalendor to seek the Slayer of the Stormblade. There she believes she may find the Slayer and the hooded man.

Corvus stared at his son with his black eyes and they glistened like the moon. When a luminous glare flashed across his eyes, the great book floated back to its resting place in the palm of the statue's hand. Corvus stood and then strolled down the dais a few feet from Black Dawn and looked down. He peered through the shiny translucent floor, past the clouds and onto the green earth of Merridia.

"You have won a great many victories against some of the most powerful foes that we have ever faced. Yet, in the lives of the mortals of Merridia you have taken little interest. Swift judgment may be exact, but it is not always the most apt course of action," said Corvus looking up again at Black Dawn.

"Could you have stopped the man from killing Aygron?" asked Black Dawn almost lamenting the loss.

"Of course," said Corvus quite straightforward.

"Then why didn't you?" asked Black Dawn.

"I had already assisted Aygron once," said Corvus emphatically.

"The Black Moon Gems," said Black Dawn motioning a hand in the direction of the glowing eyes of the statue.

"Yes," said Corvus looking at Black Dawn inquisitively.

"So you mettle in the affairs of mortals when you see fit and other times you leave them to die at the hands of a coward," said Black Dawn as if accusing Corvus of the murder himself.

"Is it not my right as Chieftain of the Gods to do as I see fit," said Corvus his voice booming in the hall like a roll of thunder.

"Do not question it," said Gorgon Ray to Black Dawn. His eyes glimmered as if he hoped to save Black Dawn from a terrible punishment.

"Have no mind to it uncle," said Black Dawn assuring his uncle that his intentions were not to challenge his father's rule; "but if he would mettle then why would we be stopped to mettle when the actions of but one could bring forth great calamity to our home." Black Dawn raised his eyebrows to his uncle for an answer and when none came he continued to speak. "You have seen what I have seen for you can see further than even I. Scicremeon must be stopped," said Black Dawn loudly.

"Gorgon Ray has spoken to you of my true power. He is a master maker, but even he could not construct a device powerful enough to supplant me, not here. Have comfort in knowing that while I am here there will be none powerful enough to stay my hand," said Corvus with great pride.

With a resounding boom and crackle of lightning, Corvus was gone, leaving Gorgon Ray and Black Dawn together again in the throne room.

"He has spoken his words," said Gorgon Ray. "Be obedient and take heed to them."

"I think my father's heart is softer than he puts on," said Black Dawn with a glimmer in his eyes.

"How so?" asked Gorgon Ray.

"You're still alive," said Black Dawn with a sneer. "But...," Black Dawn took a step back, "maybe not for long," As the words left his mouth he turned the palm of his hand toward Gorgon Ray and a blaze of black energy with red cords of light exploded out and smashed into Gorgon Ray's chest sending him hurling into the large double doors opposite the throne.

"Like father like son," said Gorgon Ray.

"Really," said Black Dawn squinting one eye taunting his uncle.

"Yes, sneak attackers," said Gorgon Ray.

Quickly standing, feeling little pain from the blow, Gorgon Ray's scepter transformed into a trident as he rocketed toward Black Dawn, his teeth grinding in a wild grimace. Black Dawn stood calm with a toothless smile on his face waiting for the impact.

God...Man...It Makes No Difference

The village square was littered with dozens of people paying very little attention to what was going on outside their field of vision. That's how it was in Marside, the largest village on the eastern bank of Hormand's Rock. While everyone liked to put off that they were nothing more than farmers to anyone not from Marside, most people knew better. No one snuck up on anyone in Marside, because almost everyone was a warrior and it was considered spineless. In Marside, being called spineless could get you killed by your best friend. Only those too old or too small to carry a sword didn't call themselves warriors. All others knew it was wise to pick up a sword, and if one wasn't available, a stick or a rock large enough to crack a man's skull. If a challenge didn't happen by midday, it was sure to happen by sunset before most turned in. No one stayed out late in Marside, no one but those looking for trouble.

The grass throughout the village was a bright green and the wind always blew westward coming in from the Blue Sea. Across the shore men fished while others lied on the beach, eyes to one of the three suns of Merridia. Always in the light of the three suns made the people of Marside a shade darker than all others on Merridia, who usually only saw one sun during the daytime. The villagers of Marside had planted hundreds of thousands of trees around the base of Hormand's Rock to keep as much sunlight out as possible.

There were only eight hours of nightfall in Marside and most spent them sleeping. During the day they would train hard and work the fields to keep strong. Even when war wasn't brewing, the villagers of Marside kept prepared for it. The Chalendorans had come far too often in the past for them to ever let their guard down. With that in mind, they smiled at the three suns for making them have to be harder than most. For it was said by all the villagers of Marside that; *"weak people don't belong here, and if a sword don't kill you, the heat surely will."*

The market was full of people buying meat and spices. A woman leaned on the side of a tavern clad in thin dusty clothes. She had obviously been working the fields. Dirt covered her from the tips of her fingers to her elbows, and the knees of her pants were spotted with green and brown from kneeling all day. Around her waist was a flimsy looking belt holding up a sword that looked made for the hands of a much larger man. The weight of the sword pulled one side of the belt below her hip, but it didn't seem to bother her. She lifted a large mug up to her lips and sucked down a gulp of sweet ale.

"Ah," she said as the bubbling liquid ran down her gullet and into her belly. She slapped her belly pleased and ran her hands through her bright auburn hair.

"Another one Scicremeon?" said a boy with a girl's voice.

"You read my mind Aton," said Scicremeon her voice sounding muggy.

Scicremeon licked her chapped lips and spit out a heavy glob of saliva. The saliva fizzled out of existence when it hit the grassy floor, hot from the touch of the suns.

"I don't know who pissed the gods off to make them curse us like this," said Scicremeon yelling toward Aton who was filling another mug.

"Can't argue with the gods," said Aton running toward Scicremeon with a large mug, twice the length of his scrawny hand. His body looked half starved, teaming with sweat, as he wiped his forehead with the bottom of his sleeveless shirt.

"Well I'll curse them just the same for all the heat they've wrought upon us. I mean this is ridiculous," said Scicremeon as she rustled Aton's black locks after taking the mug from his hand. She handed him three small gold coins.

"It's just one," said Aton.

"Take it," said Scicremeon with a mean grimace. "You're one of the few people I happen to like."

"Thanks, mother will be pleased," said Aton glossing over the extra gold and then stuffed them into his pocket.

"I'll have to beef you up if you're ever to take to the road with me," said Scicremeon.

"I know I'm quite the runt, not even a quarter of a real man of Marside," said Aton with a discouraged curl of his lips.

"In due time you'll be as grand as Aygron ever was," said Scicremeon.

"It's the dream of all men," said Aton happily.

"And women in my case," said Scicremeon taking a swig of ale. "Run along now, trouble seems to be brewing," said Scicremeon turning her mug up and pouring all the ale down her throat as fast as she could, taking care not to spill what was left.

Aton turned to see a hulking figure walking toward them swinging an axe in front of him from side to side. His right eye was missing and a long scar lined his face from the top of his head just below his lips, where his eye should have been. He was shirtless, sweat cruising down his chest, and his great big belly bounced up and down as he made his way to the market. His pants were made of leather and Scicremeon wondered to herself why he would wear them in the blazing heat of Marside.

"Ale," said the hulking man in a deep gargling voice as he approached the tavern, resting the shaft of his axe over his shoulder.

"Coming right up," said Aton sprinting toward the tavern half in fear and half in service to the request.

It took the big bulk of a man another two minutes to close the distance from where he was to stand in front of Scicremeon. He eyed her with a lustful stare, grinning wide, the four center teeth missing from his smile. Scicremeon could smell salted meat on his breath as he grunted a laugh looking at her up and down, eying her as if he would eat her alive at any moment.

"Can I help you friend," said Scicremeon feeling that he had invaded her space. She had already positioned her feet to be ready to defend if he decided to swing his axe.

"Not unless you're supplying ale or know where I can find the great warrior Scicremeon. Everywhere I have gone I have heard of his feats," said the mass of man, breathing hot meaty breath in Scicremeon's face.

"The little one there is making your ale and I'm Scicremeon," said Scicremeon dropping her mug and letting her hand dangle next to the pommel of her sword.

"Ha ha ha," said the man stretching out the last huff of his laugh. The very sound of his laugh was an insult.

"What is funny?" said Scicremeon staying her anger.

"If you're Scicremeon, then I am Corvus himself," said the hulking man doubling over in laughter.

Aton strode up along the side of the man slowly, his body quivering with fear. He had learned long ago that fat strangers with axes that weren't from his village couldn't be trusted. Especially when the first thing they wanted was ale and the name of the most feared warrior in all of Marside was on their tongue.

"Your ale sir," said Aton holding up the cup shaking. A little of the ale spilled over the top.

"Ah!" said the man happily hoisting the cup in the air and tipping it over. The wooden mug never made it to his lips, but the ale splashed past his tongue and down into his gut. Aton was sure that more hand landed in his curly brown beard than the hole in his face.

"That'll be one gold coin," said Aton sticking out his palm.

"The Great Gustain does not pay for ale boy," said Gustain and backhanded Aton across the cheek with a closed fist.

Aton fell back, legs in the air as Gustain's blow lifted him from his feet.

"Now where is Scicremeon, I've come to test his metal," said Gustain removing the axe from his shoulder. He looked around the village square and didn't see anyone approaching. He'd thought that his striking of the boy would garner the attention of his intended target, but none moved. Most of the onlookers who had begun to pay him any mind simply rolled their eyes and shook their heads *no* in annoyance. Soon their attention was turned back to whatever they were doing before. Someone being slapped wasn't enough to earn their undivided attention. Not in Marside.

"I told you, I am right here friend," said Scicremeon removing her sword from her belt.

"No woman could be the greatest warrior this side of Hormand's Rock," said Gustain still amused at the thought.

"Sorry to disappoint you, but-," said Scicremeon and then she heard his annoying laugh again.

"This will be the shortest fight of my life," said Gustain crouching.

"That I can be sure of," said Scicremeon mockingly.

"I'll let you take the first swing," said Gustain feinting.

"You sure, my name alone should warn you otherwise," said Scicremeon.

"Prove your reputation girl," said Gustain feinting again.

"Sure," said Scicremeon feinting with her sword and then drawing it back.

Gustain swung at her head with surprising speed but wasn't quick enough to catch a reeling Scicremeon. She took her own stance, her sword over her head while her other hand was extended directly in front of her, palm facing up. With her fingers she motioned for Gustain to come closer and he quickly obliged her. Raising his axe over his head, he swung with all his might.

He laughed as he swung, but missed, jamming his axe into the dry ground as Scicremeon sidestepped. With the tip of her boots she kicked him in the fruits and he wrenched in pain.

"Won't last very long with that technique," said Scicremeon as she tapped him on the butt with the blade of her sword.

"I'm just warming up," said Gustain yanking his axe from the ground.

Again and again he swung missing wildly. Scicremeon got a laugh out of watching his belly move and she taunted him, rubbing her flat gut as he missed and missed. If she were a lesser warrior she knew he might pose more of a danger. But his bulk was not his friend, it slowed him down. She could see the blows coming before he grunted his swings.

Finally when she grew bored with the exercise, she caught his axe by the shaft with the blade of her sword and then elbowed Gustain in the throat. He reeled from the blow, gurgling as he tried to catch his breath, but it was too late. Scicremeon's sword plucked his left eye from his head and his mouth flew open in surprise. Gustain reached for his eye and with a mighty thrust, the tip of Scicremeon's sword stuck out the back of his neck, and the lids of his missing eyes went wide as his mouth gaped open.

Life had only left him for a few moments as Scicremeon held his body up and then yanked her sword from his throat. Gustain collapsed in a heap, warm blood running into the grass below her feet. Slowly under the heat of the suns his blood boiled, making the puddle under his big neck bubble as he bled out.

Aton's eyes were wide with fear. The palms of his hands were covered in dirt as he stared at the blood pouring from Gustain's throat. Gustain's eyelids were open, a petrified look still on his face as his mouth hung open, his tongue sticking out to one side. Aton thought the man was still alive stalking him, even without his eyes, but he didn't a move a muscle. He heard footsteps and he scrambled to his feet as fast as he could, brushing grass and dirt from his shirt as he balled up his fists in anticipation of a strike. Aton recoiled when he felt two hands grasp his shoulders from behind. Twisting, he stumbled and nearly fell but felt a jolt as he was yanked by the collar of his shirt.

Hot breath with the hard smell of ale danced all over his face and he cringed from the smell of beer and meat, but mostly because he was afraid. People in Marside who let their collars be twisted inside a balled fist were punched in the eye soon after. He closed his right eye, as it was closer to the free hand of whoever had him by the collar and they were sure to strike him. For a moment he waited. No punch came and he felt his collar loosen and fell back onto his heels.

"You had better toughen up if you expect to live long," said Scicremeon.

"I thought he was going to kill you," said Aton in his girly boy voice.

"Ha! Not that miserable oaf," said Scicremeon laughing.

Aton looked her over, impressed. She had barely broken a sweat and was already rummaging through Gustain's pockets. Scicremeon patted him down, but didn't find anything in his pockets and then pushed him over onto his back.

"Here you are," said Scicremeon cutting a small purse from his belt.

Shaking the bag of coins in her hand, she marveled at the weight. The bag had seemed a lot smaller to her when she looked at it, but the coins inside were folding around the palm of her hand.

"What did he owe you?" said Scicremeon.

"Just one," said Aton knowing better than to ask for more than his share.

"There, nine," said Scicremeon shaking the coins into the boy's hands.

"All this," said Aton shocked.

"You took a good lick," said Scicremeon rubbing the side of Aton's face where Gustain's good nature had introduced itself. "Surprised you didn't cry like a girl," she said rustling his hair.

"I'd be laughed out of Marside," said Aton smiling for the first time.

"Do yourself a favor and don't die in this wretched valley," said Scicremeon.

"Why not, this is home," said Aton curious.

"No one will care," said Scicremeon bending down over Gustain's body and wiping her hands over his eyelids to close them, after stuffing the eye she cut out back in the socket.

The fat man looked peaceful with his eyes closed, almost jolly. She glossed over his face for a long moment. He wasn't as ugly with his mouth closed and he didn't seem so stupid to her now that he couldn't speak. Aton looked at her dumbfound, because it seemed that she had pity for him. What he did notice was that she was right about not dying there in Marside. No one had even flinched at the commotion and Gustain was dead long before the fight was interesting enough for anyone to take notice. Scicremeon had killed enough men for any sane man in Marside to want to test his metal against her. Only a fool would try his hand with her and take her lightly.

"Wouldn't they bury you," said Aton as he watched over everyone going about their business as if a man hadn't just fallen dead.

"Me? Ha! They'd spit on me and sing songs of praise to the gods," said Scicremeon standing up and slapping her hands cleans.

"Huh," said Aton stumped.

"Men don't like losing to women," said Scicremeon.

"I think you're grand," said Aton still in awe.

"How about you grab his other leg and help me drag him to the river," said Scicremeon.

"Sure," said Aton scurrying to Gustain's feet.

Scicremeon stuffed the purse into her shirt and exhaled feeling miserable that she had to lug Gustain a half mile. She stood there looking at Aton for a moment, as he crouched over Gustain, his arms relaxed on his knees waiting patiently. She shook her head as a feeling of adoration washed over her. Half smiling, she rolled her eyes at herself and grabbed Gustain's right leg.

"You've got the left," said Scicremeon.

Aton looked at her eager, but his eyes betrayed his true thoughts as he curled his lips knowing a tall task was ahead of him. He huffed out a gust of air as Scicremeon had and with all his might, grabbed Gustain's left leg. Hefting it, he tucked the leg into the fold of his arm and pressed it against his hip and leaned back as Scicremeon had. As they began moving, the leg didn't seem as heavy as it originally had. He watched Scicremeon whistle a tune as she strode backward, the exertion seeming effortless though her brow held a thin sheen of sweat. Thinking that she whistled to keep her mind off the pain that began to creep through his arm, that she must have felt as well; Aton began to hum a song his mother used to sing to him when he was a baby.

"A fine tune that is," said Scicremeon looking at him out the corner of her eye.

Aton just nodded, not wanting to break his focus.

"Tomorrow I'll teach you to fight," said Scicremeon.

"I'd like that," said Aton.

"You need it," said Scicremeon wrinkling her face in a way that told Aton she wasn't looking forward to it.

He was sure he'd break after a few minutes, as sure as he was ready to drop the leg from his grasp. In the distance he could hear the river running, but wasn't quite sure how far it was. From the feeling in his arm he guessed it would take him an eternity to make it there. Gustain's calf had begun to stick to his forearm and sweat was running into his eyes. The suns didn't help as they grew further away from the protection of the trees into an open valley that began to incline downward toward the beach. Sand upon his feet, even as hot as it was, was a welcomed sign, but cold water still seemed far off.

"Just a little further," said Scicremeon, her breath sounding labored.

"Ok," said Aton sounding like he was ready to drop the leg at any second.

"I'll send you down the river with him if you even think about letting go of that leg," said Scicremeon giving the boy a sharp look.

His eyes nearly popped out his head but he grinded his teeth together and screamed with his mouth closed. He sounded like a large beast though he was barely bigger than most girls his age.

After another twenty feet Scicremeon dropped Gustain's leg and said, "There."

Aton let the other leg go and tumbled back in exhaustion.

"You passed the first test," said Scicremeon nodding her head yes.

"Test?" said Aton lost.

"You didn't give up," said Scicremeon extending her hand and pulling Aton to his feet. "Now roll him."

Aton dusted the sand off his backside and dug his feet into the sand. With his arms extended he pushed Gustain's arm across his body and began to push with all his might. When the fat man didn't budge, he turned his back and leaned into him, digging his heels into the sand. For a few minutes he pushed and huffed with no progress and then suddenly the fat man began to roll. Aton sped up his feet and pushed and pushed until he felt water hit his knees and ran in the opposite direction. Turning around he saw the body floating belly up. Two of the suns began to drift out of sight and his mood quickly changed.

He had been impressed with his feat of endurance, but soon felt for the dead man. As much as he was a warrior, he wasn't much different from the other men who paraded around Marside sticking their chests out. He knew that far more than a handful of them had found their end at the hands of Scicremeon. It amazed him to think that such a small woman could prove so dangerous to fighters as much as three times her size.

Aton studied her frame realizing that as much as she seemed to tower above him, she was shorter than six feet tall. Her hair was long, auburn, colored like the day changing into the night sky, tied at the back of her head in a ponytail. A few loose strands of her hair traced the sides of her face and he finally realized just how beautiful she was. Scicremeon's face was the color of the pale sand and didn't have a single blemish. Her eyes were a near crystal blue and her lips always seemed glossy, no matter how hot the weather would get. He then remembered that she would always dip her hand into a jar tucked into her coin purse and spread it across her lips just before making a loud puckering sound.

"How did you become so good with a blade?" asked Aton curious and half scared.

"I had to," said Scicremeon looking at Aton quizzically.

"For what?" said Aton unsatisfied.

"I live in Marside," said Scicremeon in a matter of fact manner that made Aton cringe.

"Is that all?" he asked pressing harder for information, his eyes wanting.

"Why are you all interested in me all of a sudden?" said Scicremeon scowling her inquisition of his interest.

"I'm sorry," said Aton looking at his feet defeated.

"Don't apologize," said Scicremeon softening her scowl.

Aton looked at her squinting one eye, Scicremeon's head shielding the rest of the bright light from his face as she had come to stand over him, her hands on her hips.

"Here's the deal," said Scicremeon extending her right hand that Aton took a bit reluctantly. Pulling him up she said, "You learn how to fight properly and I'll answer three of your most burning questions, deal?" A stern stare appeared on Scicremeon's face and she titled her head to one side and then the other observing Aton. She noticed that he hadn't flinched but just glared at her blue eyes as if he wanted to pull her in to him. Shaking his hand she barely heard him.

"Deal," said Aton and shook her hand tightening his grip.

"Now that that's settled, let's find some food and get you to your mother," said Scicremeon, a smile wrinkling her face.

Aton smiled and followed a few strides behind her. He wondered what he had gotten himself into, but figured if Scicremeon was going to teach him to fight; he'd eventually be able to handle himself well enough to survive until he was a man. The prospect of being batted around the market didn't suit him very well. Gustain hadn't been the first beast of a man to put the back of their fist to his face. Now that he thought about it, he'd been smacked around one too many times. Aside from the blacksmith and the butcher, ale was the only reason outside of killing that made men come to the market. When his brother offered for him to help out, he thought he'd be friend to many. It turned out that only Scicremeon cared for the scrawny boy who poured the drinks. Even his brother went off to test his metal against men of note. What came of him, Aton never found out, though he heard stories of his brother's demise.

Half the way back to the market, the last sun of Merridia had nearly set and the Black Moon began to creep into view, casting its dark light onto Marside. Both Scicremeon and Aton looked up marveling at the massive orb, nearly twice the size of Merridia herself.

"We ought to speed up a bit," said Scicremeon extending her hand behind her for Aton to grab hold of.

"Wouldn't it be faster if we ran?" said Aton growing fearful.

"You'd never manage to keep up," said Scicremeon exasperated.

"I helped you carry the fat man," said Aton abruptly not wanting to be seen as helpless.

"Huh, I did most of the work. . .and it was a test anyway," said Scicremeon almost chuckling and hunching her shoulders.

"What kind of warrior am I supposed to become if I can't carry my on weight," said Aton harshly.

"Hope you find your way home," said Scicremeon as she began to run.

She was faster than he thought anyone should be and wailed in dread as the thought of being left behind washed over him. He'd heard stories about the bad things that happened in the dark.

"Wait!" he bellowed and Scicremeon laughed at the top of her lungs as she turned backpedaling, waving her hands for him to come on, almost playfully.

"I said keep up," she yelled back at him.

Then suddenly a loud boom sounded off in the distance above them, about a hundred yards ahead of their position. As they looked up, they could see something falling from the sky and Aton thought it was moving ten times faster than Scicremeon had been running. Above the falling figure where the boom originated, a circle of wind pushed the clouds away from the center of the sound.

The object fell faster and faster until a louder boom reverberated in their ears and a wave of energy blew out in all directions. Again it was just air, but Aton and Scicremeon nearly lost their footing as the wave swept over them.

"What is it?" said Aton.

"Probably a rock of fire," said Scicremeon.

The two of them approached the place where the object landed slowly, Aton behind Scicremeon looking around her arm. She had to nudge him every few seconds because he would step on the back of her heels.

After what seemed like an eternity, they came to where the object had fallen, dust still skirting around the crater that the falling object created. Scicremeon focused her eyes and in the center, she saw a man shrouded in a cloak with a hood covering his face. Instinctively Scicremeon drew her sword and pressed herself against Aton, making sure that he was firmly behind her.

"You are quite the caretaker, for a ruthless killer," said a mellow voice filled with arrogance.

The voice sounded like music to Aton and Scicremeon.

"And you look like the man from my nightmares," said Scicremeon glaring at him.

"Revenge is sweetest when it has not been tasted," said the man, his arrogant song-voice filling the air again. "You'll find the flavor to be quite bitter and unfulfilling."

"I'll be the judge of that when I've had my fill," said Scicremeon wrapping two hands around her sword.

"Always so eager to prove yourself," he said as he lifted a hand with his palm facing Scicremeon. He waved his hand from left to right and the mist of dirt and grass floating in the air around him dropped to the ground.

"I don't know who you are, so I have no need to prove anything. You know well my name obviously," said Scicremeon flattering herself.

"And you know well mine," he said, his voice growing deep and echoing through the valley as he stepped out of the crater, standing five inches over six feet.

"Sorry, it escapes me at the moment," said Scicremeon sniggering with every word.

Without warning, the man zipped toward her, his speed un-natural. Scicremeon barely had time to react when his sword col-lided with her own. The impact of the blow pried Aton's hands from the back of her shirt and sent him flying thirty feet in the air. Scicremeon pitched hard into the ground, her right shoulder slam-ming down violently.

Turning on her stomach Scicremeon watched in horror as Aton's arms and legs flailed in the air hoping to catch hold of any-thing that would ease his fall. More dread dressed Scicremeon's face when the man came to stand under Aton with his sword pointed toward the boy. Scicremeon stood quickly and dashed toward him, running faster than before. Aton took a moment to marvel at her, but quickly remembered the awful feeling of falling that already had a hold of him.

The man plunged his sword into the earth and with a short blow of breath the sword began to barrel toward Scicremeon. Aton screamed, fearful for himself, but his heart poured out more for Scicremeon. He wished there was more he could do, but in a few seconds, he'd be on the ground with a broken bone or two.

Twisting his hands upward under Aton, a clear substance floated from his hands forming a bubble. When it touched Aton, it wrapped itself around him, and left him floating, suspended in the air.

"What the…," said Aton punching the surface of the clear substance unable to make a dent. As soft as it looked, it was solid and immovable. "Watch out," he screamed to Scicremeon as he watched the sword ripping through the ground as it made its way toward her.

Scicremeon kept running with all of her speed, eying the sword as she saw the ground splitting apart in its wake. A mere ten feet away from the sword she screamed raising her sword over her shoulder. Just a foot away, soon to be torn in half, she shifted to one side and knocked the sword at the hilt sending it careening the opposite way.

Spinning around she was charging again toward her second enemy of the day, her sword at the ready, the blade's tip pointing forward. She cast her vision above her for a moment seeing Aton wrapped inside of what looked like a bubble of liquid. She could see his mouth moving, but couldn't hear a word. Her mouth folded harder in anger, her cheeks pressing her eyes closed from the bottom as her brow fell onto the top of her eyelids.

To her left she could hear something spinning, the same sound her sword made when she twirled it too hard. Yet, she paid it no mind and kept her eyes set on her mark. A few yards separated them and she swore that she could see his teeth under his shroud twisting into a large grin. *Now* she thought to herself when she was close enough and swung her sword.

Clank. It was the only sound she heard before she felt the jolt of pain shoot through her arm assailing her muscles as she forced herself to keep pressing against his sword; the weapon having made its way back just as she arrived. Her hands gripped tighter and tighter as she pressed against his sword with her own. She began to sweat profusely from the effort while he stood there holding his sword with one hand, seemingly with no effort. The idea that he didn't have to try hard bothered her.

For what seemed like minutes they stood there, Scicremeon pressing hard while the shrouded man stood calm as a statue. Intensely curious she looked at his sword averting her attention for a moment. As a child in Marside she had been told that a lot could be told about a person from their sword. The blade was black and hummed without ever ceasing and around its sharp edges was a glowing light that was dark as the Black Moon. In the pommel of the sword sat a jewel as red as blood and just above the hilt was another jewel as red as the other.

"Who are you?" she asked.

"Your worst nightmare," he said mocking her.

"Not scared."

"What if I told you that I am a god?"

"God...man....it makes no difference."

"Is that fact?" he said with the first hint of feeling in his voice.

"I'd sooner kill a god than I would my worst enemy."

"Wouldn't that be a sight?" he said letting out a haughty laugh.

"Everyone will fall before me until I have my revenge."

Scicremeon's eyes welled in anger and two tears rolled down her face as her emotions roared inside of her. In her mind she saw Aton trapped in the bubble again and grew angrier. Her body grew hot from the inside and the hairs on her arm stood up. Her blue eyes grew a slightly darker shade. The heat in her body drew to the center of her chest. The shrouded swordsman turned his head slightly to one side.

"So you are special," said the shrouded man sounding enthused.

"Very," said Scicremeon. With a loud scream the heat that had risen to Scicremeon's chest shot out in a rush of hot blue flame. When the flame struck her enemy, Scicremeon slid back five feet, her chest heaving up and down as sweat poured all over her. All she could see in front of her was seared grass and a cloud of dust. The man was shielded from her view but she was sure he was dead. No one had ever survived.

Her arms felt heavy from holding her sword and she allowed the tip to fall to the ground. Leaning on the pommel, she allowed herself to relax, breathing deeply, while still trying to peer through the dust of her destruction. Grabbing the hilt with her fingers facing forward, Scicremeon dropped to one knee and wiped her head with her forearm. *Aton* she thought and quickly ran through the mist of dirt. He was still floating in the ball still unharmed, but looked grim. His eyes were wide as he turned in a circle searching the area. Scicremeon looked at him and mouthed, *its ok*, hoping Aton could read her lips. When he stopped turning he stared deep into her eyes. Scicremeon nearly recoiled from the harsh stare.

"He's not dead," said Aton. She couldn't hear him, but the weight of the soundless words echoed in her ears and her body tensed. Aton's eyes went wider just over her shoulder.

Scicremeon turned swinging her sword finding only air. As her fist hit her shoulder she felt a hand close in around her neck and squeeze. Her gasp turned into choking and she felt her feet leave the ground.

Pain shot up every inch of her being as her shoulders crashed into the ground two feet deep. Tears rolled into her hair as she lay on her back suffocating, the hand still closed around her neck. The sword she wielded had left her grasp on impact. *My revenge...* but her thought trailed off and her eyes slowly began to close as she felt herself falter. There was a feeling of finality in the air and the confidence she had had abandoned her. Through the narrow slit in her eyes she saw the whitest set of teeth she had ever seen gnashing in a ferocious grimace. *Kill me and be done with it*, she thought. She'd never been one for slow death and torture. Misery was reserved only for her revenge. Today the shrouded man had bested her. *In what world could I have killed the man that killed Aygron Stormblade?* A wave of tears flowed from her eyes as she accepted defeat. Then she heard the same voice of arrogance that had taunted her, but this time there was a measure of sympathy filtering through the haughty musical. And then the voice changed all together to something of a song with a deep rumble, greater than any she had heard.

"I am not a man," the voice said.

Scicremeon felt his hand leave her neck and her lungs fill as she drew in breath. She sat up slowly on her haunches and pulled her sword from the ground. Something occurred to her then.

"Can you read my mind?" said Scicremeon.

"That I can and a great many things more," he said smiling.

"Who are you?" she asked the question for the second time.

When he threw his shroud aside there was no need for him to answer. His eyes told the whole story and she shuddered at the thought. None of his boasts had been arrogance. All of his actions were calculated and she was never going to win. His golden eyes pierced hers and a touch of fear even greater than the thought of dying washed over her. His black armor was luminous and the red phoenix looked as if it were ready to pounce at any moment. His hair was black as the Black Moon and seemed radiant, even in all its blackness. His features were strong and striking, more beautiful than she imagined a man could be. The stubble upon his almond face made him seem even fiercer than the stories of his exploits.

"You're Black Dawn," she said still afraid and enamored all at once.

"Yes and it made the greatest difference in your defeat for you are not strong enough to best a god," said Black Dawn without arrogance or pride.

"Why?" asked Scicremeon. It was beyond her ken to fathom why a god would pursue her.

"I had to see why my father would not allow me to kill you," said Black Dawn nonchalantly.

"You were going to kill me?" said Scicremeon, her eyes bulging.

"I thought that you were a danger to Merridia. But I see now that you are a danger only to yourself. Yet, your heart is bigger than you know. Your love for the boy is honorable. While your revenge may be your downfall, it is the driving force of your goodness. When the time is right, you shall put others before yourself," said Black Dawn opening his hand.

Scicremeon pushed back with one hand, grabbing her sword and brought it up to defend herself, still not able to stand.

"If I wanted you dead I would only need a thought," said Black Dawn sharply. He took a step forward and crouched in front of Scicremeon and she could see a white gauntlet adorned with purple jewels. The largest jewel would fit into the center of her palm, while the other would sit atop her hand between her wrist and knuckles.

"What is it?"

"It is the Hand of Destruction, once worn by my mother."

"What does it do?" Scicremeon asked as she took the gauntlet from Black Dawn's hand and glossed over it for a moment

"It will help you get what most you crave, but it comes at a cost," said Black Dawn a bit grim.

"No cost is too great for my revenge."

"If you put it on, it will never come off. From that moment on you will be bound by the Laws of the Gods," said Black Dawn with strict authority. "Think long on it, for that which keeps gods at bay is far more treacherous than that which mortals fear," he said and waved his hand.

Aton floated over Scicremeon and then the ball of energy vanished and he dropped into Scicremeon's lap. He wrapped his arms around her neck hard and she cradled him tight to her bosom.

"I expect great things from you Aton," said Black Dawn and the boy looked at him with eyes of wonder.

Then the ground cracked slightly as Black Dawn rocketed toward the clouds and was gone from their sight.

Home Of The Souls

The assembly of Our Union had come to gather in the Palace of Eternity where Aeon had long rested in stasis without sharing so much as a thought with any of them. It was the first time that all of The Twelve were gathered together in the presence of one another. The walls of the great hall were ten times taller than Thutmos, who could hold a small planet in the palm of his hand. Thutmos stood in awe of the great hall as if he had never set foot there before. From where he stood he could see his entire quadrant as if he were on all the planets at once.

There was a place for each of them to sit. Pillars rose up out of the floor, dimly shining, a golden light emanating from what appeared to be a stone structure. Atop the flat portion where they would sit were two symbols. One represented their quadrant and thus each member of the quadrant would sit next to one another. Along with the symbol of their quadrants was a symbol that represented their name. Quadrant One shared the left side of the hall with Quadrant Four, while Quadrant Two and Three sat opposite them.

Seated with Chasm and Everdon, Thutmos sat directly opposite Primsec, who sat next to Carnok. Carnok's face was red as blood and he wore red robes to match his skin. His eyes were menacing, burning like two fiery comets and his lips were dark as space. Next to him was Forecon, adorned in white robes smiling. He had no eyes and looked much like a skeleton though his hands looked like those of a man half burned by the sun. Next to Forecon was Trurow, her robes a dingy looking grey thing that seemed to have a life of its own. Her face was the most beautiful among all of The Twelve, an uncanny depiction of perfection. Her grey eyes seemed old and wise as if they were able to tell a story without her ever uttering a word. Luminar sat next to Trurow nearly as beautiful, but her robes were far more radiant, shining brighter than the illumination from the pillar that she sat upon. Her hair was a bright orange, producing ultraviolet rays and her eyes burned almost as menacingly as Carnok's.

Unlike the others, Asteron stood on top of his pillar wearing no robes. His skin shimmered, made of sparkling crystals and when he moved, it seemed like he folded in and out of himself. Cowlran and Thracno of Quadrant Four sat next to the pillar where Asteron stood. They were twins, identical in every way, except that Cowlran's eyes were as white as pearls and Thracno's were emerald green. Both had long flowing black hair and fair skin. Their faces wore stoic expression and they appeared to be uninterested in the assembly that they were a part of. Whenever they spoke it was only amongst themselves and the last of their quadrant, Kinozl. Kinozl's hair was long like the twins but her hair was violet. Her skin was fair like the twins' and her eyes held the same color as her hair. Between her hands she played with an orb of energy. A few times she passed the orb to Primsec with a great smile and he would catch it, smiling just the same. The twins would scowl at her and then Thracno would whisper in her ear with a spell so that no one could hear.

To Thutmos, time seemed to stand still in the Palace of Eternity. He felt like he was suspended in a vacuum of wonder that didn't exist. He felt great peace and all of the chattering around him sounded like a faint whisper. Only Carnok's voice was able to break his concentration.

"Did you feel that?" asked Carnok his voice deep and dark.

"I'm sure we all did," said Thutmos motioning his hand around the great hall and nodding his head at the others.

Carnok looked at the others and then closed his eyes turning his head to one side as if in pain.

"Uh," they all said as a great weight pressed them against their pillars. Even Asteron, who had been standing, fell upon his pillar in a seated position.

The Palace of Eternity shook as if it had been struck by a violent earthquake. A roll of thunder boomed and the hall filled with the screams of The Twelve.

"I've never felt this before," said Kinozl happily. She and Primsec were the only ones smiling while the others seemed distraught and uncomfortable. Among them all, only Thutmos was calm and quickly able to compose himself.

"Why didn't you warn us?" asked Carnok again accusingly.

"You felt it, as we all did. There is nothing to fear," said Thutmos, his brows drawn down slightly over his eyes.

"Of course I am not afraid," said Carnok arrogantly.

"You know well his feelings," said Chasm to Thutmos. Everdon nodded *yes* slightly, looking at Thutmos gravely.

"Have no mind to it," said Thutmos calmly.

"You are wiser, beyond measure," said Aeon, his voice erupting into the great hall, making the twins shudder. It was the most emotion they had shown since gathering.

Aeon appeared bathed in a radiant light brighter than any sun that burned in the cosmos. Thutmos marveled at The Creator as he did whenever he was in his presence. Each time felt different and new. Tears ran from his eyes and he kneeled and then bowed in submission, pressing his head against the pillar, weary of looking up again. His brothers and sisters followed suit, Chasm weeping in adulation, while a great deal of the others entered into song, evoking Aeon's name in blessing and worship.

"Behave not like servants, but as children," said Aeon as he swept them all up in his hands and embraced them. With his mind he spoke personally to them all. Each of the short conversations was intimate and none of the others could hear.

"I am glad that you are pleased," said Thutmos when Aeon finished speaking.

"My expectations were never in question," said Aeon knowing Thutmos's mind.

"Will you remain with us longer this time?" asked Thutmos.

"I am afraid that I will only be here for a very short moment," said Aeon somberly to them all. "I have robbed from myself the great rest that I require in order for the Universe to be sustained. My stasis was replaced by a great work; The Laying of the Fire-," said Aeon cut off.

"Why would you deceive us?" asked Carnok.

"Because my work required for the first time again, the very contemplation that brought the Universe into being as you see it now," said Aeon hoping to satisfy Carnok's inquisition.

"Will you show us this work?" said Carnok as if begging.

"You know well of it. You have known long before you had form to call your own. The word of my greatest creation has been in the mind of Our Union since the moment Thutmos called forth Chasm and Everdon," said Aeon.

"Home of the Souls," said Primsec, his face lighting into a dozen colors, his expression filled with joy.

"It is done..." said Thutmos as if breathless.

"May we see it?" asked Forecon.

"Please," they all said at once. Even the twins' usual stoic expressions seemed to be lightened.

Carnok was the only one who hadn't smiled. He sat brooding, cutting his eye at Aeon and Thutmos, visibly angry.

Aeon whispered and the floor parted. The darkness of space appeared before them spotted with stars that glowed alone while others made wonderful constellations. Aeon placed his radiant hand above the opening in the floor and whispered again. Slowly, a planet began to ascend toward them. To Thutmos it seemed small compared to the great many that he had seen. Merridia was four times its size. Thutmos wondered what was there as he watched the planet approach. Aeon had spent his entire stasis on such a small planet. The Home of the Souls didn't seem so gravely important to Thutmos, even though much of it was shielded from him like a veil placed over the eyes.

When the planet finally rose up into the great hall, they all glossed over it intently, studying every rivet of the sphere. Most of the planet was covered with the water of raging oceans. One of the land masses was totally covered in ice and one of the great oceans too was largely ice. The land masses were scattered about the sphere at varying distancing, but it seemed that at one time they were all joined as one. At certain points, they appeared to fit together like a puzzle.

"This is The Home of the Souls," said Aeon with great pleasure.

Thutmos had never seen him so happy for the coming of any planet. Even the birth of Corvus from Merridia seemed to pale in comparison to the adoration Aeon held for the new planet.

"What is this place called?" asked Kinozl, her violet eyes glittering.

"It is called Earth," said Aeon.

"Where will it be placed?" asked Carnok quickly after having heard the name.

"In the newest galaxy of the universe," said Aeon. As he waved his hand, the Palace of Eternity faded from existence, and only the pillars remained. They floated in space atop their pillar-seats and drifted into an unknown region of the universe. Names and images began to flash before their eyes, imbedding themselves in their minds as Aeon opened the truth to them. With a third whisper Earth drifted back into its orbit and then its solar system sprang up around it.

At the center of the system was a great sun shining brilliantly, its rays shooting off of its surface. Closer to Earth on its dark side was a great moon that provided light to its inhabitants.

"In what quadrant shall this Earth lie?" asked Carnok.

"You've been quite the inquisitor of late," said Chasm harshly.

"Speak your own mind Thutmos," said Carnok.

"We are of the same mind," said Thutmos casually.

"Indeed," said Everdon solidifying Thutmos's assertion.

"Then you wonder as I do, who shall have governance," said Carnok impetuously

"None shall," said Aeon calmly.

"Surely the balance must be kept," said Carnok with an incredulous look on his red face which had begun to darken.

"The balance will be kept, for that precision is vital to the health of the universe. But those of the Earth will be sustained by my power just as you are. The very life force that flows within them is the same that flows within you. My life force," said Aeon beaming with delight.

"Are not all things sustained by you?" asked Primsec clearly confused.

"Yes all things are sustained by me and you through Our Union," said Aeon at an unhurried pace. "Yet, most are sustained simply by the energies that flowed from The Spring of Creation. What they became was not intentional or of my doing per se. The others simply exist as a part of a chain reaction, left to grow like a wildfire. Every facet of the people of Earth is of my making. I molded them in the same way that I molded Thutmos and through that molding you all came," said Aeon stopping for a moment.

"Is that why he is The Most Favored?" asked Forecon.

"Yes," said Aeon nodding.

"Then they are just like us," said Asteron his crystal face shimmering as he spoke.

"No," said Aeon emphatically.

"No?" said many of them at once confused.

"They will never know the universe as intimately as you do. Where you are mighty and everlasting, they are fragile and short-lived. Death will always haunt them. Their very own lives they will hardly understand and their only comfort will be in the bosom of another. Many of you have found comfort in only yourselves, even amongst the members of your quadrant. While you are connected in Our Union you are each aware of all things and thus need not search for much. Only that which I keep from your eyes and thoughts can you not uncover. There has been very little that has been shielded from you. The people of Earth will know great tribulations and will ponder the greatest mystery of life for many ages to come. Thus while I have given them the greatest gift, I have also assailed them with a great calamity. For the balance of life is both a gift and a curse. So while they have not asked for life, giving them of my own spirit has given me great pleasure," said Aeon digressing.

"What have you called them Lord?" asked Thutmos in earnest.

"They are called humans," said Aeon.

"If these humans are the possessors of your life force, then they have great potential for power," said Carnok harshly looking around the great hall for a supporter. Aeon spoke before any could be roused.

"Thutmos has told you not to fear, but you have not heeded his words. You have always been passionate, but you reach when you should stay your hand. Humans are no threat to your position. Our Union shall endure for all time," said Aeon and then vanished.

Thutmos had watched Kinozl chase Primsec around until they disappeared from his view. Their departure compounded the loneliness he felt when he could no longer hear their laughter. Aeon no longer whispered to him from his stasis and every meeting with him seemed fleeting. He had begun to loathe his position as The Most Favored. Around Aeon he always felt like a child seeking approval, wishing to be cradled and assured that everything would be fine. His instincts told him to be weary, but Chasm insisted that he remain calm and remember his duties. She hadn't said it aloud for hours, but the words continued to echo in his head, and no matter how hard he tried he couldn't escape them.

Everdon was very little help as he always seemed to agree with whatever Chasm said. Everdon sat in silence and never offered Thutmos any words of encouragement. He only offered assertions that seemed to be the workings of Chasm and not a concert of their one-mind. Any time he thought he was in control, he would eventually lose himself in a sea of confusion. There was a longing in his heart that he couldn't escape. As Aeon continued to be absent the longing became a void he didn't quite understand how to fill.

More disconcerting than his own feelings was the fact that Carnok had stood next to him since Aeon had vanished and never moved. Anger seemed to spew from his very aura and Thutmos wished he would return to his quadrant where he could loathe without feeling it. It wouldn't have been so bad, except Carnok hadn't spoken or even tried to commune with him through his mind. His red-faced brother seemed to be closed off from the entire universe, yet sought the comfort of company. When Chasm became aware of his annoyance with Carnok, she laughed at him, hoping that Everdon would join in, though he never did. Thutmos could sense his emotions and there always seemed to be a bit of elation there, but his face told nothing of the sort.

"Are we really supposed to endure for all of eternity?" asked Carnok.

Finally he's broken his silence, thought Thutmos, though he had barely been listening to anything Carnok had said. He was glad the question registered in his mind.

"That is what has been said by The One Above All," said Thutmos as if pained. As far as he was concerned, Carnok had inquired enough of Aeon that he needn't ask him for clarity.

"Do you want to exist only as you are now? A piece...a pawn to be used at the whim of his master," said Carnok as if hoping for an ally.

"What else is there but duty?" said Thutmos though he didn't entirely believe himself.

"We are all keenly aware of your desires. You divulged them to your precious Corvus millennia ago. Those cravings still stir unsatisfied within you," said Carnok looking at Thutmos with a smirk, his eyes giving away the intense thought in his mind. "Would you journey with me to this Earth, to find the truth of our father's plans?" asked Carnok. It was as if a savage beast raged inside of him, waiting to burst free from his cage.

"You think he tells us lies," said Thutmos, with an air of judgment in his voice.

"He does not give us all of the truth. We are supposed to be the only ones who share in Our Union. Has he not given these humans what he has given us," said Carnok, his voice still grave, filled with longing and a tone of anguish.

"Feelings of betrayal often spawn anger and retribution. You would do well to tame your emotions," said Thutmos, his words hot and accusatory.

"Do not speak to me in riddles. You are not in a position to lecture me. Names and titles mean nothing...," said Carnok trailing off as he turned his back to Thutmos. "He may call you The Most Favored in your presence. But even you have not enough favor with The Creator for him to share with you the making of his greatest creation. A multitude of creatures made in the image of himself. Endowed with his very life force," said Carnok loudly as if addressing a large crowd. "If that does not stink of betrayal, then you are an all-knowing fool," said Carnok storming off and then vanishing in a swirl of black mist.

"He has always been headstrong," said Chasm softly, her voice like a lullaby.

"There is some merit to what he speaks," said Thutmos squinting.

"It is not our place to question Aeon's actions. He is The Creator," said Chasm touching Thutmos's shoulder.

"Indeed he is. Wise beyond measure and father to us all," said Everdon his heavy voice booming in the great hall as he shook his head yes and closed his eyes. He turned to the stars and leaped into the blackness of space and then vanished.

"We must go to Earth, to make sure Carnok does not behave recklessly," said Thutmos to Chasm.

She felt the weariness in his heart and closed her eyes, her hand still on his shoulder. "It is your burden to shoulder as The Most Favored," said Chasm as the two of them vanished from the Palace of Eternity.

Lesson Twelve

Scicremeon had stared at the ceiling for more than an hour, lying flat on her back; her hands tracing the lines of the Hand of Destruction. For the last few days she had tried to pry the jewels from the gauntlet, but they wouldn't budge. The thought of a large purse of coins to buy ale made her try everything from fire to a large hammer. Her efforts were unsuccessful in producing even the faintest scratch. Yesterday she had given up on the effort when she remembered that Black Dawn had said the gauntlet would never come off if she put it on. She figured there was nothing a mortal could do to destroy it. The prospect of being attached to the small piece of armor bothered her. The only feeling that was more unsettling was being bound to the gods. She was never good at following rules and she thought laws were a waste of time, especially being from the battle torn village of Marside.

Since her mother's passing two years ago, she had only been bound to herself. Up until recently, she cared for nothing but herself and her unquenched thirst for revenge. Other than the taste of ale and the want of blood, there was nothing else that drove her to wake in the morning and leave the two room shack she called home. Her life was a bore if there was no fighting and she spent a great many days in bed hoping anyone would come knocking on her door to offer a challenge. The days she spent in the market were spent mostly with her eyes on the same people repeating the same mundane activities. Yet, in the market she found conflict and with it came a sense of peace.

What a foolish brute he was, Scicremeon thought of the man who called himself The Great Gustain. The memory of him crept into her mind as she continued to caress the Hand of Destruction. Shaking her head she thought of how formidable Gustain must have been in battle. As easy as it was for her to dispatch him, he was a fine warrior. Closing her eyes, she breathed in deeply. *Amazing it is how at one moment you stand in victory and then in the next, you are lying on your back not so ready to taste defeat.* When she opened her eyes a tear fell from each one. She wiped them away quickly, but the memory of loss haunted her. Black Dawn had spared her life when he could have taken it. The very thing that she held in her hand was not a reward of victory, but one of defeat. Never had she fallen under the sword of anyone. Not even in the training ring.

It doesn't matter if he is a god; she thought bitterly and hurled the gauntlet into the wall with all of her might. The wooden wall cracked and she watched the gauntlet hit the bed with a faint thump and quickly wiped the tears from her face again.

She sat up and grabbed a large wooden mug from a small table set by her bed. Opening her palm she tipped the cup over and felt three drops of liquid hit her hand. She was hoping for a little more but happily lapped up the few drops of ale that had fallen onto her hand.

"I'll need more of that soon," said Scicremeon aloud as she stood up.

Sniffing her arms pits, she shrugged her shoulders and then pulled her sword from under her pillow. She strapped her sword belt to her waist and then stuffed her feet into her boots. Seeing the dirt and blood on them, she remembered her mother saying, *you ought to be more of a lady.* She smiled at the thought and rolled her eyes storming toward the door.

The door slammed against the side of the shack as she stepped out.

"Well at least you haven't dropped dead yet," said Scicremeon as she saw Aton standing just ten feet beyond the door, crouched in a horse-stance with a sword in either hand, arms outstretched. "How many times have you dropped your arms?" asked Scicremeon.

"Not once," said Aton panting. His hair was matted to his head and sweat ran down his bare chest and back. His legs were vibrating and they looked like they would buckle at any moment.

"You wouldn't lie to me would you?" said Scicremeon turning her head to one side eyeing him.

"Never," said Aton his parched throat scratching, sounding like a cat in pain. He coughed and hoped to spit but his mouth was too dry to produce any.

"How many days has it been?" asked Scicremeon looking up into the sky at the three suns that seemed to settle directly over them.

"Haven't you kept count?" asked Aton his eyes full of fear.

"Oh right," Scicremeon began cheerfully. "A full three," she said beginning to laugh as the color disappeared from Aton's face.

"I thought I was going to have to start the lesson over," said Aton a bit of hope entering his eyes as he smiled.

"What lesson?" said Scicremeon visibly confused.

"Lesson twelve," said Aton, his brow falling over his eyes, "you told me to get ready for lesson twelve and then you made me squat like this for the last three days," a look of anguish taking hold of his face.

"Ha!" said Scicremeon her voice a high-pitched mockery of everything Aton had said. Scicremeon loosed a villainous laugh that echoed into the air as she walked past Aton to a well a few yards behind him. Removing the lid she dropped a bucket in after hitting the lever above her head. Hearing the bucket hit, she waited a minute and then drew the bucket back up with her hands.

The water squished and splashed over the sides of the beat up wooden bucket, as she tugged the line until the bucket sat on top the uncovered well shaft. She dipped a small cup in the bucket and pulled it out, the water dripping down her hand. Walking toward Aton, Scicremeon took a few sips from the cup. In her other hand, she carried the bucket by the handle, dangling next to her knee.

Standing over a sweating and shaking Aton she locked eyes with him. His eyes were wide with pain and wonder as she stared at him. Her lips curled to one side as she forced back a smile and took another sip from the cup.

"Open your mouth," said Scicremeon as if upset and Aton complied. "Good," she said as if she were satisfied. "Now drink," she said forcing the cup to his lips and as she poured she crooned, "don't swallow, don't spill, or you'll be sorry."

Aton's cheeks puffed and blushed as his eyes opened wider trying not to swallow. His mouth felt like it was stretching, but he fought the want to ask for comfort.

"Ready for lesson twelve," said Scicremeon seeing the fear seeping into Aton's already flushed face. "That was just the warm up," she said answering the question that registered on his face that he couldn't speak.

Aton nodded his head *yes*, his eyes giving away the fear in his mind and heart.

"Last obstacle," said Scicremeon basking in Aton's fear. Taking her sword from its sheath, she cut the rope from the bucket and let it fall to the ground. Hoisting the bucket, she sat it on his head. She clapped her hands together to dry them of water and then rubbed them on the back of her pants. "Ten laps," said Scicremeon pointing her finger at Aton sternly, "and not a drop on you, in your belly, or on this ground or you'll pay." Inclining her head, she raised her eyebrow.

Aton shook his head yes as he stood up.

"Oh no, with them bent," said Scicremeon touching his shoulders and pushing him back down into a squatting position. "Off you go," she said turning him to the mile long circular path she had carved into the dirt around her small shack.

Scicremeon sat under the shade of two large trees on a swinging net with her legs crossed. She slid a stone across the edge of her sword slowly sharpening it. Her eyes were glued to Aton who trudged along slowly, grunting and grinding his teeth together in exhaustion. Looking at Aton reminded her of her own struggles when she was a child learning the way of the warrior. She was eleven when she began her training, just a year younger than Aton. His painful expressions made her smile at the memories. In his eyes she could see same the determination that once drove her never to quit. While their wills seemed to be similar, what drove them was totally different.

Scicremeon had never wanted to impress her teachers or make them proud. She had nothing to prove to them other than that she could learn their lessons without making mistakes. In her there was no fear of death as with others. Only a cold want to inflict pain and taste revenge drove her through each arduous task until they each had nothing to teach her.

Her thoughts of the past forced her to remember her first real fight with a sword. The hour had grown late and a storm had swept through Marside, pelting the ground with drops of rain. She'd begun to make her way home when a band of three thieves approached laughing and splashing ale about their beards and bare chests.

A sweet piece of meat we have here she remembered the shortest man saying as he eyed her, her clothes plastered to her body by the rain. His smile was half toothless and one of his eyes was missing. When he took a half step to approach she held up her hands in submission.

"I don't want any trouble," Scicremeon had said beginning to step backward slowly.

"Trouble has a mind of its own in Marside girl," the short toothless man had said.

"Move," the tallest man had said pushing toothless aside and stepping forward with an ugly scowl. He stood well over six feet with big sinewy muscles from head to toe. In his hands he held a large mace with three skulls tied just below the head. The big man's teeth were plastered with brown and yellow gunk, though they were perfectly straight in his mouth. What Scicremeon noticed about him immediately was that he didn't wobble like his two companions. The other man with them held a large container in his hand barely able to stand. His eyes were glossed over and the line of hair on his otherwise bald head bobbed from side to side.

"Hey!" toothless had said and the big man jabbed him in the fruits with his mace.

"Shut up," the big man had said as toothless doubled over in agony.

"I just want to go home," Scicremeon had said as her back touched to the wall of a house.

"That's a nice looking sword," the big man said smiling.

"It was my father's-," Scicremeon had said slowly before being cut off.

"I want it," the big man had said walking quickly toward her.

"No!" Scicremeon had screamed and then her sword found the soft flesh above the big man's knee and then the hard muscle below his chest. Her sword slashed up quickly and split his face in half. The big man fell to his knees as his mace dropped from his hands. By the time the big man's face hit the ground; Scicremeon had removed the toothless man's head from his shoulders.

As she stepped over their corpses, she saw their drunken companion's eyes wide with wonder. He wasn't afraid and Scicremeon wasn't sure he was aware of what was going on. Standing in front of him she wiped the blood from her sword on her pants and looked dead into his eyes. He smiled wide and laughed his funk into her face nearly toppling over.

"Is that ale?" Scicremeon had said as she felt herself beginning to shake, as the rush she felt had begun to subside and the drumming of her heart took over.

The drunkard laughed harder still.

Scicremeon snatched the container from his hand and stuck her nose in the opening. The liquid inside wreaked of the ale the men in Marside drank. She had heard rumors that it was rank and should only be drunk by those with a strong stomach. Shrugging, she tipped the container over her open mouth. The taste was worse than the smell, but she closed her eyes, swallowing hard and fast. Licking her tongue out as if choking, she was almost totally disgusted with the taste, but the toxic stew of a beverage eased the shaking of her hands and the rapid beating of her heart.

That's when we fell in love, she thought as she opened her eyes leaving the memory behind. *Good thing there are others to choose from these days,* she thought as she sat up and dropped her legs around the swinging net holding her in place.

Looking around the path, she couldn't see Aton. At first she assumed he was behind her shack, but two minutes had gone by and he hadn't come out around either side. Her first thought was that he had dropped dead and she'd have to go and scrape him off the ground. As she cursed him to the gods, he spoke.

"I've been here for a little time now," said Aton on his knees, the bucket of water still balanced on his head.

"But you've swallowed," said Scicremeon, a devious smile creasing her face.

"No," said Aton as he held up a cup full of water mixed with his saliva.

"Who told you to stop?" said Scicremeon dropping both legs to one side of her net.

"Well I did twenty five rather than ten," said Aton beginning to smile. "You were out for a while."

Scicremeon stood towering over a kneeling Aton and huffed her displeasure at his relaxed demeanor. She grabbed the bucket of water from his head and checked the weight of it. She made another sound within her chest and Aton cackled.

"Laugh at this," said Scicremeon as she splashed him with the bucket of water.

"Oh thank you," said Aton happily as if a huge pressure had been lifted from his shoulders.

"You're too much like me," said Scicremeon scowling.

"Really," said Aton beaming.

"Yeah, you don't know when to quit," said Scicremeon grabbing him by the back of his collar and dragging him to the well.

Horror struck Aton's face as he tried to fight against her, but his body had nothing else to give. He ended his struggle and allowed himself to be dragged across the ground.

"Ready for lesson twelve," said Scicremeon ferociously.

"I thought that was-," said Aton afraid.

"I lied," said Scicremeon as she kicked the lid off the well. "That was the rest of the warm up," she said as she grabbed the back of Aton's pants, lifting him from the ground. "If you die, I'll have to kill your mother because she's sure to seek revenge. You wouldn't want that on your conscious now would you?" And with one swing of her arms she let Aton go.

He looked back at her, his eyes ready to jump from his head as he slowly looked down and realized there was nothing he could do about falling. The feeling was familiar, but there'd be no floating crystal sphere to stop his descent this time. Darkness took over as he passed through the opening of the well. Mud crept under his nails as he reached to grab hold of anything to slow him down, but the slick stones only served to twist him in awkward positions as he continued to plummet.

The air grew colder as it whipped past his face and made the short hairs on his arm stand up at attention. The three suns of Merridia had no dominion in the darkness of the well. As his fall seemed to last forever, he began to hear the rushing river outside the well. The air grew cooler still as he finally let out a frightful scream as he felt his body falling faster. He closed his eyes in anticipation of a hard smack and his inevitable death atop a bed of liquid, for he was sure he was going to die on impact.

SPLOOSH!

The water whisked around him and he flipped twice under water, his cheeks stretched past his eyes. Aton kicked hard to the surface and burst out, taking in a gulp of air that brought on a fit of hiccups. Trying his best to ignore the hiccups, Aton sucked in and blew out as much air as he could until his breathing slowed. When his eyes couldn't see the top of the well, he realized how daunting his task would be. He could only see just in front of him and when he finally made it to the wall, he found that the grooves between the stones were barely wider than the follicles of his hair.

His mother loved to run her fingers through his hair and wished that her hair was as fine. At that moment he wished that the grooves between the stones were as thick as her coarse locks.

How many times will I have to do this before she shows a little mercy on me, he thought as he remembered that there were only two suns still shining over Marside when he finished his twenty-fifth lap. He estimated that he had just over two hours to complete his task, before his taskmaster of a teacher chucked him headlong back into the watery asylum he began to try to escape from. Digging his fingers into the space between the stones, he pressed his lips against his teeth and grunted his effort.

Don't look up, he told himself as he climbed without thinking, losing himself in the sea of darkness that was the shaft of the well. Every rivet he could fit his fingers and toes into he called friend.

"That'll teach you to outdo me and take a break after doing it," said Scicremeon aloud as she clapped her hands together as if cleaning them of some vile slime. "I've never done twenty five laps around this thing," she said quietly to herself. She peaked back at the well and her mind set upon Aton for a moment and then her eyes fell to her feet. *If he makes it out on time, I might just throw him back in for sport. Persistent little. . .,* her thought trailed off as she kicked her feet into the air, her hands pressed into the warm earth, strands of her hair kissing the dirt.

Balancing on one hand, she pulled her sword from her scabbard and placed the blade across the arches of her feet. She began to move slowly around the track whistling as she went.

The second sun of Merridia drifted from view and the world cooled around Scicremeon's blood filled head as she counted thirty to herself softly. Her arms were vibrating by now with every walking motion she made with her hands around the track and she had rolled her eyes up in her head to better focus. She knew that closing them would have caused her to think too much and thinking allowed fear and doubt to creep into your mind, or so she believed.

Half way through lap thirty-one she saw a crude stick of wood between two ashy ankles above a dusty pair of sandals that appeared ready to snap in half at a moment's notice. Kicking her sword into the air, Scicremeon flipped backward into a standing position and caught her sword in the air. Sliding the sword in its sheath she saw a weak old man standing before her hunched over, making him a full head shorter than her.

"You're interrupting my work," said Scicremeon bothered.

The old man hackled, clearing his throat, an ugly smile creasing his pale face nearly closing the wrinkles and bags completely over his glazed brown eyes.

"There is no one here to kill," said the old man with a wide grin. The top row of his teeth had obviously decided to flee his mouth along with all but two from the bottom. Scicremeon cringed at his empty mouth. "And you are only in the business of blood," said the old man gravely squinting his eyes further.

"Who are you...since you seem to know who I am," said Scicremeon flatly.

"I am Cale," said the old man revealing his name.

"What is your business here in the woods," said Scicremeon motioning to the trees around the small patch of dirt where her home and makeshift track sat.

"I have come to deliver you the most pertinent information you have ever received," said Cale grunting joyfully, his skinny bones shaking as he titled to one side nearly losing his balance.

"Oh have you," said Scicremeon setting her hands on her hips.

"Indeed I do. The very words you have been waiting to hear since you learned of how your father truly died," said Cale cutting his eye as he read Scicremeon's reaction.

Her mouth parted and he saw her teeth pressed together hard. Her hands left her hips unhappy with their placement, her nails now digging into the flesh of her palm as if the two parts of her hands were at odds with one another.

"A name," said Scicremeon as she approached the old man. "Give me his name," she said in a threatening manner, her hand now on the pommel of her sword. Her heart was racing faster than the tide of anger that swelled in her chest. She could taste blood on her tongue and was ready to cut the knowledge from his very head when a labored voice broke into the air followed by a thumb.

"...finished...there's a sun...there's still one up," said Aton lying on his back panting, one hand pointing to the darkening sky, reaching for something to help lift himself from the ground.

"Tell me the name," said Scicremeon after turning her attention away from a wheezing Aton.

"The name you are already familiar with. It is the news that involves that name that will make your heart flutter," said Cale as if savoring the very words.

Scicremeon pulled her sword from its cover and pressed the blade to Cale's neck grimacing as if pained. "You talk too slow old man," said Scicremeon. Her hand would have squeezed the life from her sword handle if it drew breath. The tightness of her grip made her arm vibrate violently as her eyes welled deeper than the shaft that Aton had just climbed from.

"There is no honor in killing an old man," said Cale as he slowly pushed Scicremeon's blade away from his neck. Clearing his throat again and coughing he said, "The great King Chale of Chalendor has gone to the land of the dead."

Cale smiled at Scicremeon as the weight of his words registered on her face. The angry grimace on her face turned to one of wonder and excitement.

"The king's pact no longer stands," said Scicremeon spinning in half circles not knowing what to do with herself. The delight in her mind burst out through her limbs as she waved a hand this way and that, still not knowing what to do with herself.

"Revenge is yours," said Cale.

"Why, why have you given me this news?" said Scicremeon puzzled.

"I was there to watch the treachery of your father's demise. No warrior as honorable as he was deserved to die at the hands of a trickster. Even worse, it was a coward that supplied the ruse," said Cale, his voice deeper than the cracking and gurgling he had been pushing into the air.

Scicremeon sensed that he was on the verge of tears, but stopped herself from reaching to console him. "If ever you are in need, I will be yours," said Scicremeon.

"Perhaps I shall be," said Cale.

"Hi, I'm Aton," said Aton extending his hand for Cale to shake.

"Cale," he said and extended his own hand.

Aton felt a rush of cold air grip him and what felt like a thousand needles stab at his mind. It felt as if the world around him had left and he had been pulled into a dream. His eyes saw the scraggly old man standing before him hunched over, his sandy face wrinkled to oblivion, the skin around his eyes folding atop it. But in his mind he felt an unbridled fury that he could not escape, no matter how much he tried to pull away. The force that invaded his mind gripped him and forced his mind to see what was before it. He hoped to fold himself into his mind where his oldest memories had evaded him, but with every effort to fight, the pulling grew more intense. The thought to scream pressed itself against his subconscious and he yelled inside his thoughts with all the will of his mind's voice. And then he saw them, two burning eyes delving into his soul. The pain was intense and felt as if it tore the very essence of his being.

"No!" Aton yelled in his mind at the top of his lungs and then a powerful voice spoke to him.

"I have you," the voice said and then it was gone and he saw the old man again.

Aton shook his head and realized that he was smiling and saying *nice to meet you,* as the old man had turned and began to walk away.

Scicremeon wrapped her arm around Aton's shoulders and kissed his head. He looked up at her confused though he smiled through the fogginess in his head. He felt hungry, but not for food, though he rubbed his belly as the two of them turned back toward the well.

"I have somewhere to go," said Scicremeon to Aton solemnly.

"On an adventure?" said Aton hopeful.

"Yes. One of blood," said Scicremeon severely.

"I want to come, I'm ready," said Aton hungry for a journey out of Marside.

"While you have been more than a good student, you are not yet ready to wield a sword against warriors and brave the likes of Chalendoran magicians," said Scicremeon removing her arm from

Aton's shoulders and leaning over into the mouth of the well. "But maybe you can come as far as the palace with me," said Scicremeon.

"Why do you have to go to the palace?" said Aton.

"I need to speak with the emperor. I'll need one of his ships if I am to go to Chalendor," said Scicremeon.

"Who was that old man?" asked Aton.

"Cale. Didn't he tell you his name?" said Scicremeon confused.

"Yes, but," said Aton trailing off for a moment. "Didn't you see his eyes," said Aton squinting and blinking fast as the burning eyes flashed across his mind.

"He's old. They start to look wicked like that," said Scicremeon dismissively. "You have other concerns," said Scicremeon looking from the opening of the well to Aton and back.

"What?" said Aton as he approached the well and leaned over the opening. "I don't see anything," said Aton lifting up on the ledge higher.

"I leave at sun down!" said Scicremeon as she pushed Aton over.

"Ah!" Aton bellowed as he tumbled back into the dark shaft.

Scicremeon roared with laughter as she walked away toward her shack.

"No one's ever climbed out of there faster than me," she said as she opened the door to her shack. "Sun down!" she screamed as she let the door shut behind her.

Watchful Eye

Black Dawn stood at the edge of a precipice a mile from the gates of Algar, the great palace of the Merridian gods. The palace's high walls were imposing, shining in gold, arrayed with green and red jewels sparkling in the light of the suns. He eyed a great statue of a beast standing guard at the gate. Its head was large, tucked neatly under a furry mane, with six horns curving out from the sides at razor sharp points. The hands were clawed, and so massive that the beast could squeeze the life out of two men at once. The beast stood twelve feet tall on two sturdy legs leaning forward, his broad chest protruding as if the rest of his body followed behind it. Sharp horns lined his spine and two horns protruded from where his elbows should have been. He carried no weapons and looked fully capable of maiming an opponent with great ease without one.

Black Dawn turned toward the beast and lifted his palm and the statue began to move toward him, breaking the stone and pushing pieces of rock to the side. When the beast settled just a few feet from the edge, Black Dawn pressed a hand to one of the beast's cheeks and rubbed the stony mane as if it were soft fur. Sighing, Black Dawn looked at the beast in his eyes deeply, and locked there for a few moments. The creature's eyes were alive, brown orbs vibrating in its sockets. There was a faint rumble in the beast's chest as Black Dawn rubbed his hard mane.

Turning his back and stepping toward the edge of the precipice and then kneeling down, Black Dawn looked, appearing as if it were difficult for him to see through the white clouds below him. Yet, he saw the world below as clearly as the closest rock at his feet. He gazed down to the surface of Merridia for a long moment and shook his head *no* and then rolled it as if to remove a crick from his neck.

Standing up fast he turned in a half circle and massaged his hands and cracked his knuckles while kicking dust and rocks off the cliff. The air seemed to cool slightly and Black Dawn noticed. Inclining his head to one side, his ear moved, and his hearing sense heightened intensely.

In the distance he could hear a howling wind that he couldn't feel but suspected that it was what had made the air cooler. When he searched with his eyes into the clouds he couldn't see anything. They had turned grey and began to converge on one another unnaturally and he immediately took notice, standing and readying himself for a conflict.

"Always on edge," said a deep woman's voice.

"Phray," said Black Dawn dismissively as he turned away from the golden hair swaying in the wind, piercing the grey clouds that began to turn white again.

Phray descended onto the precipice from the skies with a great smile of perfectly white teeth. Her eyes were gold like her hair and her beauty was nearly infectious. Her head was not adorned with a crown of jewels, but only a simple band of rope knotted at the back of her head that flowed down to the base of her neck like a ponytail. Her silk golden robes were simple looking compared to Black

Dawn's detailed armor and blade. Phray carried no weapons and wore no jewels on her wrists or fingers.

"What mischief are you up to?" said Black Dawn with a faint smile as he plucked a morsel of dirt from the ground in a crouched position.

"Do you still think so lowly of me?" said Phray smiling her perfect smile.

"Low?" Black Dawn said confused and then chuckled. "I've never thought low of you, just never very high," he said chucking a rock into the sky.

"That just warms me inside," said Phray as she watched Black Dawn fumbling with a handful of rocks.

"Is there a reason for your visit? You tend to keep a great distance away from Algar of late," said Black Dawn with an unmistakable undertone of suggestion in his voice. He waved his hand and sent the beast at the edge of the cliff rumbling back to its original resting place.

Phray scoffed and rolled her eyes as she looked down upon a crouched Black Dawn, still not giving her the attention of his eyes. A frown arrived on her face as she dropped down into a squatting position opposite him, grabbing the rock his fingers were approaching. When he looked at her she smiled and tossed the rock into his breastplate with a lazy hand.

"Still don't like being ignored?" he said.

"Can't say that I do."

"Then let your voice be heard and be gone."

"You seem content in breeching every law that your father has put into place," said Phray following Black Dawn with her eyes as he rose to his feet.

"I've broken no laws."

"Not quite. But since when does a god mix it up with mortals. There is no contest. You should be but a shadow to these people. Coming and going like the wind. Only those who are without their minds or scratching the surface of death should see us. The days of glory are over. I know that must hurt your heart as your days have been shortest among us," said Phray standing a head shorter than Black Dawn but bearing down into him with her eyes and the weight of her words.

"This is laughable. My record of victory speaks for itself. Do not forget that it was me who saved you from becoming a...," said Black Dawn stepping closer. His voice had deepened and the clouds grew darker as his agitation turned to anger. A bolt of lightning cracked a section off of the cliff just to the left of Phray, tumbling into a free fall. "That does not matter now does it? I have seen many futures and they are all troubling," said Black Dawn flatly.

"None of them are set in stone," said Phray standing her ground as Black Dawn stood over her.

"Be that as it may, your gifts are not as strong as my own. You can see into the future far as my father, and even read the thoughts of many as much as a year from now. But your mental gifts are confined to Merridia and its inhabitants. I can see the coming calamities from those outside of Merridia. Everything that threatens our home is my burden. My father will not listen to reason," said Black Dawn as if he were hurt.

"Trust in his power and leave this girl alone," said Phray in a caring way.

"That is none of your concern," said Black Dawn sharply stepping to the edge of the cliff.

"Is that love permeating from your aura?" said Phray surprised.

"I love all of my father's children," said Black Dawn breathing in deeply and looking down into the clouds below.

"Lies!" said Phray forcefully while laughing. "I too am fond of some of those pests down below more than others. Yet, I give none the watchful eye that you are giving this girl."

Black Dawn turned his head to his right as Phray had come to stand next to him. His gaze went back to and through the clouds, his eyes moving from one side to another. He rubbed his chin ruminating and smiled faintly. Phray watched him intently and then shook her head no, slowly, as she caught the smile from the side of his face.

"Where is she going?" said Phray as her brows descended onto her eyelids. She leaned forward slightly, nearly slipping from the cliff and inclined her head forward as she squinted. "Tell me!" she said as if ordering a servant.

"Don't act like a child, you know the path," said Black Dawn dismissively.

"Why is she…," said Phray slowly and then finished, "she has learned of his death hasn't she."

"Yes," said Black Dawn happily.

"You fool, you told her," said Phray and her eyes began to glow white and six bolts of lightning struck the ground around Black Dawn's feet.

The ground dropped from under him in two dozen pieces and he dropped a half inch before suspending himself in the air. Drifting away from the cliff a bit, he turned to face Phray with a look of boredom.

"It was an old man," said Black Dawn. "Your jealousy is flattering but it is misplaced," he said as he descended back to solid ground.

"I don't want you. I want you to exercise a morsel of reason. It never ends well when gods mix with mortals. You are going to get this girl killed. She will die on Chalendor. That much I know, that much I can see," said Phray with great trepidation.

Black Dawn's head shifted back at her sudden burst of emotion. He had never seen her so passionate about anything before. Her interest in him had been a faint memory for well over a thousand years. She hadn't entreated him as a consort after he last turned her down, but he knew the mention of it would anger her. But her reaction to his calm demeanor and snide remarks weren't enough to bring on such an outburst. She believed what she was saying.

"You have not spoken in puzzles today," said Black Dawn leaving behind his playful nature.

"Not in the least," said Phray still noticeably angry.

"She is more than a mortal," said Black Dawn plainly. Phray gave him an awful look that was more disbelief than anger. "She was able to touch me," he said offering his hands in submission.

"I've touched you in battle before. Gorgon-Ray is still nearly your match, and you are still hoping to scratch your father within the next ten thousand years. It is harder now to touch you, but not so great a feat," said Phray as if appalled by the notion that Black Dawn thinks himself untouchable.

Black Dawn stared at her for a moment and let the echo of her voice retreat into solitude. His face cringed and then he burst out into a bellowing laugh as he watched Phray's face flush bright red. With some effort, he stopped laughing as quickly as he could before she grew angrier and began shooting bolts of lightning at him again.

"None of you are mortals and she is not a god. She has inherited the Fires of Aygron and so much more. I choked her. I slammed her deep into the ground and her bones did not shatter. She did not cry from tears of pain, but from the taste of defeat and the looming heaviness of an inevitable death at the hands of something she could never overcome, no matter how hard she tried. And even with the knowledge that I was a god, she would still try her hand, no matter how futile the effort," said Black Dawn with a great sense of pride and admiration.

"Prove it," said Phray in disbelief.

"What, should I engage her again? I've asserted that I am not her enemy and no longer want to see her dead," said Black Dawn folding his arms across his chest.

"No, she's proven she can match you," said Phray sarcastically, hoping to get a rise out of Black Dawn. He only smiled at her declaration.

"Then what?"

"Send The Ragnon," said Phray pointing toward the beast near the gates of Algar.

"This isn't a game," said Black Dawn incredulously as he unfolded his arm. His voice was dark and filled with seething authority.

"No it's not my precious prince of the gods. But if she goes to Chalendor she'll face far worse," said Phray trudging headlong in the direction of The Ragnon beast at the gates of the palace.

"Read my mind and see for yourself," said Black Dawn, a hint of fear registering on his face.

"I've already tried. Only when your father still called us babies did you ever let me," said Phray, a glimmer flashing in her eyes.

"Long before you became a treacherous villain," said Black Dawn, his face curling into a scowl trying to press away the anxiety that had dampened his mood.

"We are all what time makes us," said Phray raising her eyebrows waiting for Black Dawn to act.

"Fine," said Black Dawn. Without warning he grabbed Phray by the throat and closed his hand. She bared her teeth like a ferocious animal ready to pounce and gripped his hand with an unimaginable force but he didn't so much as flinch. The angry scowl left his face and his normal resolve took hold of him, relaxing the muscles in his face as he marched her closer to The Ragnon. Phray wrenched her hand in his grasp trying to free herself, but could not loosen his grip. She kicked him in the stomach, but it did not stop his march toward The Ragnon. Black Dawn only reacted with a soft toothless smile. "You've never been stronger than me," he said to anger her by reminding her of the obvious truth.

"I thought you said this wasn't a game," said Phray already having ceased trying to fight against Black Dawn's might.

"It isn't a game. You've spied on me one too many times. You claim to be over your infatuation, but you watch my movements below these heavens. My interactions with mortals are my own. I only answer to my father. You'd do well to remember your place in the coming storm, for my visions rarely falter," said Black Dawn as his eyes flashed and he pressed a thousand images into her psyche so she could see what he had, while shielding himself from her mental powers.

Phray gasped and recoiled, again trying to free herself.

Black Dawn grunted and hammered Phray into the statue of the Ragnon. He ascended above the cliff and waved his hands in a circular motion. Around the cliff, a barrier of red light ascended up a thousand feet and then closed at the top.

Phray blinked fast and shook the dizziness in her head and rolled onto her back. The world had seemed to go dark, but the great suns of Merridia were still bright around her. Looking up she saw The Ragnon ripping through the stone that had held him in place. The Ragnon rose up from out of stone, three times the size of the statue that had held him at bay. The Ragnon roared and shook the remaining stones off below his knees, sending shockwaves through the rock of the cliff. The rock split in three distinct paths toward the edge of the cliff.

"If you can bring down the barrier before The Ragnon tears you apart, he'll go and see that she proves herself to you. If not, my mother may have to put you back together," said Black Dawn as he flew through the barrier and disappeared.

"Games," said Phray exhaling hard.

The Ragnon roared again and then lifted his foot. Phray saw the descending bulk of his great foot and rolled out of the way just in time.

"Games!" she bellowed as she stood up. "I'm going to make you uglier," she said as she ran toward the hulking beast.

He roared again, lifting his arms into the air and then pounded his chest. He ran toward her and swung his great fist.

A loud boom echoed through the air as their fight began.

The First Of Us

Thutmos and Chasm made themselves smaller in order to walk upon the Earth like its many inhabitants. Thutmos stood a few inches taller than fifteen feet, while Chasm stood just over nine feet tall.

They strolled along a beach lined with palm trees a few feet inland, just above where the waves broke onto the sand. The air was cool and calm, blowing at inconsistent intervals, pushing Chasm's hair around her face. She often had to move it from her eyes so it wouldn't be a constant distraction.

Unlike the many planets they had visited, Earth was quiet and only seldom did they see a creature walk past them or come close enough to the shore for them to see. The presence of life was there, but it remained largely out of sight, most creatures having domain under the blue and black seas of the new planet. There were great beasts of variety, some calm, others quite ferocious, but they stayed mostly in the forest lands that the two had walked through yesterday.

Today was the fourth day that they had spent on Earth and they had seen no sign of Carnok or any others of Our Union. A great deal of their time had been spent talking about Carnok's anger over Aeon hiding the existence of Earth from them.

"There is nothing here to rule," said Chasm looking off into the distance.

"Not now, but humanity will be great," said Thutmos.

"They are so few and know not of civilization."

"But they will."

"It will be a long time coming, thousands of years from now."

"A short order of time for us," said Thutmos in a matter of fact way.

"Very short," agreed Chasm.

"And our presence is not needed here," said Thutmos looking toward the great yellow sun of the Earth.

"Aeon is always here. I felt him from the very moment I set foot down and shifted the dirt under my boots," said Chasm closing her eyes and inhaling deep, the stream of air filling her diaphragm.

"Amazing how breathing is comforting for even those of us who need not air," said Thutmos breathing in as Chasm had.

"We've been more in concert since being here," said Chasm a bit apprehensive.

"That is because you have not been at odds with me, but as one as we should be," said Thutmos with a soft smile.

"Would you remain here then?"

"I will not dwell where there is no need," said Thutmos pausing for a long moment.

Thutmos walked over to the edge of the beach and kneeled down. Looking across the great body of water in front of him, he reached down pulling a flat rock from under the surface. Standing, he tossed the rock across the surface and watched it skip atop the water for a mile and smiled. "There is surely a serenity here that I do not find in the blackness of space," said Thutmos seeming rather melancholy.

"The balance must be kept," said Chasm without emotion.

"Everdon would have accepted the notion," said Thutmos hoping to cheer Chasm up. He knew that she loved Earth far more than he did, as much as it felt like a place of solitude from the rigors of his duties; he knew that they could not stay.

"Can we stay a little longer," said Chasm calmly, but her eyes begged for an affirmative answer.

"I suppose we can," replied Thutmos turning around and re-joining Chasm.

They continued to stroll and day began to turn to night. The sky had turned a dark orange and the blue waters became black. The light from the stars and the moon began to reflect off of its surface and the surf became more violent. Giant swells of waves formed and crashed upon the sand, making a great rumbling song that would always fizzle before rising again like a crescendo. White long-beaked creatures with wings had come to walk along the beach as they sat there and stared as the bright light of the sun walked away from the lands. The screeching sound that they made was deafening, but their beauty and elegance was unlike any other on the planet.

Chasm sat and regarded the creatures, stroking their necks and back, studying their movements as they played in the sand. Her mood grew darker by the second as she felt Thutmos's mind ready-ing for the journey back to their quadrant.

"Can we not fly back," begged Chasm.

"So that you may look upon her as you leave," said Thutmos laughing softly.

"You know my mind well dear brother," said Chasm grinning like a child.

"I suppose so, at least until we reach the edge of the galaxy," he replied as if issuing an order.

"Fine," said Chasm feeling slightly deflated.

Thutmos levitated into the air and hovered there as Chasm kissed a bird goodbye. She waved to the rest of the lot who screeched their awful call to her as she rose into the air to join Thutmos.

"Do you have closure?" asked Thutmos sarcastically.

"As much as I'll get," replied Chasm flying higher into the sky.

When Thutmos and Chasm broke through Earth's atmosphere into open space, Chasm turned and began to watch the planet as she drifted further away from the blue sphere. A tear streaked the left side of her face, glistening as the light from the far off sun hit the clear liquid. The stars around the galaxy shimmered around her, making the darkness of space comfortable. Thutmos did not turn, but watched the beauty of Earth through Chasm's eyes.

"I fear that if I look with my own eyes, that I'll never be able to leave this place," said Thutmos as his heart began to grow heavy, beating in concert with Chasm's rapid drumming that felt as if it would burst through her chest at any moment.

"It is you who must remain steadfast; Charm of the Sacred. Dragging me back might very well be in your future," said Chasm trying to smile through her growing anguish.

"Our Father has put a great burden upon our hearts. I think it may have been better to not have shown us this Earth at all. It permeates with his perfection," said Thutmos closing his eyes.

"Let's-," started Chasm before she felt a jolt of energy erupt around her, She heard Thutmos gasp above her and then heard a loud reverberating boom and then a sonic wave erupted, rocketing toward them. Looking left and right, she saw that the boom originated from Earth as she lifted her hands to shield herself from the energy.

BLOOSH!

A light green-yellow wave of energy collided with her invisible force field and pushed itself against her trying to break through. The waves began to collapse backward upon the coming storm of energy and produced more booming sonic waves. Her arms began to shake as the energy continued to try and force its ways through her defense.

Grunting, she exhaled a short breath and her force field grew in power, appearing like a shield of glass and floating cloud with no sense of direction. She continued to increase the strength of her force field, but there seemed to be no cease to the onslaught of energy carried by the wave of energy.

"What is this?" screamed Chasm, feeling weak for the first time.

Thutmos shot toward her and then settled just behind her and watched her intently for a moment. The throng of power he felt continued to rise and he could see two balls of energy colliding just above the surface of the Earth.

"This cannot be-," he began baffled.

"It is, so please a little help," said Chasm, her arms shaking violently as she fought to hold back the energy.

"It keeps reinforcing itself as-," she cut him off again.

"Brother!" she yelled.

"Yes, right," said Thutmos snapping out of his mystified stupor. Touching Chasm's left shoulder he uttered a single word and a jolt of energy shot through his hand and into Chasm.

"Huh!" She could not finish the line of words that began to shoot from her mouth as the energy surged through her and into her force field with a whooshing sound, evaporating the unending wave of energy coming toward them. "Who else is here? Why couldn't we feel them?"

"We must go now!" said Thutmos with great alarm.

"You will not continue this," said Asteron. His body still shimmered under the light of the moon. The soft lunar light seemed to flow through him and reflect the light back outward as his crystal form glowed in the darkness of night.

"I have always done as I pleased," hissed Carnok with anger. "It is not your place to order me."

"Then use your reason and be guided by the word of Our Lord and cease your conquest of this fertile grove," begged Asteron.

"Your weakness is appalling," said Carnok. His black lips creased in anger as he stepped forward slowly approaching Asteron. "Either move or fall here now," said Carnok, his pace quickening to a purposeful march. A mass of dark energy flowed from his red skin like rising fumes. His fiery eyes were trained on Asteron.

"And your treachery will be the ending of the world," said Asteron facing his palms together.

A current of yellow-green energy vibrated between his hands. Asteron turned his fingers toward Carnok, thumbs above his palms, and a jet of energy shot out. The stream of crackling energy slammed into Carnok's chest, turning the ground below him into a half-mile crater at the point of impact. Carnok didn't seem phased by the attack and continued to press forward, The ocean current was pushed in the opposite direction, a towering tsunami drove backward into the vastness of the sea, rumbling with awesome power. A belt of Asteron's yellow-green energy shot upward and out of the Earth's atmosphere at a rapid pace. The trees that lined the beach were pulled up from the root, and the sand rose up with the energy that left the Earth.

"When are we going to fight?" asked Carnok with a wicked grimace

"Listen to reason," said Asteron, his hands still leveled toward Carnok.

"I have listened to my reasons."

"Is there no turning you from this course?" said Asteron gravely disappointed.

"Join me, or be the first of us to fall," said Carnok emotionless.

"We are one," said Asteron harshly. His tone didn't suggest anger. He was trying to remind Carnok of their eternal bond.

"Right, Our Union," said Carnok as if the very words polluted his guts.

Carnok now stood face to face with Asteron who had finally allowed his arms to rest at his sides. Their eyes were locked, both glossy with the fervor of overwhelming emotion.

"Appease my conquest of this Earth. Stand by my side and rule. I would make a world so great that even Merridia would have no choice but to envy its magnificence. Take my hand, serve me as your lord," said Carnok softly, though with great pride.

"There is but one above us all and he is not you," said Asteron as his fist slammed into Carnok's chest sending him sliding back a hundred feet into the sand.

"Now you're angry," said Carnok, laughing hideously as he rose to his feet. "Show me more."

Asteron readied himself as Carnok roared toward him in a blur. A thunderous boom echoed as Carnok's forearm slammed into Asteron's while swinging a hammer fist. Carnok's left hand shot up clawing at Asteron's face. Asteron pulled back avoiding the blow by an inch as he pushed back at Carnok's right arm.

The two circled each other, levitating as rain clouds began to form above them, thunder rolled as grey clouds covered the black skies. A steady flow of large rain drops began to pelt the ground as lightning crackled across the heavens of the Earth. A violent wind pushed the falling water sideways, pelting Asteron and Carnok. In this moment Carnok seemed like a predatory creature while Asteron appeared to be his prey.

Grunting, Carnok flew at Asteron again, this time with his fingers at the ready, waiting to grab Asteron. Asteron opened his arms as if awaiting a hug and then whipped backward, kicking Carnok in the chin, sending him flying higher into the air.

Asteron followed in haste and caught Carnok by the ankle. Whipping his arm over his head, he flung Carnok to the ground. The dirt and rocks below Carnok cracked, sinking in ten feet. Folding his arms together, levitating upright, Asteron descended faster than he had risen through the air to catch Carnok and drove his feet into his chest, pushing Carnok down another ten feet, before rising again.

Asteron looked down eyeing Carnok's red face that looked calm and at peace with closed eyes.

"This is not my purpose," said Asteron aloud as his feet touched the ground again. "This is not the way of Our Union." Turning, Asteron began to walk away slowly leaving Carnok behind in the twenty-foot crater. Asteron walked with his head down in great distress. "We are one. None can exist without the others." He stood still for a moment and then lifted his head to the sky, rain slamming against his crystal skin. His eyes welled, but no tears fell. Then his emotions erupted in a forceful scream, a jet of yellow-green energy shot from his mouth into the sky and formed a disc of energy as it broke through Earth's atmosphere. Thunder and lightning roared louder and with more frequency than before.

He continued for two minutes when he felt warm breath on his skin and heard a low pitched voice like a whisper just over his left shoulder.

"There is no us, only me, and I shall endure forever," said Carnok softly.

Asteron turned quickly, swinging both arms at Carnok who slipped under grabbing him by the throat and driving him through the ground.

"You do not deserve your station. You are weak and wretched," said Carnok his fiery eyes burning with anger, the red skin around his eyes, darkening more.

Carnok's eyes began to glow with more fury and comets began to shoot out of his eyes assaulting Asteron's crystal face in rapid succession. While the balls of comets were small, they hit with enough power to destroy a planet, ripping through the ground as they bounced off of Asteron's crystal face.

More than just comets flew; chips of Asteron's face began to fly from his body. Dents and scrapes lined his face in every direction.

"What will you gain by my demise?" said Asteron weakly.

"All that you are," said Carnok with pleasure.

Carnok lifted Asteron from the ground and held him up with one arm. A thousand comets shot from his eyes and ripped through Asteron, sending pieces of his crystal form in every direction, polluting the ground below them with foreign objects.

"How?" said Asteron. He looked weak, his arms dangling by his sides, his eyes barely able to stay open.

"I took it all. All the power you used. All the anger you tried to hold back but could not has joined with me. The power you saw radiating from me was not my own energy alone, but also yours. You made me the instrument of your own destruction and I thank you for it brother," said Carnok releasing Asteron who remained suspended in the air.

Carnok opened his arms and ascended into the air, floating face to face with Asteron. Touching one hand to Asteron's chest, Carnok began to draw out his life force. Yellow-green energy came to one point in Asteron's chest and drifted from him into Carnok's hand. The top layer of Asteron's skin cracked and fell to the ground in tiny grains. And then a dozen more times it happened. More power, more of Asteron's life force joined with Carnok.

"The balance will be destroyed," said Asteron struggling to speak.

"That is where you are wrong," said Carnok smiling deviously. "We will truly be one now and the balance shall be maintained. I will be the architect of a new order. A new Law of Power will be written by my hand," said Carnok.

"You will fail," said Asteron mustering every bit of strength he had left and then his eyes closed.

"Goodbye dear brother," said Carnok as he drew out the last of Asteron's power and life force.

With no more light inside of him, his skin turned black as he fell to the ground in a heap. Carnok looked at the fallen Asteron, shedding a tear. He smiled as the tear rolled down his red face and then vanished in a black spiral.

Chasm and Thutmos breached Earth's atmosphere. As they continued toward the source of the power surge that they'd felt. They felt another jolt that sent Chasm careening into Thutmos knocking him off course. He caught her after regaining his balance.

"Did you feel that," said Chasm. A look of fear registered on her face that had Thutmos taken aback.

Thutmos did not answer but held Chasm tighter. He broke the sound barrier as he whizzed to the location of the surge. In a matter of seconds the two reached the ground.

"My worst fear is realized," said Thutmos as he stared unbelieving at Asteron on the ground, black as the night sky. The rain had stopped falling, but thunder still rolled around the grey skies and short bolts of lightning crackled before it.

"Is this possible," said Chasm, confused and weeping on her knees. She touched Asteron's black and broken face with her hand. His body was cool to the touch and it unnerved her.

"No, we cannot die," said Thutmos assuredly.

"Then what explains this," said Chasm looking for an answer.

"Almost all that he was…was taken by another of us," said Thutmos clenching his jaw.

"Who would do such a…," said Chasm as the truth came to her quickly.

"But our dear brother Asteron has fallen. He is the first of us to have fallen. Never to rise again as he was," said Thutmos gravely, kneeling down beside Chasm and touching Asteron's face.

The black of Asteron's face began to fade back to the original crystal shade as Thutmos caressed his face like a loving mother to her child. Asteron's eyes began to glow a stark gold and there was a gold energy radiating from his head outward, piercing the darkness around them.

Reaching inside Asteron's head, Thutmos pulled a circular ring of energy that hummed a sad song in his hand.

"Do not ask questions to which you know the answers," said Thutmos when Chasm began to speak holding up a hand for her to be quiet.

"You know it well," said Chasm.

"That I do," said Thutmos, placing the loop around his head like a crown. The energy glowed more radiant for a moment and then seeped into Thutmos's head slowly.

Asteron's face turned black again and then slowly his black crystal form began to sprinkle into the air, small as a grain of sand until he was no more.

"We must put an end to this," said Thutmos calmly.

Chasm nodded and Thutmos ascended into the air and vanished from her sight. She stood there still reeling from seeing Asteron fallen. The rolling thunder unsettled her, making the weight of the moment all the more heavy. She heard a voice in her head, but she chose to ignore it. There was nothing she wanted to hear. There was no one she wanted to talk to.

"Is this tiny planet worth it?" she asked herself aloud. She heard the voice again and closed her mind.

"I have to save us all, Our Union must endure, the Chain of Balance must be kept," she said aloud looking around her.

The voice in her head grew louder, imploring her, sounding like an order.

"I understand," she said quietly.

A bird flew past her as the grey clouds began to turn white, and sunlight began to creep over the horizon. Another bird flew past her and then a flock of white birds flew overhead chirping their song as they batted their wings. Behind her a lion roared and she turned to see a female cat standing guard, four cubs at her heels. The lion roared again and Chasm smiled at the surly mother.

"Take care," she said and vanished from the Earth.

One Request

"I do not have time to scrape you up if you fall," said Scicremeon almost angry, looking down at Aton who held on to a rock with one hand, dangling from a tall mountain. Rocks were still tumbling down against the mountain where he had lost his footing. His breathing was labored. His chest was rising and falling rapidly as the fear of falling to his death invaded his mind. "I'd owe you at least a proper burial for allowing you to come with me this far," said Scicremeon as she began slowing her speech, "so please save me the trouble," she said in a harsh tone.

"I'll be more careful, I promise," said Aton afraid of Scicremeon's wrath. She had pushed him hard through the forest and even harder when they reached the mountain.

His feet burned and the mountain had been unpredictable at every turn. It snaked upward like a spiraling tornado, but every incline seemed to disappear as quickly as it began, becoming flat with no ground to fall onto if his grip waned. He'd surely find himself broken on the ground below if he failed to hold on.

"And stop apologizing," said Scicremeon loudly from above as she moved with ease.

"I'm sorry I," said Aton starting, but stopped himself.

You already promised, Scicremeon thought to herself shaking her head with her eyes closed at his incessant acts of kindness in the face of hostility. She couldn't understand why he wanted to be around her. She knew there was no way she could tolerate herself for even half as along as Aton had, as demanding as she was. Whatever pleasure he derived from being in her company she failed to comprehend.

Watching him swing his arm in defiance of the mountain, and grabbing ahold of the rock with both hands made her proud. The fight inside of him was much bigger than his scrawny little body.

That's the limit of my admiration, she thought to herself as she turned her attention back to the mile of rock between her and the top of the mountain.

The moon hid behind the pointed top of the crag. As it descendent out of view, a faint line of light flew outward around the rock. Sunlight had begun to break over the horizon behind Scicremeon, warming the cold air that had been blowing all night high above the ground. Reaching up Scicremeon pulled harder at every rock, moving faster up the vertical rise taking in long breaths to steady herself.

She had come to find comfort in the howling winds and Aton's grunting from below. The echoes of his struggles were quickly swept away in the wind, but there was some comedy in them. Scicremeon had giggled a number of times when his manly grunts would turn into girly squeals when he had to reach higher than his arm would allow. Twice he had to jump and Scicremeon was sure he'd miss his mark and plummet to a bone crackling demise.

Each time he conquered the mountain. As she continued to ruminate on Aton's will and bravery, she came closer to thinking that he was stronger than she was. Only his defeat at her hands time and time again at swordplay, and hand to hand combat made her think otherwise. And as tough as people in Marside were, she was no longer so sure that any of them were tougher than Aton.

He kept pushing harder, now faster than before, and everything in his big wide eyes said that he wanted to catch her. He'd want to get his head above her boot, and be able to smell the fragrance of the sweat that rolled down her back. His size was his primary foe. His arms were boney and appeared all too breakable. But when she looked back again to see that he was still alive, he smiled wide as if there was no place he would have rather been at that moment. And reach and reach and reach he did as he kept his eyes on her for as long as she looked at him.

He'd happily fall from here in adventure, she thought as his face poured out the determination in his heart. There was a sparkle in his eye. Never had she met anyone who loved dangerous things as she did. *I would be angry to fall,* she thought to herself, reminded again of the stark contrast between them.

Aton's every effort seemed to be out of want and love, hope for something more than handing ale to mean brutes that happened upon the market. It was rage and revenge that drove Scicremeon. She hadn't known her father; but never did a killer, who also wore the title of coward or trickster in Marside, ever make it out unchecked. Giving your name and showing your face to your enemy was more important than the quality of your swordsmanship. If he did not pay with his life, then he would pay with a limb.

For all of our savageness, we have our traditions. That is simply how it is. I must walk this path, she assured herself for the hundredth time, as time slipped from her mind and only the work of her limbs meant anything.

"Catch up," she yelled down at Aton, who still hadn't gained any ground.

"I will," said Aton.

He never argues, Scicremeon thought. She had always been a back-talker. She wondered if her teachers tolerated her because of her namesake.

"Don't give me words, give me action," said Scicremeon in a mocking tone.

"Yes mam," said Aton.

The grunts from his chest grew louder as he pushed himself harder. After a few minutes, his grunts turned into breathy moans as he forced himself up the mountain at a faster pace.

"Do I look like your grandmother," said Scicremeon annoyed that he had called her mam. Only women more than a hundred years of age were called mam in Marside. Most would still consider her a child, even at her age.

"No mam…I mean no, um, what should I call you?" replied Aton worried, hoping he had not insulted her.

"Master," said Scicremeon calmly.

"Master?" said Aton surprised.

"Yeah, master. I like the sound of that," said Scicremeon with a smile.

"You seem more like a sister," said Aton blissfully.

Grabbing a handful of rocks, Scicremeon flung them hard at Aton's head.

"Ah," he extolled covering his head with one head.

"Would a sister do something like that?" yelled Scicremeon.

"Yes, my cousin's sister would," said Aton dodging the rocks.

"I suppose so. Move," she screamed upset that he'd lightened her mood. *Other men aren't half as brave*, she thought of his playful nature. He had seemed emboldened since they left the village. He walked with his chest poked out and even jogged in order to keep up with her. By the time she slowed down he was usually panting and out of breath. She'd look at him out the corner of her eye and he'd smile back as if he weren't exhausted.

A dozen or so minutes passed and Scicremeon grabbed hold of a ledge and pulled herself up to the top of the spiraling mountain. The pointed apex's surface was flat and slopped downward into a steep incline.

Scicremeon slid off her backpack made of some unlucky animal's hide and reached inside, pulling out a flask. She uncorked the top of the flask and poured a swig of water down her throat. It was warm and didn't give her the refreshing feeling she was looking for, but it did serve in quenching her thirst.

Aton climbed over the ledge ten minutes after Scicremeon had set foot down on the top of the mountain. She turned around to find him standing up slowly. Aton smiled wide hoping for a look of approval, but Scicremeon never failed in offering him an eye of disdain. Curling his top lip into his mouth, he slapped the dirt off of his hands making a clapping sound as he did.

Scicremeon rolled her eyes. She was beginning to see too much of herself in him. His calm demeanor didn't stink of her prideful nature, but told her that the mountain climb wasn't as treacherous as he originally thought. He was too comfortable at its top, happily awaiting whatever was next to come.

"Where do we go from here?" asked Aton interested.

"Down."

"The other side?"

"No, down the arm and up the other," said Scicremeon, pointing to a nearly identical mountain opposite their position.

"It really exists," said Aton excited.

"Of course they do. Not everything's a myth."

"I've just never met anyone who's actually gone across."

"Do it today and you'll never have to."

"What if we die?" said Aton visibly alarmed.

"Then the climb was for nothing and we'll be just two more fools that tried to cross the Hanging Hands Mountain that never lived to tell the story."

"But it's really two separate mountains," said Aton sure of himself as he looked at the gap between the two rock formations that appeared to be hands with the finger tips touching.

"Looks like one from afar," said Scicremeon in a condescending tone.

"We ought to move before it gets too hot," said Aton looking up and wiping his brow. The second sun of Merridia had begun to come into view and the first was nearly at its highest peak for the day already.

"We're on my clock not yours," said Scicremeon dropping to her butt, crossing her legs and gulping another mouthful of water. "You're just along for the ride," said Scicremeon cracking her neck to both sides.

"Ride? We've been walking the whole time," said Aton sitting down cross legged in front of Scicremeon and pulling a flask from his own bag.

Scicremeon gave him a threatening look and Aton turned his eyes from her hiding a smirk.

"Don't forget who the student, and who the teacher is here. You've not yet learned the lesson on how to fly off of a mountain," said Scicremeon motioning her hand toward the edge.

"My apologies master," said Aton with a bit of sarcasm.

"I've got to get you away from me," said Scicremeon exacerbated.

"Why?"

"No one will ever like you again."

"You will."

"Probably not."

Aton smiled at her dry comment and half drained his flask of water to Scicremeon's dismay. He hadn't often seen her eyes go wide and they were almost literally popping out of her head.

"The next water supply could be miles from here," said Scicremeon with a look of disbelief.

"Sorry," said Aton flatly punching the cork into his flask.

"Haven't you learned anything?" she said dumping her flask back into her backpack.

"Sorry," said Aton standing up quickly before she did.

"Stop apologizing, it is becoming rude," said Scicremeon.

"I thought it was good-," began Aton.

"Manners won't save you out here and thinking will get you killed most of the time," said Scicremeon swinging her bag over her shoulder to rest on her back.

"If I'm not thinking then-."

"You're doing...following my lead," said Scicremeon sharply grabbing him by the collar. "It's about the only thing that's sure to keep you alive."

"What about the Hanging Hands?"

"That'll probably kill us both," said Scicremeon earnestly releasing his collar.

"I promise to follow," said Aton clapping his heels together and saluting like a soldier.

"You'll never learn," said Scicremeon deflated as she turned toward the incline at the edge of the Hanging Hands.

"Steep," said Aton peering over the side. His body jolted forward as a strong gust of wind swept across the mountain top.

"Well at least don't die being swept away by air," said Scicremeon catching him by the back of his collar.

"Thanks," said Aton breathless.

"Let's go," said Scicremeon rolling her eyes back and trudging past Aton.

They took to the Hanging Hands slowly. The incline was far steeper than it appeared to be. Scicremeon moved slowly below Aton, his feet resting on her shoulders, both of them with their backs and butts pressed to the side of the mountain. Their movements were slowed by the constantly shifting gravel and rock. Scicremeon checked every step three times to make sure she wouldn't lose her footing.

Aton's vibrating legs didn't make it any easier to steer them slowly down and his weight she thought would eventually become a problem if they had to maintain such a slow pace. But she'd rather the discomfort than tumbling through the air to her death.

The third sun had crept over the side of the mountain and shined through the center of the Hanging Hands. There was no way to avoid the heat with no tree for shade, or river for a cool drink. The heat was suffocating and every few minutes a flock of birds would fly pass and squawk, making Aton tremble more as their wings came terribly close to his face. The first time they passed he swatted at one and nearly fell from Scicremeon's shoulders. If her words and sword mastery hadn't caused him fear in the practice ring, her eyes did the trick on the slope; as he hadn't swatted at them again.

Maybe we should just risk a slide, Scicremeon thought to herself as the sweat climbed out of her pores faster, racing down her arms and soaking her palms. If it were not for the dirt between the rocks, her hands would have surely slipped a dozen times. *This is going to take longer than coming up,* Scicremeon thought to herself and grew tired thinking about it. It had taken them half the day to make it to the top and she now realized it might take them a full day to get to the bottom of the first hand, which was four times shorter than the entire mountain.

Day quickly slipped into night and the two were three quarters of the way down. Warm air filled Scicremeon's lungs as she breathed in slowly, comforted by the light of the moon. The heat had fatigued her a bit and she had nearly fallen asleep, firmly dug into the ground. Had it not been for Aton's weight, she might have dozed off and fallen from the mountain.

"I'm sure I can make it the rest of the way down myself," yelled Aton, though Scicremeon was right below him.

"You'll need your energy for the climb up," said Scicremeon. *Brave little runt.* He annoyed her to no end. She had cursed herself a hundred times for allowing him to tag-along. While his company was a comfort, he was too easy going. *His confidence grows at every turn. I guess I would have asked the same,* she thought forcing back a smile and the urge to look up at him impressed.

"I'm well rested. You've done all the work," said Aton beaming with confidence.

"My word, my way," said Scicremeon.

"Won't you need energy to make the climb up as well?"

"I'm a lot stronger than you are."

Aton curled his lips to the side in thought. He couldn't argue her strength. He'd seen it first hand, and had the great misfortune to experience it in the practice ring. And then he thought she was too strong; far too strong for a woman. His mother was twice Scicremeon's size in every way and she often struggled to lift two buckets of water at once. Scicremeon shrugged off tasks that would have taken two men to do.

"Will I ever be as strong as you?" said Aton hoping she would give him more information than his question begged.

"Not at the rate you're going," said Scicremeon with great joy. "Just hold still."

"Right."

"Good."

When they reached the bottom they walked on the first hand for a mile before coming to the tip. At that moment, Scicremeon and Aton now knew why so many people knew of the hands, but never made it across. The gap was too wide for anyone to jump and make it across. *Fifty yards,* Scicremeon thought to herself and continued to stare at the gap between the Hanging Hands Mountain. *At least fifty, maybe more,* she thought and looked at Aton with a hint of fear in her eyes. *He'll never make it.*

Aton watched her closely, studying her face and the way her eyes darted from one place to another. He guessed that she was thinking that he should turn back. But he wasn't sure he could make the climb alone. He wondered if she would force him to go home or if they'd sit there waiting to die. Even he thought there was no way they could make the jump. Even with all Scicremeon's strength and speed, he'd never seen her jump much more than any man could.

Scicremeon dropped to her butt and crossed her legs as she always did. Yanking her backpack off, she began rummaging through it. Aton sat next to her and pulled his sack off slowly. She eyed him softly and he looked back up and smiled to show that he was comfortable, though there was great fear running through him. She forced a toothless smile back, pulling her lips into her teeth.

From her bag she pulled out two thickly rolled leaves and set them on the ground. After setting her flask on the ground next to the leaves, she began unrolling the black leaves revealing cooked meat and nuts.

"It's cold, but you won't starve," said Scicremeon lifting the larger piece and biting a huge chunk out of it.

"Thank you," said Aton grabbing a handful of nuts and shoving them in his mouth. The left side of his cheek was bulging and he chewed happily.

Scicremeon ate fast, her attention pressed to the gap between the hands. They appeared to be so much closer from a distance, as if you could step from one to the other with little effort. That was the story of Heartless Vern, who was the first to cross the Hanging Hands Mountain to brave Hormand's Rock and attack the village of Marside. Seeing the Hanging Hands for herself made her think Vern's story of crossing the mountain a ruse, something to sensationalize his story. What was true was that Hormand and his warriors killed all of Vern's men. Heartless Vern crossing the mountain a second time was even more farfetched than the first. *No one will ever know and they won't believe me. That story's older than my father,* she thought of how stories became fact and nearly law in Marside. You didn't challenge what was older than yourself without proof. Everyone needed to believe it or you'd be gutted.

She turned to find Aton sprawled out on his back humming a tune with the mouth of his flask kissing his lips. His eyes were closed and he appeared to be at peace. If he wasn't flustered, Scicremeon was flustered for them. She still hadn't managed to figure out how she'd get them both across without getting them killed. *Best to do anything... rather than nothing at all.* Lance, her first teacher of the sword would always say that. He had never backed down from a fight, and his missing eye was proof of that. It was he who impressed upon her never to surrender to an enemy unless already dead. *And when you're dead, you really can't surrender to anything now can you?* Scicremeon chuckled thinking of his words.

"He'd jump," she said quietly to herself. "Get up," she said kicking Aton's leg.

He stirred quickly and rose to his feet. "Are we leaving?" he said confused looking around.

"Yes, we're crossing."

"How?"

"We're going to jump."

"We are?"

"Yes."

"Yes?"

"Well," she began and looked at him with a devious grin.

"You're scaring me," said Aton gravely.

"It's about time," said Scicremeon chuckling.

"About time for what?" asked Aton shoving his flask back into his bag.

"That you show a bit of fear," said Scicremeon shaking a finger at him.

"I can't make that jump,' said Aton lifting a hand to the gap.

"I'm going to throw you," said Scicremeon as she gathered her things and started toward the edge of the hand.

"You've got to be kidding me right," said Aton with half a grin mixed with the look of impending vomit that would spew from his mouth at any moment.

"Like you said, you can't make the jump," said Scicremeon without care.

"No offense, but I'm half-grown, and that's," started Aton not knowing the distance. He only knew he couldn't jump it.

"Fifty yards give or take," said Scicremeon as if the distance were short.

"Fifty-."

"Yup, fifty, get ready," said Scicremeon swinging her bag onto her back.

Aton strapped his bag on and came to stand at the edge of the hand with Scicremeon. He looked down and realized how high up he was. Death would be the only result of a fall and he began to quake with fear, his knees going weak at the prospect of falling. There was nothing to grasp, no rope to burn his hands on, not even a sharp rock that might cut through his flesh, but save him from a painful thump. The only good thought that registered in his mind was that he'd probably die on impact and only feel something for a split second before the world went black.

The color flushed from Aton's face and his heart began to pound. Scicremeon looked at him and saw the fear resonating from his being. She rolled her eyes and looked into the sky, rolling her head around trying to fight back her emotion.

Scicremeon grabbed Aton and pulled him into her bosom, and stroked his hair. He wrapped his arms around her tight and a single tear fell from his eyes.

"I promise nothing will happen to you," said Scicremeon, pained by her moment of weakness for the boy.

"May I tell you my one request?" begged Aton.

"Request for what," said Scicremeon pulling back from him confused.

"My dying request, don't I get one in the face of defeat?" asked Aton seriously, his eyes still glossy.

"What defeat? You aren't in battle," said Scicremeon with a deep frown.

"Yes. We're up against the mountain," said Aton assuredly.

Scicremeon could do nothing but smile. He was more than she had ever hoped for in a student. At every turn he found some way to conquer a portion of his fear. His heart still beat rapidly, but it had slowed a bit since she first grabbed hold of him.

"If you say so," she said to dispel his notion of some great battle against the mountain. She thought his deduction of the situation was appropriate, but she'd never confess it to him.

"Ready," he said cracking his knuckles and licking the ash from his lips.

"Good, I know I can get you at least twenty yards out, give or take," said Scicremeon dusting off her hands.

"What about the rest of it?" said Aton his eyes wide with shock.

"The rest is on fate. If you pray, do so now," said Scicremeon as she snatched him by the arm and pulled him up, his face level with hers. "Do you trust me?"

"Not right now," said Aton. He wanted to shake himself loose, but what he'd do after being free didn't appear in his mind. He'd wanted to go on an adventure and he had it. "But that's what adventure is all about right," said Aton and then produced a lie of a smile on his face.

"Yeah sure," said Scicremeon and grabbed one of his ankles with her free hand.

Here we go, Scicremeon thought as she began to turn in a circle. Her turns began slowly as Aton slowly rose from her ankles to being level with her shoulders. Faster and faster she turned until she could hear the air whipping around her in her ear like a howling beast. Faster and faster she went until the rocks of the Hanging Hands Mountains became a blur. Her eyes began to tear from the air whipping against her, but she didn't want to close them.

"Uh!" with a grunt she released Aton into the air sailing over the gap.

Up he went quickly in an arc toward the opposite hand of the mountain. And then quickly his upward movement ceased and he felt himself suspended in air for a moment. Fear rose in him quickly and without warning the feeling of falling caressed his limbs as he began to shoot toward the ground below. There was no rock formation below him, only the green of a distant patch of grass.

There was a flash of light and he closed his eyes. He didn't want to look at his coming doom. Crack. He heard it, and then all the air left his body. There was no pain, only numbness in his back and chest as his eyes rolled up in his head and all that he once saw went black.

Lovely Face

A resounding boom erupted; rocks flew in every direction, floating in the air and then gravity enveloped them, forcing them to tumble to the ground. Where they hit he could not tell, as he was too far up, seeing only black. His head was ringing and though they were open, his eyes were hazy. He saw a figure sailing over him, sword at the hip, wearing a single-strapped backpack across the right shoulder and a satchel across the left. Sunlight helped to blur his vision further as he squinted harder to avoid the radiant light.

To his right, he heard a grunt. It was the severe rumbling that rose from the chest of a man. He never thought any woman could sound that way. He turned to look and saw her faintly. She rose from a crouched position, one leg slightly ahead of the other after bracing for the landing. He recognized the dingy boots from the field near the two-room shack that had been his home for several weeks, even though he never had the pleasure of sleeping under the ramshackle roof. Somehow, he always ended up sleeping outside.

"I'm alive," said Aton rubbing his eyes with both hands. He grabbed at his forehead and massaged it for a long moment. Blinking rapidly, the world slowly came into focus.

"Are you hurt?" asked Scicremeon

"No," said Aton sitting upright. "Ah." He recoiled when he pulled his back from the mountain.

Scicremeon opened his shirt from the collar and peered in.

"Just bruised, you'll live," said Scicremeon releasing his collar.

"Did you jump?" asked Aton curious as he remembered seeing her sailing over him.

"Not quite," said Scicremeon as she reached into her backpack and pulled out a wooden box.

"How did you get across alone?" begged Aton with a fierce look of want.

When she opened the box, a rank odor jumped from it. Inside of the box was a green colored cream with all manner of lumpy looking things that Aton didn't recognize.

With two fingers Scicremeon swiped some of the green goop and pulled Aton's shirt open again. Finding his bruise, she rubbed the cream on in circles quickly, not taking into account the discomfort he may have felt.

Grinding his teeth, he groaned as she massaged the cream in aggressively. His back began to burn as if on fire and then the area around the bruise began to tingle. Slowly the hot intensity turned cold, and it felt as if someone was digging into his back and pulling the pain out inch by inch. Aton breathed a sigh of relief and smiled as the remedy that Scicremeon rubbed into his bruise seemed to give comfort to his entire back. Some of the fatigue that he felt had gone and he prepared himself to stand up.

"Rest a moment," said Scicremeon touching his shoulder and softly pressing him back down.

"So how did you do it?" asked Aton again, the question still at the forefront of his mind.

"A gift from my father," said Scicremeon closing the lid over the green cream and stuffing the box into her bag.

Aton gave her a puzzled stare. The expression on his face begged her to elaborate.

Scicremeon rolled her eyes as she always did and sat back on her heels.

"Have you heard the great tales of my father's exploits?" asked Scicremeon.

"Everyone in Marside has," he replied in a matter of fact way.

"So you've heard the saying that Aygron Stormblade could kill a thousand men with one blow?" asked Scicremeon expecting the nod of *yes*, as Aton began shaking his head before she finished her sentence. "There is no man, not even my father, who could kill a thousand men with a single blow. But there are forces in this world that can do that very thing, and so much more."

"Like the man from the beach," replied Aton as he thought of being trapped in a bubble of energy.

"Like him. Yet, he was no man," said Scicremeon.

Aton stared at her in puzzled amazement for a long moment. "Then what was he?" said Aton with great curiosity.

"He was a god," said Scicremeon flatly.

"You fought a god!" said Aton astonished.

"Black Dawn himself," said Scicremeon with a hint of pride that nearly made her smile.

"Then that explains it," said Aton without thought.

"Explains what?" replied Scicremeon.

"Why you lost. If he was anyone else, you would have crushed him," said Aton with a wide smile holding up a clinched fist.

Scicremeon rolled her eyes and forced back a smile before saying, "Any way, my father was blessed with something called The Blue Ember. The talent became known to those who lived in those days as The Fires of Aygron. It allowed him to shoot blasts of blue flame from his chest and roast his enemies on impact."

"It's what you tried to do to Black Dawn," said Aton.

"Doesn't work very well on gods."

"But it got you across the hands?"

"The stronger the blast, the more force. The more force, the further back I go. So I figured I'd give it a shot," said Scicremeon looking at the gap between the two towers of rock called the Hanging Hands Mountain. "Here I am, still breathing," she said closing her bag.

"Thank the gods," said Aton inhaling deeply.

"Let's move."

The stories had all been wrong. The other side of the Hanging Hands Mountain was no treacherous stretch of winding rivers and falling rocks. It was a quiet forest descending onto flat land. The ground had begun to level off slowly as they marched down the last couple miles of the incline. The way down was quick, a comfortable slant of soft dirt and fallen branches. Wide rays of sunlight slipped through the forest, as the trees seemed to be evenly spaced, as if they were purposely planted at their distance from one another.

The forest wasn't a simple boring green with beams of light from the suns. There were hundreds of different flowers growing in an array of colors. Buzzing insects with wings and scurrying creatures that paid them no mind. The place seemed to be too at peace for a forest, a place that usually held mystery and danger at every turn. They'd encountered none on their trek and Aton seemed comfortable and at home.

Scicremeon wore a focused scowl the entire time, turning her head at the slightest sound she didn't recognize. She kept her hand on the pommel of her sword and walked about ten feet behind Aton who was struck with wonder, trudging along and exploring the behaviors of the many creatures he had seen. She had smiled once at his carefree nature and then cursed him for all of his mindless freedom. Revenge weighed heavy on her mind, allowing her no ease.

Serenity is a dream I cannot find, she thought to herself as she touched her sword with her fingers, feeling the contours of its shape. *This is the only comfort I find in this world,* she thought and then her eyes turned to Aton. She turned them quickly away as he looked over his shoulder with a smile. *I cannot remember the days when life was such as you make it seem boy.* Tears welled in her eyes and she rubbed them briskly hoping he didn't turn again to see her in a weakened state of mind. *It's not as if he can read my mind,* she thought and then smiled to the heavens as two tears rolled. Her heart had become heavy with all of the anger boiling in her gut and the beauty sprawled around her; surely designed by one of the gods or even Corvus himself. *Who else could paint such a beautiful picture but the gods?*

"Stay where I can see you," Scicremeon yelled ahead to Aton who had begun to chase a black bird with white wings that was half his size.

He didn't respond and only kept chasing the bird. Scicremeon began to jog. Her nose flared as she began to pick up speed, closing the distance between Aton and herself. Just as she reached to grab Aton, he turned and jammed the palms of his hands into her stomach.

"Fifty two steps, ha," he said in victory.

"This isn't time for games," said Scicremeon angry that she didn't notice him twist.

"I was practicing," said Aton.

"Good student," she said smiling with her hands on her hips. "I'll have to think of more ways to snap you in half."

"That's not going to-," Aton began but felt his legs fly from under him as Scicremeon kicked him in the knees with her shin.

The hand came from behind a tree. The claws were long and looked sharper than her sword. She could hear the air whisk as the beastly hand cut through it toward her face. She twisted and leaned back and felt the air blow past her. Her shoulders hit the ground hard and a drop of blood rolled from the tip of her nose down the right side of her face. Aton lay at her feet, looking at her startled.

"You're bleeding," he said in horror looking at her angry face.

"Move," she said, her voice nearly screeching.

Aton rolled quickly to one side just before a foot the size of his body came down denting the dirt six inches deep.

"Behind me now," said Scicremeon as she stood and pulled her blade.

Aton scrambled forward to his feet nearly tumbling over, kicking up dirt as he ran behind Scicremeon. He held on to her waist, looking around her, his eyes wide with fear. He'd never seen anything so big.

"What is it?" said Aton in horror.

"I have not the slightest clue, but don't you think he has a lovely face," said Scicremeon with a hungry smile.

"Lovely?" said Aton looking up at Scicremeon who had looked in his direction.

"We are never in agreement," said Scicremeon as her blood began to boil hot. Her heart beat slowed as she inhaled deeply and licked her lips as if looking at a hot meal after a long day's work.

"Huh," said Aton with a furrowed brow, his nerves frantically colliding with one another.

"Scicremeon," said the booming voice of the giant beast that had just tried to kill them.

"I've been really popular these last few weeks. More so than usual," said Scicremeon as she pulled Aton's hands from her waist and strutted forward slowly with her sword dangling at her side nearly touching the ground.

"The gods have given me your name. It is time that you are judged," said the big voice of the beast. While his appearance was ferocious under his furry mane, his voice was regal and measured.

"And you are," said Scicremeon in an uninterested tone.

"I am The Ragnon," said The Ragnon.

"That's a dumb name," said Scicremeon.

The Ragnon's eyes narrowed in contemplation as he studied Scicremeon. He looked her up and down. When he was done surveying her, he titled his head to the left and kept it there for a few minutes. He then titled his head to the right and kept studying her.

"I think he likes you," said Aton, whispering to Scicremeon still staring at the beast, grabbing her waist.

"He probably wants to eat me."

"Choose your weapon," said The Ragnon in his booming voice.

Scicremeon swung her sword in a circle as she pulled her back pack off and tossed it to the side. She pushed Aton's hand off of her waist again and grabbed him by the front of his collar.

"Hide," she said assertively hoping not to scare him.

He shook his head yes, his eyes wide with fear and confirmation of her orders as he back pedaled looking around frantically for where he would shield himself from the eyes of The Ragnon.

When Aton was gone from her sight, Scicremeon returned her attention to The Ragnon who'd begun to slowly approach her. The ground looked as if it would give way under his bulk, each time his massive foot struck the earth. He towered over her with teeth bared, claws at the ready with his eyes trained on her.

Boom, boom, boom; The Ragnon's feet began to pound against the floor of the forest as his speed increased. The distance between him and Scicremeon closed rapidly. Scicremeon crouched with her sword at the ready, level with her hip, pointed toward The Ragnon.

Ten feet now separated them and Scicremeon began to run toward The Ragnon. Her eyes narrowed as she trained them on The Ragnon. She screamed at the top of her lungs, her body temperature rising slowly as she sprinted toward her adversary. The Ragnon's arms swung; his razor sharp claws singing their malice in the air. Scicremeon felt the air pass her face as she titled backward and slipped between The Ragnon's legs, swinging her sword at his left leg.

A jolt of discomfort shot through her arm from the tips of her fingers to her shoulders. She'd heard her blade ringing as if it had clashed with another sword. No blood ran from The Ragnon's leg as she looked back at her failed attempt to wound the beast who'd begun to turn on her already growling with anger, his long hooked teeth protruding from his mouth. He roared again and a cloud of smoke issued from the hole in his face.

Scicremeon stood and gazed at The Ragnon, feeling angry that her sword made no impression on his leg. She knew now that his flesh was as hard as her sword and wouldn't be easy to scar. *How can I beat him,* she asked herself the question only once as the hulk of a beast bared down on her again, swinging with intent to kill her where she stood every time.

She rolled once and again, and what began to feel like a thousand times, as The Ragnon kept coming, seemingly more energized from his relentless exertions. Her breathing had begun to become labored and she found herself leaning against a wide tree, trying to hide herself from his never ending assault to catch her breath and regain her composure. Her only comfort was that the suns of Merridia had begun to descend out of sight.

Minutes passed without the booming sound of The Ragnon's feet descending down upon the ground. Scicremeon began to grow anxious and her caution began to wane. She wondered if he had grown bored and departed from what seemed to be a need to kill her. *But he's no mindless beast,* she thought as she remembered his voice. His regal tone had said; *I'm important and you ought to fear me.* She hated him. For as much as he was a beast, he was one that could reason.

"Watch out," screamed Aton, his voice breaking her calm, setting her blood boiling again.

She ducked, expecting the blow to tear through the tree and severe her head, but there was a cracking sound from under her. And before she could get to her feet, the tree was falling. She could hear The Ragnon grunting his effort. His leg was pressed into the ground as he leaned on the massive tree pulling its roots from the earth below.

Death, that was all that crossed Scicremeon's mind as she began trying to scurry from a seated position. *Not enough time,* she thought realizing how big the tree really was. It was ten feet wide and she wouldn't make it in time. The weight of the tree would crush her and end her hope for revenge. *I'll never make it to Chalendor.*

She turned quickly and lied flat on her back.

"What are you doing, get out of the way," said Aton screaming from atop a tree just a few yards from where Scicremeon lay on her back awaiting a terrible death. "You're not supposed to give up," he yelled at the top of his lungs. Tears rolled down his cheeks as he began to scramble from the branch he was perched on.

Aton hugged the tree and began sliding down as fast as he could. He didn't care for his comfort as he allowed the tree bark to rip into the palms of his hands, removing flesh every few inches on the way down. His already tattered shoes barely fared any better as he used his toes to steady his descent. He turned his head to look back as he slid down, but couldn't see Scicremeon.

"Don't give up," he yelled, but this time he didn't know if it was for Scicremeon or himself. He let go of the tree and dropped through the air. He thought that he'd gotten far enough where he could jump, but he misjudged the height of the tree and fell head-long into the soft dirt. "Uh," he moaned and saw the tree fall hard into the ground above Scicremeon just before his eyes closed.

Aton slipped into a dark oblivion. A ferocious voice called out to him and began to speak in a language he had never heard. The boy tried to shake loose of the voice but as he fought, its power increased and pressed harder upon his mind. He knew he wasn't dead, but with every moment that passed, he wished he was. Aton suddenly stopped trying to fight and the pressure in his head slowly subsided and the voice in his head became clearer. He understood its words, foreign as they were. They weren't commanding or invasive, but he felt that all the control he had over himself had been lost. And then he saw them again, those eyes that he'd seen when he shook the old man's hand. They made an impression in his psyche and he could feel an ominous presence binding with his essence, breaking apart who he was and making something new. He fought it and his entire body felt as if he'd been gripped by a thousand hands, wrestling him down so he couldn't move. He heard, saw, and felt a thousand voices, a thousand images and a thousand emotions flooding in on him. Just as he felt himself going crazy, he could see the stars in the sky.

Looking over to where the tree had fallen, he could see Sci-cremeon climbing out from a hole in the tree, the perfect circle between the bark still smoking with little fires rippling about slowly dying down. The scowl on her face made Aton smile. She was still beautiful, her auburn hair mangled in every direction with small pieces of shattered bark entangled in her locks.

"The Fires of Aygron will not save you," said The Ragnon haughtily.

"They've saved me twice today," said Scicremeon sarcastically as she jumped from the fallen tree.

The Ragnon laughed hard, his broad sinewy chest rising and falling fast.

"Whoa," said Aton breathlessly as Scicremeon shot toward The Ragnon faster than he'd ever seen.

She plunged her sword into the center of The Ragnon's chest and felt a more painful jolt shoot through her arm than the first time she'd struck The Ragnon. She heard the same singing of metal on metal, but this time she heard The Ragnon grunt and heard his foot give way to her blow. A smile slipped across her lips, but it was short lived as he swatted her to the side as he stumbled back slightly. Her satchel flew from her shoulder as she barreled through the air before slamming into a tree.

"Oh," she yelped as she hit the ground.

"No," said Aton as he saw Scicremeon reaching for her sword.

"Wha…you…what…" she kept trying to speak, but decided she should first catch her breath before she tried. The Ragnon was far enough from her for now that he was no danger. "Didn't I tell you to hide," she yelled with an angry expression.

"I know, but I thought you were going to die," cried Aton. "I was trying to save you."

She looked at his watery eyes and felt her heart drop, the scowl attempting to flee her face, but she maintained her hard stare. She looked at him with wanting eyes.

"Will you just do as I say," said Scicremeon, her face as mean as The Ragnon's, but her eyes pleading with him, incessantly begging for him to listen to her request.

"Yes," he said softly, only his eyes assuring Scicremeon of his intention to remain as far away from The Ragnon as he could. Her eyes reminded him of his mother's when he'd hurt himself.

Aton began to scurry back up the tree slowly and as he neared his perch, he heard The Ragnon's feet marching again toward Scicremeon's position. He saw Scicremeon's eyes change, and he saw her sword held at the ready. She'd pulled a knife from her boot. Aton felt a pang of pain in his head and closed his eyes as he shuddered. The revelation came quick and he spoke to himself twice before he yelled.

"They won't work," said Aton with all haste.

"What are you talking about?" screamed Scicremeon to Aton.

"Your weapons, your father's gift; none of them will work," said Aton batting his eyes confused.

"How do you know this?" said Scicremeon as she slipped to one side as The Ragnon's foot dented the bark of the tree she had fallen in front of. He swung again, and she used her sword to defend his blow and was sent stumbling off to the side.

"I don't know," yelled Aton.

"Then what am I supposed to do without a weapon," she said ducking again and lunging forward with her sword.

The Ragnon parried her blow and slapped her across the shoulder, sending her sprawling to the ground. She cut her arm twice on a stone before rolling over onto her back.

"Only what you were born with can aid you in this fight," said Aton still confused at where he'd gotten the information.

"If I die it's on you," said Scicremeon as she threw her sword and knife aside. Her eyes turned to their normal shade as she watched Aton settle onto his perch in the tree.

"If you die, I don't think I'll be too far behind," said Aton with a smile.

Little prick always joking when we're facing death, Scicremeon mused as The Ragnon swung a fist at her face.

She pushed her arms up in front of her face and felt his massive wrist press into her arms knocking her onto her butt. His flesh was hot to the touch and soft as any animal she'd ever cut open for dinner, yet her sword could not make his blood run.

Again he swung and she parried, moving her arm in a circle trying to absorb as little of the force from the blow that she could. The Ragnon's balance shifted slightly and Scicremeon kicked him in the bend behind his knee and watched his leg buckle slightly.

"Pesky little mortal," said The Ragnon as he stepped around and kicked at her.

She slipped under and punched him in the back of the thigh. He grunted again.

"Not as weak as you thought," said Scicremeon proud of causing him a bit of pain.

"You will die," said The Ragnon.

"I don't think so," she said as she ran toward him.

He reached out to grab her with both hands and she somersaulted forward, landing on his forearm. Scicremeon ran up the length of his arms and saw his eyes go wide as she reached his shoulder.

Crack!

The Ragnon's head twisted to one side and he began to stumble to his right. His arms flailed and Scicremeon jumped to his other arm.

Crack!

Crack!

Twice she kicked him and sent him stumbling in circles. He reached to grab her, but she was too fast, flipping backward and landing smartly on her feet.

The Ragnon steadied himself and attacked again moving toward Scicremeon faster. His sharp claws knocked chunks out of big trees, and fell others as Scicremeon used her speed to keep out of reach of his sharp claws. As she continued to evade him, she began to smile and the comfort she usually felt in battle began to rise inside of her. She ran in a circle keeping The Ragnon moving and clawing and she began to see that he was tiring. His breathing had become labored. Half an hour had passed since she kicked him in the head three times.

"Stand still," he roared as he hefted a tree, raising it over his head.

"Ha," she laughed again as the tree sailed over her head and knocked over another.

The Ragnon hefted another tree and raised it over his head.

Running at full speed, Scicremeon lifted a large branch from the ground without breaking stride and ran away from The Ragnon. With great purpose he ran behind her, his feet booming on the ground, shaking leaves from trees as the stars shined brighter across the darkening sky.

Scicremeon was headed toward a tree and then heard The Ragnon grunt. She could hear the howling wind as the tree sailed through the air, The Ragnon pounding behind it. Scicremeon ran up the tree in front of her, and pushed off with all of her might.

Crack!

The thick branch in her hand shattered against The Ragnon's head and he toppled over, thudding against the forest floor. Scicremeon came down on his chest, her eyes locked with his. The piece of branch left in her hand was sharp, and she raised it over her head. The Ragnon's eyes rolled into the back of his head and his eyelids fell over his eyes.

His chest still rose and fell, air slipping out of his huge snout, and she could hear the loud thumping of his heart behind his chest.

"He really does have a lovely face doesn't he," said Scicremeon smiling at an approaching Aton.

"He looks nice when he sleeps," said Aton as he stood over The Ragnon's head.

Suddenly The Ragnon's eyes opened wide and his eyes flashed dark black, glowing like the moon. Scicremeon slammed the sharp branch into his chest, but it shattered against him as his body began to rise.

Scicremeon rolled off of him and landed on her feet crouching, preparing to fight. The Ragnon's body began to turn to stone as it ascended into the air. He rose slowly for a while and then rapidly until it was a blur that quickly vanished from their sight.

A few long minutes passed as the two of them stared into the sky not speaking a word. Scicremeon gathered her weapons and bags and strapped them around herself and readied to continue out of the forest.

Aton rubbed in another layer of Scicremeon's green cream before wiping his hands on his pants. He then took a sip of water from his flask and closed the cap.

Scicremeon began to lead them out of the forest and then stopped and looked up. She turned around fast and cocked her head to the side, staring at Aton with a puzzled look.

"How did you know my weapons wouldn't work?" asked Scicremeon.

"Because they're enchanted," said Aton blankly without think-ing.

"I thought you said you didn't know," replied Scicremeon.

"I just remembered when you asked," said Aton like a kid hop-ing to quiet a prying parent.

"How did you know that they were enchanted?" said Scicre-meon.

"Someone told me."

"Who?"

"I don't know."

"I guess it doesn't really matter," said Scicremeon as she turned and begin walking again. *That makes no sense*, she thought.

Aton shrugged his shoulders and jogged up beside Scicreme-on, pulling on the strap to his book bag. He looked up at her and smiled. She rolled her eyes and mushed the side of his face and he smiled wider, looking up at the stars as they left the forest behind them.

No Return

Thutmos's tears ran hot as he watched them lying there together, their faces blackened on the surface of a bright burning star. The twins; Cowlran and Thracno were unlike most of the others, enjoying only each other's company and that of Kinozl, the third member of Quadrant 4. However, they communed with Thutmos from afar every once in a while enlisting the advice of The Divine Witness. He knew it was his station as the Charm of the Sacred and his closeness to Aeon that made them treat him differently. And as much as he knew them not, he knew them well as members of Our Union, and continued to weep for them as he approached the hot burning star that was their resting place.

As Thutmos grew closer, the twins' black faces seemed to blend in with their jet black hair, making them seem as one. Only the light from the star allowed Thutmos to see the lines that broke them apart. Even now they were inseparable, holding hands, their heads touching from chin to ear. Thutmos lifted his hands and a soft humming began. Cowlran and Thracno began to float toward him. As they drifted toward him, their hair swayed and their heads titled downward into their chests. Their eyes were closed and the expressions on their faces were calm. It seemed that they had accepted their fate, embraced it even. Thutmos remembered Asteron's face still holding the scowl of battle and resistance.

Asteron had always been strong of heart and his power pushed Chasm to the brink of losing control. Thutmos's weeping grew in intensity at the memory of his fallen brethren, but he made no sound as the tears rushed from his eyes like a waterfall into the abyss of endless space.

Thutmos touched the twins on their cheek and their faces brightened again, glowing a stark gold as Asteron's had, when he'd touched him fallen on the surface of the Earth. Like Asteron, from their head came a gold ring of reverberating energy that Thutmos grasped in either hand. He put the rings together and they became one. He then placed the ring of energy on his head and waited as it seeped in. At that moment he pulled his hands from the twins' faces and the black took them again; and like Asteron they began to dissipate into nothingness, scattering into a million tiny grains until they were no more.

Chasm began to weep when Cowlran and Thracno disappeared. Disbelief invaded her mind. She watched Thutmos as he turned. She saw his tears falling and didn't bother to look at the others around her. She could feel their grief inside herself.

"There is but one way to end this," said Everdon the only one among them without watery eyes.

"We must reason with Carnok and bring him to his senses," said Chasm looking at Everdon confused.

"He has chosen his path Chasm," said Thutmos trying to reel in his anguish.

"The hammer must fall," said Everdon.

"Will you not heed my words?" begged Chasm.

"Do you believe that Carnok listened to the words of Thracno and Cowlran? He has removed himself from Our Union, keeping his thoughts shielded from us, his whereabouts unknown. When was the last time you felt his presence? Yes..." said Thutmos adamantly, "...when he slayed our brother upon the Earth. Has he exercised reason or care for the Chain of Balance?" said Thutmos angry, his voice rising with each sentence. "It must be war."

"Indeed," said Everdon solidifying Thutmos's notion, casting a sharp eye upon Chasm as he shook his head up and down.

"The three of us are to be of a single mind," said Chasm narrowing her eyes and staring deeply into Thutmos's eyes.

"You are to be only a guide for my indifference. Everdon exists to solidify my notions. For many millennia, it has only been your notions that he has found reason to accept. Today I am set upon a course to meet Carnok head on and bring him to heel. He has taken from Our Union. He has tainted the purity of the Home of the Souls by slaying our brethren upon its sacred ground. He has invaded a quadrant that was not his own and spread malice upon its breast. What he has planned next escapes the communion of Our Union. His path is no longer the path of Our Lord, but a path beset by him. We know not of Kinozl and-," said Thutmos before Chasm's voice broke into the air.

"Give him a chance to answer for his transgressions," said Chasm narrowing her eyes as a great light broke into the darkness of space.

"He whose eyes are like mine own does not have a heart the same," said Luminar flanked by Trurow who was sorrowful, her grey robes seeming more drab than usual.

"Carnok has slain our brethren and must pay for his crimes against Our Union," said Trurow, her voice faint and weary.

"We do not exist to be set against one another," said Chasm loudly hoping someone would hear her.

"Carnok shall feel the wrath of Our Union," said Thutmos his voice booming, sending a rumbling shockwave across the cosmos as he looked at each of them starkly. "Will you stand with me sister?" he asked Chasm with wanting eyes.

"It is the righteous path," said Everdon quietly.

"We shall," said Luminar and Trurow together.

"Please, allow me to enlist the purity of Primsec. He may be able to deter Carnok from this path. Everyone has always listened to him," said Chasm pained, her eyes begging Thutmos to accept her request.

There was a long pause and everyone's eyes fell upon Thutmos who rubbed his face with his hand, ruminating. He closed his eyes for a short moment before opening them.

"There can be no return to what we once were. There has been a rift that has reshaped the Chain of Balance. It has been made anew and I fear that not even The Smile of Our Union may be able to suture the fissure of this great calamity," said Thutmos shaking his head as he locked eyes with Chasm.

"Then I am overruled and must continue to perform my duty with you, the Chieftain of The Ripples of Time and Space. It is your path I must follow now, for Our Union is strongest in you," said Chasm bowing her head to Thutmos.

"Then let there be no further discussion on it, our course is set," said Everdon.

"How then will we proceed?" asked Luminar her voice soft, though akin to a rippling fire.

"As a single unit," said Thutmos.

"Indeed," said Everdon.

"We could cover more of the universe if we split up," said Trurow.

"Carnok's strength has grown many times over. There is nothing any of us could do alone," said Chasm giving a sharp look to Thutmos.

"She is right," said Thutmos flatly.

"But I will go and seek out Primsec. He may soon come to stand on our side," said Chasm.

"If you do not find him quickly, then return to us," said Thutmos fearfully.

"Indeed, for Carnok is surely watching," said Everdon.

In a flash, Chasm was gone and a great silence fell over the four of them. The star that had been the resting place of Thracno and Cowlran spewed hot streams of liquid from its core, warming the open area around them.

"Why is Primsec now keeping himself shielded from us?" said Luminar curiously.

"I do not think he has joined Carnok in his quest to dominate us," said Thutmos appearing to be in deep thought.

"It is highly unlikely," said Everdon as he eyed Luminar.

"He would never harm any of us," said Thutmos rubbing his chin.

"Indeed," said Everdon shaking his head yes.

"Therefore, all that I know and all that I feel tells me that he will stay as far away from this battle as he can. Many of us may soon fall in Carnok's wake. I would hope Primsec's righteousness could extinguish the fires of Carnok's trepidation. Yet…when has Primsec done much more than muse and watch the cycles of life?" said Thutmos to Luminar directly while giving his attention to all of his companions every few moments.

"Is it truly wise then to allow Chasm to go alone when we don't know Primsec's position," begged Trurow.

"As the Charm has said, we know his heart," said Everdon sternly.

"Hearts have a tendency to change on a whim," said Trurow in opposition to Everdon's hard assertion.

"We are far too old to be whimsical," said Thutmos shaking his head *no*, his eyes closed as he inhaled deeply. "It is our nature to focus. To have our eyes ever cast on the Chain of Balance."

"What part of the balance then is Carnok's eye set upon?" asked Trurow with hungry eyes.

"The same as it has always been," said Thutmos.

Luminar gave him a sullen look but spoke no words for a long moment. She rubbed the tips of her fingers together and then smiled. A laugh built up inside her and her shoulders began to shake with laughter as tears began to fall from her eyes. "We've allowed all of the signs to go unnoticed," she said angrily.

"What is done is done," said Everdon loudly.

"Yes, we must begin on our course," said Thutmos.

"Where does this new path begin?" said Luminar.

"We shall commune with The First Born. His sight is nearly as keen as our own from the perch of his tree. Whatever Carnok's plans are, it includes the whole of the universe. There will be none who are not touched by his transgressions. Thus, his vision may be even better than our own in this circumstance, as Our Union has become splintered and layered with veils," said Thutmos.

"Indeed," said Everdon with a vicious scowl.

Old One

Looking directly across the throne room, Black Dawn noticed that Gorgon Ray sat leaning to the left, his elbow resting on the arm of the throne between the feet of a statue that was made in his likeness. The face of the statue was not an exact replication of his current self, as he wore a great black beard, and there were a few wrinkles under his eyes that were not apparent on the statue. He had changed it himself since he last looked upon the statue in disgust. Black Dawn found a bit of humor in his uncle's actions. As much as he often gave good advice and crafted the weapons that the gods wielded; his thirst for aesthetic beauty was truly unmatched.

To Gorgon Ray's right was Phray, whose calm face turned into a sneer when she locked eyes with Black Dawn. He smiled when she frowned at him and rubbed the tip of his nose. Phray's nose wore a nick that had mostly healed, but Black Dawn's mockery of her imperfection made her grind her teeth together as she flinched to stand. Black Dawn waved his finger at her as if to say *no* as he sat there laughing silently.

Opposite the large throne atop the dais were two thrones, one holding a man and the other a woman in between the legs of statues of their likeness. The man sitting just to the right of Phray was thick, wrapped in a heavy looking black armor, holding a large golden chalice adorned with red jewels. His face was big and muscular looking, shaven clean, handsome, but quite uninviting.

"Mastadon," said Black Dawn nodding his head once.

"Brother," said Mastadon with a big gurgling voice, that seemed to carry with it, the sound of impending doom.

"Have you noticed the jewel that Phray is wearing upon her nose," said Black Dawn with a sly smirk, looking at Phray again.

"Another run in with The Ragnon?" said Mastadon with a great smile, narrowing menacing golden eyes as he leaned forward a bit on his throne.

"You should see what I did to him," said Phray to Mastadon with a grimace pressed on Black Dawn.

"He was in more pain after his second fight," said Black Dawn leaning forward and staring at Phray for a long moment.

"You fought The Ragnon? That is child's play," said Mastadon laughing hard with a half-surprised look on his face.

"Of course not, he is my companion these days," said Black Dawn dismissively.

"She never did quite understand how his power works. Too persistent eh Phray…" said Mastadon.

"I understand the beast quite well. He caught me by surprise," said Phray defending herself.

"I want to know who it was then," said Mastadon sipping a golden liquid from his chalice.

"The Ragnon was set upon a mortal at the behest of our good friend Phray," said Black Dawn happily. "She was able to best him rather quickly."

"Outdone by a mortal," said Mastadon laughing his mockery.

"Will the three of you ever quit with your competition?" said a quiet female voice to the right of Mastadon.

"Pearl, dear sister, my sincerest apologies," said Black Dawn bowing his head to the woman on the throne next to Mastadon.

Her hair was white as snow and one could get lost in its beauty if their eyes were set upon it for too long. Her face was a perfect almond shape, her skin pale, though it held a glow that couldn't be missed. Like most of the other gods her eyes were golden, but her eyes were closed most of the time, her hands folded in her lap. Pearl sat upright, almost as stiff as the statue above her. She was arraigned in all white robes like Gorgon Ray, save for a jewel set in the center of a necklace as black as the eyes of the statue behind the throne atop the dais.

"Do not apologize," said Pearl, her voice soft as a whisper, "but please spare me when we are in council as I cannot leave."

"I thought you enjoyed my company?" said Black Dawn as if hurt.

"You're just a bore," said Mastadon turning his head to face Pearl. He delivered his words slowly, putting extra emphasis on the last.

"We can at least agree on that," said Phray rolling her eyes at Pearl.

"You say there are troubling things on the horizon, do you not?" said Pearl a tad snappy to Black Dawn, paying Mastadon and Phray no mind.

"Yes," said Black Dawn quickly.

"Then should you not be more couth when we are in council," said Pearl, her face a mask of stern authority.

"Point taken," said Black Dawn sitting upright and crossing his left leg over his right.

Black Dawn didn't utter another word for a long moment, taking in the beauty of the throne room and the faces of his companions. Phray had looked upon his face a dozen times, turning her gaze away from him when he noticed. He never smiled, as he knew it would give her satisfaction to know that he didn't mind her incessant gawking. There was a moment many years ago when he thought he'd make her his bride. But that time had long since passed and many wounds had been inflicted that he could never forgive her for.

Among the gods, Black Dawn's affections rested solely on his sister Pearl with whom he'd do anything to please. They were closest among the gods of Merridia, even more so than his brother Mastadon who had been trying to win Pearl's attention, leaning over his throne to babble in her ear. Black Dawn knew that Mastadon's only hope was to unseat her calm, and spark a violent reaction that had been her way when they were very young. He admired her ability to act only out of reason and discretion, where he himself was a more emotional creature, acting largely on impulse. Everyone knew it of him and often never failed to remind him. Pearl was his confidant, the one who could calm his nerves and help him to see reason. Though more times than not, she failed.

As the five of them sat there, Black Dawn became more impatient, almost restless, shifting and turning in his throne. Gorgon Ray hadn't uttered a word, and Pearl had even entertained Mastadon twice, answering the most sensible questions he had asked.

Again Black Dawn was left alone with his thoughts and the visions that had plagued his mind. His visions were the very reason that they were there. He couldn't understand why the throne to his right was empty; as well as the throne upon the dais that his father would occupy.

"Why is he never on time?" said Black Dawn thinking aloud.

"Everything upon the dirt of Merridia is a mirror of its maker," said Gorgon Ray.

"What does that even mean?" said Phray, curling her face in confused annoyance.

"Kings arrive when they choose," said Pearl. Gorgon Ray smiled at her response, nodding his head in approval.

"There are things that even kings are on time for," said Black Dawn.

"Only that which threatens the crown," said Gorgon Ray coolly.

"Well," Black Dawn began, trailing off as he heard a latch move behind Corvus's throne.

The dais floor began to move in between the throne and the massive golden statue in the likeness of Corvus. The sound of the heavy floor could be heard grinding as the mechanism pulled it open. The clattering of shoes could be heard on the hard surface as someone made their way up the staircase under the floor.

Streaks of golden hair rose from out of the dais floor and around the throne. The floor slowly slid back into place and sounded as if it had slammed shut when the grinding ceased. Golden robes sparkled as the sleek body that had ascended out of the dais floor sat down upon the throne. One of her eyes was gold, while the other was black as the jewel in the necklace that Pearl wore around her neck. She bore a startling resemblance to Pearl, but looked much more mature.

The Merridian gods stood and bowed to the woman seated on Corvus's throne and sat back down, with the exception of Black Dawn who stood to full height slowly. The gaze that he casted upon the woman seated on the throne might have been mistaken for one of malice, had it not been for the words that followed the hard stare.

"You are sitting in the wrong place, mother. Your chair is here on my right hand," said Black Dawn gesturing toward the empty throne.

"That is accurate," she replied, her voice a beautiful sultry alto that floated into the air, echoing as it went.

"Your voice is as intoxicating as ever Maji," said Gorgon Ray who seemed to be mesmerized by the sound.

"Thank you Gorgon, you are always too kind," said Maji smiling.

"Spare us the flatteries," said Black Dawn in anger and annoyance looking around the room. "Where is father?" said Black Dawn his tone demanding, his anger still rising.

"He has been detained," said Maji.

"Detained?" said Black Dawn. His face wrinkled as if he were going to be sick as he screamed the word again. "Detained!" he said his voice growing louder, "by what, by whom; what could be more important than being here at this moment?" A bolt of lightning flashed onto the transparent floor and was sucked in, disappearing.

"Sit down," said Maji sternly.

Black Dawn's face curled into a scowl while his lips pursed in anger like a toddler being denied a toy to play with.

"Dorrin, sit down," said Maji calling Black Dawn by his birth name. Her tone was commanding as she motioned with her hand for him to follow her order.

Black Dawn breathed in and out deeply, his shoulders rising and falling with every breath. His anger was boiling, but he slowly sat down, jaws clinched together tightly. His forearms were on the arms of his throne, but they weren't at rest. His hands were clinched in palm grinding fists. Any mortal would have bled as hard as Black Dawn was pressing his nails into his skin.

"Corvus could not be with us, as he has been detained by powers far greater than our own," said Maji locking eyes with Black Dawn for a short moment and then panning around the room. "He has seen the visions that have haunted my dear son Dorrin, as he too sees the threats that may harm Merridia long before they come to pass. In the past a great many wars have been averted due to our king's foresight, but this threat is far greater than any we have seen before," said Maji trailing off for a moment looking down at her hands. She touched the fingers of her hands together as she looked up. "Thus, by order of the king, none are to leave Merridia until this great calamity that is set upon us passes."

Black Dawn's eyes regarded his mother for a long moment and he then looked around the room. None of the others had made a noise; none of them moved or seemed uncomfortable with her words. He stirred in his chair as he began to shake his head no rapidly. He stood fast and half stepped toward the dais with his fists balled.

The statues off to the sides of the throne began to move, their spears pointed at Black Dawn, crossed in front of Maji to protect her. The statues stood motionless now, their dead eyes trained on Black Dawn.

Maji stood and the statues took another step forward to maintain the distance between mother and son.

"This is an outrage!" said Black Dawn hot with fury.

"Orders are orders," said Maji, her intoxicating voice deepening.

"The orders of madness need not be followed!" said Black Dawn nearly hysterical. "He sits on his laurels consulting powers that no one has ever seen. None are greater than father on Merridia and I've met none who could even withstand the might of my own hand," said Black Dawn gesturing hard with his chest and hand.

"Everything is not for you to understand boy," said Maji showing a morsel of weakness. She lifted her hands slightly, nearly reaching to embrace her son, but pulled her hands back to her sides.

"I understand much well mother. I understand that while our world hangs in the balance, we are to sit back and wait for our end," said Black Dawn turning to his companions still looking for an ally.

"Mother has spoken," said Pearl flatly and disappeared from her chair in a gust of wind.

Gorgon Ray followed Pearl's disappearing act and Phray quickly followed, rolling her eyes at Black Dawn. He didn't expect an ally in her.

Mastadon stood and poured what was left in his chalice down his throat. He slapped his armor hard where his belly was and burped a laugh as he strode toward Black Dawn. Mastadon wrapped his bulky arm around Black Dawn's shoulder.

"When father speaks, even when the words do not come out of his own mouth, those words must be obeyed. As hard as it may be," said Mastadon, his jubilant nature never dulled. "You know where to find me if you want to hit something," he said grunting a laugh as he bowed to Maji and walked past the dais and out of a door behind the throne. The door crunched closed loudly as Mastadon disappeared behind it. Only the clanking of his boots could be heard in the distance.

"Are you sure that father is the one who said those words," said Black Dawn softly, trying to subdue his anger.

"Has my hand been too soft of late?" replied Maji.

"How do we know that he has even spoken with you?" said Black Dawn questioning his mother again.

"His absence has been long, but I know well the whereabouts of my husband," said Maji stepping down the dais steps closer to her son.

The statues moved with her.

"Do you fear me too mother?" said Black Dawn as he watched the sharp points of the statues' spears inching closer to him.

Maji pushed the spears from in front of her and descended the dais quickly and embraced Black Dawn tightly pressing her head against his chest.

"You are the youngest of us all, though you are now only weaker than your father. But you will always be my son," said Maji kissing Black Dawn on both cheeks.

The golden guards backed away slowly and took their resting place, back on the flanks of the throne. The Black Moon gems set in the eyes of the likeness of Corvus flashed as the two statues settled back into place.

"Is he watching us?" said Black Dawn.

"He is always watching my son," said Maji turning as she released her hold on Black Dawn.

"Then he finds reason to torment me," said Black Dawn sighing.

"Learn patience and do not defy your father," said Maji as she turned and followed the same path out of the throne room as Mastadon had.

Black Dawn found himself walking up the side of the mountain Zar'dos, facing the sky. Its terrain was treacherous, rocks falling every time he took a step up the slope. He wondered how Aygron was able to make it to the peak of its great height. As talented a warrior as Aygron was, Black Dawn was sure he would have been hard pressed to reach the top without much trouble, especially fighting against Chalendoran warriors and magicians. The weather was constantly changing, and the three suns of Merridia at certain points had no dominion on the surface of the mountain.

Black Dawn then thought that Aygron likely never made it to the top of the mountain, though his vision of the event told him otherwise. There were shelves every few hundred feet with enough space for thousands of men to wage wars with room to spare for a convoy of merchants.

One thing that was unmistakable was that there was great energy swirling about the mountain, inside and out. Black Dawn could feel it radiating all over. He knew that The Black Moon Gems being there was no accident. Zar'dos seemed like the perfect place for them to be found. The energies he felt there were potent, with no source that he could pin point. It was all around him at all times; rising and falling in strength, always moving, never ceasing.

"I have denied you notice," said Black Dawn to Zar'dos as he continued to scale her side. "Father is at least right in that," said Black Dawn thinking aloud.

He reached the top and stood on Merridia's highest peak and marveled at how much of the land could be seen from there in all directions. With his godly vision he could see further than any mortal, but even still, much could be surveyed from Zar'dos' peak by anyone who might reach her top. It was the perfect watch tower; and it made sense that Aygron chose it for the decisive battle against his greatest enemy.

"What would father have me do?" said Black Dawn aloud.

"He would have you obey," said the raspy voice of a woman, deep, slow and measured.

The ground in front of him began to move, shifting slowly and began to rise up. Small rocks slid in every direction, some stopping quickly, while others fell from the top of the mountain. A face began to form from the rock, clear features of a woman with long curly locks. The eyes seemed to be tired and uninterested, but alive with life and zeal.

"Old One," said Black Dawn as he recognized the voice of The Mother Merridia.

"Young one," said The Mother Merridia.

"What do I owe the honor?" said Black Dawn bowing in reverence.

"My child is gone from my bosom while a great storm rises to bring its wrath upon my shores. Would you meet such a threat with fury," said The Mother Merridia.

"I would risk all that I am," said Black Dawn kneeling before the rocky face of The Mother Merridia.

"Then heed not the words of your father through your mother. Heed only the words of the mother of your father and go. Meet this great calamity head on and see the torment go from your sight," said The Mother Merridia.

The rocks that were her face fell back into place and the mountain Zar'dos became as it once was.

Black Dawn rose and leaped from the peak of Zar'dos with furious speed, shooting through Merridia's atmosphere.

Favors

Aton had never seen so many books in his life. There were so many shelves of books in the room that the walls seemed to be made of them. His mother only had a handful of books that no one ever read. He never bothered to read much after learning how to; as he spent nearly all of his waking hours providing Marside with ale. His face was alight with happiness, as he flipped the pages of a red covered book detailing the exploits of a mad magician hell bent on destroying his master's greatest enemy.

"Have you ever heard of Hal the Mad?" said Aton beaming.

"Was he a swordsman?" said Scicremeon with a bored expression.

"No, a magician," said Aton his eyes pressed upon a page.

"Then no. I am only interested in killing magicians."

"Because of your father?" said Aton somewhat saddened by the thought.

"Is there any other reason?" said Scicremeon curling her lips in boredom, as frustration began to build inside her.

"Do you like to read?"

"For what purpose?"

"Any purpose at all," said Aton blankly, shrugging his shoulders.

"Strategy, swordsmanship, and war."

"What about stories?"

"I have enough of my own to tell haven't I?"

"I suppose so," said Aton curling his lips to one side thinking. "Do you think you'd ever write them down?"

"And bore myself half to death," said Scicremeon letting out a hearty laugh.

Aton smiled wide at her laughter and chuckled a bit himself. He really couldn't imagine Scicremeon sitting down to write. He guessed she'd quickly grow bored and set the papers on fire before she got to the heart of one of her many adventures. But he did love to see her smile. Often, she seemed to be in deep thought whenever she wasn't barking orders at him.

"Guess you're right. Maybe I could write them for you after our adventure is over," said Aton, as he came to sit next to her on the opposite side of a large wooden desk, that sat in front of a large window.

Aton squinted from the sunlight that lit up his face as he leaned back in the chair. He shifted his chair closer to Scicremeon to avoid the hot rays.

"You might as well start writing tonight," said Scicremeon.

"What do you mean?"

"This is where your adventure ends," said Scicremeon patting his head like a dog.

"You don't mean to leave me here," said Aton his eyes wide with shock.

"It will be too dangerous," said Scicremeon her eyes becoming glossy.

"What could be more dangerous than the Hanging Hands?" begged Aton.

"Magic. Trained soldiers," said Scicremeon.

"I'm trained," said Aton hotly defending his untested skill.

"You have no experience," said Scicremeon, the skin on her forehead wrinkling as her face squeezed into a bewildered scowl.

"You trained me," said Aton forcefully.

"That means nothing," said Scicremeon moving thoughtlessly to the edge of her chair.

"Who is better than you?" said Aton turning hard to face her with big hungry eyes, his head sweating as he slammed the book shut in his hands.

Scicremeon bit the inside of her bottom lip and breathed in deeply through her nose. She rubbed her face starting from her chin and pushed her hair back tightly. Tilting her head back, she took in another deep breath and calmed herself. *You little brat,* she thought with her teeth ground together.

"You're a runt, but you're an excellent student. Brave...maybe too brave," said Scicremeon cringing as she spoke. Aton began to open his mouth to form words and she held up her hand to silence him. "But you are not ready for this trip," she said with finality.

"You may need my help," said Aton, his eyes pleading with her.

"I cannot risk it, your mother would be heart broken," said Scicremeon forcing back a ball in her throat. *And so would I,* she admitted to herself. She wrapped her arm around his neck and kissed him on the head.

"Please-," said Aton cut off.

"My way," said Scicremeon holding up her index finger to silence him.

They sat in silence for what felt like an hour. Aton tried twice to change Scicremeon's mind but she wouldn't broach the subject with him. He was reduced to reading the large book, while Scicremeon filed her nails with her feet kicked up on the desk. There was a wooden fixture with three unlit candles in the grooves. Aton had been sure Scicremeon was going to knock it over as she kept pointing her toes toward it.

Aside from the large mass of books aligned along the walls, the room was rather bare and quaint. The floors were wooden like all of the other furnishings. There were a few bureaus just by the door behind Scicremeon, both with a sword on a stand.

Click!

Scicremeon heard the knob twist behind her and heard the door creak open, telling its age as a draft of cool air entered the room. Slowly approaching her she could hear the sound of boots against the wooden floor. Just beside her chair the approaching steps stopped and she felt eyes on her. Cracking her neck, she slipped her nail file into her bag on the floor and crossed her hands in her lap. Then from behind her more steps filled the room. The door closed abruptly as a man rounded the desk and looked at Aton suspiciously.

Aton swallowed as he shifted in his chair and then looked to Scicremeon as he touched his hands to the armrest, preparing to stand. Scicremeon touched his chest and pushed him back softly into his chair.

"Would you deny the boy to show his manners?" said the man standing at Scicremeon's side.

"And you'd be," said Scicremeon to the man standing at her side, though her eyes were pressed upon the man standing behind the desk motioning his hand to someone behind her.

"I am Elio Van Taven, the emperor's advisor and personal bodyguard," said Van Taven.

Scicremeon turned her eyes toward him and took him in for a moment. His eyes were a dark green and his hair was brown and full. He was strikingly handsome, his skin almost pale, though there was a peach-red tone to his skin that gave him a nice color. He stood tall, just over six-feet, his posture perfect with his hands behind his back. He wore no weapons but his face looked stern and determined. Van Taven wore a thin goatee and a relatively thick beard along his chin.

"Then you're one of his lackeys. I didn't come to speak with you," said Scicremeon averting her attention from him with a roll of her eyes.

Van Taven's hands floated to his sides, lips pressed into one another. Scicremeon caught him out the corner of her eye; looking to do everything he could to remain calm.

"You possess your father's good humor," said the bald man behind the desk. His voice was deep and commanding, though filled with a hint of excitement.

Scicremeon listened to the tone of his voice and knew he enjoyed conversation. He was light hearted, enjoying the jab that she threw at Van Taven; but he was visibly comfortable, knowing full well that he was in charge.

His skin was a light brown. His head was bald and he wore reddish brown robes with a matching shirt and pants. The fingers on his right hand were covered with jeweled rings; while his left only held one ring to signify his marriage to a woman. He wore no crown, but it was obvious that everyone was there to answer to his whims.

While his demeanor seemed light, the visible part of a scar he tried to hide on his neck showed that he had been wounded in battle. Only a very sharp object would have left such a scar. The knuckles on his hands were large and old scars lingered there as well. The truth about the emperor was written on his body. There were no books or stories that needed to be written for those around him to know. He hadn't inherited his place upon the throne of Merridia. He'd fought for it.

"Larnaxe is it?" said Scicremeon as if she were unsure.

"Who else could it be?" said Larnaxe opening his arms wide and smiling.

He pulled the large wooden chair from under his desk and plopped down, and then scooted himself closer to the desk. He folded his hands together on top of the desk and leaned forward.

"Hi," said Aton extending his hand.

"You do indeed have manners," said Larnaxe happily, grasping Aton's hand and shaking it. "Firm grip...did your father teach you?"

"No," said Aton pointing to Scicremeon.

"How did you manage such a feat? Aygron was never known for his pleasantries, as likeable a figure as he was. And where would a girl learn to shake hands without a father in a village of killers," said Larnaxe turning his head sharply and locking eyes with Scicremeon.

"Times have changed," said Scicremeon titling her head to the side.

"That they have," said Larnaxe snapping his fingers.

A servant off to Aton's right scurried to the desk and set down a cup of water a few inches from Larnaxe's hand.

"Can we cut the small talk?" said Scicremeon raising her eyebrows.

"The man died long before you were born, yet you managed to inherit almost every character trait that he owned," said Larnaxe exhaling hard as if preparing for a wrestling match.

"I've heard a lot of stories," said Scicremeon sitting up in her chair.

"But you didn't come here for tales," said Larnaxe leaning back in his chair and taking a sip of water.

"Of course not," said Scicremeon smiling, "but the tales told I imagine have much truth to them. Especially the tales concerning your rise to power," she said still smiling wide.

Larnaxe gave her an unsettling look, half a smile, the other part of the expression a threat of the highest order. It was the first time he seemed uncomfortable. His eyes shifted to his servant and he quickly scurried over and filled the emperor's cup. The boy's head was down, his eyes never making contact with Larnaxe as he quickly shuffled backward to his position.

"I guess you believe I owe you something," said Larnaxe slow and measured, "that somehow you should profit from the things that I owe your father.

"What you owe him is too much to ask for. And I'm sure you've grown quite accustomed to the throne that was supposed to be his," said Scicremeon shifting sideways in her chair.

"It sounds like there are still some of the old boys left," said Larnaxe with a sly smile.

"There are few who know that you followed my father; very few who know that the throne was his to take for his own; and fewer are there those who know that he gave it to you because home was more appealing than ruling," said Scicremeon with her eyes dead on the emperor's. "Now there are just a few more who know the truth of your ascension."

"The truth is overrated, and most people have no problem with perspective," said Larnaxe setting his cup down on the desk. "If you are not here to make some claim for position or rank, what is it that you want?"

"My lord," said Scicremeon sarcastically, "you'll find that I'm not as fickle as others. I require one of your ships."

"You want to sail the open seas," said Larnaxe with a confused smile.

"I didn't cross the Hanging Hands Mountain for a boat," said Scicremeon with a scowl.

Van Taven scoffed, and began to laugh, but suppressed it quickly. He clasped his hands together in front of him and cleared his throat turning his eye quickly to Larnaxe and then looking away again.

"My young friend here means you no disrespect, but what you speak of is impossible," said Larnaxe with a look of indifference. "See your father destroyed the bridge that connected those two mountains many years ago."

"That explains how Heartless Vern was able to cross back over after losing his whole army," said Aton excited with his hands balled up under his chest.

"To think I had to throw you and shoot you," said Scicremeon as if coming to a revelation.

"Building a bridge would have taken too long," said Aton with a huge smile. He was happy to know that all the stories he'd heard were true.

"You can always say you were the first to do it without one," said Scicremeon

"Even before you," said Aton, lifting his brows, his index finger pointing to the ceiling in a matter of fact tone, as if to say *ah ha*.

"I went over unassisted," said Scicremeon slapping him on the back of the head. Aton's shoulder sunk, his jolly mood deflated. She hadn't needed his help and he wouldn't have made it across without her.

"Is this little spectacle over?" said Larnaxe, disbelief covering his face.

"Apologies my lord," said Aton as Scicremeon stared at Larnaxe with a look of boredom on her face.

"So you want a favor," said Larnaxe, his voice measured again, giving Scicremeon a bored look of his own.

"Of sorts," said Scicremeon.

"Favors come at a cost, even when they are owed," said Larnaxe blinking rapidly.

"No cost is too great," said Scicremeon hard.

"May I ask why you need it?" said Larnaxe interested.

"So that I may go to Chalendor to avenge my father. I'm sure you don't need me to enlighten you of the circumstances surrounding his death," said Scicremeon, anger beginning to boil up inside of her.

"You mean to stir up old hatreds," said Larnaxe regarding Scicremeon with surgical eyes.

"I mean to kill two men," said Scicremeon.

"And then return home?" said Larnaxe leaning forward with his eyes narrowed. "To serve me until I see fit to release you from duty," said Larnaxe finishing.

"Is that all?" said Scicremeon standing up and gathering her bags.

"No, my man Van Taven will be going with you," said Larnaxe strictly as he stood up.

"I don't need him," said Scicremeon looking Van Taven up and down in disgust.

"On Chalendor, you may find him handy in a tight spot," said Larnaxe nodding his head at Van Taven.

Van Taven lifted his right hand, palm facing up and turned his eyes on Scicremeon. He nodded and then a small fire burst out from his palm, flickering slowly. Lifting his hand to his mouth he turned toward the desk and blew into the fire in his hand. Three balls of fire shot out toward the desk and hit the wicks on the candles light-ing them. Van Taven then turned his fingers toward the fire and ice drifted from his fingertips, dousing the fire in a ball of ice. Raising his hands as if to surrender, the ball of ice floated into the air. With every move of his hand the ball of ice followed his instruction as if it were a living being, able to take orders. Van Taven then snapped his fingers and the ball of ice shattered against the floor turning into sand.

Scicremeon cut her eye at Van Taven, curling her lips into a mad grimace. Every fiber of her being wanted to pounce on him. She hated magicians. A magician was the reason she never knew her father. She stepped directly in front of Van Taven and looked him square in the eye. He shifted, looking uncomfortable and she enjoyed it. Scicremeon breathed in and out slowly, making sure that he could feel her breath on his face.

"If I didn't need his ship and if I had my sword, I'd severe your head from your neck right now," said Scicremeon slowly in nearly a whisper. She clenched her jaw twice before she spoke again. "However, since I must tolerate you we'll work together under one condition. You do as I say and nothing else. Clear?"

Van Taven looked over at Larnaxe and the emperor nodded yes. Scicremeon cut her eye at the emperor and scowled at him and then pressed her eyes back on Van Taven.

"Clear," said Van Taven softly.

"Here," said Scicremeon. She reached into her bag and then tossed the wooden box with the green goop inside onto Larnaxe's desk.

"What is it, poison?" said Larnaxe eyeing the box unsure of its contents.

"Healing cream of the Naheim root. You haven't been home in a long while," said Scicremeon looking at the box and then at Larnaxe.

Larnaxe lifted the box and pulled open its top and sniffed in the hideous aroma as if it were a sweet fruit. Aton cringed at the emperor's enjoyment of the cream that healed his back.

"So you do have manners," said Larnaxe closing the lid on the box.

"Only where necessary," said Scicremeon bowing her head slightly to the emperor. "Remember what I said," she said to Van Taven.

Scicremeon turned hard and walked fast toward the door. The guard near the door pulled the door open and she stormed past him. "Aton," she screamed, and the boy quickly followed. As she got past the first guard in the hall a second guard lifted her sword. She snatched it from him without giving him any notice.

Van Taven jogged out of the door and caught up with Aton who was just a few steps behind Scicremeon.

"Is she always so on edge?" said Van Taven with a slightly worried look on his face.

"You haven't seen edge yet," said Aton with a smile.

"I doubt she could cut my head off though," said Van Taven haughtily.

Whiff. The blade sung in the air and stopped abruptly. Aton gasped and fell back onto his hind. Van Taven's cheeks were inflated with air, his stomach tensed as he recoiled backward. His fingers were frigid and blue, ice slowly pouring from them. A trickle of blood fell from the skin on his neck, touched by Scicremeon's sharpened blade.

"Men have doubted me all my life. And all my life I have beat them to the punch. Just as you stand here now with those powers you have dancing on your fingertips. A great many heads have rolled before they had the chance to draw their swords. You'd do well not to test the limits of my patience," said Scicremeon forcefully with a mad stare on her face.

Scicremeon pulled her sword from his neck and kept the tip pressed in front of his chest.

"Bah!" Van Taven released the air he was holding in his mouth.

"Are we clear?" said Scicremeon moving her head around as if asking the question more than once.

"Crystal," said Van Taven as he wiped at the small cut on his neck.

"At least it's not only me anymore," said Aton standing and looking up at Van Taven's bewildered face.

Scicremeon turned hard and sheathed her sword with a smile on her face. *That little runt will teach you.*

"Only you what?" said Van Taven confused still wiping at his cut.

"The only one she beats up on," said Aton shaking his head in sympathy of Van Taven's new plight.

"No one's ever been able to touch me with a sword before," said Van Taven blinking slowly and cringing all at once.

"As far as I know, she's only ever lost a fight to a god," said Aton clapping Van Taven on the small of his back and walking past the distraught magician.

"She doesn't know where she's going; why is she walking so fast?" said Van Taven following behind Aton confused with Scicremeon's behavior.

You've got a lot to learn about me magician, Scicremeon thought to herself able to hear Van Taven even ten feet away. She walked with her head held high as if she owned the floors of the castle she walked upon. She treated the emperor as if he had no control, as if the whole of Merridia wasn't his to order. *Everywhere I go belongs to me until I bring my father's killers to heel. The world will answer to my whims,* she clenched her jaw tight and continued to stride down the long corridor having no mind to where she was going, but not allowing her hosts to lead. She'd make the choice on where she'd stay until her ship was ready. *That is my way.*

Revenge

Aton's head was pressed between her breasts, warm tears staining the skin-tight white uniform that Scicremeon wore. His arms squeezed tight around her waist, fingers clasped together, and he had held them there for nearly five minutes. Scicremeon tried to push him away, but he'd squeeze tighter, yelling *no* each time. She wanted the embrace to end long ago, but she feared that she'd push him harder than she intended. Her heart was beginning to melt, and her resolve had nearly weakened. Her love for Aton had grown in the short time that he had been her student and her heart pounded in her chest. She hoped that he couldn't hear the incessant drumming in her chest, but she knew better. *He'd probably think I was growing angry any way,* she thought unsure of the truth.

As the two of them stood there, Aton nestled into her, Scicremeon hoping to be as comforting as she could without feeling weak; begged quietly to herself for Van Taven's presence. The day before, she'd been hoping to cut his head off, but now he was the only one who could save her. He'd be accompanying her on her trip to Chalendor. As much as she'd stomp around the castle looking for the ship, he'd know exactly where it was. He couldn't come sooner.

All she wanted was to be done with this display of heartfelt emotion. The only emotions she wanted to embrace were anger and rage.

What Aton offered her were things that only applied to her when her mother was alive. Feelings that were easy to have before she knew the cause of her father's death. Happiness and compassion; those were the things that were only afforded to children in Marside and her time with them was cut short. The sword became her only refuge and it was there that she felt like herself. *How did I allow this boy to break my resolve?*

"Are you going to cry all day," said Scicremeon in the most annoyed tone she could muster. It was all she could do to try and cool her warming heart.

Aton sniffled and pulled away slowly looking down at his feet defeated.

"I'm sorry," said Aton wiping his tears with the back of his hands.

"Uh," said Scicremeon looking up and forcing back tears and the lump forming in her throat. "I told you to stop apologizing. To me and most certainly don't apologize here. Not even to the emperor," said Scicremeon still looking at the ceiling afraid to reveal her weakness to Aton.

"Yes master," said Aton woefully, biting and licking his lips trying to calm himself.

"Good," said Scicremeon almost sounding jovial, breathing into her nose deeply as she finally reeled her feelings in enough to look Aton in the eye.

She looked Aton over, and closed the top button on the new shirt one of the emperor's servants brought him during the night. It was charcoal with a matching set of loose fitting pants that appeared to be some kind of uniform along with a pair of black boots.

"What will I do while I'm here?" said Aton feeling out of place.

"You'll practice with your sword eight hours a day and make sure that you exercise. Eat everything and stay away from girls. A warrior needs to focus on the mastery of his weapon," said Scicremeon, running her fingers through his hair to fluff it after having been matted to his head.

"I feel out of place," said Aton looking around at the well-furnished room. All of the chairs had cushions and the bed was fluffy and soft. There was a washroom and a small study down a short corridor. A window on each wall allowed them to see out to all parts of the castle and the surrounding landscape for at least a mile.

"At the very least you'll be comfortable."

"Will I ever see you again?"

"We've been over this all morning."

"What if you die?"

"I don't plan on dying."

"I know, but what if you do."

"Then you can tell the stories of my adventures."

"But I only know about this one."

"Then make it a good story," said Scicremeon exasperated rolling her eyes. *You'll never make this easy for me will you, you little runt,* she thought twice to slap him for his prodding.

"At least you're well dressed," said Aton of Scicremeon's new attire.

She was dressed in a skin tight white uniform with the emblem of the Merridian Empire. It was a purple phoenix with two swords crossed behind its body, wings out stretched, talons ready to pounce on its prey. Her sword was sheathed in her scabbard attached to her back by a thin strap. Her satchel had been refashioned so that it could fit on her hip like a pouch. A knife was sheathed on her left boot.

"You think you feel out of place. I'm not a soldier of the empire," said Scicremeon. "If it were not for Larnaxe's insistence and his threat to deny me his ship, I would wear my own clothes."

"They look better."

"Do they?" said Scicremeon cutting her eye at Aton as if she cared for fashion.

There was a hard rapping at the door and then the latch loosed, the door swinging open letting in a warm draft.

"Lord Van Taven awaits you mam," said a brown-eyed soldier dressed in similar white attire to Scicremeon. His hair was long and black, tied into a pony tail. He wore a sword on his back as Scicremeon did, and his hands were gloved white, while hers were exposed.

"Do I look like your grandmother?" said Scicremeon with wide eyes and a disgusted expression.

Scicremeon walked outside of the door and turned around facing Aton who had followed her to the threshold. She closed her eyes slowly and then opened her arms. Aton slammed himself into her, but let go after only a few seconds. *Thank you for not tormenting me,* Scicremeon thought and smiled inside.

"I'll miss you," said Aton.

Scicremeon rolled her eyes and turned to the soldier at the door. "What is your name?"

"Casca," said Casca with a boy's voice, leaning into the wall as Scicremeon inched toward him.

"If any harm comes to him, I'll hold you personally responsible," said Scicremeon with a smile. "Understood?"

"Yes mam," said Casca and then cringed when Scicremeon's expression turned grave.

Casca closed the door and left Aton behind. He stepped slowly around Scicremeon.

"I'm not going to bite you unless you give me reason to," said Scicremeon with a bemused stare at his fearful behavior.

"Your reputation is well known my lady," said Casca taking extra care not to call her mam.

"Even here?" said Scicremeon surprised. She'd traveled quite far in her efforts to find suitable challengers, but this was her first trip across the Hanging Hands Mountain. She never thought that anyone as far away from Hormand's Rock as those on the opposite side of the Hanging Hands Mountain, would have ever heard her name. She was flattered, but didn't show it.

"Yes," said Casca in his boyish voice as he scurried in front of Scicremeon and led her down the hallway.

Casca pushed hard against the giant double doors forcing them to swing out into a large courtyard. The sunlight from outside filled the long corridor that they had traversed, nearly blinding Scicremeon's vision as she made her way through the door. The grass was the darkest green Scicremeon had ever seen. As she walked upon the grassy courtyard, the grass seemed to be springy as the mattress she'd slept on the previous night. There were two lines of trees stretching for hundreds of feet to the edge of the courtyard. In between the trees were white ships with the purple phoenix emblem of Merridia. There was a lone ship in between the isle of trees about a hundred yards in the distance and she could see people moving around it at a rapid pace.

Only two of Merridia's great suns were showing and she'd noticed that those who lived in the castle never saw the third. As she turned she could see a main tower rising up at the center of the palace, never allowing the third sun of Merridia to shine its brilliant light. The stone structure seemed to have no end and seeing the very top was almost impossible from where she stood. Purple flags flew from the battlements of the squared structure on all of the six tiers until the big tower shot up. A lone flag was blowing in the light breeze, making the top of the tower apparent.

Scicremeon neared the ship in the isle and she could see Larnaxe and Van Taven engaged in conversation. She clasped her hands behind her back as she began to close the distance between them. Van Taven was dressed in a uniform identical to her own; except his was black and he wore no weapons. Larnaxe wore a red robe with no shirt, his hand making sweeping motions in the air as his mouth moved quickly. She could make out some of the words but was still too far away to make any sense of them. Van Taven continued to nod and she could at least read that each of his responses had been yes.

"Scicremeon," said Van Taven, bowing as she came to his side.

"Emperor," said Scicremeon bowing her head slightly to Larnaxe. "Lackey," said Scicremeon to Van Taven with a sly smile.

"Your manners improve by the day," said Larnaxe sticking out his chest with a joyful expression, clapping his hands together. "I wonder what a year might do for you."

"You'd likely find me insufferable," said Scicremeon with a smile playing to Larnaxe's ego.

"At least she is not a liar my lord," said Van Taven cutting his eye at her before looking her up and down.

"Still nursing that wound," said Scicremeon without turning her attention to Van Taven.

"No it is healed," said Van Taven in quick response.

"I didn't mean the physical one," said Scicremeon laughing at once.

"Wit, guile, and from what we hear a good sword," said Larnaxe ecstatic at her bandying of words, "you might make a good ruler one day."

"Perhaps," said Scicremeon.

"I hope your stay here has been enjoyable. It is regrettable that you could not stay longer, though if you return you'll spend many days within the walls of Phoenix Helm. Your father built this stronghold many years ago when our wars with the Chalendorans began. From here we were able to keep their troops at bay while we fashioned a strategy against their magicians. They were few in number but quite potent. Many a great soldier fell to their powers and deceptions. I hope you do not suffer the same fate," said Larnaxe, his tone seeming serious and grave for the first time. "For as long as this great fortress stands, Merridia shall see no defeat. It has been given its own enchantments over the years by our own magicians like your friend Van Taven here to protect us against magic. It is a shame that you will not have the same protection once on Chalendor. Your sword and Van Taven will be all there is standing between you and their crippling power. Think of that the next time you have mind to place your blade upon his neck," said Larnaxe with a hint of care, though his tone was also laced with threats.

"Then I'll wait until the ride home," said Scicremeon meeting Larnaxe's eyes.

"That is if you make it," said Van Taven with an ugly scowl.

"You seem tense magician," said Scicremeon finally giving her eyes to Van Taven.

"Because I now know that you take us on a suicide mission to avenge your father," said Van Taven harshly.

"You think I am reckless," said Scicremeon in a matter of fact tone.

"That's obvious," said Van Taven sharply.

"Those who know well of me know that I am measured and calculating," said Scicremeon in a threatening tone.

"I can calculate how long it will take one of their spell casters to separate your mind from your body," said Van Taven turning to face her fully.

"I'll let you in on a little secret magician," Scicremeon began, "I only go there for two; the one who dealt the killing blow and the coward who distracted my father long enough for the blow to land. The rest of their wretched planet is of no concern to me," said Scicremeon her shoulders rising and falling fast as her last statement ended forcefully.

"Revenge never serves the purpose it is intended to serve," said Van Taven.

"Revenge serves tradition where I am from. It will serve in giving me peace of mind," said Scicremeon challenging his statement with great fervor.

"Is there nothing more important?" begged Van Taven loudly.

Aton, she thought.

"Nothing," she said lying to Van Taven but more so to herself. Aton was more important to her than her revenge, and every day with him made revenge seem less important. But she had already set her course. She could not go back on the promise she made many years ago. Tradition demanded it. And though the thirst for it had begun to wane, her heart still beat for the man who gave her life, even though she never knew him.

"Is there nothing that could change your mind?" asked Van Taven with a measure of hope in his voice.

"Nothing that can be said by any magician," said Scicremeon as if her words were made of acid.

"Then I await your boarding of the ship," said Van Taven. He turned and marched up the hatch at the back of the ship, disappearing inside.

"Safe travels my dear Scicremeon," said Larnaxe pointing toward the ship's hatch with his hand.

"Take care of Aton. I hold you personally responsible for his well-being," said Scicremeon raising an eyebrow to the emperor.

He turned and walked away with his hands behind his back flanked by four guards, two on either side. "You have my word," said Larnaxe pointing his finger in the air and shaking it.

"You'd better," said Scicremeon as she boarded the ship.

As she stepped onto the flat surface inside, the men who had been scrambling around the ship pushed the hatch closed. Inside the ship, Scicremeon marched toward the front where she could see Van Taven sitting there waiting, his eyes pressed forward, looking out of the glass window. There was another chair just to his right and another two chairs directly behind them. Everything inside was purple save for some of the buttons on the control panel that lit up yellow, green, and red. Aside from the few chairs inside, there wasn't much to the ship. There was little cargo, and not much else on board and Scicremeon hadn't noticed any weapons mounted to its structure.

"So it's just you and me," said Scicremeon as she sat down in the empty chair beside Van Taven.

"Regrettably," said Van Taven looking at her out of the corner of his eye.

"How long?" said Scicremeon.

"On The Runner. . .luckily, just twelve hours," said Van Taven.

"Then my revenge will come sooner rather than later,' said Scicremeon.

"Or you'll die," said Van Taven with a hearty laugh.

"Better to die, sword in hand, than wrinkled old, cold in bed," said Scicremeon as if singing a song.

"I never took you for a poet," said Van Taven surprisingly impressed, looking at Scicremeon quizzically.

"I'm not. They were my father's words," said Scicremeon leaning back and latching on the straps connected to the chair. She leaned back and kicked her feet up on the console as she placed her hands behind her head.

Van Taven stared at her for a long moment and then looked forward at the controls. Lifting his hands over the control panel, it lit up and the engines fired. The ship began to vibrate softly as Van Taven waved his hands around the control panel. "Plot a course for Chalendor," said Van Taven aloud as he strapped himself into his own seatbelt. A screen slid up from the center of the control panel and lit up, showing a map of the solar system that Merridia was part of. A line from Merridia was drawn on the screen from Merridia to the closest planet to her and a lively woman's voice entered into the ship. *Course plotted for Chalendor. Prepare for takeoff.*

There was a ding, and then a second, and then a third. The engines roared louder and then Van Taven and Scicremeon were shot down the isle of trees at incredible speeds. Their backs were pressed into their chairs as they began to ascend.

Wooosh!

The Runner quickly broke the sound barrier and shot quickly through the clouds.

"Uh," Scicremeon moaned breathing hard.

The ship's voice rang into the air again, *preparing for hyper drive.*

The Runner shot through the Merridian atmosphere and kept gaining speed. The ship hardly shook, and only a faint whistling sound was apparent once they were in the blackness of space. Scicremeon's eyes went wide with wonder, being so close to the stars she had watched many nights before.

"It's beautiful," said Scicremeon, allowing herself to feel for a moment.

"True."

"May my revenge be sweet," said Scicremeon with a smile as she watched the stars flit by.

Prepare for light speed.

Van Taven looked at Scicremeon with a devious smile. Her brows descended onto her eyes in a confused stare. Van Taven burst out into a hearty laugh as there seemed to be an explosion in the engine. Scicremeon felt the jolt shoot them faster than anything she'd ever imagined, now pressed deeper into the chair. She screamed at the top of her lungs, feeling an intense adrenaline rush.

Just twelve hours.

No Reason

An entire galaxy seemed to flit by in the blink of an eye. There was hardly any life there as Chasm flew through a portal. She had been trying to find Primsec for days, searching the vastness of space with her mind, hoping to feel even the faintest glimmer of his presence. But the harder she tried, the larger the universe seemed to be. For all her power, she felt powerless to do anything. She knew she too could become invisible to her companions if she wanted. But she had never had any purpose to do so. There was nothing she could point to that would make Primsec shield himself, unless he was among those with Carnok; for none of them could now be seen.

As she flew through portals, and in and out of dimensions she remembered how they once were as one. The twelve of them were always able to hear one another's thoughts over vast distances. Pinpointing one's exact location took a matter of seconds. Even when they traveled faster than the speed of light, their companions could sense them coming, even if they were a million galaxies away. No one hid, not even the twins, Cowlran and Thracno, who seemed only to enjoy their own company.

Chasm couldn't put her finger on the exact moment when everything changed between them so much that Carnok would desert them. He was always brooding and setting some awful plan into motion, but she had never thought him capable of killing one of Our Union. She hadn't even known it to be possible, but now knew that their physical form was able to be destroyed. How he found out how to do it, still escaped her. Even though she'd seen her brothers fallen, she still didn't believe she was capable of doing the same. At first she thought she was not strong enough, but then thought more so that she was incapable of inflicting such harm on one like herself. Her heart poured out to them all and more so to Primsec, who she begged to hear her.

Chasm hadn't noticed how far she'd come, until she looked upon the beauty of the Earth, and remembered how much at peace she felt being there. When she pierced the atmosphere, the feeling of exhilaration, and then an intense calm came over her. She felt happy.

Sitting atop a snow capped mountain, she watched a large flock of birds circling overhead squawking. She wished to be like them, free of responsibility, living by the impulses that drove them. Never had she known hunger or pain. Desperation and fear were figments of her imagination. She thought that she might thank Carnok, for allowing her to understand things that she only knew by name, or by the knowledge she had been given.

Through the creatures of Earth radiating Aeon's force, she felt closer, thought she understood more the meaning of life. Until Asteron had fallen, she never quite saw herself as a part of it, only giving it, allowing others to endure for a short while. Death she thought was a great teacher, and even though she knew there were still some parts of her brothers left. She knew they'd never be the same.

Chasm felt a mind brush against her own as she continued to keep herself open to feeling Primsec's presence. She had hoped it was him, but she noticed that the connection was one way.

She could seem him climbing the mountain below her. His head was covered in ragged brown locks and he was naked, save for a cloth to cover his loins.

Into his mind she delved and found much of it empty, focused only on the task at hand. She could sense his fear of falling, but also his determination. His mind was set on a blue berry just a few feet above him that would satisfy his hunger. Searching his memories, she could see that he had already eaten. But the berries would be a treat for him and his family who waited at the base of the mountain.

Like the birds that flocked above her, she could feel that all he cared for was satisfying his impulses. Yet, unlike the birds he felt a great need to help those who were close to him. While the birds flew together they would pluck food from one another to satisfy their own hunger. This man would make sure all around him were satisfied first.

His thoughts were on those below him. Their happiness would be his happiness, and she could feel their fear for him. All they wanted was for him to be safe. The berries were welcomed, but his life was their greater concern. The children among them cheered his efforts. In their minds he would succeed. He had done it so many times.

Chasm smiled as she felt his joy when he stuffed a handful of the berries into his mouth, the sweet juices flooding his senses. He breathed in deeply, ignoring the cold, basking in his triumph of the mountain. The man grabbed another handful and filled his mouth again. He then began to fill a bag hanging around his shoulder with enough to share with his family.

Chasm disengaged from his mind as he slowly began to descend down the mountain. She noticed that she was still smiling as she watched him. For the first time she was aware of how different she was from them. The sensations that the people of Earth felt, were ones that she only experienced second hand.

Letting down her guard, pushing her powers deep into her core, she plunged her hand into the snow. The cold gripped her skin, goose bumps dressed her arm from her wrist to her elbow, and she began to shiver. Closing her hand she pulled it from the snow and opened it. The snow in her hand slowly began to melt as she held it to the blazing sunlight.

Chasm felt the cold of the snow begin to warm as it melted away into water. She smiled at the process. She watched intently as the snow transformed into water and began to dribble off the sides of her palm and through her fingers.

Amazing isn't it, she heard a voice and then felt a powerful mind brush against her consciousness.

Her concentration was broken and she pushed her powers outward, putting up her guard and closed her mind against invasion.

"Who is there?" said Chasm aloud and then stood. She looked around for a few moments and felt the consciousness brush against her own again.

The mind that pushed against hers was familiar, but still veiled against her power to see it clearly.

Have you forgotten me already, said the voice again pushing against her consciousness.

Slowly the veil over the mind communing with her mentally, allowed her access. She knew the mind well. Chasm burst into tears recognizing Primsec's consciousness.

A swirling wave of colors flashed in front of her. Primsec's physical being appeared before her, his face changing from red to white to black, in reflection of his mood.

"Your passion still burns deep for Our Union brother," said Chasm wrapping her arms around his neck.

"Yes it does, but I feel a deep emptiness that can never be filled," said Primsec as Chasm released him from her grasp.

Primsec sat down upon the mountain and Chasm followed, placing her hand in his. Primsec eyed their surroundings, not really in awe, but he seemed to be pleasured by it as Chasm was. She watched him without speaking, touching his mind, feeling his emotions manifesting as he took in the beauty of the Earth.

"I can always feel our Lord Aeon here," said Chasm softly.

"Of course," said Primsec flatly.

"Will you help me to bring an end to this conflict?" said Chasm almost begging.

"It is not my place to stand at odds with my brethren," said Primsec sharply. "You feel the same as I do, you should not ask such a thing." Primsec's face flashed red for a moment and then quickly to black. He closed his eyes softly, his lips became one line. "Thutmos must stop his conquest of Carnok."

"To what end?" said Chasm pleading as her confusion grew.

"That the balance may remain intact," said Primsec surprised by Chasm's question.

"Carnok will not stop, he is killing us," said Chasm letting go of his hand and standing fast preparing to leave.

"Know this before you go if that is your intention sister," said Primsec standing slowly, his face flashing a thousand colors in rapid succession. Chasm turned her back to Primsec, her chest rising and falling fast. "I know you wish for me to go and take sides with you, but I must not."

"Tell me quickly then," said Chasm, not wanting to face Primsec, hoping to quell her growing anger and disappointment by looking away.

"There is a great calamity coming that will befall us all. Even Thutmos's beloved son Corvus, and Corvus's own son has seen it," said Primsec turning Chasm around by the shoulder to peer into her eyes. "Yet, they do not see nearly as well as we do. And we cannot see that which The Creator does not allow. This you well know. But this great calamity he has not shielded from my eyes. Nor will he shield it from you if you would like to see it," said Primsec with a severity in his voice that couldn't be mistaken for anything else but fear.

"Show me," said Chasm.

Primsec's mind pushed hard upon Chasm's consciousness and pressed on her a million images. The images came in chronological order. There was war everywhere; famines and plagues. She could see planets exploding and shifting abruptly off course and out of their orbits. Entire galaxies ceased to exists, billions of beings fell dead and then she saw Earth. It was bathed in a blue flame, turning black, devoid of any color or the blue of its waters and skies. There was no life there, nothing of Aeon's presence, only horror and death.

"War with Carnok will be the cause of this?" asked Chasm.

"You know well the answer to your own question," said Primsec without sarcasm.

"Why won't you show him yourself?" said Chasm as if pleading.

"Thutmos must see it for himself. It will mean nothing if I show him. Your bond is stronger than you wish to accept. Even in him finally taking a stand on one notion, his heart can very well change," said Primsec.

"But you've shown me," said Chasm, her eyes imploring Primsec to change his course and come with her.

"He is the Charm of the Sacred," said Primsec forcefully.

"And you are the-," said Chasm beginning to fire back, but quickly interrupted.

"I have no reason to smile any longer," said Primsec in a whisper, "Our Union is broken and the new Chain of Balance will determine our future."

"I will give you a reason to smile again brother," said Chasm pulling Primsec into a tight embrace, tears falling from her eyes.

"We can only hope," said Primsec.

Chasm sat down again on the cold snow and allowed herself to feel again like the people of Earth. She wished again that she didn't have to leave, but she knew that her duty meant their survival. She could not bear to see Earth burned to ashes.

Primsec sat down beside her and cradled Chasm in his arms. He stroked her hair with one hand and held her close to him. Together they watched the sun set and the black sky consume the bright blue as the moon took the place of the sun to light the Earth. The stars drifted into sight and Chasm felt that all was right in the world.

Far Too Brave

There was no resistance when they crossed into the Chalendoran atmosphere. Seven hours had passed since they first touched down on the surface of the planet. The Runner had rolled through a desert and then floated across a large lake before taking to a valley with more hills than Scicremeon had ever seen.

Chalendor was half the size of Merridia and sparsely populated. The few people they'd passed paid them very little attention. One thing that stuck out to Scicremeon was the eye color of the people. Everyone's eyes were a shade of burgundy.

Van Taven had said that their eyes were that way because all the Chalendorans possessed some form of magic. Most of them were healers and shape shifters he said, but those in the employ of the king were far more powerful. The darker the eyes, the more power a person wielded; at least that was the theory.

Scicremeon had her feet resting on the control panel, her fingers locked behind her head. She tried to contain her boredom by whistling old war songs. Van Taven gave her a sideways glance every few seconds hoping she would stop. She was happy to be able to annoy him.

"Why aren't your eyes burgundy magician?" said Scicremeon sort of mockingly.

"I am not Chalendoran, fully," said Van Taven staring at a screen in the center of the control panel that he was tapping on. Scicremeon watched images pop up on the screen, uninterested in what they were. She then stared blankly at Van Taven who finally looked her way. "My ancestors were Chalendorans who stayed behind after the first wars."

"Then that makes you one of them," said Scicremeon feigning sickness.

"That was hundreds of years ago," said Van Taven with a stern look.

"Then how did you learn to use magic. Surely there are no Merridian magicians," said Scicremeon in a matter-of-fact tone.

"Merridians have their own brand of what you could call magic as you very well know," his eyes full of accusation. "However, what I know comes from books left to me by my ancestors."

Scicremeon turned her attention back to the monitor Van Taven was still tapping at. "Are you trying to beat it into submission?" said Scicremeon ready to chop off Van Taven's fingers.

"I am trying to find the mark of a building's structure and civilization, but I am getting nothing," said Van Taven finally slamming the screen shut into the console. They'd seen people, but those that they'd seen were too far away from one another to be even a small clan. Clans stuck together and didn't wander too far off.

Scicremeon laughed at the top of her lungs at his frustration. Nothing made the boredom of riding alongside a magician more bearable than seeing him struggling. Their inability to find more than a handful of people put her revenge off. She had grown antsy, but another few hours didn't much matter to her. Every nerve in her body was itching for the inevitable moment, a moment that she was sure would come soon.

"Perhaps we might try the old fashioned way," said Scicremeon hoping to insult him.

"And what might that be," said Van Taven swiftly, hearing the mocking tone in her voice.

"Asking the next person we see the way to the king," said Scicremeon, rolling her eyes around in her head and whistling.

Van Taven scoffed and turned his eyes forward.

They came to a hill far taller than the others that they had scaled and ascended for more than an hour. As they appeared to reach the top, the hill began to ascend further up. Suddenly the ship's power shut off and the entire landscape changed. No longer were they in a valley of hills. They were being pulled by an unseen force through a sprawling city that stretched out for miles.

Beautiful homes made of wood and stone stood as tall as three floors. Other more magnificent homes had as many as five floors. Where there were no homes there were beautiful trees, rising up out of the dark green grass. At the edge of the city stood a magnificent palace that made Larnaxe's fortress seem small.

Though unlike Larnaxe's palace, there were no battlements with men standing guard, or a drawbridge. There was a massive stone wall encircling the entire palace. Colorful stones rose up on all sides shimmering in the bright sunlight. Winged serpents circled the highest point of the palace that stood more than twenty floors high.

Scicremeon tried to stand, but Van Taven quickly held his hand up and she felt herself being pushed back into her seat. She was ready to pounce on him, but he held a finger to his lips for her to be silent. His eyes were wild with fear and suspicion. He kept panning his head from one side of the ship to the other, trying to find what was controlling their ship.

This time Van Taven waved his hand frantically for Scicremeon to remain silent as she fixed her lips to speak. He could see the lines of irritation on her face, but he shook his head so slow that she couldn't mistake his meaning. Van Taven remained on edge as the palace grew closer. His ears moved, his eyeballs slid side to side behind his lids, and his head would never remain in one place. Scicremeon's face was a mask of anger and confusion as she watched an unsettled Van Taven. Everything in her told her to move, to react; to do something as she had always been instructed to, but against all of her impulses, she decided to listen to the magician.

Larnaxe said you'd be good in a tight spot, don't disappoint me, she thought of all the torturous things she could do to him. Feeling powerless wasn't something she could get used to. Having to trust Van Taven, a magician, wasn't something she wanted to get used to. *Is my life in his hands*, she wondered as she touched the pommel of her sword.

"Try to relax," said Van Taven in a whisper.

Scicremeon gave him a hard stare, audibly sucking in air through her teeth, hard set against one another. *I should have cut off your head when I had the chance*, she thought still unnerved watching him flinch and shift as if he couldn't control his own body.

Time seemed to drag on as the beauty of the Chalendoran city drifted by. The enormity of the Chalendoran palace came into focus and in front of the gate, Scicremeon could see a group of people standing in lines at the opening of the stone wall surrounding the palace. A tall figure stood between the lines of people who Scicremeon could now see were holding long spears, dressed identically. More of them filed out of the gate and fanned out in a half circle formation.

"What is the meaning of this?" said Scicremeon no longer able to keep silent.

"I don't know," said Van Taven wide eyed.

"I thought you'd been here before," said Scicremeon beginning to whisper.

"Never," said Van Taven frowning.

"Then how would you know how long it would take to get here," said Scicremeon nearly bursting.

"Mathematics," said Van Taven sarcastically.

The Runner began to slow down as it approached the tall figure standing in between two large lines of guards. His head was covered by the hood of a burgundy cloak and his hands were covered with black gloves. Scicremeon estimated that there were at least a hundred guards in lines and another two hundred fanned out on either side in the half circular formation. Behind the cloaked figure were another three cloaked figures, standing watch of the one at the center.

As The Runner came to a halt, Scicremeon saw a half dozen cloaked figures walk from under The Runner. The six of them joined the others standing behind the tall man at the center who began to move his hands in awkward movements above his head.

The hatch on the ship opened and at least four dozen guards sprinted toward the door. The tall man walked slowly behind them, followed by the others dressed like him. Scicremeon saw their dark burgundy eyes, haunting and hungry. She drew her sword and stood at the ready, as Van Taven turned to face the hatch.

Quickly, the guards rushed in, moving fast to the lower level of the ship, spears forward with focused expressions. The tall cloaked figure walked into the ship and marched forward until there were just five feet separating him from Van Taven and Scicremeon.

The cloaked figure pulled his hood down slowly. His face was pale and skinny, his cheek bones visible, his eyes set deep in their sockets. Fatigue seemed to dress his face, though he looked even younger than Van Taven; yet his eyes appeared focused and determined. He locked his eyes on Scicremeon. His eyes were so burgundy that they were nearly black. He looked at her quizzically and then quickly turned his puzzled stare on Van Taven.

Van Taven crossed his arms in front of his chest, his fingers caressing his shoulders, and bowed to the tired looking pale faced man.

"What are you doing?" said Scicremeon screaming at Van Taven, her voice growing deeper.

"He is The Erudite," said Van Taven still bowing.

"I am Mysticgo," said Mysticgo with a warm voice. "And your friend is correct in his deduction of my station." Mysticgo continued to stare at Van Taven drawing in breath. "How are you aware of this thing, Merridian?"

"Your robes are different from the others. The white stripe down the center tells me who you are. As well as the white pearl ring on your right forefinger," said Van Taven.

"Either you are well read Merridian, or," said Mysticgo and raised an opened palm to Van Taven, a terrible glower taking over his face.

Van Taven went stiff, rising onto the tips of his toes, his back arching in. The veins in his neck and arms bulged. He screamed, writhing in pain, as steam began to rise from his body. Van Taven's dark green eyes began to glow, expelling a beam of light to the ceiling of the ship. Darker and darker they grew and then quickly his eyes flashed, the green light dancing on and off of The Runner's ceiling. Slowly the hue of the light changed as it began to flash, growing brighter and then cycling to brown and then pink and finally to a light shade of burgundy.

"There you are," said Mysticgo pleased with his find.

Van Taven dropped to his knees, steam still rising from his pores. Slowly he rose to his feet like a haggard old man, leaning against the control panel. He looked into his hands, his eyes flashing burgundy light into his palms. His breathing was labored and he fell back each time he tried to stand up straight, his knees weak.

"What have you done to me?" said Van Taven weakly.

"I have unlocked your full potential," said Mysticgo with a warm smile. "Your Chalendoran power was suppressed by your Merridian blood. It has been a long while since your family moved there so many years ago. I doubt that your children's children would have shared your gifts had you never have found your way home. I must apologize for the pain."

"How do you know these things," said Van Taven still huffing out each breath as if it were going to be his last.

"The Erudite can read the blood history of any Chalendoran," said Mysticgo rather disappointed, "I thought you would have come across that in your readings," he said as he turned his attention from the nearly breathless Van Taven, "and as for you," said Mysticgo turning to Scicremeon and taking a step forward.

Scicremeon pointed her sword at him, falling deeper into her fighting stance, her eyes trained on Mysticgo, the scowl on her face becoming a ghastly grimace of rage. "Another step and you're dead," she said grinding her teeth together.

"Why are you so hostile?" said Mysticgo taking another step forward.

Nine cloaked figures had come to stand among them behind Mysticgo, looking fiercely at Scicremeon. Each of them had their right hands raised, with their palms facing Scicremeon. Their burgundy eyes were glowing, illuminating their faces.

"I am here for my revenge," said Scicremeon twirling her sword and sizing up her opponents.

"Who has harmed you here?" said Mysticgo seeming bewildered.

"I am here for my father's killers. One of you dirty magicians tricked him," said Scicremeon exasperated. Every one of the cloaked figures behind Mysticgo angered her to no end. She judged them, made them responsible for her father's death. *He wants to try and soothe me with his kind words*, she thought to herself as she allowed her anger to overtake her.

Scicremeon's blue eyes grew darker and glowed, and the heat rose inside of her as her rage took her in. Mysticgo's eyes narrowed as he looked at her. The Runner shook violently as Scicremeon roared like a savage beast. "Die!" she yelled at the top of her lungs and a jet of blue flame ripped from inside of her chest at Mysticgo and the cloaks behind him.

Van Taven lied on the floor writhing in pain from the shockwave the blast sent back after colliding with Mysticgo's force field. He reached for the control panel to pull himself up, glass from the cockpit sprinkled around him. His hands were scarred from the glass that tore into his flesh, along with a harsh cut down his left eye.

Scicremeon cut him a sideways glance, as she shook her eyes into focus. She wanted nothing more than to strike him down, but she had made a deal with the emperor. She would at least honor it until they had gotten off of Chalendor. *Think you'll scare me with magic do you*, she thought as she slid down off the control panel, her boots clapping against the floor of the ship.

Her sword swung and dispatched the first guard who came running through the hatch toward her, his body flying into the mess of cloaked magicians on the floor. Another came, thrusting his spear. He was too slow as Scicremeon shifted to her left and dispatched him with a thrust of her sword. Another came, and another, and another until she no longer bothered to count them as they fell at her feet.

The opening to the hatch was swarming with Chalendoran guards, each rushing toward Scicremeon with murderous intent. She struck down two with one stroke of her sword and stood still, daring the next to come. He was a big man, twice her size, roaring his battle cry, spitting as his teeth gnashed together. His speed was incredible for his size, his skill with a spear unparalleled compared to the men Scicremeon had already downed. The rest of the guard watched, standing calm, knowing he'd win. *He must be one of their best;* she thought to herself and grew disgusted. *Men never think highly enough of me until they are moments from death;* she frowned as she ducked again and slipped to her right, avoiding two more his blows.

"Do you have nothing else," said Scicremeon making a mockery of his skill.

The guard grunted wildly, swinging like a madman with no care for life or limb. Scicremeon smiled and allowed him to press her backward, deeper into the ship. Her leg pressed against the control panel and her eyes went wide with fear. Her opponent smiled his victory pulling his spear back to strike the killing blow. *Amateur,* Scicremeon smiled back at him as she slipped under his thrust. She twisted and jammed her elbow into the small of his back, sending his face crashing into the control panel.

He made a gurgling sound that muffled his scream as Scicremeon's sword slipped through the back of his neck and back out.

The guards at the hatched marched up toward her slowly, the two at the front looking at one another trying to decide who'd go first.

"This is suicide," yelled Van Taven who'd finally gotten to his feet, still leaning on the ship's control panel.

"I'm just getting warmed up," said Scicremeon with a cold smile on her face.

Her blood was hot for more death and each time she killed a Chalendoran guard, she fell deeper into a drunken trance, hell bent on spilling blood.

As she stepped forward, she felt a rush of energy surge behind her and watched five guards slam into the men behind them, rattling the line they were forming to attack.

"I didn't ask for your help," said Scicremeon looking back at Van Taven as she rushed forward. She pulled her sword over her head and swung down at the guard on the floor.

Clap.

Her hand fell into Mysticgo's palm who was staring at her with a puzzled scowl shaking his head *no*. He pushed her back hard into the back of her chair. Her eyes went dark blue again and she roared.

"Not this time," said Mysticgo, waving his hand in a back-slapping motion.

Scicremeon pitched backward over the chair from the rush of energy that slammed into her chest. She heard Van Taven roar above her. *Traitor*, she thought and steadied her sword in his direction. Before she could react she heard Mysticgo.

"You are nowhere near your potential yet," said Mysticgo twisting his left hand toward the ceiling.

Scicremeon watched as Van Taven flew into the ceiling of The Runner and fell onto the floor in a heap. She watched as Mysticgo marched toward her. Unlike the guards he was unafraid of her strength and skill with a blade. She rolled backward and up onto her feet, just in front of where Van Taven lay unconscious.

Scicremeon marched backward slowly with her sword at the ready. Her eyes panned between each of Mysticgo's hand. What he was capable of she wasn't entirely sure, but she at least knew he could move her body without touching her. That was unsettling enough. But his closeness to her blade made her wonder whether she could harm him with it. "Fight me fair magician," said Scicremeon feinting at him with her sword. *He'll bleed like the rest of them*, she said to herself as she watched Mysticgo recoil at her fake attempt.

"There are no fair fights with the daughter of the *Stormblade*," said Mysticgo smiling at her. "You showed no mercy as you expelled The Fires of Aygron upon my brethren."

It had to be him. Even if he appeared to be younger than Van Taven, it had to be him. Who else would know about her father's gift but someone who was alive to have witnessed it? *Only one from Merridia. Only someone old enough who had marched with him.* His recognition of her gift was enough to convict him in her mind. He had to be the trickster who snuck up on her father, in aid of the hooded coward. Since in truth, there was no one in all of written or spoken memory who was as skilled as Aygron Stormblade with any weapon made for cutting, hacking or smashing. He was a magician. He could conceal his true age, and his true identity. The strongest Chalendoran magicians had been known to live twice as long as Merridians because of their intense magical training. That much she had cared to learn of them, as much as she despised them.

Her eyes went dark again and the ship shook more violently this time. Mysticgo twirling his hands in a circular motion in front of himself as The Fires of Aygron burst from Scicremeon. The two of them fell back into the walls of the ship. Scicremeon watched

Mysticgo tuck his back in, obviously in pain as her eyelids shut, and she drifted off into blackness.

No, was all she could think of as her eyes tried to focus, a haze covering her sight as her head swirled around, her shoulders rocking, as she tried to steady herself. She was astonished at her predicament, but none of it mattered. She would have happily died, knowing that so much Chalendoran blood had been spilled by her hands. It would have been enough. There was nothing else to drive her. Mysticgo himself had barely gotten to his feet.

In what world could I have subdued he who could deceive my own father? My stories had been told, but no one ever placed me above the Stormblade. All that they were sure of was that I was of his bloodline. This was the one magician who he could not thwart. And she knew that tradition would give her respect enough for trying her hand. What more could it have asked?

Though, as she heard Mysticgo bark his orders for the guards to seize him, she knew she was still alive. The fight wasn't over, but she found it hard to move. His sword was short, but true, sharpened to a razor's edge. He moved with good speed, and his thrusts were strong and precise. The guards fell in his wake as he yelled his fury, marching toward the cockpit.

Nothing but pride could have made her smile at that moment as she watched another fall as he avoided the blow from behind. The lessons had paid off. Only a few strands of his hair floated in the air when the sword swiped at his head. Those brown eyes were as big as they were when Gustain had slapped him across the face. But this time, there was no fear in them. Only a wild happiness as more blood smacked him in the face from another throat slit on his blade.

But he wasn't supposed to be there. Aton was supposed to be with the emperor. Larnaxe was supposed to be watching him. *I'll kill him I swear it*, she thought as she pressed against the floor with her hands trying her hardest to get up. There was nothing else she could do as she hacked away at a guard's knee and continued to crawl toward Mysticgo.

Mysticgo, she thought and screamed in agony as her back cracked into place when she rose to her feet.

"Aton!" she screamed louder than ever before as Mysticgo caught his sword hand and batted him to the floor.

Mysticgo turned on her and backhanded her across the cheek as she struggled to get her sword ready. Scicremeon grunted as she hit the floor in a heap, her sword clattering away from her. She stretched her hand out to grab it and felt it being crushed under the weight of a boot. Her fingers grew hot as she moaned, praying inside for him to release her.

"Everyone out," cried Mysticgo and the guards quickly filed out of the hatch, leaving him alone with Scicremeon, Aton still unconscious behind him on the floor. "You are truly blessed, for I cannot kill you myself." Scicremeon looked at him puzzled as he lifted her sword and tossed it onto the control panel. "I can however make this ship your grave, with no air to breathe. Eventually you'll be in so much pain, that you will wish you were dead," he said grabbing her with both hands by the neck, and lifting her onto her feet.

Scicremeon's head bobbed lazily from side to side. Her arms and legs were limp, ready to give way to her weight. She would have collapsed if it were not for Mysticgo holding her up. "I had thought you killed yourself with that beautiful gift your father passed down to you. That would have eliminated you as trouble here, and there would be no need for these measures," said Mysticgo looking her face over, sympathy filled in his eyes.

Scicremeon struggled to speak, but could say nothing. The glaring look she tried to make was more than words could describe. Mysticgo knew she wanted nothing more than to kill him.

If you did not kill my father who did, she thought having heard what he said about not being able to kill her himself. For surely if he could not kill her, he could not have killed Aygron. *You're still as guilty as the rest,* she said to herself, fighting to keep her eyes open.

Mysticgo took his hands off her neck and she remained suspended in the air. He marched over to Aton and lifted the boy from the floor and slung him over his shoulder.

"For what it's worth, had you not attacked my men, we would not be at this point. But your temper it seems is far worse than what the stories have said of your father's," said Mysticgo as he began to march toward the hatch.

Scicremeon heard him, but her eyes glossed over the face of her only student. Rage boiled inside her, mixed with fear and sorrow. A single tear fell from her left eye, wetting her cheek. *You're too much like me little boy.* She thought to herself as Mysticgo waved a hand above his head, and the metal of the ship began folding in on itself and around Scicremeon. Mysticgo waved his hand again and Van Taven went sliding down the hatch at the feet of the guards, who lifted him from the ground. *Too much like me you are Aton, far too brave.*

The hatch slammed shut as Mysticgo stepped down and waved his hands again.

She heard his voice inside the ship as if he were there with her. *Goodbye. I will weep for you.*

The force holding Scicremeon up released her, and she crumbled to the floor of the ship. *Save your tears,* she said to herself as she felt the ship begin to move. It was moving fast, but not nearly as fast as they had come. But she guessed that it wouldn't be long before she got to space and ran out of air. *If you have to go, go out in a heap,* she thought of Lance and smiled as she turned over on her back and closed her eyes. Where the ship was going she would go with it, until life chose to abandon her.

She crawled to the control panel and found her sword, looking it over with tears in her eyes. The blood soaked blade was testament to her fury, rage, and thirst for blood. Revenge wasn't as sweet as she had expected, but the dead bodies around her were enough to make her smile. Having the knowledge that Aton was responsible for part of the pile of dead men, made her weep with joy.

"Better to die, sword in hand, than wrinkled old, cold in bed," said Scicremeon aloud. "That is my way."

Faster

Had his father been there, he would never have been allowed to leave. But it was the one thing his grandmother was able to do that no other Merridian could. She could find ways around Corvus's power. Even away from Merridia, Corvus's word was law and held sway at great distances. Whatever he spoke while on Merridia could not be changed even in his absence. Yet, the longer he remained away, the more measures The Mother Merridia would take to ensure the survival of the planet and all its inhabitants.

Black Dawn flew away from Merridia in defiance of his father's orders. He believed that Corvus was not doing enough to stop the coming disaster that he saw in his visions. Taking matters into his own hands was something Black Dawn was used to doing. Defying his father entirely was something new.

The older gods had quarreled with one another for ages. In their youth they had been reckless and headstrong. Even Gorgon Ray had tried to unseat his brother Corvus as the ruler of Merridia. There were other forces that also grew out of The Mother Merridia. They were forces of the nature of life on Merridia that could also work their way around Corvus's power at times. Black

Dawn knew his father often had to work tirelessly to keep peace on the planet. He'd always sided with him and never believed he could truly be at odds with him.

As he passed a bright red star he felt the presence of two beings following him. He recognized them immediately and slowed down. When he turned he saw the faces of his siblings. Mastadon slowed down his bulky frame and came to a halt a few feet from Black Dawn, flanked by Pearl on his right.

"How did you-," said Black Dawn cut off abruptly by Mastadon.

"We followed you," said Mastadon twirling his hammer in his hand.

"Where do you plan on going?" said Pearl crossing her arms.

"To find Scicremeon," said Black Dawn coolly.

"You are love struck," said Pearl shocked, her face scrounged in amazement.

"Why would you be searching space brother?" said Mastadon confused.

"She's not on Merridia," said Black Dawn as if Mastadon should have known.

"I'm sorry that I don't keep tabs on mortals," said Mastadon.

"She's gone to Chalendor," said Black Dawn rubbing his chin and thinking hard.

"For what purpose?" said Pearl inclining her head, looking at Black Dawn's perplexed stare.

"Revenge," said Black Dawn.

"Nothing wrong with that," said Mastadon with a big smile looking at Black Dawn and then Pearl. Pearl rolled her eyes at him and turned her attention to Black Dawn.

"Dorrin," said Pearl, always using his birth name when she was frustrated with him, "you were carrying on in council about father's priorities; but it seems your priorities rest on your love for a mortal who might get herself killed over a father she never knew. How does that have anything to do with this calamity that you keep blabbering on about," said Pearl hunching her shoulders and shaking her head looking for an answer.

"It has everything to do with it," said Black Dawn irritated with his sister's inquisition.

"What have you done?" begged Pearl, her lips curling in anger as she moved closer to Black Dawn. He inhaled deeply, his chest rising as if he were trying to make himself appear larger. "Tell me," said Pearl, always insistent when it concerned Black Dawn.

"You're not his mother," said Mastadon sneering at Pearl as he glided toward Black Dawn and wrapped an arm around his shoulder. "She prods too much, I know," said Mastadon, whispering in Black Dawn's ear as he looked at his sister as if he were telling a secret she couldn't hear.

"I'm afraid of what father will do to him when he finds this out," said Pearl exasperated as Mastadon continued to smile at her. "Father will find out, he always finds out. It will be better to go home now while you're not so far away," said Pearl looking at Black Dawn, her eyes begging him to listen to her. She always kept his best interest at heart, as demanding as she was. Often following her recommendations produced favorable outcomes for Black Dawn, especially those concerning Corvus. But she could see in his face that this time was different. He wouldn't listen. Mastadon never made it any easier.

"Ah, as hard to kill as my little sister might be, she has the emotions of a mortal woman," said Mastadon laughing hard as he usually did, his voice a pit of mockery.

"In this instance, I don't think it wise to be beguiled by this warmonger," said Pearl softly, trying not to be too bossy.

"If I could see all the details, I would show you. I know simply that Scicremeon is a piece to the puzzle," said Black Dawn, his eyes urging Pearl to listen.

"You should have killed her like you planned to, it would have made father's anger worth it," said Mastadon shaking his head as if truly disappointed with his brother. He remembered Black Dawn being lectured by Corvus on orders and the Law of the Gods. "This time he'll probably strip you of half your powers, so we might as well go on," said Mastadon.

"Might as well go on," said Pearl disbelieving.

"He had The Mother Merridia break father's barriers, that is a direct condescension of his authority; he'll be punished gravely," said Mastadon laughing.

"So he should compound his indiscretion by further disregarding father's orders?" asked Pearl.

"Yes," said Mastadon fervently.

"Have you thought about our punishment?" said Pearl facing Mastadon, knowing he hadn't.

"We tried to talk him out of it," said Mastadon looking at Black Dawn, raising his eyebrows.

"Just go back," said Black Dawn to Pearl.

"We'll tell you about it when get back," said Mastadon.

"You think I'm going to let him go to Chalendor alone with the likes of you. You'll pollute his mind with your stupidity and aloof nature," said Pearl with mean intentions.

Black Dawn looked at them both shaking his head *no*. He knew Corvus would be angry with him. For dragging his brother and sister along, he'd be furious. It was he who sought the aid of The Mother Merridia; they only followed him. They wouldn't accomplish anything by going. Pearl was right about Mastadon, he was a warmonger, always looking for a battle, and some action for his hammer. Pearl knew Black Dawn enjoyed battle as much as Mastadon and the two of them together had caused great destruction.

"Can I not talk you out of this?" asked Black Dawn, their faces quickly registering the answer. Mastadon would go with him anywhere just to cause some trouble or mischief. Pearl would go truly, to shield him from Mastadon's poor discretion.

"No," said Pearl and Mastadon together.

"The one time the two of you agree on anything," said Black Dawn with a defeated smile.

"Lead the way brother," said Mastadon turning toward the direction Black Dawn had been facing before he sensed their presence.

Black Dawn turned around and began to lift his arms in the direction they would travel and suddenly felt a jolt of energy surge in his chest. He felt a decrease in life giving energy. The jolt brought misery screaming to his features. It pulled at the love in his heart, slowly breaking him into pieces. Everyone was right about his feelings. Though he would never validate their claims, it was the utter truth.

Pearl seeing him in distress immediately asked him what the problem was. Never had she seen him so pained, so fearful, even in the face of a near scornful father full of disappointment. None of the chastisements that Corvus berated Black Dawn with ever produced nearly as frightful a result. The strongest of the Merridians, save for Corvus was gripped with a haunting feeling.

Tears were welling in his eyes when the mood in the pit of his stomach rose up to cast away the misery. The glistening liquid in his eyes began to evaporate as his eyes glowed.

"Tell me what is wrong. I can feel your anger growing," said Pearl in a commanding voice.

"She's dying, Scicremeon is dying," said Black Dawn, his anger forcing his voice to grumble.

"How do you know brother?" said Mastadon with a concerned look.

"I can feel it," said Black Dawn his breath rapid, "it's all happening now. I have to save her, we have to save her. We have to move faster," said Black Dawn giving a hand to each of his siblings.

A shockwave burst from within Black Dawn and propelled them forward through space. Stars seemed like small candle lights as they roared past, constantly gaining speed. The dark matter that was space seemed to fold around them and appeared as a tunnel. Charges of energy shot in all directions around them and Black Dawn's own energy shot out, colliding with the black wall of dark matter, propelling him forward faster still.

"I should have left sooner, I should have made haste even though I let her go," said Black Dawn his voice echoing in the tunnel.

"We make haste now," said Pearl, feeling Black Dawn's sadness and anger pouring out into the tunnel of dark matter they were traveling through. Her sweet voice she hoped was a comfort to him. It usually had a calming effect to anyone who'd ever heard it.

"We'll step on the fleas responsible," said Mastadon, a mood of excitement growing in him. His love for war and conflict was never so hot as when his brother's wrath was ready to boil over. He could feel Black Dawn's emotions churning like a great windstorm. The love he held for the mortal Scicremeon was obvious. He'd never forgive himself if a hair on her head was harmed. In his heart, Mastadon didn't care whether she lived or died. But if she were important enough for his brother, it made her important for him.

"It won't be long now," said Pearl.

Black Dawn knew they'd arrive on Chalendor in less than an hour, but Scicremeon's life force was fading faster. Death could happen in a matter of seconds. And on Chalendor there'd be nothing he could do to save her, for the Chalendoran forces would have dominion over life and death. He cursed himself for not being there. His heart poured out anger again and propelled him forward faster.

Smaller Divide

Forecon stood on a fiery comet, circling Luminar with a devious smile on his face. His black hands were ablaze with the fires of the comet as he watched Luminar's every movement. The blackness where his eyes should have been was burning with white fire, flickering inside of his head. A planet just behind him was black as death, burnt beyond repair, a mass of the war between the titans of Our Union. The moon of the planet was falling to pieces, floating outward around Forecon and Luminar in ragged pieces of rock.

Luminar's orange hair was bursting with ultraviolet rays, as if it had a mind of its own. She hadn't moved for an hour, deflecting the fiery attacks of Forecon. The bottom of her illuminate robes were stained with the celestial fires that Forecon kept assailing her with.

He didn't seem to be actually trying to destroy her, only keeping her busy. Forecon hadn't fully engaged Luminar. He was content with keeping his distance and Luminar decided to oblige him. When she had tried to close the distance between them he'd flee until she ended her pursuit.

"Whenever you are ready to begin, please inform me," said Luminar brazenly flicking away another of Forecon's fiery attacks.

He didn't reply, he only smiled wider and then white ropes of fire ripped from his eyes toward Luminar. The rays of her hair shot out toward the white ropes, colliding with them. The energies wrestled with one another, pushing back and forth, a ball of energy forming. The white fires and ultraviolet ropes of energy grew and grew and then exploded outward into the cosmos.

The stars around them absorbed their blazing energies, shining brighter for a moment and then subsiding.

"I can keep this up for eternity," said Luminar.

"No doubt, but it shall not take that long," said Forecon laughing hideously.

Forecon closed the distance between them, still circling Luminar, his eyes trained on her as he orbited her never changing position. She didn't bother to watch him, finding it to be a waste of time. He moved closer again, throwing balls of fire in a myriad of sizes. Each one bounced off of Luminar's robes and she found enough humor in it to laugh.

"Engage and let's be done with it," said Luminar pressing her eyes onto the white flickers in Forecon's face.

"Death should not be an abrupt consequence of existence," said Forecon. The fire around his black hands subsided as he clasped them behind his back.

"I do not plan on dying, in any form."

"There is but one who shall endure forever."

"We are all part of that endurance. Has your master forgotten his place among us," said Luminar with a disgusted look on her face. "He makes war where there need be none."

"This is not a war."

"Then what is it?"

"It is the proper shift in the Chain of Balance."

"The Chain of Balance was made long before any of us had come. It was broken and made anew in the treachery of Carnok."

"There is no treachery in Our Union. Everything is as it must be," said Forecon, his skeletal face appearing to register annoyance.

"Are these the lies that he told you, in a rousing speech to change your mind," said Luminar closing her eyes slowly.

"We have been shielded from you true, but what lies need be told by those such as us," said Forecon stopping his circular movement for the first time. He settled a good distance away from Luminar, in her direct line of sight.

Forecon remained quiet, his hands still clasped behind his back. The flickering white fire in his eyes dissipated as if blown out, a small line of smoke floating out into space, fading into nothingness.

Luminar studied him carefully, her eyes narrowing as she watched his behavior. Thutmos had called them evil, ravenous animals seeking only death. Forecon's words and demeanor offered a different perspective. The calm in his voice seemed to purport the truth. She still could not fathom the necessity of them shielding their minds from the rest of Our Union, if this were the way of things.

"Are you and Carnok the sole wielders of this new purpose?" asked Luminar, a hint of sarcasm in her voice.

"The Charm of the Sacred knows it well, but has been unwilling to accept it," said Forecon as if sure.

"If it were the proper purpose, he would have followed the same course. Your words are the honey of treachery," said Luminar disbelieving, shaking her head *no*.

"It happens as it must. You should know well that everything isn't always apparent, even to us," said Forecon as a buzzing mass of energy began to form in front of him.

Out of the mass of energy came Kinozl, her face a mass of pain and indignation. Kinozl faced Forecon, one hand outstretched, holding something. Luminar struggled to see what it was. She called to Kinozl, but she did not respond. Kinozl's mind was open, her feelings were unmasked. Luminar could feel her despair and sought to connect with her.

Please tell me how I can help you, Luminar thought to her, hoping Forecon wasn't listening.

There is nothing; it would be best that you leave or you shall suffer the same fate, Kinozl thought back to her.

A small force pushed against Luminar's mind. Trurow was near and she thought out to Luminar. *Listen to her and go, please.*

"Or suffer the same fate," said Forecon reaching forward with one hand.

Luminar heard Trurow gasp and watched as Kinozl and Forecon shifted sideways. Each had one hand wrapped around Trurow's neck. Trurow hung there, limp, not putting up a fight. Her face was nearly a mass of blackness; her eyes were full of tears.

The flickering flames returned to Forecon's eyes, quickly bursting out like a smoldering fire, swirling around his head. Kinozl's eyes illuminated. Together, Kinozl and Forecon loosed the energy from their eyes assaulting Trurow's face. Her body shook violently as Kinozl and Forecon drifted backward slowly as the energy overloaded Trurow.

There was a sound like shattering glass and then Kinozl and Forecon stopped. Trurow's head bobbed to one side as her eyes closed, life gone from her body.

Luminar was dumbstruck, more than shock taking over her face as it happened. Forecon had kept her so busy to the point that she had decided not to move. All of his attempts were futile. But they served a purpose. He was stalling; waiting for Kinozl to bring Trurow to him. At first, she didn't move because of Forecon's unwillingness to engage. Now she could not move because Trurow was there in front of her, devoid of life.

Forecon rushed toward her on his fiery comet, the trail of fire splitting into two streams, whipping around in front of him. The lines of fire blazed toward Luminar who remained still as a statue.

She watched them coming, but her heart was gone. She would let the fiery rays of malicious intent have her. They would consume her until she was like Trurow. She would be dragged to an unknown place that they could never have dreamed of themselves. There they would lie in the bosom of Aeon comforted for all of Eternity.

Those were her thoughts. That this existence had changed too much. Whatever the new Chain of Balance was she didn't care. She only understood the collective of Our Union. It was perfect.

Let them come, Luminar thought to herself. Rage was there inside her, but there was no heat to stoke the fire. Grief was a terrible storm showering down upon her, dousing whatever fire that might burn inside of her to force her hand to action. *Strike true in your new purpose servant,* Luminar thought to Forecon. *Do not stand idle, take part in further treachery, for your hands have been stained and it cannot be washed away,* she thought to Kinozl.

Kinozl's tears had been welling since she'd held Trurow. There was grief inside of her, showing itself in falling tears. Luminar sought to make her feel shame with her words. She showed Kinozl images during The Assembly of Our Union, when she was with Primsec. Each of them was there together, comforted by Aeon, being in utter happiness.

Forgive me, Kinozl thought to Luminar and then turned away, not able to watch the comet's fires assault Luminar.

Whoosh.

The shockwave was intense when it struck, deflected back toward Forecon. He avoided it narrowly, jumping from his comet. Watching it as he flipped backward, he saw it explode into a thousand speckles. Then a voice like a billion raging storms filled the cosmos.

"Your victories today have come to an end," said Thutmos who had shielded Luminar from Forecon's attack.

"The weight of your voice is frightening," said Forecon with a smile, drifting backward away from Thutmos toward Kinozl. "It is shameful that you hold back your true power." Forecon took Kinozl by the wrist and looked at her with his eyeless face. "It is time that we go my dear."

Kinozl nodded and then looked back at Thutmos with wanting eyes. Space folded around them, twisted, and then they were gone as it folded back in place.

Thutmos turned to Luminar, his eyes sharp baring down into hers. His eyes flashed in front of her and she snapped out of her stupor. She burst into tears, whaling and shaking, sending shockwaves of energy rippling out into space.

"Listen to me," said Thutmos taking her by the shoulders, "go to Everdon and tell Chasm that her time is up." Luminar continued to sob and didn't respond. He shook her. And his voice began again, sounding like a billion raging storms, "Heed my words," said Thutmos and Luminar shuddered.

"Yes lord," said Luminar and began to fold into space.

Thutmos regarded Luminar for a moment as he watched her shift space around her to depart. His eyes narrowed and he pressed his lips together. He ruminated for a long while and then turned.

Seeing Trurow suspended and bobbing in space grieved him immensely. He went to her and stuck his hand into her head as he had with the others. He watched her form dissipate and drift apart.

It was the fourth time it had happened. Each time was the same, yet different at once. For the first time he had felt the singularity of these titans that had been laid to rest. *This must stop here; there is a smaller divide between us. Enough has been wasted.*

What You Most Crave

Cold had crept into her bones, slowly inching its way toward her soul. Death she thought would be a comfort to her. There was no pain in death once it arrived, though the process toward it was often taxing and wet with blood. That truth of it, she was finding out first hand pressed against the cold metal inside of the lifeless ship, propelled only by the powers of Mysticgo. *I would rather have had my head lopped off, or a sword in the guts. Bleeding out would not have been nearly as bad,* Scicremeon thought to herself as she tried to force herself to sleep. But the cold wouldn't allow her any reprieve.

Never had she thought that she'd curse the resilience of her own body. She'd suffered through the cold before in relative comfort. *It was a lot easier dressed in the fur of a beast,* she thought trying to smile through chapped lips. Her lips were a mass of blood and peeling skin. Licking them was painful, and the crusting feeling annoyed her.

Looking toward the hatch, she saw the mass of bodies that she'd laid to waste. *Poor souls; never stood a chance,* thought Scicremeon to herself. Inside she wanted to weep for them. They were men with families somewhere on Chalendor. They weren't her real enemies, only obstacles that had to be traversed. *Acting on orders,* she thought and spit what little saliva on the floor that she could produce.

Don't look at me like that, she thought as the dead burgundy eyes of a young soldier stared blankly at her. Scicremeon knew he was younger than she was, barely past his eighteenth birthday. There was no hair on his face. There were no wrinkles or hard lines under his eyes that soldiers usually got. She guessed he must have only just begun his long days standing idle, watching and waiting for something to happen. She didn't remember his skill, but if she had to judge from the rest of the lot, he wasn't very good at all.

His face appeared to be pained, not by the hurt of injury, but the look of one who died too soon. It was the look of one who knew that they're time had come. The look of one who wished they'd been somewhere else rather than at the opposite end of Scicremeon's blade. The list of victims was long and bloody. *I'll remember you forever,* she thought knowing she couldn't escape those eyes.

There were others like him, young and old, kind and mean; unlucky people who had been in the wrong place at the wrong time. Now she too was in that predicament, floating toward space in a mass of metal, with no way out of the enchanted scrap heap. She'd tried to burn through it, but she didn't have enough energy left to produce a blast strong enough. She could barely grip her sword, for if she could have, she'd have tried to hack away at the metal. *Likely a futile effort,* she thought smiling knowing well that she would have happily passed out doing so.

To think I should have already been dead, Scicremeon thought remembering her run in with Black Dawn. She'd been forced to read tales about him by Lance, who'd first taught her the sword. She admired his bravery when he defeated the Levian beast that swallowed up all the seas of Merridia, beginning a draught that lasted an entire summer. It was how she recognized him. The sword, the armor; it was all identical to the stories.

He hated me, she kept thinking to herself, *called me a savage killer. I guess I am;* she thought looking at the bodies scattered about the ship. Yet, he had let her go for a reason that seemed silly at the time.

Compassion had never been her strong suit and love was something she hadn't thought of since her mother died. Surely he had been joking, she thought at the time as she cradled Aton in her arms. Her being a killer was the one thing he was right about. Many men had fallen dead at her feet. It was the only thing that made her feel that life was worth living, until Aton.

Aton, she thought of him and smiled wide, splitting her lips in three places as her chapped lips cracked. He'd done her proud as a teacher and she must have done well, for he had no experience at all. Yet, he moved with the precision of a practiced artist, painting his victims on the canvas of The Runner's floor, as if the ship were a fabulous masterpiece meant to be hung on the wall of the emperor. On no occasion had she ever been more proud of anything or anyone, not even herself.

He gave me a gift, she thought of Black Dawn, knowing her want for revenge. In his own words he'd said, "It will help you get what most you crave," she remembered Black Dawn saying to her. And all that she craved was revenge, though it slowly began to escape her that day. Aton had grown on her before they drug Gustain to the ocean. He was her company in the marketplace where she waited for challenges and drank herself silly.

Each day that he'd been with her he'd grown on her. Aton always pushed harder than he needed to in order to please her, to be the perfect student. For some reason he seemed happy around her and forced her to be happy as well. She hid her feelings at every turn, for she'd always believed that a killer couldn't have a soft heart. It'd make her weak, and weakness had no place in the warrior's heart.

But you're more important than my revenge, thought Scicremeon, remembering the lie she'd told Van Taven on the ship as they made their way toward the planet that housed her greatest enemy. The faceless trickster and swordsman who destroyed her father no longer seemed to matter as much. Only Aton mattered, and she'd lost him to a magician.

A tear invaded her face as she sniffled, suffocating the whimper that tried to climb into her throat. *But how,* she begged herself.

"Do anything...," she could hear Lance in her ear, his words of reckless wisdom. He'd never told her to act without thinking, but the scars on his body were no indication that he ever did much thinking himself. Though in her current predicament, she couldn't argue with the other half of the phrase he always repeated, which was, "...rather than nothing at all."

Scicremeon knew death would eventually come crawling out of some unknown hole she'd never be able to find. He'd grip her and pull her into the miserable oblivion that she believed he must live in. There was no escaping his grasp, no matter how strong you were. With all of her gifts, the skills she'd acquired through intense training, none of them could save her from the suffocating grip of death. She was mortal and all mortals ceased to wake for some reason or another.

After a short struggle and forcing her aching fingers to obey, she slid her sword into its sheath. Both her sword and sheath were cold, unwelcomed guests against her tight uniform, but she'd tolerate their freezing presence rather than leave them behind. Even on a ship where she was sure to be the only thing alive, life had taught her to never take unnecessary risks.

Crawling as fast as she could against the cold floor, she made it to where the cargo hold door should have been. *The good thing about a battlefield is that there is no need for doors.* Reaching over, she closed the eyes of the man who'd given her his dead stare. She kicked one guard off the back of another, his body rolling to the right. Then, with all of her might, she pushed the soldier covering the door to the hatchway.

Breathing out hard after her exertions, she forced herself up onto her knees and grabbed the lever to the hatch. *Stuck,* she thought as it didn't give way as she yanked at it.

Letting the fire build up inside of her, her blue eyes glowing dark, she let out a focused blast of The Blue Ember. Steam rose as she let the fire burn into the cargo hold latch and with a forceful tug the door sprang open.

Whoosh.

The freezing air struck her with hatred, forcing her to recoil and turn her face away. She scowled and scoffed at the cold gust of air.

Grabbing hold of the ladder she climbed as quickly as she could, hoping to divorce the ladder as soon as possible. She held no love for the cold slippery metal.

The floor of the cargo hold was twice as cold as the cockpit. Scicremeon could feel the cold creeping into her boots. She crept around feeling for the walls in the pitch black square of the cargo hold.

Finding one, she crept along it slowly feeling with her hands as she rotated her head around, her eyes wide looking around as if she could see. *I wonder where they put it,* she thought to herself of the satchel that she allowed the emperor's men to carry. In her lifetime she'd had to do everything on her own, and thus it was hard to refuse service, especially when everyone was afraid of you simply because of your name.

She took note to how most of the men in the emperor's employ tried hard not to look her in the eye. In Marside they had heard that a long enough stare signaled a challenge. *The stories people tell, most of them are true*, she thought knowing that this particular one had not been. Eying someone in Marside was only a signal of your courage, for to not look one in the eye was seen as cowardice. Yet, challenges could only be made with the heart and the heart could only be heard when words were spoken, or when tears were shed. And in Marside, it was only acceptable for mothers of dying or dead children to cry outside the company of family.

Coming to a shelf, Scicremeon felt around, touching boxes and hard chests. She reached low and high and didn't feel what she was looking for. She continued to move slowly down the shelf, reaching and prodding with her fingers, blind in the darkness of the gripping cold.

A soft handle fell onto her forearm as she reached her hand back. Deeper she pushed her hand and squeezed. It was her ragged beige bag, knowing it the moment her hand folded. They'd only improved upon the handle at her request. And she knew there was nothing in it, except for the one thing that'd been there since the day Black Dawn handed it to her.

She pushed a box aside and pulled the bag from the cold shelf.

"It will help you get what you most crave," she heard Black Dawn's voice in her head again.

At the time when he'd given it to her, revenge was what she most craved. But now, as she pulled the Hand of Destruction from the satchel it was Aton. She missed his presence miserably, and the only thing left for her in the cold abyss of the ship was death. *He has to be closer,* she thought of death, feeling her body shaking, her teeth chattering together. Purpose had allowed her mind to wander, but as she found what she was looking for her eyes rolled and the stifling cold crept back into her bones.

BANG!

She dropped to her knees hard. Her fingers would have been clattering if they were metal, cold ripping through them, causing them to knock into one another as her body shook. Cold as they were, she forced her fingers to trace the lines of the Hand of Destruction. She heard Black Dawn's voice again, "...but it comes at a cost," she remembered him saying. *No cost was too great then*, she thought and then said aloud to herself, "No cost is greater than Aton's life, not even my own."

Her hand was at the opening to the Hand of Destruction. There was another thing that he said that gave her a bit of a pause. She never enjoyed being bound to anything or anyone until Aton. It was the reason she followed no men of power, or great warriors, and though she'd promised her service to the emperor, agreement with him was only out of her need for a ship she'd have never been able to procure on her own. It was a necessary compromise to her thirst for revenge. Still, the words echoed in her mind, "If you put it on, it will never come off."

No cost is greater, she reassured herself as she slipped her left hand through. Hot air swept through the gauntlet, and then the jewels on the top of her hand and the larger one in her palm squeezed onto her hand. The white colored metal squeezed onto her forearm, pressing down tightly.

Her blue eyes began to glow, her eyelids blinked rapidly out of her control. Sounds that she didn't recognize flooded into the room. They were voices whispering and yelling all at once. A golden light burst into the room illuminating it and then barreled toward her.

Marvelous warmth overtook her, pushing the cold away. The voices became clear, they were kind to her. The uniform she wore became as hard as the Hand of Destruction. The jewels set in the gauntlet turned blue, identical to her eyes. Inside of the jewel, a gold string of energy roamed around between both jewels. The white uniform she wore slowly transformed into the blue color of her eyes.

Inside of her she could feel The Blue Ember rising as it did when she was ready to attack. Yet, this time it was different. Instead of pushing through her chest, she could feel it coursing through every part of her body. Her ears flexed and she could hear everything around her, inside and outside of The Runner.

The golden light left the cargo hold, but her eyes were no longer covered in darkness. She could see everything as if the light of a radiant sun were shining through the metal of the ship.

The voices that were in the room had begun to quiet. But she remembered all that they had said and could recall every word without fail, though they were all talking at the same time. *More will come later*, she remembered one saying, but what she now knew was enough. And she knew what she'd do first.

Turning her gauntleted palm toward the ceiling and closing her eyes, she thought of one word, still feeling The Runner sailing through the air. *Stop*, she thought softly to herself and the ship came to a sudden halt. Scicremeon smiled inside as she felt the surge of energy as the heap of flying metal adhered to her demand. Whatever was forcing the ship toward space and her impending doom succumbed to the whims of the single thought in her mind.

She remembered one of the voices speaking of The Blue Ember. And another responding, calling it The Fires of Aygron. Scicremeon already knew the names of her gift well. Yet, what stuck with her was that it would no longer be the same. It would shoot from anywhere she'd like it to now. *The Blue Ember has no limitation*, one of the voices said. With that statement Scicremeon's mind began to see her escape.

Raising her hands just above shoulder level she screamed. The energy of The Blue Ember coursing through her body swelled up in a matter of seconds and burst out from all sides, a whooshing sound invading the room and then she watched as the entire ship shattered into pieces.

Scicremeon landed on her feet as the remains of the ship fell to the ground around her. Looking forward, she knew the way she'd been going, for the ship had not changed course at all. She stared for a long moment, taking in a new world as her senses had heightened to incalculable levels. Closing her eyes, she saw the face of the boy she loved and frowned in anger grinding her teeth together.

I am coming for you Aton and all of Chalendor shall quake with fear.

There Will Be No Quarter

Scicremeon began walking back toward the palace slowly, taking in the landscape around her. Chalendor didn't seem so much different from Merridia. The earth was alive with miles of green grass, colored flowers sprouting up in its midst, and great trees were scattered about the landscape ahead of her.

Her stride was slow as she examined the planet she had spent all of her life hating. She'd dreamed of the day she could exact revenge, and when it came she almost failed. Dying wouldn't have been so bad, but her new-self seemed more equipped to finish the job she'd begun a few hours ago. More men would fall at her feet and she would take the boy back home who taught her how to love again.

In the distance she could hear the pattering of boots coming in her direction. Caution crept into her heart, beginning to feel the rush of excitement that she was used to. She drew her sword in anticipation of a fight and smiled as she kept marching forward slowly. As the boots continued to patter, she focused, and she could feel the beat of their march as if they were touching her on the bottom of her bare feet.

Interesting, she thought to herself and smiled wider. She could perceive the cadence of the soldiers' march and hear the inconsistent bang of a boot not in step with the rest of the cohort. *They must have heard the ship explode,* she wondered as the marching soldiers grew closer to her position.

She quickened her pace and then saw the top of the tower of the palace. *I was never going to make it back to space,* she realized. She hadn't gone very far in the time that she'd been on the broken Runner. Mysticgo had to have spelled it to freeze her to death. He said he was sorry, but she now knew he had no intention of making her trip to the afterlife a pleasant one.

I'll have to repay him the favor, she thought as she smiled in anticipation.

The boots grew closer and Scicremeon quickened her pace. The first helmet came into sight and then she began to see the full line of them. She had felt the number of them and guessed the group would be large, but not as big as the eight hundred she stared at. Surely all of these men wouldn't be needed for a single explosion.

As the men came closer she swung her sword in circles. As her blade cut through the air, the swinging sound was louder than ever. She realized she was hardly putting in any effort to keep the sword balanced, and it twirled three times faster than usual. The feeling of power intoxicated her and drove her anger wilder, but there was a great pleasure in the pit of her stomach.

The soldier at the front held up a fist as he stopped. Others behind him followed suit and the word *stop* began to drift into the entire crowd of men. *I only needed the word once,* she thought to herself, the pride of her feat making her heart flutter.

"Clear the way," said the soldier at the front of the perfectly lined group. His voice was a high pitched soprano sound that informed her of his youth. It seemed that Chalendor only employed their youngest for combat. When she kept coming toward them, twirling her sword, he screamed, "What business do you have here?"

"I'm looking for Mysticgo," said Scicremeon closing the distance between herself and the soldier in charge.

"Lord Mysticgo is at the palace," he began looking Scicremeon up and down with a puzzled stare. He inclined his head to one side saying, "You'll have to make a request if he isn't expecting you." He shook his head and blinked hard as if the gesture alone would improve his vision. Pulling his shoulders back, he looked up slightly, and then turned his head to the side.

He didn't think I heard it, thought Scicremeon to herself of the gasping sound he made. No one else had, but she did and just before his eyes fell on her she had him by the throat.

They are at least coordinated, she thought as she lifted the soldier from his feet with one hand. His comrades stood at the ready, spears pointing forward as they watched their commander's feet dangle by Scicremeon's knee.

Scicremeon saw the muscle in his forearm twitch, long before his hand made its way to his sword. She twisted her lips to one side in disgust. Twice she could have stopped him, but she allowed the events to unfold as they would have before. He'd get his swing halfway to the top of her head before she caught his wrist with the pommel of her own sword.

Crunch!

The veins burst in his neck, the bones cracked, his arms went limp, and his chin rolled into his collar bone. The sword clanked against the soft earth below him and she tossed him fifteen feet to the side as if he were a weightless pebble.

Half the men who watched from the front gasped their astonishment aloud, taking two steps back into the carefully constructed lines of their formation.

"Hold your line," one of the men said as the soldiers at the front kept pedaling backward into their comrades.

Scicremeon slipped her sword back into its sheath, quickly realizing she wouldn't need it. Her perception of the man's movements happened before his body moved. Had she not been looking at his arm, she wouldn't have seen it, but the knowledge of it was still present. It was as if she could read his body.

The other men pushed back at the retreating men at the front, and their backward motion ceased.

Scicremeon stood front and center, her arms resting at her sides. The lot of them angered her, the very color of their Chalendoran uniform she saw as an insult. The stories of fearsome Chalendoran warriors now sounded like a lie. Surely her father must have killed all the soldiers who actually earned their uniforms. Those who saw her snap their commander's neck were in a panic. *They wouldn't last in Marside*; she thought and grabbed two soldiers by the head.

Their heads molded together like clay as she slammed them ear to ear. Gruesome expressions of surprise and agony dressed their faces as their eyes bulged from their heads and their tongues hung to one side.

The two of them fell to the ground in a heap, blood pouring from the holes in their faces, soaking into the dry dirt, turning it to mud. More panic ensued as others tried to flee, before they were swept up in Scicremeon's powerful hands.

A pathway began to open as Scicremeon kept marching forward, snatching men by the throats, the arm, catching the spears of those who had a measure of bravery. The blood of her victims began to run, creating a trail that she walked on, as if a carpet laid out for royalty. As more blood spattered, her lust for it grew even more intense. A spear snapped against her belly, unable to even nick the Merridian uniform that had become armor.

Three men were struck down at once as her forearm collided with their breastplates. The metal folded into their chests and guts, spilling their entrails out. The smell of metal laced blood filled the air. She knew none of the men could smell it, but she savored in its aroma. Scicremeon hadn't had a taste of ale since she'd left Merridia, but she needed none. Basking in the death of so many Chalendorans was all she needed for her head to lighten and for her heart to pound.

The sea of bodies on the field of battle was far larger than the mess she and Aton had made on The Runner. This time there'd be no need for a door. They could lie there and decay for all she cared.

The grand palace grew larger and larger as she marched forward alone. Smash, crack, snap, crunch; twenty men fell and she stepped over them coolly. Faster she went, snapping necks, breaking bones and smashing heads.

Hundreds of them were fleeing in all directions, dropping their spears and shields as they went, screaming into the open field. *There's no wonder why my father laid waste to these men for so many years,* Scicremeon thought as she watched another group of them fleeing. Here she was, something much more than she had been, remembering when she crossed blades with a god. There was no fear in her before what seemed like her inevitable end. She was not fearful of him like these men were of her. She thought of him now. He was her savior. Black Dawn, the giver of the gift she wore that gave her the power to crush her enemies without breaking a sweat. *Stories will be told of this day,* she thought as she kept the count in her head.

More than two-hundred Chalendoran soldiers lie dead behind her. The lot that wasn't dead was too afraid to advance on her. It would be futile for them to try. She felt a small bit of sympathy for them knowing their every effort would be in vain. But the creed she lived by remained true and she realized that she expected the same of everyone. It was where Aton never disappointed her. *All the more reason to save him from this villainous sphere of cowardice and magic,* Scicremeon thought as she saw the massive gate in front of her closed, three magicians standing in front of it.

"There are less than a handful of you here," said Scicremeon to the band of magicians.

"You're supposed to be dead," said the one on the right, wearing a grimace.

"And you will be soon," said Scicremeon in response.

"Turn from here and be gone. You escaped once with your life, you will not get a second chance," said the short man in the center.

"Perhaps you didn't hear what I said," replied Scicremeon in an unpleasant tone.

"Mam please, for you own good be gone," said the short man again.

Her face wrinkled in anger, as she tried to keep her rage at bay. She breathed in air slowly, in and out of her nose; loud enough that it could be heard. She wondered if they noticed how beautiful she was, her auburn hair perfectly straight behind her ears, not a strand out of place. Her blue eyes were stark, more brilliant than any sky she'd ever seen. And her face was young, and it didn't hold a single scar or wrinkle. So she had to beg the question as she always had, "Do I look like your grandmother?"

The short magician stammered as he tried to answer her question, knowing she was angry, seeing her face still visibly annoyed by the use of the word *mam*.

"Go now," said the two magicians standing on either side of the short magician in the center.

"Fools," said Scicremeon as she began to march forward.

The three magicians' right hands went up facing Scicremeon, pleading with her to stop, but she kept coming. There was another warning that went unheard and then she felt a barrier push against her chest. She could still move but her progress was slowed. The magicians' faces were strained and she could hear them grunting and moaning, trying to force her back.

Their left hands flew up and the barrier pressed harder against Scicremeon, slowing her down more. But she continued to move forward about a half a step each time she moved her feet.

"How is she able to do this," she heard one of them say in despair.

She wanted to tell them to stop, but her curiosity in testing her new powers overran any ideas of mercy. Knowing what she could withstand was important, especially concerning magicians. Scicremeon was well aware that she could perceive the intentions of men's physical actions before they were aware of them. However, magicians were a different breed. Where men fell to her even as she was before slipping on the Hand of Destruction, Mysticgo had had very little trouble with her. He was able to dispatch her quickly, though for some reason he knew he'd be unable to kill her with his powers.

Looking at the Hand of Destruction, she saw the swirling string of golden energy. *Let's see what you can do*, thought Scicremeon with a devious smile. Opening her palm, the swirling gold string of energy shot out like a rope, wrapping around the magician's neck at the center. Narrowing her eyes, she looked at the man to her left and the rope of energy split in two, another string circling his neck. And then to the right she looked, and the center line of energy split again, encasing the third magician's neck in its grip.

The ropes of energy began to hum and the life force of the magicians began to be sucked away from them, coursing through the golden strings of energy. Scicremeon could feel their life force pouring into her through the Hand of Destruction. The faces of the magicians grew old before her eyes, their skin wrinkling, the muscles in their bodies weakening, slowly turning to mush. Their life's energy made her want more.

The magicians dropped as the golden strings of energy released them and fled back to the Hand of Destruction where it appeared again as a harmless spiraling energy. But now Scicremeon knew its true nature.

At the gate she eyed the stone wall surrounding the palace of the Chalendoran king. She knew Mysticgo was inside, holding Aton hostage, probably performing some dastardly spell on him. And Van Taven, her mind remembered him, even though he had no place in her heart. He'd come there with her and she did promise to keep him in one piece, at least until they returned to Merridia. And because she didn't make many of them, never did she make a promise that she didn't keep.

"Mysticgo!" roared Scicremeon at the top of her lungs. The stone walls shook, the power of her voice ripping into the structure. Small pieces of stone crumbled to the ground. Scicremeon watched the chips of stone fall to the earth and giggled aloud. *Magnify*, she thought to herself and then screamed his name again, "Mysticgo!" This time she dragged his name out as if singing a song, but this song had no melody or harmony. It was nothing of beauty; but a high pitched ballad of frustration, anger, and rage.

The ground began to shake as if an earthquake had begun beneath the crust. Chips of stone began to fall from the walls as cracks ran along the structure. Larger cracks occurred and then larger pieces of stone began to fall. *More*, she thought and her voice rose like a crescendo and each time she thought the word, more of the wall would fall. The ground began to crack; the earthquake shook the entire structure of the palace. The ground under the wall sunk in as the ground continued to crack around it.

The top portion of the wall began to fall, larger pieces breaking off and then the gate fell backward as the rest of the wall went tumbling down.

Mysticgo appeared at the window of the largest tower that rose up out of the center of the palace. He watched in horror as the wall around the palace continued falling. Focusing his eyes, he saw Scicremeon standing there alive.

Scicremeon eyed him from where she stood, and seeing the horror in his face, she smiled. He didn't make a sound, but she could read his lips as he mouthed *how*, flabbergasted at her still being alive, and then the destruction that she had caused alone.

"You will bring me the boy and that wretched magician or I will come in there and make everyone suffer," said Scicremeon. Though she was new in the use of her powers, she had been given a great deal of knowledge on how to use them by the faceless voices that had come, whispering and yelling at her in the cargo hold. The magicians at the gate had fallen to her easily enough, and thus she knew she posed a greater threat to Mysticgo than she previously had. Every soldier there would easily fall and she was also sure that Mysticgo could see the river of bodies for half a mile beyond the fallen gate. In her experience, a spoken threat meant more than the one you thought of, so she told him, magnifying her voice so he and everyone inside could hear, "There will be no quarter given to anyone; man, woman, or child!"

Scicremeon stepped over the rubble and into the courtyard of the palace. Mysticgo still watched her, studying her fearless stride toward the door of the palace. "Time is running out," said Scicremeon, still magnifying her voice.

"You will not like what you'll find here if you continue these hostilities," said Mysticgo gravely.

It didn't sound like a threat, but Scicremeon took it that way, speaking her own in return, "And you will not like what I've become," she said casting a dirty look his way.

"The king will give you audience," said Mysticgo frantically, almost begging.

"That is a start," said Scicremeon walking up a staircase toward the large doors to the palace. "He has five minutes to satisfy my demands, or I'll bring this wretched collection of rocks crashing down on his head with him inside it."

Heed My Words

"If it had not been for the momentary lapse in Forecon's judgment, none of us would have known where you were," said Thutmos fuming, his face a mass of anger.

Luminar cowered before him, his voice unbearable as it rolled through the throne room of the Palace of Eternity. He towered over her like an angry parent, chastising their child without regard for their imposing size. Thutmos was twice as large as Luminar, who stood there with her head down weeping for Trurow. Tears were wet in her eyes as Chasm stood against a pillar, trying to keep her own grief at bay.

"She's apologized a thousand times," said Chasm in Luminar's defense, her voice pleading with Thutmos.

"Do you not understand the gravity of the situation," said Thutmos turning fast to Chasm who had stood up tall.

"Of course I do," said Chasm striding toward Thutmos as if she were going to strike him. Standing fast just a foot from him, she looked him in the eyes. "Are you sure you understand what is taking place, brother," said Chasm, adding emphasis to the word *brother*, her lips pursing forward, as her passion welled up in her chest.

"I know that our advantage has been cut down by one," said Thutmos and Chasm looked at him bemused.

"Our advantage?" said Chasm bewildered as she drew her head backward and touched her hand to her chest.

"We are at war," yelled Thutmos, full of rage, the throne room answering back his emphatic statement in an echo.

"Indeed," said Everdon softly with a grin.

"Have you both gone mad?" asked Chasm as she turned to Everdon who stood off to Thutmos's right, close to the throne atop the dais that was meant for Aeon.

"What is this if not war?" begged Everdon, speaking nearly as many words in a single string as he had for all the millennia he'd lived. He'd been content over the years to simply listen. "Sides have been taken," he said stepping down onto the floor where the others were standing. Thutmos regarded him for a moment with a smile and then looked at Chasm.

"This is not our nature," said Chasm.

"The very nature of things is this," said Everdon furrowing his brow.

"We all thought of ourselves as immortal, incapable of dying; even the matter that holds our essences," said Thutmos speaking as if trying to rouse a group of fearful soldiers. "But Carnok has taught us that all physical beings have their end. Our brothers and sisters shall endure after this existence, in the comfort of The One Who Eclipses All and so shall we," said Thutmos closing his eyes as he looked up to the ceiling. "You are right that this isn't how it should be."

Chasm smiled for a moment, hearing Thutmos utter the very words that were beginning to form in her mind.

"But this is how is must be now," said Thutmos his voice growing in volume again.

"Primsec believes that you are blind," said Chasm as if accusing Thutmos of a crime.

He laughed short at her words and rolled his eyes turning around and taking a seat upon the throne set there for him, as Charm of the Sacred on the right of Aeon's throne. Thutmos leaned to one side as he relaxed into his throne. Looking around the room, he regarded each of them for a moment. Again he panned, studying their faces, feeling their hearts, and reading their minds. And then, his eyes settled on Chasm.

She looked back at Thutmos as if he were her enemy. Chasm knew what was coming. She could feel his emotions and hear his thoughts coming to his tongue.

"I love him dearly, but he has always been a child, loving and liking things as they are. He wants no change and he knows not of it. War is not for his heart, I know this. But he ought to stand with those who would not see our Father's will come to such tragedy," said Thutmos solemnly.

"I wonder if you know what that is anymore," said Chasm.

"You go too far," said Everdon quickly.

"Indeed," said Thutmos, a hint of a threat in his voice.

"The two of you have become more like Carnok than you know," said Chasm, her lips turning her calm face into a frown.

"If that is such, you would do well to know your place then," said Thutmos rising from his throne. "For if that is the truth of matters, what makes you think that we would not wipe you from this existence," said Thutmos.

He watched the tears well in Chasm's eyes and closed his own. His head dropped toward the floor.

"Primsec's fear has poisoned your mind against me, against this new collective of us four. He is foolish to believe that there is some other way this can end. Follow me and find hope in the new

Chain of Balance that has been struck. True by treachery, but it is made anew still, in me. Let us remake the world as we see fit," said Thutmos moving toward Chasm with his hand extended.

Her head said *no* as it swung from one side to the other, the word came out quickly, each time behind its identical self at a different pitch. Chasm looked at his outstretched hand and though the word would no longer allow itself to be spoken, her head continued to say it.

No, he could read her thoughts and *no* was the only thing her mind was filled with.

"The chain has been made anew, but not how you see it," said Chasm, trying to keep her composure, mustering the fortitude she had left to shield herself from Thutmos's rousing words. She wanted everything to be with him as they once were, but she knew that time had long gone. "If this war is not stopped, I fear that a great calamity shall befall us. It will not only be us who suffers, but all shall suffer," said Chasm turning away from Thutmos.

"Then you shall not follow?" said Thutmos inclining his head down and narrowing an eye to her.

"Never will I take sides. I will disengage from you so that the balance may be struck and this war may end. Perhaps then will you find the truth in your heart of what I am saying," said Chasm.

"This is a mistake," said Thutmos angrily.

"You would do well to heed my words brother," said Chasm as she began to walk away, her shoes pounding hard against the floor.

"Go not from my sight," said Thutmos his voice akin to a billion raging storms.

"Uh," said Chasm feeling the weight of his voice. Luminar crumbled to her knees in fear.

Chasm turned hard to face Thutmos, and Everdon positioned himself at his side, turning his head sideways, a ball of energy rising up in the palm of his hand as he scowled at Chasm.

"Even our union together in Our Union is broken by this," said Chasm, a wave of disappointment sweeping over her face.

Thutmos was floored by her words, touching Everdon's arm and looking at him intently. "We will not force her brother," said Thutmos calmly. "Go where Our Lord might lead you and be in peace," said Thutmos, his rumbling voice subsiding. His words and the weight of them eased from Chasm and she walked out into the darkness of space.

I bid you a farewell; she thought to Thutmos and went her way into the depths of space and time.

And I you sister, he thought to her, splitting The Ripples of Time and Space so that she would be able to read his thoughts as she traveled away from the Palace of Eternity.

Thutmos would like to have had Chasm at his side as she always had been. But he knew she would never agree to fight on his side or the other. Forever she would remain a neutral party until one side subdued the other. He was sure that he knew Carnok's heart and that if he were the victor; he'd surely destroy her as he had with all the others. He would never be merciful in his conquest of Our Union. Those who stood opposite him must fall. Thutmos knew this and in his mind his stance was the same. What he had watched come into existence at the whim of Aeon was now beginning to unravel in the wake of those who were tasked to keep the balance. The first chord was struck by Carnok. Thutmos promised himself that he would end it and set things right.

"Your orders Lord," said Everdon quietly to Thutmos.

"We'll go to where the rift began," said Thutmos.

Everdon smiled and bowed his head. "Luminar, the time has come," said Everdon turning and giving her his hand to take.

Luminar wrapped her hand around Everdon's and Thutmos turned to look at her. She read his mind before he open his mouth to speak and said, "I will do my duty or die doing your bidding Lord," said Luminar still reeling from Trurow's death and Thutmos's chastisement. Everdon held out his other hand for Thutmos to take.

Thutmos waited for a moment and then reached out and locked hands with Everdon. He looked over at Luminar and smiled. "I know that you shall do what it takes to please me," his face hiding the joy building up inside him, "I am content," said Thutmos looking forward.

Thutmos pressed his mind out in every direction, his mind's eye reaching with the weight of his voice. They were all fighting hard to keep him from their minds so he couldn't pin point their location. He felt them faintly and smiled. Thutmos could feel the smallest glimmer of Kinozl's fear. *It is good that you are afraid of me, for I will bring forth a tide of retribution that shall shake the very fabric of the universe,* he thought to Kinozl whose mind had nearly allowed him in. He could feel Forecon's presence, looming over her, fighting hard to shut him out. He laughed to himself, Everdon and Luminar feeling his jubilation, grew emboldened by it.

Wherever you are brother, know, know it well, I am coming for you.

A King's Son

The palace was twice as big on the inside as it appeared to be from outside. The walls were ivory; so shiny that Scicremeon could almost see her reflection. The emerald jewels inside the walls sparkled as they were touched by firelight. The two men leading her had been polite, but she suspected it was out of their fear. She'd never felt the sensation before, but she swore that she could smell their fear in the droplets of their sweat.

When they'd first opened the heavy doors to the palace, they backed away quickly. Mysticgo had surely seen the carnage lain out before the palace gate and it'd have been foolish not to warn them to take caution. It wouldn't have mattered as slow as their rapid steps were. She saw their knees buckle before their minds told them to retreat and she'd have smashed their skulls together.

Why go back on my word, I could always kill them later, she thought to herself as she had watched their fear with satisfaction. She'd told Mysticgo she'd come quietly if he gave her Aton. Opening the door without hostilities was a first step toward that end.

The guards led her around two corners and then down a long hallway. At the end of the hall were two large wooden doors. As they drew closer to the door, the fire on the lamp posts flickered faster and shot upward in hot streaks. Scicremeon pushed her ears out to hear better and swung her eyes from one corner to the other. There was no one there, but she didn't put anything past a magician. Even though she had made quick work of them outside the palace, her hatred of them would never allow her to put down her guard around them.

When the guards were ten feet from the door it swung open slowly. The guards leading Scicremeon set their backs against the wall of the hall on either side and allowed her to pass.

The door closed behind her hard as she stepped across the threshold. An unsettling feeling of capture swept across her body as she surveyed the room, a gust of cool air whipping in as the door clicked shut.

There was a sturdy wooden chair at the center of the room, empty where she had expected to see someone. Over the chair was the portrait of a man arraigned in maroon robes, wearing a crown of gold with a crimson jewel set in its center. In his hand he held a scepter of gold and wore the haughty look of an aristocrat. The fingers on the hand that held the scepter were adorned with jeweled rings. His other hand rested on the pommel of his sword. On his face he wore an expression of cool control, a weak smirk hoping to disguise the confidence inside him that his chest revealed as it stuck out.

There were others portraits there, all of different men, wearing the same crown, wielding the same scepter. Some of them were old, some very old. Very few were as young as the portrait hanging over the wooden chair.

The vanity of kings, she thought to herself as she crossed her arms and continued to examine the room. To her left were two tables, each with containers of colored liquid, still at the bottoms. There were all manner of herbs and animal hairs scattered about in jars atop the tables. A dozen or so relics hung on the wall behind the tables. Some of them were funny looking things of which their origin she had no idea. Others were swords and pieces of armor, and she was well aware of their functions.

Aside from the wooden chair and tables, there was no other furniture in the room. To her right high up on the wall, she noticed a set of empty manacles. By their design, two would go around the wrists and the center manacle around the neck of a prisoner.

Torture chamber, she thought as she looked again at what was there in the room. To either side of the manacles on the wall were sharp blades and gauntleted claws, spears of varying size, and a rugged looking axe.

Interlocking her fingers, she cracked her knuckles and rolled her neck, the joints making a snapping sound. She'd felt no discomfort or pain, but did so out of habit. Her boredom was beginning to peak and she had been waiting for what felt like far longer than ten minutes. Scicremeon began to tap her foot against the floor, breathing in deeply. *My patience is wearing*, she thought to herself.

It had been a long time since any of them had seen the carnage they now saw before the gates of the Chalendoran palace. They'd fought many wars of their own, and watched a great many more unfold, endure, and end abruptly. But Merridia had been in relative peace for many years.

Black Dawn was flanked by Pearl and Mastadon as they crossed the rubble of the fallen gate. There were footprints of blood in a trail going toward the double door entrance of the palace.

"I can't feel her presence anymore," said Pearl.

"She's inside. Their enchantments are blocking our connection," said Black Dawn looking at the palace wearily.

"Then what are we still waiting here for," said Mastadon who began charging forward.

"No....," began Black Dawn, but Mastadon was already twisting past him, screaming in flight.

Mastadon thumped hard against the ground and moaned as he sat up, his face wearing a great deal of surprise. Pearl approached him with her hand out stretched. Clapping his hand into hers, she pulled him to his feet.

"One day you are going to break into a million tiny pieces and father won't be able to stitch you back together," said Pearl in a fit of anger at his recklessness.

"That only happened once," he said with a big smile.

"Don't be foolish," said Pearl thrusting his hand out of her own, knocking his arm into his chest.

"The Erudite must be inside," said Black Dawn, who touched his hand to the invisible barrier that had struck Mastadon. The barrier began to radiate, and the energy of the barrier began to surge. Crackling bolts of energy shot out around his hand.

"The Erudite?" said Pearl bothered by the title she recognized.

"Yes, this may take a little while, depending on how strong he is," said Black Dawn taking a step back and pulling his sword from its sheath. He pressed the tip of his sword against the invisible shield and the energy rippled from it, wrapping itself around the sword, as if trying to penetrate the metal. Black Dawn's arm vibrated as he looked at the energy intently. "Strong, very strong this one," he said with a toothless smile, much impressed.

"Show off," said Mastadon with a grunt as he folded his arms across his chest watching.

"Don't be grumpy, you're at least tolerable as the miserable oaf you are," said Pearl clapping Mastadon on his big shoulder.

There were at least three men coming down a stone staircase. Scicremeon could hear them behind the wall that held the picture of the young man with a jeweled crown, set over the lonely wooden chair. A door she couldn't see behind the wall clicked, and it whispered its age into the room, a foul odor seeping in along with it.

She recognized him immediately, his chest protruding, with the same weak smirk and jeweled crown. He cast a short glance at her and quickly turned his attention away. *How about I pluck those eyeballs out of their sockets?* Scicremeon's face was wearing her anger at his dismissive gaze. She watched as he plopped himself into the wooden chair thoughtlessly, throwing his right leg over the arm rest. The cup in his hand was steaming, the rank odor floating into the air.

Settling in on his left side was a man wearing a grey hooded cloak, who kept his gaze at the floor at all times, leaning over a bit. Scicremeon didn't mind his unwillingness to look at anything but his feet. He was likely some kind of bodyguard who'd pounce the moment anyone threatened the arrogant man in the wooden chair.

Last to enter a few moments after the others was a man she recognized. His young face had seemed to regain some of its color, and he no longer appeared to be wilting away. She knew his appearance was no indication of his strength, because he had nearly killed her. Had she'd not been able to find the Hand of Destruction; she'd be an ice sickle by now.

Mysticgo kept his darker-than-blood eyes trained on Scicremeon as he found himself on the right side of the wooden chair. With his eyes still pressed upon her, he leaned over and whispered something in the haughty man's ear as he sipped from his funky cup. His eyes went wide with interest and fell onto Scicremeon, taking her in from head to toe.

"So this is the great Scicremeon," said the man in the chair, his voice a smooth baritone.

"And you are?' said Scicremeon.

"I am King Hann, son of Chale, and ruler of all Chalendor," said Hann, handing the steaming drink to the man to his left.

"I haven't come for your conversation," said Scicremeon giving him a hard stare.

Hann ignored it, pulling the leg he had resting on the arm of the chair, across his other leg. Folding his hands on his chin he titled his head to one side and regarded Scicremeon for a long moment. "You've come making demands of Lord Mysticgo," said Hann as he raised his hand to stop her as Scicremeon looked to be ready to speak, "but you've come here a hostile party." He stood up and turned, walking to his left where Scicremeon had noticed the manacles. "Should there not be some recompense for the suffering of the families of many dead soldiers?"

Mysticgo waved his hand and Van Taven appeared; locked in the manacles apparently battered. Dried blood was spattered down his neck and chest. His head hung low and his eyes were a mass of swollen flesh.

Scicremeon laughed softly and spoke with a big smile, "So you beat a magician half to death and expected me to weep?" The golden string from the Hand of Destruction shot up and slipped under the manacle around Van Taven's neck. *Strangle*, thought Scicremeon and the golden rope squeezed around his neck. Van Taven's head wrenched back as his futile efforts to free himself from the suffocating grip made the pain worsen. He gasped for air, reaching for the manacles around his wrist with his fingers, their rugged edges digging into his arms. "I'd have helped you," said Scicremeon looking at Hann with angry pleasure as Van Taven struggled.

"Are you mad?" said Hann, his face a wrinkled mass of indignation.

"I came here for the boy," said Scicremeon.

She drew the golden string of energy back into the gauntlet and turned to Mysticgo.

"You came here for revenge," said Mysticgo angrily, his eyes hard as if they could pierce Scicremeon's very flesh.

"It is because of the disgusting magician that tricked my father," said Scicremeon, her anger rising uncontrolled. A wave of energy swept from her mouth and cracked the wall in front of her.

"What harm did any of the dead men outside do to your father?" said Mysticgo stepping closer to Scicremeon, after looking at the wall behind King Hann.

She watched him, waiting for him to attack, but he never did, he only stood there.

"They're all dirty Chalendorans," said Scicremeon, scowling at Mysticgo.

"The men who killed your father have long been dead," said Hann, shaking his head exasperated, sighing hard as he walked slowly back to his chair.

"You lie," said Scicremeon elongating the second word as Hann plopped himself down again in his chair.

"I told you I was not your enemy," said Mysticgo moving back to stand by the king's side. "Neither is my king."

"Lies," said Scicremeon harshly, as her eyes met them both.

"What he tells you is true," said Hann taking the steaming cup from the cloaked man. "Our peoples have been at war for centuries. Who began the hostilities...well, that is a matter of which side you favor." Hann took a sip of his drink, seemingly refreshed and began again. "I'm quite sure you know that it was the death of your brothers that made Aygron take up his sword again. Vengeance it seems is a way of life for you Merridians," said Hann as if disgusted. "He was like you, relentless, unforgiving, but in the end he met his undoing," said Hann appearing to take some pleasure in

Aygron's demise. "It wasn't until my father was on his deathbed that I knew Aygron had had another child, and that's when I knew one day you'd come."

Scicremeon stared at Hann intently, her anger slowly subsiding as she listened to his tale. His voice was soft and measured. She'd noticed the joy that rose up inside of him at the mention of her father's demise, but what enemy dislikes the fall of his greatest adversary. Her want to pounce on him was still there, but she wanted to listen to what he had to say first.

"As I said, vengeance seems to be the Merridian way. And like all people we have our own traditions. One of those traditions is the passing of the crown on my head. A burden I have to wear. A king's son inherits his father's kingdom, his riches, his servants, and all the power he once held. These are the good things, the things that everyone wants, though they may not admit it. But I being the new king also inherit all of the negative aspects of my father's reign. Anger, discord, rebellion, enemies," said Hann as he paused and looked hard at Scicremeon, his eyes locking onto her own. "Retribution," said Hann, pronouncing clearly every syllable of the word.

Minutes passed as Hann and Scicremeon stared at one another. Scicremeon's chest was rising and falling slowly as she took in breath after breath of warm putrid air in the small room. Her eyelids blinked rapidly as she looked down at the floor, shaking her head as if to say *no*.

Aton, the single thought crept into her mind. Revenge had been the reason she'd come, but saving Aton had become more important. The blood bath on The Runner had been enough, nearly costing her life. The line of bodies outside of the palace was more for sport than it was for revenge. With her new power came a new hunger to destroy things. Her hatred of the Chalendorans made it more pleasurable to satisfy that hunger.

"Give me the boy and I will go," said Scicremeon coming to the revelation at that very instance.

"Then your thirst for blood has been quenched?" asked Mysticgo sharply.

"If what your king says is true then there is no reason for me to be here," said Scicremeon, "I hunger only for Aton."

Mysticgo began toward the door that he'd come through with the king and the cloaked man beside him. As he reached to grab the knob, he was thrown forward into the door. He turned hard on Scicremeon, his face pushed forward in anger.

"Who else has come with you?" begged Mysticgo, his voice far more severe than the expression on his face.

"No one," said Scicremeon defensively, closing her hands into fists, the golden rope from the Hand of Destruction swirling around rapidly, ready to race out.

King Hann rose and marched toward Mysticgo, falling in behind him. The cloaked man followed slowly behind the king, his eyes on Scicremeon the entire time.

"Come quickly, take the boy and leave," said Mysticgo pulling the door open and storming through, Hann and his cloaked servant behind him.

Scicremeon fell in behind the cloaked man, as she turned to see Van Taven still hanging on the wall a captive. Something inside her made her have pity on him. *I made a promise*, she thought to herself, reminded again that she guaranteed his safe return to the emperor.

Remembering something the voices had told, her mind seemed to expand. *I'll return for you*, thought Scicremeon pressing her mind toward Van Taven, touching his mind with her words. His head rose, and had he been able to see her, he would have looked directly in her face. *Don't go anywhere*; she thought with a smile inside knowing it would anger him as she rushed headlong up the staircase.

The Host

Black Dawn's sword was spinning so fast that it appeared as a blur. If it were not for the barrier radiating its energy and the grinding that sounded like a saw against wood; perceiving the sword's presence would have been difficult. There were two piles of the barrier's dust-like particles collecting on the ground on either side of the sword. They were silver in color, sparkling in the light of the sun. Though they appeared like snowflakes, the particles were warm to the touch, but harmless once separated from the whole.

Pearl and Mastadon had settled near the barrier with Black Dawn and watched as the sword continued to breech the barrier. There was a hole the size of a small fist where Black Dawn's sword was working its way through.

The pommel of the sword began to disappear into the barrier, the grinding decreasing in volume. The barrier's radiating energy began to cease as the sword began spinning in open space. Black Dawn's sword continued to move forward, touching only air as it passed the barrier.

On the opposite side of the barrier, the sword ceased its spinning and bobbed in the air, its tip pointing toward the sky. The blade began to hum, and the jewels set inside the hilt and pommel began to glow. Black Dawn smiled as he watched the sword through the breech.

"Let's go," said Black Dawn.

One by one they floated through the barrier in forms of mist, each the color of their outerwear. Black Dawn grabbed his sword and marched toward the palace doors followed by his brother and sister.

"I can feel her," said Pearl.

"Yes, she's alive," said Black Dawn moving faster.

The door swung open, the top side coming off of the hinges by the force of the blow. Three guards stormed toward them. With an outstretched palm, Black Dawn pushed a clear mist like bubble toward them, encasing them in it. He wasn't there to do harm, only to find Scicremeon.

Another set of guards rushed forward and Black Dawn stopped them the same as the last.

The three of them turned left and headed down a long corridor lit by firelight. There were no guards there, only a set of armor with a long burgundy colored cape flowing down its back. Black Dawn covered half the distance of the hall in a flash, Pearl on his heels and Mastadon behind her a few strides.

Black Dawn surveyed the armor and rounded the corner. He expected it to move, but it stayed an ornament-statue, adding a bit of flare to an otherwise dim and boring hallway. Pearl paid the armor no mind as she followed Black Dawn around the corner.

"Sad, armor with no one to wear it," said Mastadon as he grew closer to the end of the hall, slowing down to walk. He rounded the corner, his big boots thudding against the floor. Two steps into the new hall; he felt a cold hand grip him by the neck.

Crack!

Mastadon slammed into the wall. Still on his feet he watched the armor come to life, a pair of glowing eyes under the helm of the armor. The statue grabbed the massive sword that was hidden behind it and swung it at Mastadon. The sword took a big chunk of stone out of the wall as Mastadon ducked from the blow. He laughed hard, turning fast to his left.

Clank!

His hammer slammed into the breastplate of the unmanned armor, sending it crashing to the floor. The glowing eyes disappeared, and a cloud of smoke drifted from the armor.

Mastadon looked down the hall and saw Pearl standing there with her hands on her hips, lips pursed forward in frustration.

"Can't you go anywhere without being knocked around?" said Pearl screaming down the hall.

"I wouldn't be me if I did dear sister," said Mastadon grunting a laugh as he stepped over the pieces of armor at the end of the hall. "You know I love a fight, even if it's a short one."

"Come," said Black Dawn as he rounded another corner.

Pearl and Mastadon raced behind him, sprinting to catch up. The hallways seemed to be the same, except the décor was slightly different each time they turned. Guards continued to pop out every few minutes and Black Dawn would encase them in bubbles. Some tried their swords against the surface of the clear prison to no avail, while others tried to kick and punch their way through.

"This way," said Black Dawn as he came to a staircase. "Up the stairs, I can feel her."

Soon he realized that the staircase wasn't a typical staircase at all. It was a spiraling march up the center tower. Ever few hundred steps, there was a floor that extended to the end of the castle. On each floor, there were battlements that featured different weapons that could attack an enemy from a distance. From the outside of the palace, it seemed to have been only built for luxury. That façade however masked a much more dangerous defensive structure.

"There's not much resistance," said Pearl noticing that there were no more guards popping out to attack them.

"I think most of them are dead, and we've missed the action" said Mastadon.

"Not to mention, this place is massive, even by our standards," said Black Dawn looking up at the top of the tower. "Faster."

Up they went, as fast as they could without missing a step and plummeting between the spiraling stairs. They were heel to heel, taking each floor in less than a minute.

The cloaked figure pushed the door open and sunlight slammed into Scicremeon's face. She could feel the heat of it, but it didn't bother her. She walked into the room, looking at the bare stone walls. There was no furniture anywhere. If it were not for the sunlight coming in through a window at least thirty feet high, the room would have been freezing.

King Hann sauntered into the room and turned to his right. Mysticgo followed and stood on his left side.

Scicremeon heard a chain rustling against the hard stone floor, and heard a weak grunt as someone slammed into the stone wall behind the door. She watched Mysticgo take a step forward and then heard a familiar voice. *Aton*, she thought and in a flash she was in front of Mysticgo. She'd arrived in front of him so fast that he stumbled back a step, pulling his head back in anticipation of a blow. *I'd have knocked your head off*, Scicremeon thought to herself, having seen his every movement.

"Scicremeon!" said Aton screaming at the top of his lungs. She turned around to see him, his big brown eyes staring at her in amazement. They were the eyes of someone who thought they'd never see you again. Tears welled in his eyes and sprinted down his cheeks as he began to cry. Scicremeon took him in her arms and squeezed him tightly, forcing back her own tears.

"I thought I lost you," said Scicremeon softly, her lips kissing the top of his head.

"I thought you were dead," said Aton still weeping hard into her chest.

"Almost," said Scicremeon still trying to force back her tears. *Still these tears*, she thought to herself and the effort to control her emotions came in an instant. "Did they hurt you," begged Scicremeon of Aton. Looking at him, she knew the answer, but she wished it had been opposite of what she suspected. He didn't seem to have a scratch on him anywhere, though he was a bit dirty, and stained with dried blood.

"No," said Aton as Scicremeon thought.

"Why do you have him in chains?" said Scicremeon turning on the three men behind her.

"You saw what he did with that little sword. He's obviously been well trained," said Mysticgo shocked at Scicremeon's question.

"He's still just a boy," said Scicremeon. Deep down inside she was hoping for a fight. Any reason to crack another skull would suffice to cool the anger that she was feeling now that her fits of nearly weeping had ceased. Reaching between his wrist and the shackle, Scicremeon gripped the cold metal and yanked it off his wrist. She did the same to the other and looked him over again. "Are you ready to go home?"

"Yes," said Aton wrapping his arms around her waist, watching Mysticgo from the corner of his eye from Scicremeon's side.

"He won't hurt you, don't worry," said Scicremeon feeling Aton's hands around her waist, and the fear in him. Though Mysticgo had never done anything to harm him, his presence was unsettling.

Among dozens of soldiers, he had easily bested Scicremeon and took Aton captive. Even now, with a great deal of new power that she had just begun to understand, she wasn't fully comfortable around the magician.

"Safe travels my boy," said Hann in what Scicremeon read as a genuine tone of kindness.

Aton took the king's hand and gripped it firmly, still holding on tight to Scicremeon's waist. Scicremeon slipped around to her right and Mysticgo took a step back. Scicremeon shot him a dirty look that warned him not to come any closer. *I said I'd go quietly, but I didn't guarantee that no one would die along the way*, she thought, knowing that she'd try to snap the magician in half if he tried to offer any pleasantries, regardless of good intention or not.

They approached the door and the cloaked man was standing there holding it open, his head still facing the floor.

"Farewell child," said the man in a hackling cough of a voice. He extended an old wrinkled hand, with dark spots just below the knuckles. Scicremeon looked at his hand and squinted as Aton outstretched his own. By the look of the man's hand, Scicremeon swore to herself that even Aton might shatter the man's hands if he squeezed hard enough.

The sound of a small clap dissipated quickly into the air as Aton and the cloaked man gripped one another's hands in a show of courtesy. By now Aton had settled in front of the man, and looked up, wanting to see who he was exchanging a goodbye with.

Aton's lips parted in surprise as his eyes met the man's eyes behind the cloak. He couldn't see the man's face wrapped under the hood, but he couldn't mistake those eyes. Recognition began to pour over him and he craned his neck more to get a closer look.

"Cale," said Aton quizzically seeing those glazed over brown eyes that he'd seen by the well Scicremeon pushed him into one too many times.

Aton felt that rush of cold air devour him again; the needles came and assaulted him. It was more intense this time as the voice began to pour into his mind, taking over. He shook his head rapidly and tried to pull away, but the grip of the old hand was strong like frozen iron. Aton's body wrenched with agonizing pain as the man held onto him. Reality slipped from him and he folded into himself, afraid, so very afraid of what might come. Those eyes were there again, and he shut his own eyes to shield himself from them. He believed that if he looked at them for too long, they'd kill him.

Scicremeon's eyes went wide when she saw Aton's body convulse. She'd been told the name first, and suffered the old man to speak, to tell her the information she'd wanted to hear. *But he lied*, she thought to herself, having been told by King Hann that the men who killed her father were dead. *Or perhaps the king's lying*, turning her eyes toward the king and back onto Aton and the cloaked man who she now knew was Cale.

Scicremeon struck Cale's forearm, breaking his grip, Aton's hand coming free. The boy scrambled back on his haunches as he came to his senses. Scicremeon pulled Cale's hood off and the old scrawny man's face came into view.

"Did you lie to me," said Scicremeon her eyes wide with fury as she grabbed him by the collar.

"Of course I lied to you," said Cale who gripped Scicremeon's wrist with an angry stare, and pulled her hand from his collar.

He's strong, too strong for an old man, thought Scicremeon as her arm flailed toward her side.

Cale gripped her by the collar of her uniform with both hands and flung her through the door against the hard stone wall.

"No," yelled Aton as he scrambled to his feet.

Mysticgo stalked toward Cale, pushing Aton aside. "Stay in the corner boy," said Mysticgo as he reached for Cale. Just as he was going to grab the old man by the shoulder, Cale turned on him and stuffed a foot into Mysticgo's gut, sending him stumbling back, falling onto his rear in jarring pain.

Cale set his feet toward the door and grimaced hard at Scicremeon who was standing from a crouched position. Her face was a wrinkled mass of anger.

"Come and get some old man," said Scicremeon standing there with her arms wide like someone looking for a hug.

Cale laughed a throaty ugly laugh that usually would have been owned by a big husky man. He stalked hard out of the door into the hallway.

Scicremeon took a step and swung; her fist singing like a blade as it cut through the air. Cale parried it coolly with the edge of his hand and slammed his opposite fist into Scicremeon's chest.

"Uh," said Scicremeon shocked and alarmed at the pain that shot through her. *You will be indestructible,* she remembered the voice saying. *I guess that doesn't count out pain,* she thought as she smiled still able to feel pain.

Cale took another swing at her, this time she ducked. Whatever the Hand of Destruction had made her, Cale was strong enough to damage her. Even though he appeared to be old and frail, his movements suggested vitality and great dexterity. He attacked again, fast, swinging blows consecutively that Scicremeon had to make some effort to avoid.

I can still read him, thought Scicremeon to herself as Cale punched through the stone wall that she slipped away from. In the distance she could hear the drumming of boots. As they drew closer she could feel the presence of whoever was coming. *Guards, I'll have to deal with them quickly,* she thought as Cale wrestled his hand away from her grip.

He reached and pulled her sword from her sheath and her eyes went wide as the blade was aimed at her neck. She ducked and slipped under Cale's arms. Her knee caught him in the guts and then her head slammed against his chin, sending his head backward into his neck.

Mysticgo was on his feet, Scicremeon could see him above Cale's shoulder. His hands were out stretched and Scicremeon looked at him angrily. He shook his head *no* in submission and she drove her fist into the side of Cale's head. Pulling her sword from his limp hand, she jammed it into his throat. He began to croak, a line of blood trickling from his lips as he swayed in pain.

The feet she had heard earlier had drawn closer. It didn't matter; she had work to finish. The golden string shot out from her gauntlet and found Cale's neck, gripping it tightly. Scicremeon turned her palm up, and then wrapped her fingers around the string. *Kill,* she thought to the rope and it began to radiate. She could feel Cale's life force seeping into her.

The staccato of feet entered into the hallway she was standing in and she turned to see who was coming. They were far too fast to be guards, and their clothes were different. There was a woman among them, too beautiful to be natural. Then she recognized Black Dawn who's hand was outstretched, his mouth was wide with wonder, a hint of fear washed over his eyes and then she heard the word, *no.*

Turning her head back to Cale she smiled as his eyes closed and his body began to decay before her. Mysticgo came toward them, and stood just off to Cale's right. He watched intently but did not disturb Scicremeon, though he didn't think she should have been enjoying Cale's death as much as she was.

Her smile was devious, almost packed with lust and a hunger to keep hurting. Cale's body went limp before her and she loosed the golden string and allowed his body to fall. Scicremeon had expected his body to fall in a heap of bone crackling noise, but it didn't.

When Cale's body hit the floor it became a black mist. It glided toward the room Cale had thrown Scicremeon out of. She followed the mist and watched it rise and then it plunged toward Aton. She began to run toward him, but was pulled back. The grip was tight and when she turned to see, it was Black Dawn holding her back. His other hand was outstretched, keeping a disturbed Mysticgo from going any further.

Scicremeon could only watch as the black mist zipped toward Aton, and plunged into him.

Aton gasped in pain, his body rising into the air, a wicked voice rolled like thunder and crashing waves from his mouth. His eyes flashed black, a fiery orange, clear and then back to his normal brown. A hundred times it happened as he descended back toward the floor. Aton's fingers were flailing about in every direction. Scicremeon could see that he was fighting to stop whatever assailed him but it was stronger than him.

Aton touched softly against the floor on his back, his eyes closed, his body unmoving, flinching once every few moments.

"My lord, Cale was possessed," said Mysticgo to King Hann who was curled into a ball in a corner as he stepped forward from behind Black Dawn's arm. "Whatever it is, the boy has become the host."

"I think I know what this is," said Black Dawn as he released Scicremeon's arm.

Answers

Aton kept turning as he lied on a bed, his brow wet with sweat. Every so often he'd utter something that no one could make sense of. Scicremeon sat next to his bed in a chair, holding his hand, rubbing his knuckles. When her emotions tried to overtake her, she'd force them to stop, and then whisper an order to Aton as if they were back at her home training.

"There's nothing I'd like to do more right now than to throw you down that well," said Scicremeon softly, trying to smile.

By now she'd known his moans were the result of whatever was assailing him on the inside. She wished it were the well, and the makeshift track outside of her home that were the source of his pain. *Why*, it was the one word that appeared before every thought in her mind as she looked back on the recent events of her life. And while the questions kept coming, she knew the answer to every one of them without thinking.

It was her fault Aton had gotten on The Runner. He loved her too much to risk not seeing her again. They'd grown too close on their journey to see Larnaxe. Aton had been everything she needed to feel again. He was everything she was and everything she wasn't all at once. He was brave, unyielding, hungry for adventure, and an accomplished student, pleasing to his teacher. His need for adventure was as insatiable as her need for revenge. How could she thrust him into danger and then try to hold him back. *I'd have never stayed behind either,* she thought to herself growing teary eyed again.

Yet, unlike her, Aton was kind and welcoming to everyone. He believed that people wanted to do well and were mostly kindhearted. Her first thought was of shedding blood, where his was of company. To her, everyone was an enemy first, while to Aton, they were a potential friend. Even his incessant apologies were a reminder of who he was deep inside.

"I'll get you out of this mess," said Scicremeon whispering to him again.

"Can I get you anything?" asked Mysticgo who was standing against a wall at the head of Aton's bed.

"No, thank you," said Scicremeon raising her eyes to Mysticgo slightly. Her hatred for the magician had subsided over the past few hours, but she was still weary of him.

"Do you want to see what's keeping him," said Pearl, sitting on the frame of the single window in the room.

Mastadon looked at her suspiciously, his brow furrowed in disbelief. "It takes ages to pull him out of meditation. Do you think me stupid?" said Mastadon balancing the handle of his hammer on his thumb.

"Well I didn't want to do it," said Pearl huffing.

"Why does he need to meditate?" said Scicremeon confused, looking at Pearl, "I thought he knew what this was."

"Ha," said Mastadon beginning to laugh.

Scicremeon looked at him hard, her face saying; *quiet,* as she looked at him and then Aton. Mastadon scoffed and resumed toying with his hammer.

"What Dorrin sees isn't always what is there," said Pearl before Scicremeon cut in.

"Dorrin?" said Scicremeon, her eyebrows trying to touch the line where her hair began.

"Black Dawn," said Pearl laughing quickly as she rolled her eyes around in her head. "I rarely ever use that ridiculous name. I address him by the name our mother gave him." Pearl walked toward Aton's bed and rested a hand on his forehead. "Are you sure you don't need a moment alone, he'll be safe with us," said Pearl in the most endearing tone she could muster.

"Yes I'm sure, thank you" said Scicremeon.

Another three hours seemed to fly by like minutes as they sat there watching Aton struggle from inside. None of them had moved much in the time that passed. Mysticgo had gathered for himself a chair and table to write upon. Mastadon was still playing games with his hammer, while Pearl watched the sun fade out of sight just as the moon began to rise. A few servants had come and gone, making sure Mysticgo was tended to; and King Hann had come to check on Aton's condition once.

Mental fatigue had begun to set in on Scicremeon and she felt like she was going to burst. While her mind was solely on Aton's condition, she came to wonder on Black Dawn. She wanted to know where he was and what he was doing. *Why has it taken him so long to come back*, she thought to herself growing angry. Feeling powerless wasn't something she enjoyed. She had far more strength than she'd ever had; and thus it drove her mad that none of it could help Aton.

After thirty more minutes passed, Black Dawn's boot broke the threshold of the room as the door swung open slowly. Mysticgo looked up and Pearl half ran from the window to Aton's bedside. Mastadon wasn't nearly as animated, gripping his hammer tightly, and resting it on his shoulder. Scicremeon turned slowly and met Black Dawn's eyes.

Paying little attention to everyone else, he looked at Scicremeon, "Will you come with me for a moment," said Black Dawn extending his hand.

"What about-," said Scicremeon cut off.

"He'll be fine here with my sister," said Black Dawn.

Scicremeon placed her hand in Black Dawn's and he led her out of the room.

He led her down a familiar staircase that she'd traveled not so long ago. But instead of coming down, she had been going up to rescue Aton. When she entered the room, it was as murky as it had been before. Nothing had been moved, not even Van Taven, who she noticed was still hanging by the manacles Mysticgo had locked him in.

Van Taven's breathing was labored, his eyes were still swollen shut, and the bruises on his body were darker, slowly beginning to heal. The wound on his neck was fresh where Scicremeon had set her golden string of energy upon him. She closed her eyes, and breathed in, surprisingly sympathetic to Van Taven's plight.

It's no fun being captured, she thought to herself as she watched him. She took a step forward, and Van Taven struggled to get out of his chains.

Black Dawn strolled over and stood under Van Taven. He waved his hand over the manacles and they opened, freeing Van Taven from their grasp. Black Dawn caught him by his arm pits as he fell from the wall, powerless to stop himself. Guided by Black Dawn's eyes, Scicremeon cleared the table on the opposite end of the room.

Lying Van Taven on the table, Black Dawn and Scicremeon stood over him, looking at his wounds. He'd obviously been tortured, but those wounds were going to heal. Scicremeon could see that the wound she inflicted was still growing. Slowly eating away at Van Taven's flesh and life force, and it wouldn't be much longer before death took him.

"I've done this to him?" said Scicremeon in shock as she watched Van Taven fading slowly on the table.

"Yes, with the Hand of Destruction," said Black Dawn.

"I only meant to scare Mysticgo and the king, so that they knew not to cross me. I had to make them believe," said Scicremeon looking at Black Dawn gravely.

"The damage can be reversed," said Black Dawn with a smile.

"How?" said Scicremeon her eyes darting from Van Taven to Black Dawn.

"The same way you hurt him," said Black Dawn.

"No, it only takes life," said Scicremeon shaking her head *no*.

"They only do as you will," said Black Dawn grabbing her gauntleted hand. He looked at the top of her hand and then turned her hand over so that her palm was facing up. "This is the Hand of Destruction, crafted by my uncle, wielded by my mother. Within the jewels are the Strings of Fate. With it, you are able to take the life force and power of anyone they come into contact with. Conversely, you are able to heal those with the life forces that you have absorbed."

"I have wanted nothing but blood," said Scicremeon looking at Black Dawn concerned, "since I have worn it, I have wanted it more."

"The gauntlet magnifies your desires tenfold. Whatever it is you want, it forces you toward that end. It is the reason why my mother has parted with it," said Black Dawn.

"Why did you give it to me?" begged Scicremeon, remembering how she felt like she was losing control.

"Because I couldn't bear the thought of losing you," said Black Dawn looking away.

Scicremeon stared at him blankly, floored by his statement. The only other time they met was when he bested her many moons ago. But the tone of his voice, and the words therein she couldn't mistake. The undertone of it was apparent. The side of his face she stared at as he looked away. When he turned back, she cast her gaze down on Van Taven. *Never could I,* she thought to herself and then something struck her.

"What has this thing made me?" asked Scicremeon, her eyes finding Black Dawn's face.

"It has made you like me," said Black Dawn.

Scicremeon's mouth was wide with amazement and Black Dawn said *yes* as she mouthed *a god.*

"Shall we get to the task at hand," said Black Dawn gesturing toward Van Taven.

"Yes," said Scicremeon with a girlish smile as she looked at the god who she had read stories about all of her life.

"Slowly," said Black Dawn as he watched her intently.

The Strings of Fate crawled from the Hand of Destruction and found the wound on Van Taven's neck. *Heal;* thought Scicremeon and the string wrapped around Van Taven's wound and began to suture it. As the wound sutured, the Strings of Fate flickered and Van Taven's bruises began to clear. His swollen eyes subsided back to their normal size and his skin flushed to its natural color.

A smile took over Scicremeon's face and a feeling of accomplishment washed through her. Van Taven began to sit up slowly, looking around bewildered for a moment as his eyes adjusted to the little light that was in the room. He looked at Black Dawn and squinted, disbelief jumping into his expression and then he turned to Scicremeon. He noticed that she was the same, but aside from her clothes he noticed that something about her was very different about her. Looking again at Black Dawn, the disbelief on his face grew in intensity.

"No way," said Van Taven as he swung his legs over the side of the table where Scicremeon stood. She took a step back, the smile on her face growing larger as she looked at Black Dawn, ready to burst into laughter. "Black Dawn?" said Van Taven dipping his head low and whispering the name.

Scicremeon shook her head *yes*, enjoying his bewilderment as Van Taven sighed, the sound of the air from his lungs saying *too much*.

"You were going to kill me," said Van Taven an accusatory stare coming over him.

"That wasn't my intention," said Scicremeon as if to calm him down, holding up her hands in submission.

"Could have fooled me, you were sure I was a traitor," said Van Taven still accusing her.

"It crossed my mind," said Scicremeon with her usual look of bloodlust and warrior's ambition.

"What made you stop, I'm sure you're still not very fond of me," said Van Taven, his face no longer a mass of accusation.

"I may still kill you once we're on Merridia, but I promised the emperor I'd at least get you back in one piece. Now that I know you're part Chalendoran, you most certainly can't be trusted," said Scicremeon with a smirk, half playful and half serious. "You should have been left on the ship like me, but that Mysticgo unlocked your full potential. You'll have access to all your Chalendoran powers. That I am not particularly fond of," said Scicremeon as if disgusted.

"I still think I am no threat to you," said Van Taven pausing for a moment, looking downward, "obviously even The Erudite couldn't kill you."

"Mysticgo is The Erudite," said Black Dawn happily surprised.

"Yes," said Scicremeon and Van Taven at once, both confused.

"There may yet be a chance for the boy and the rest of the world if we can get him back to my father," said Black Dawn rounding the table, making his way toward Scicremeon.

"Can you save him?" said Scicremeon hopeful, grabbing hold of Black Dawn's arms as he came to stand in front of her.

"There are no guarantees, but I'd die trying," said Black Dawn, his eyes boring into Scicremeon's.

Scicremeon wrapped her arms around his neck and squeezed him tightly. His arms enclosed her waist and for the first time in a long time she felt comforted. A tear ran from her eyes and she turned her face to hide it from Van Taven's view. She wouldn't let him see her cry. Even knowing what she now was, she refused to show him her vulnerability.

"Do you know what it is that has him," said Scicremeon drawing back, confident that there were no tears still falling from her eyes.

"I wish I knew the answer to that question. This is the moment where my vision becomes hazy. I do know that whatever has subdued the boy has the power to destroy worlds. I have seen this thing that the boy has inside him destroy our world. If we cannot put a stop to it, it would wipe Merridia from existence," said Black Dawn, his voice slightly shaken from what he said. The prospect of Merridia no longer existing scared him.

"Then we must leave right away," said Van Taven growing fearful when he heard Black Dawn's voice crack.

"We'll leave in due time," said Black Dawn calmly.

"I know fear when I hear it," said Van Taven cutting his eye at Black Dawn.

"We all have need of fear," said Black Dawn turning to Van Taven slowly, "even gods."

Pearl had taken Scicremeon's place in the room next to Aton's bed. When she entered the room, Pearl was wiping his forehead with a warm rag. Pearl stood, seeing Scicremeon followed by Black Dawn. Scicremeon thanked Pearl for sitting with Aton and gave her a warm hug. Leaning over him, she kissed Aton's forehead and whispered in his ear.

"Hold on you little runt," she said forcing back another fit of tears. *Caring for someone is taxing,* she thought as she closed her eyes for what felt like forever.

"I apologize for keeping you all waiting so long," said Black Dawn looking around the room.

"It is fine," said Mysticgo to Black Dawn and then looked happily at Van Taven, who'd come in behind him. "Good to see you back to your normal strength."

"No thanks to you," said Van Taven sneering at Mysticgo.

Scicremeon smiled at Van Taven, satisfied at his anger toward his fellow magician. She almost enjoyed the dissention among two magicians as much as the thought of killing them.

"If we're to save the boy, I need the two of you to work together," said Black Dawn to Van Taven.

"How can we help?" said Mysticgo standing and stepping from behind the small table he'd been writing at.

"An extraction spell," said Black Dawn.

"Do you even know what this thing is?" said Mysticgo.

"No, I am not entirely certain," said Black Dawn.

"Surely you felt the weight of its power," said Mysticgo, his eyebrows folding down over his eyes as his voice rose.

"Surely I did," said Black Dawn a bit puzzled. "Yet, I find it troubling that this being lived under the nose of The Erudite for so long, and he took no notice of it."

"What are you accusing me of?" begged Mysticgo stepping directly in front of Black Dawn.

"Hold fast magician, your power isn't as potent as your books might have you believe," said Black Dawn his lips pressed hard into a line of brewing rage.

"Now, now, we're all here to get along," said Mastadon seeming bored, finally stepping away from the wall.

"You speak sense," said Pearl drained, "finally it's not only me."

Mysticgo began to back away, looking Black Dawn up and down. Black Dawn took a step back, his eye still trained on Mysticgo.

"I have my moments," said Mastadon clapping Black Dawn on the shoulder.

Black Dawn regarded Mastadon and smiled, clapping his brother back on the shoulder. He then turned his attention back to Mysticgo who still had his eyes pressed upon him.

"I need you to come with us to Merridia," said Black Dawn.

"If the extraction spell does not work, the boy's personality could be splintered if this being is too strong, you know this," said Mysticgo, his tone grave and cautious.

"I've taken that into consideration, but we cannot risk allowing this being to take over; and your powers will be more potent on Merridia," said Black Dawn.

Scicremeon's eyes darted toward Mysticgo and then to Black Dawn. Van Taven had turned his head and wouldn't look her way when she turned to him. Confusion dressed her face and she stood fast, angry in her bewilderment.

"Why would a Chalendoran be more powerful on Merridia?' said Scicremeon, growing anger apparent in her tone.

"Do you remember when I said that I could not kill you with magic?" asked Mysticgo of Scicremeon.

"It's the reason why you tried to freeze me in the ship," she replied.

"That is because you are the carrier of The Blue Ember. It is the source of our power. To deal a killing blow to the physical body of one such as you with my magic would have destroyed me, and all of my power would have been yours," said Mysticgo looking into Scicremeon's startled eyes.

"Where does The Blue Ember come from?" said Scicremeon looking around at the gods and Mysticgo.

"Merridia," said Black Dawn wearily.

"Why would it be given to the Chalendorans?" begged Scicremeon.

"We were not always enemies," said Mysticgo coolly.

"Is that why you gave me this?" said Scicremeon raising the Hand of Destruction, staring at it as she turned her hand over.

"I knew that you would find your way here. I also knew that if you encountered The Erudite he would find out what you held and find a way to destroy you. If you died, so would the greatest threat to Chalendor," said Black Dawn.

"And if I had won," said Scicremeon.

"Then you would have become The Erudite," said Mysticgo.

"Imagine that," said Van Taven rolling his eyes.

Scicremeon imagined herself dressed in the burgundy robes of the Chalendoran magicians and cringed. "I think I like what I've become far better," said Scicremeon balling her gauntleted fist.

"Uh!" screamed Aton writhing in pain, reaching up with his arms like he was snatching something from out of the air. His hands fell to his sides, all the energy gone from him, and then he fell silent again. His whining grew soft, as he shifted slightly every so often.

"I think it's time that we leave," said Scicremeon lifting Aton from the bed.

Pearl looked at Black Dawn and he nodded to her and then Mastadon. Every one began to move at once, filing out of the door.

"Stay with me," said Scicremeon touching her head to Aton's.

Behind the procession of gods and magicians, Scicremeon followed with Aton in her arms. As she trotted down the hallway, she hoped for the best, but her mind was prepared for the worst. Black Dawn was spooked enough to be concerned about what might happen if Aton remained possessed. She had always been taught that things usually took a turn for the worst, before they got better. *I hope this is not the case*, she thought to herself as her foot touched the first stair on their descent down.

Dark Angel

The trip back to Merridia took far less than the twelve hours it had taken Scicremeon and Van Taven to get to Chalendor on The Runner. Van Taven and Mysticgo were still shaken by the speed at which Black Dawn and his siblings traveled. Even Scicremeon who had ascended to godhood, felt spent by the ordeal, moving faster than she'd ever thought possible.

The gate of Algar had come into view and Scicremeon could see a figure standing there before it. As they neared the gate, Black Dawn had begun to drift backward toward her and Aton, allowing Mastadon and Pearl to proceed forward. Scicremeon couldn't believe the beauty of Algar. She'd read about it a hundred times, but she now knew the stories could never do it the proper justice it demanded. The home of the Merridian gods was massive, far too large for any mortal to describe in accurate detail. She guessed that no mortals had ever set their eyes on it.

Algar sparkled, even with none of the suns of Merridia shining. The Black Moon was enough light to set the palace alight. On a ridge high up on her left side, she could see the beast that had destroyed part of a forest trying to kill her. Black Dawn apologized softly to her, a smile dressing his face as she turned to him.

Pearl landed first and Scicremeon could see that the waiting figure was tall, his hair golden, and his eyes were dark as The Black Moon. Pearl hugged him and then Mastadon touched him to the shoulder, standing eye to eye with him. His gold and black armor glowed in the moonlight and he watched Black Dawn intently. As they descended, she could see his calm demeanor change to one of concern, the face of a parent's anger.

"Let him speak first," said Black Dawn, caution in his voice.

"Is that Corvus?" said Scicremeon close to Black Dawn, whispering as quietly as she could.

"Yes," said Black Dawn his eyes weary darting from his father and then back to Scicremeon. They had landed a great distance from Corvus and began to walk toward him.

Scicremeon drew closer to Black Dawn, honestly afraid for the first time in her life. The stories she'd heard of Black Dawn were among the most well-known to all Merridians. He was celebrated among warriors unlike any other Merridian god who had come before him. And while his might was known to all who set foot on Merridia, all knew that he had a father, far more powerful than he was. It had been said in many a tale, that Corvus could break a god with a thought. If he could crush those far older and much more practiced in their power, Scicremeon knew that she'd be easy prey for the king of the gods.

Mastadon disappeared into the castle and Pearl stood to Corvus's right, her hands folded in front of her. Mysticgo and Van Taven walked a few strides behind Scicremeon and Black Dawn.

"He's bigger than I imagined," said Van Taven.

Scicremeon heard him and shushed him with a fierce grimace. She'd taken it to heart when Black Dawn told her to allow Corvus to speak first. Even though he was probably referring to addressing him, she didn't want to take the risk in angering him. For whatever reason, Pearl and Mastadon had been happy to approach and embrace their father. Black Dawn on the other hand seemed fearful and reluctant. *What has he done wrong?* Scicremeon wondered.

Standing in front of Corvus was daunting. He was massive, with broad shoulders, making Black Dawn seem small. He was slightly bigger than Mastadon and only The Ragnon had been bigger. But it wasn't just his size that felt overwhelming. Whatever it was that fueled his power was present there. Scicremeon's knees felt weak and all she thought of doing was dropping to the ground in supplication. If it were not for Aton in her arms, she would have surely bowed to Corvus.

"You are the very image of your father," said Corvus, his voice regal and powerful. "I welcome you to Algar, now that you are one of us," said Corvus eying the Hand of Destruction and then casting a narrowed eye on Black Dawn as he turned his head slightly to one side.

"Thank you," said Scicremeon softly, her eyes meeting Corvus's.

His black eyes seemed soft, calming as she looked into them.

"Your eyes are still the color of The Blue Ember," said Corvus drawing in a deep breath, his brow wrinkling. "Quite interesting indeed," he said, casting his eye back on Black Dawn.

"Father," said Black Dawn addressing Corvus.

"Dorrin," said Corvus flatly, his lips wrinkling in anger.

Scicremeon saw Corvus's fists ball up and she knew he was going to strike Black Dawn. In a flash she shifted in front of Black Dawn, giving Corvus a fierce stare. Whatever he was going to do to Black Dawn, she was willing to endure. He'd saved her and his promise to help Aton was more than enough to offer her protection, even if it was futile.

"You have made an ally out of the very person you thought was the greatest threat to our home," said Corvus with a smile.

"The world changes fast," said Black Dawn stepping from behind Scicremeon, and standing toe to toe with his father.

"You have not been able to stop this great calamity," said Corvus looking at Black Dawn sideways. He looked at Aton and saw him struggling and whimpering. "For you have brought it to our very doorstep," said Corvus as he took Aton from Scicremeon's arms. His right hand began to glow a radiant gold and he touched it to Aton's face. Aton's discomfort seemed to wash away, and he was still, sleeping peacefully.

Scicremeon was floored by Corvus's display of power. Nothing they had tried on Chalendor seemed to work to ease Aton's discomfort. Her fear of him had slowly washed away, but she had guessed right that his powers were truly potent.

"Bring the magicians to the Chamber of Fires," said Corvus to Black Dawn as he turned and entered the palace in haste. "We will determine your punishment later."

"Good that we had company," said Pearl to Black Dawn as she ran over and hugged him.

"I'll have to suffer in waiting. He's going to think about my punishment," said Black Dawn looking grim.

"Uh, that can't be good," said Pearl as she drew back, cringing, letting go of Black Dawn as if he were contagious. Turning to Scicremeon she smiled and wrapped her arms around her. "Thank you for standing between them," said Pearl with a smile. She held up a finger, her face holding the look of revelation, "However, you may have made it worse. He never allows my assistance either and always steps back around in front of father."

"It was the only thing I could think of at the moment," said Scicremeon forcing out a smile, thinking of Black Dawn's eventual peril at the hands of his father.

"Follow me," said Pearl waving for Van Taven and Mysticgo to follow.

Mysticgo and Van Taven walked fast to catch up with Pearl who'd disappeared behind the open door to the palace. Both of their eyes were panning everywhere, still taking in the wondrous home of the Merridian gods. Van Taven nodded to Scicremeon and she returned the gesture. She found it alarming that she had begun to tolerate Van Taven. In meeting him, her hatred bubbled against him simply because he was a magician. His presence being thrust upon her on the trip to Chalendor made it worse. Whatever tight spot he was supposed to help her out of never materialized; as it was her who had to bring him back from the doorstep of death. She at least knew where his allegiance had lied, even if his show of respect for Mysticgo made her weary. He tried his hand at defending her, as pointless as it seemed at the time. *That at least earned you my tolerance,* she thought and then smiled as he pressed his eyes forward, *we'll see how long it lasts.*

Mysticgo casts his eyes on Scicremeon and Black Dawn, but he didn't offer a nod as Van Taven had. Scicremeon was happy he didn't. She wasn't quite sure how she felt about Mysticgo being there, but if he could help Aton she was willing to accept his presence.

Aton could feel himself being carried against the warm breast-plate of Corvus's armor. He could hear Pearl and Mastadon whispering to one another behind Corvus, but he couldn't make out what they were saying. Though the pain he felt had subsided since Corvus touched him, each time he tried to climb out of limbo, he felt himself being pulled back down.

He remembered sleep, and in it he had never been aware of everything around him. Only dreaming had informed him that he was sleeping, but soon after the most vivid memories of a dream flooded in, he'd awaken to his reality. This was different, for he was able to feel and hear the presence of those around him, but they could hear only his whimpers and moans, as if he were unconscious and dreaming.

Screaming didn't help; he'd realized early on in the ordeal that no one could hear him. Around him there was nothing but an open desert with exploding volcanoes, pouring into rivers of molten lava. He'd walk for miles, near the point of dying, and then a small lake of fresh water would appear and he'd drink in renewed strength and vigor.

The same voice that had come before questioned him of his wants and dreams. Made promises to him that he'd give Aton everything in the world if he granted him control. The voice was calming, soothing, quite welcoming, and Aton wanted to believe him. But he wouldn't trust what he could not see and begged the voice to show him who he was. When he did, he saw those eyes. The eyes that he saw when he'd touched Cale. The same eyes he'd seen in the forest that told him the secret of The Ragnon's power. Each time Aton saw his eyes he refused his request. But each time he asked, he reminded Aton how he had helped him save Scicremeon from The Ragnon beast. *Does your friend not owe me her life? And you would have surely died if she had fallen. You owe me.* Aton could not argue with the truth of the statement, but his fear allowed him to remain steadfast in his choice.

The door in front of Corvus opened as he approached, swinging into the hallway. Intense heat rushed into the hallway, and Aton curled closer to Corvus. Van Taven and Mysticgo recoiled from the touch of the intense wave of hot energy coming toward them. At once they spoke a spell out that cooled the air around them. Scicremeon like the other Merridian gods were unaffected.

Behind Corvus they strode into the room and the door shut behind them, trapping the heat inside. Van Taven and Mysticgo felt themselves becoming quickly fatigued and short of breath, and their spell failed. Pearl touched them both to the chest and cast a force field around them to protect them from the suffocating energy of the fires around them.

Around the room there were fires of every color, flickering quickly, and roaring high into the air every few seconds. The walls of the room were gold, the reflection of the fires lighting up the walls, bouncing back their color in every direction. The fires reflecting off the walls lit the room into the form of a kaleidoscope.

Mysticgo's mouth was hanging open in wonder and Van Taven's eyes looked around in astonishment. They were both taken by the incredible force of energy they felt radiating around them. Encased in Pearl's protection, they moved around the room, studying each fire, marveling at its movement and color.

Corvus walked to the center of the circular chamber with Aton in his arms. When he stopped, a section of the floor rose up like an altar and he set Aton down upon it. As Corvus's hands left Aton, the boy began to writhe in pain again, whimpering, and moaning his discomfort.

Scicremeon's eyes began to well and she marched quickly to the altar, standing opposite Corvus. She reached out her hand to touch Aton and a hot blue flame rushed up from below him and engulfed the altar. Scicremeon pulled her hand back, feeling the awesome power of the flame. She'd felt it before, but from inside.

"The Blue Ember," said Mysticgo in awe as he felt the heat press against the force field Pearl had encased him in. He could hear the invisible energy fighting, struggling against the flame.

Van Taven fell to one knee and tried to push himself up. Pearl rushed toward him and strengthened the force field around him. Van Taven stood, panting, holding his chest, his eyes devoid of the resolve that had always been present there. He looked at Mysticgo weakly, hoping he would have an answer for him. Mysticgo said nothing and moved closer to the blue flame.

"Come, Elio, we must begin," said Corvus.

Van Taven stumbled toward the altar, coming to Corvus's side. He looked at Mysticgo who stood at Aton's head. Mysticgo's face was hard, staring into the fire as if he too were possessed. Scicremeon seemed unaffected by the fire, concerned only for Aton's well-being. He wished he had her doggedness; she always seemed in control, ready for anything that came. Mysticgo he knew was far more powerful than him and that comforted him to know he'd have The Erudite with him. Yet, he wondered what the significance would be of the part he'd play among one such as Mysticgo, and a party of gods.

"Are you ready," said Corvus making eye contact with Scicremeon.

"I am no magician," said Scicremeon harshly.

"No you're not, you're much more," said Corvus backing away from the altar. "You possess The Blue Ember inside you. You'll be able to keep them safe while they draw from its power. Join hands," said Corvus nodding and looking at them all.

Scicremeon stretched out a hand to Van Taven and Mysticgo. When they touched her, they felt a jolt of intense power, their force fields evaporating from them. Scicremeon felt the hot power of The Blue Ember rise up inside her and burst outward, creating a barrier between the magicians and the flickering Blue Ember swirling around the altar. Within the fire she could see Aton, still struggling, hoping to break him free of whatever force was causing him angst.

Mysticgo began to speak quickly in Chalendoran and Van Taven followed, reciting each line carefully. Scicremeon's eyes began to grow darker and darker, a trace of gold energy radiating around her blue eyes. The Blue Ember began to flicker more rapidly than the other fires, as each of them rose straight up and then shot toward The Blue Ember. The walls no longer reflected the color of the flames and the Chamber of Fires went dark, save for the altar at the center. Scicremeon's corneas grew blue as well, while the golden trace around her eye radiated, and she felt herself filled with greater power than when she first slipped on the Hand of Destruction.

Aton stopped moving as The Blue Ember began to fill him. His eyes opened wide and they were burning like two fiery comets. Aton's mouth opened and a beam of bright ultraviolet light shot from it, up and out of the Chamber of Fires. His voice was not his own, but a deep raspy gurgling sound of great thunder and rage entered the chamber as he spoke one sentence.

"The time has come."

Aton found himself wandering through a maze of stone rubble. A sprawling kingdom had been razed to the ground by a horde of men carrying torches and swords. He could see their bare backs, stained with soot and blood, chanting the name of their leader. They marched ahead of him, those behind him walked through him, while others pressed forward on his flanks, as they continued to collect the spoils of their victory.

Behind him he kept hearing that voice, and each time he turned around, those fiery eyes stared back at him. He motioned with his hand for Aton to come to him. The nails on his hands were black and sharp as a razor's edge. His face was pale, almost white as ivory. When he smiled, Aton saw a perfect set of white teeth.

A young girl ran past Aton and jumped into the arms of the black cloaked man with the fiery eyes. She smiled back at Aton and motioned for him to come toward her. Aton back pedaled, keeping his eyes locked on the girl and the figure holding her.

"What do you wish for boy?" said the figure, his voice mellow, echoing into the air as he reached a hand out for Aton to hold.

"To go home," said Aton quickly.

"I will take you there, if you join hands with me," said the figure, gliding toward Aton faster, hand outstretched.

He drew closer to Aton who had slowed down. The shirtless men still hammered the ground as they ran through and around him. He wanted to run, but the eyes he looked into were more mesmerizing as they drew closer. A great light radiated from them, calming his mood, and taking away the fear that was beating hard behind his chest.

"What will happen?" said Aton moving his hands behind his back.

"We'll be free to do as we please," said the figure smiling.

"What is your name?" asked Aton standing still as the sharp-nailed figure stood over him, staring down into his face.

"I am Dark Angel, the savior of the world," said Dark Angel, still smiling, his fiery eyes glowing hot.

Aton began to feel light-headed; his eyes swirled around in his head, as he rocked from side to side, trying to steady himself. Dark Angel continued to smile, but his kind expression turned devious. Aton felt his hand moving, and tried hard to keep it behind his back, but a great force had grabbed hold. His whole body went stiff and he felt cold and petrified.

"Please," said Aton shaking his head *no*, as he tried to recoil from Dark Angel.

"I am taking you home," began Dark Angel in a fatherly tone, trying to mask his harrowing tone, "isn't that what you wanted?"

"Yes," said Aton, as his eyes rolled up into his head, only his cornea visible as he stood with no control over his faculties.

"Is that what you want?" said Dark Angel turning his palm upward.

"Yes," said Aton, his hand extending in front on him, palm facing down.

"Then take my hand," said Dark Angel kneeling down in front of Aton.

Aton set his hand in the palm of Dark Angel's pale hand. Dark Angel was cold to the touch and Aton felt a jolt of energy shoot through him as Dark Angel's hand wrapped around his own. His black nails pierced Aton's hand, blood oozing out and over the side, falling between their palms. Aton's eyes began to glow like a fiery comet and he dug his nails into Dark Angle's hand, blood rolling out and into his palm, mixing with Aton's.

"We are one," said Dark Angel.

Scicremeon continued to watch as Mysticgo and Van Taven chanted over Aton, as she focused to keep them protected from the power of The Blue Ember. Both were sweating profusely as they worked at trying to break hold of whatever was keeping Aton unconscious and in pain. Van Taven's knees were shaking from standing for so long as the air around him continued to grow hotter and hotter.

Aton stopped moving, and whatever pain he had felt was gone in an instant. The flames around the room began to flicker slower than they had been during Mysticgo and Van Taven's spell. Scicremeon relaxed and began to step forward as she watched the two magicians panting, hoping to steal what little air they could from the chamber. Pearl ran over to Van Taven who'd dropped to a knee, weak from his exertion. Mysticgo was reeling, trying hard to maintain his balance as he leaned against the altar, his arms resting on the space above Aton's head. The Blue Ember subsided and was no longer wrapped around the altar.

Scicremeon touched Aton's face and felt his skin alternating between extreme cold and warmth. She could feel the blood in his veins running hot and the smell of burning wood crept into her nostrils each time Aton breathed out. She lifted his head and sat on the altar behind him, cradling Aton like an infant. She stroked his hair and it smelled like warm amber.

Corvus and Black Dawn began to draw nearer to the altar as Pearl worked her way toward Mysticgo after having aided Van Taven in getting back to his feet. Black Dawn appeared to be weary as he came closer to Scicremeon. He met her eyes with his own and smiled an unmistakable expression of affinity. Scicremeon smiled back and then looked at Aton, hoping he would wake soon.

Mastadon sauntered over seeming bored and uninterested with everything that was going on. He tossed his hammer up into the air and caught it a dozen times before he reached the altar.

"The boy still sleeps," said Mastadon not convinced that the spell worked as everyone else seemed to believe.

"All spells don't have an immediate desired effect," said Mysticgo rumbling as he stood to his full height. "Some take time to develop."

"Is this one of those," said Mastadon challenging Mysticgo's claim. Mysticgo paid him no mind.

When Corvus was just a few feet from the altar, The Blue Ember sprang up again, wrapping Aton and Scicremeon within in its fire. Aton's eyelids snapped open, revealing a set of comet like eyes ablaze in his head. He swung his arms up, breaking Scicremeon's hold on him, knocking her back against the altar. Aton stood up and surveyed the room, his blazing eyes taking in his surroundings. When he came to Corvus, his eyes locked there and a frown took over his face. A gusting wind swept up and swirled around Aton, his hair flapping in the breeze in every direction. Corvus returned the boy's frown, and Black Dawn's eyes went wide with fear. Pearl left Van Taven's side and stood behind her father. Mastadon held his hammer with both hands, crouched, ready for a fight. Scicremeon tried to stand and felt a great weight push her back down as Aton opened his hand by his side.

Scicremeon found herself lying against the altar as Aton had been, the small boy standing over her in a stare down with Corvus.

"Who are you!" yelled Mysticgo unshaken by the boy's transformation.

"I am Dark Angel," said Dark Angel through Aton's mouth.

"Where is Aton?" asked Mysticgo.

"He and I are one," replied Dark Angel, the scowl still painted on his face, his eyes never leaving Corvus.

"Aton!" screamed Scicremeon as loud as she could.

The fiery eyes flashed out of sight replaced by Aton's big dark brown eyes. He looked around confused, aware of where he was because he'd heard it said, though the room was unfamiliar. Aton was visibly shaken as he stumbled, but kept himself from falling off of the altar.

"I guess only half the spell worked," said Mastadon relaxing as he realized that Dark Angel no longer held sway over Aton's mind and body.

"I can't move," said Scicremeon, still held down by a force she couldn't see. *Is Aton doing this*, she thought as she saw his hand still spread open over her. "Aton, are you doing this?" said Scicremeon looking at his hand and then into his face.

Aton looked down at her confused and then turned his palm so that he could see it. He felt a tingling sensation from within it and heard a faint buzzing sound coming from his hand. "I don't know, I think so," said Aton looking at Scicremeon bewildered. She seemed just as confused as he was, trying to free herself of whatever was keeping her pressed against the altar.

"Leave this boy," said Corvus loudly and marched forward reaching for Aton.

Aton's head whipped around quickly and his eyes turned back to the fiery comets they were before, as he scowled at Corvus advancing toward him. The other gods followed suit, while Mysticgo and Van Taven held their ground, standing at the ready.

"Insects," said Dark Angel, his voice taking over Aton's like an ocean wave, angry and vengeful. Waving his arms, outward, The Blue Ember exploded outward knocking everyone in the room backward against the wall. "The time has come, and all of the universe will fall to their knee in submission of your rule, great Carnok," said Dark Angel taking off from the altar and pushing through the door to the Chamber of Fires.

"Aton!" screamed Scicremeon mad with rage. The Blue Ember swelled around her. She heard a sound like shattering glass as the flames cut into whatever was holding her back. She stood up quickly on the altar and The Blue Ember climbed higher into the air, covering her head. When she tried to walk out of the flames, The Blue Ember pushed her back in. She then heard Aton's voice in her mind. *It's for your protection.*

Scicremeon's eyes went wide with grief, hearing his voice, while watching his body burst out of the Chamber of Fires. Around her she saw Van Taven and Mysticgo unconscious from Dark Angel's attack. To her left she could see Corvus stand fast and quickly take flight behind Dark Angel. Black Dawn was on one knee, shaking his head. Black Dawn looked around the room and saw that Pearl and Mastadon were knocked down, but conscious. Pearl began to move toward Van Taven and Mastadon was pushing himself up, the hammerhead of his weapon pressed against the floor as he began to try and right himself.

Black Dawn took flight as his father had and Scicremeon gasped about to speak, but doubted he'd hear her. She reached out with her mind, hoping to pierce The Blue Ember with her thoughts as Aton had, even with his consciousness suppressed by Dark Angel's presence. *Aton's still in there; please don't hurt him*, thought Scicremeon to Black Dawn.

I'll do my best, Scicremeon heard Black Dawn's voice in her head and she knew what his words meant. He'd try to save the boy, but there were no promises that could be made now. Dark Angel commanded the boy's body and a fight with him it seemed could be deadly. He'd subdued five gods and two magicians without much effort. And if his words were honest, a being named Carnok must be more terrible if it were his rule and not Dark Angel's that the world would submit to.

Please, thought Scicremeon, and it was all she could do to keep herself from crying, feeling powerless, trapped inside of the power that had always given her an edge. *Blasted Fires of Aygron*, she thought to herself as she allowed her rage to boil over. The gift from the father she never knew had become her obstacle, when for so long it had been her only ally.

With the Hand of Destruction she reached out, and her eyes began to glow darker, the golden line around her iris radiating as the Strings of Fate shot from the gauntlet. They latched on to The Blue Ember splitting in three. *Become one with me*, she thought and the

Strings of Fate began to split, a thousand lines of string connecting to the Blue Ember.

The Chamber of Fires began to shake, and the other fires around the chamber began to rise straight up, and out of the top. Harder the chamber shook and Scicremeon began to scream loudly. She could feel the intense power of The Blue Ember rushing into her and quickly felt herself losing control.

Mastadon looked at the altar alarmed and flinched to move toward Scicremeon, but Pearl grabbed him by the collar and stopped him.

"Fools rush in," said Pearl looking at him sideways.

Scicremeon watched as the flames of The Blue Ember shot up like the others had and felt a sense of dread take over her. She looked to her right and saw Pearl standing with Van Taven slung over her shoulder, while she held Mastadon by the collar.

Mysticgo was backing away from them toward the door, his eyes narrowed in intense contemplation. She could sense the fear he tried to mask with the sternness of his expression.

Pearl looked worried and Scicremeon knew she wanted to stay, but she shook her head no to Pearl and then reached out with her mind, *run,* she thought to her. The fires in the Chamber of Fires stretched out within the room until they folded together. Pearl and Mastadon slipped out of the room with Van Taven just before the fires stretched wall to wall.

Do anything, Scicremeon thought as she screamed at the top of her lungs.

Where Titans Roam

Dark Angel walked past the frozen statue of The Ragnon, smiling at the beast's ferocious face. He strolled to the edge of the mountain and raised his hands above his head, palms facing forward, Aton's little hands stretching to their maximum extension. Grey clouds rolled over and covered the blue skies, lightning crackling across the gloomy clouds casting a shadow over Merridia. A furious rain began to pour from the clouds, pattering the mountain top he stood upon.

"Can you see him child?" said Dark Angel aloud to Aton.

Yes, said Aton from inside himself to Dark Angel. Looking through Dark Angel's eyes he could see a massive being with a red face, darker than any blood he'd ever seen peering down on Merridia. Aton was shocked to see something so large; big enough to hold Merridia in the palm of his hand. His eyes were identical to Dark Angel's, burning like comets. His lips were black as The Black Moon and his robes were red as his skin. He wore a black battle armor that separated his bloodlike skin from his robes.

"That is our Lord Carnok. He will rid the world of these insects and take us all to a new home, where we shall serve his will until the end of time," said Dark Angel happily. He'd been smiling as the storm he began, grew more terrible. "Drag he will, these gods from the high horses they have sat upon for too long." Dark Angel's eyes met Carnok's and from inside himself, suppressed by Dark Angel's consciousness, he too could see Carnok.

Carnok smiled without baring his teeth, seeing Aton with Dark Angel made him happy. He pressed his consciousness to Aton and Aton tried to shield himself from Carnok, curling into a ball and covering his ears.

Your coming has made all of this possible dear boy, thought Carnok softly. *You have made it so that I may begin making the world anew, starting from here, at the very center of the universe.*

No, it wasn't me, it's him; thought Aton to Carnok, blaming Dark Angel for whatever had, or whatever was going to transpire. He wanted no part of it, and wanted dearly not to be blamed.

"It is us together," said Dark Angel aloud.

"You will do no such thing," said Corvus storming toward Dark Angel from behind.

Hearing him, Dark Angel turned around as Corvus stalked toward him, standing tall, his broad chest protruding, fists balled in apparent anger.

"I've waited ages to have another go at you," said Dark Angel, curling Aton's face into a disgusted scowl.

Corvus swung a fist when he neared Dark Angel. With the palm of Aton's hand he blocked the fist as he was knocked backward off the mountain. A massive shockwave spread out, assaulting the ground between them.

Dark Angel drifted high into the air as if in retreat from Corvus, continuing to go high above the clouds. Corvus followed, his arms balled into fists above his head, his eyes locked on Aton's body.

Remove him, thought Carnok to Dark Angel, *send him to me.*

"With pleasure," said Dark Angel shifting direction and zooming toward Corvus, diving through the clouds.

It didn't take long, their speed tremendous as they met. Rain drops shifted away from them as they cut through the pouring water, making the air move so much that the rain couldn't touch them.

Boom!

They collided and sent another shockwave screaming across the heavens of Merridia. A fight ensued, each swinging with merciless intent, trying to gain the upper hand. Corvus moved with blinding speed around Dark Angel, as he kept turning to watch for his attacks. He sent balls of comets from his eyes at Corvus, trying to knock him off his course, but the king of the Merridian gods kept coming. Another shockwave rippled, and then another resounding like an enormous fit of thunder as they warred in the skies.

Dark Angel dodged and twirled to his left as Corvus advanced again, swinging and kicking. It took every ounce of effort for Dark Angel to avoid Corvus's blows. With each exertion, Dark Angel could feel Corvus growing stronger and his own strength waning. The weight of Corvus's power and relationship with the planet began to press down upon him. Dark Angel grunted as Aton's back slammed against the side of the mountain where The Ragnon stood still. As he peeled Aton's body from in between the rocky structure, he noticed he'd almost gone clear through to the other side.

Inside of himself, Aton felt the pain inflicted upon his body, as Dark Angel jumped from the hole in the mountain. *You're going to get me killed*, thought Aton to Dark Angel fearful. "Quiet," said Dark Angel to Aton. *You're no match for him this way*, thought Aton, taking notice of Dark Angel's weakening strength. "Then join with me fully and we can end him here as Lord Carnok commands," said Dark Angel aloud.

Crack!

Aton's face twisted, his chin nearly touching the back of his shoulder as he began sprawling in a free fall toward the ground. "Open yourself to the darkness boy, or you'll die and never see home," said Dark Angel his voice deep and dark. His request sounded more like an order than a request and Aton feared what the outcome would be. But he could feel himself falling, weakening every moment that Dark Angel locked horns with Corvus. Dark Angel's powers had protected his body from Corvus, but it wouldn't be much longer before his body could no longer absorb the punishment.

Become one with the darkness and let my power fill you so that you may live to see home. Aton heard Carnok's somber voice again in his head, a great weight pressing down upon him making him grow fearful. "Listen to Lord Carnok. We'll be more powerful than Scicremeon could have ever made you," said Dark Angel aloud as he couldn't stop Aton's body from falling. *Scicremeon,* thought Aton to himself, seeing her face and remembering how much she'd cared for his well-being. He remembered how she wouldn't leave him, how she'd come for him, to save him from Chalendor. *She'd fight,* he thought to himself.

An eerie feeling swept over Aton as he felt Dark Angel's consciousness folding into his own. The voices came back, a multitude of them whispering, chanting, yelling, begging and pleading with him. Darkness enveloped him and he curled deeper into a ball. Marching toward him slowly with his hand outstretched was the massive being he knew as Carnok, his hand reaching for him as Dark Angel's had done before. But he wasn't waiting outside of Merridia, but there inside his mind. The voices began to form faces, pale and black. They wore expressions of anger, sorrow, rage, misery, and all manner of hopeless wrinkles.

Carnok stood over Aton with his hand out, his blood red palm humming a beautiful song. Touching Aton's hand as they covered his ears, a deep comfort swept over Aton and he no longer felt afraid. He felt an overwhelming power sweep into his blood, flesh, and bones. Suddenly he felt himself slowing down, and then stopping midflight as the details of the earth below him began to come into focus. He placed his hand in Carnok's and then felt an even greater rush of power.

Dark Angel watched him coming, like a golden arrow out of the sky dressed in radiant sunlight. It was going to be the last blow dealt, that would send him encased in Aton's body, spiraling out of control into the hard rock below. All of their battles in the past had ended like this, Corvus standing above him in all of his might and majesty, as he'd drag him by the cloak and send him rocketing into space.

"Not this time," said Dark Angel to himself as Corvus continued toward him.

"How?" said Corvus, as Dark Angel slipped around him and grabbed him by his cape.

"This time you lose," said Dark Angel as he spun around at incredible speeds and opened his hand sending Corvus flying upward through the clouds. Balling Aton's fists, he shot toward a reeling Corvus. Bursts of black energy shot from his fists slamming into Corvus, keeping him spiraling out of control so he couldn't regain his composure.

Propelling Aton's body forward, as Corvus neared Merridia's atmosphere, he gripped the king of the gods by the ankle and swung him again. Releasing his grip, Corvus ripped through the atmosphere and then through an invisible barrier outside of the atmosphere that protected Merridia from unwanted intruders. Gold energy rippled out of place as Corvus floated through dark space away from Merridia.

"He is yours my lord," said Dark Angel as he watched Corvus rocketing toward Carnok's hand.

"The first of many victories," said Carnok as Corvus zipped toward him. Thwack! The sound cracked across space as the back of Carnok's great hand swatted Corvus like an insect.

"Ugh," moaned Corvus as his body went limp and rocketed into deep space at the speed of light. He felt himself being pulled inside a vacuum as he went drifting out of the galaxy. His body grew weak and his eyes rolled into the back of his head. His eyelids shut and the world went black as his consciousness drifted from reality.

"Father!" said Black Dawn screaming as he saw his father struck by Carnok outside of Merridia's atmosphere. He drew his sword quickly as Dark Angel began to make his way toward him. Black Dawn wanted to keep his attention on Dark Angel, but he was divided as he saw Carnok decreasing in size, floating through Merridia's atmosphere, wearing a calm smile on his face.

Carnok's feet settled on the soil of the Merridian heavens and he dug his feet into the soil, surveying the dirt around his foot as if his toes could feel the dirt through his hard boots. He breathed in the fresh air, long and deep, tilting his head back and closing his eyes. Algar rose up from the ground not too far from where he stood and he took in its magnificent presence, his eyes moving around the structure slowly. He mused over the palace as if he wanted to know every single rivet of its design.

"No," said Carnok to Dark Angel as he prepared to strike at Black Dawn. Dark Angel glided backward, and stood off to the side, just behind Carnok.

Aton's body appeared even smaller standing next to Carnok, who Black Dawn guessed was at least twelve feet tall. Carnok began to walk toward Black Dawn, only ten yards of distance between them.

"What is your business here?" said Black Dawn his sword at the ready.

Carnok stopped and regarded Black Dawn for a moment, his lips pressed hard together.

"My purpose is bring you to your knees, voluntarily, or to break you as I take the world," said Carnok fervently.

"Here, you'll find great resistance to that end, red one," said Black Dawn.

Carnok laughed and took a half step forward and then turned, motioning his hand toward Dark Angel, and then looked back at Black Dawn. "If I could bring him to heel with but the order of my words, and he removed your father from the world upon which he sat as sovereign; what makes you believe you are any match for me," said Carnok narrowing his eyes.

"I am not my father," said Black Dawn with a touch of his own fervor.

"All great sons do seek to be greater than their fathers, but I doubt you'll find that end here today Dorrin Merrid, tamer of The Ragnon beast, wielder of The Black Moon blade, who all the people of Merridia know as Black Dawn," said Carnok lifting his chin as Black Dawn looked at him quizzically. "How do I know your histories," said Carnok watching as Black Dawn reeled hearing his thoughts said before he could speak them. "I know the power that fuels your own, for I was there with my father when he gave it to yours," said Carnok walking forward again.

"Not another step," said Black Dawn vehemently readying his sword.

"Where are my manners?" said Carnok, stopping again and bowing to Black Dawn. "I am Carnok, the new lord of the universe," said Carnok as he began to march again.

Carnok was two feet from Black Dawn when Black Dawn raised his sword and swung. The sound of metal rang out as Carnok caught Black Dawn's sword in palm. Black Dawn's eyes went wide with fear and surprise as Carnok pulled the sword from his hand. Carnok jabbed Black Dawn in the jaw with the pommel of the sword.

"Will you kneel?" said Carnok.

"Never!" said Black Dawn emphatically grinding his teeth at Carnok. Black Dawn turned his palms up and sent a surge of red energy at Carnok's chest.

"Futile," said Carnok as the energy dissipated as it touched him. Carnok shook his head *no* as Black Dawn began to send blast after blast to no effect.

"This can't be happening," said Black Dawn mustering his power and sending every manner of projectile Carnok's way to slow him down. He felt himself back pedaling as Carnok continued to march forward.

"Your father has taught you a great many lessons, but he has kept you in the dark about us, which would have been your greatest lesson yet," said Carnok as he threw Black Dawn's sword at him and watched him catch it in his hand.

Raising his sword up over his head, a shower of lightning bolts collided with his sword's blade and infused it with power. Black Dawn whipped the sword in Carnok's direction sending a blazing hot streak of lightning toward him. Carnok lifted his hand again and caught the energy in his palm, closing his fingers around the charging bolt of lightning.

With a whip of his hand, Carnok sent the energy bolting back to Black Dawn. It struck him in the chest and knocked him to the ground.

"Dorrin!" he heard Pearl scream in the distance. She called his name again and heard Mastadon calling out *brother.*

"Kneel," said Carnok as he watched Black Dawn stand to his feet again.

"I will not," said Black Dawn racing toward Carnok with his sword pointed toward him. Black Dawn slammed the blade into Carnok's chest and it sent a shockwave through his arm, causing him to lose the grip on his blade.

"This must have been how Scicremeon felt against your power. So much bravery, yet no matter how hard you try, you will fail," said Carnok as he grabbed Black Dawn by the throat, squeezing.

For the first time Black Dawn felt as if he couldn't breathe, never having need to do so before. But it wasn't breath that was running away from him. It was his life force being dragged out of him into Carnok's hand. Slowly the power that was keeping Black Dawn on his feet left him, and he crumbled to his knees, Carnok releasing the grip on his neck.

"I will break you," said Black Dawn, unwilling to accept defeat, even though the balance had tipped in favor against him.

"The lesson your father should have taught is this boy," said Carnok leaning over, his face but a few inches from Black Dawn's. "Gods should not block the path where titans roam," said Carnok, his fiery eyes began to burn outward. He grabbed Black Dawn by his breastplate and ripped it from him and tossed it aside. Touching the gauntlets of Gorgon-Ray, they sprang free of his arms and dropped to the ground. Carnok looked over Black Dawn's head and saw Pearl and Mastadon rushing toward him, and smiled. "Let's hope your brother and sister are more amicable to my commands, or they'll suffer the same fate." Grabbing Black Dawn by the throat, he lifted him from the ground and turned to Dark Angel who was trailing behind him a few feet. "Shall we send him to be with his father?"

"We should make an example out of him," said Dark Angel with a devious grin.

"Very well," said Carnok.

Carnok tossed Black Dawn into the air and blew a soft gust of air out of his mouth that pushed Black Dawn faster into the air. Placing his hands in front of his glowing eyes, he pulled two burning comets from them and released them into the air behind Black Dawn. They sailed up quickly, leaving behind a trail of gas and fire. "You would have done well in service to me, what a waste," said Carnok aloud to himself as the comets reached Black Dawn and pushed him out of Merridia's atmosphere.

When he reached space, the searing comets began to rip into him, tearing apart his flesh, ripping apart his bones, and touching his essence, which was black as The Black Moon. Black Dawn's physical body disintegrated into nothingness as the comets from Carnok's eyes reached his essence. The blackness of his essence shattered into a million tiny pieces and drifted apart across black space.

Unshielded

Thutmos had been searching the universe hoping to find a glimmer of Carnok's presence, but he found none. Everdon and Luminar were searching together, but they had also met with no luck. In the days that they'd searched, they felt Primsec's presence and found that Chasm was with him on Earth. Thutmos made every attempt to convince them to come and stand on his side, but they would not. Lately, any time he mentioned the notion, they'd cut him off from their presence. He had known Chasm's displeasure with the war between the two sides of Our Union, but Primsec was even more distraught over the circumstances. He'd pleaded with Thutmos to change his course, but Thutmos would stand firm in his decision.

Everdon had sent word that traces of Kinozl and Forecon's power had been left in a dozen galaxies. In their wake they had left dead stars, consuming their energies for whatever it was they were planning with Carnok. Yet, finding them had been difficult. They too like Carnok had remained shielded, and though Luminar and Everdon allowed their presence to be known, neither Forecon nor Kinozl would engage them.

On Earth, Thutmos found himself sitting with Primsec and Chasm after he decided that his efforts were in vain. Together they walked across a sweltering desert, where no animals roamed, and where there was no vegetation; except for a cactus every few thousand yards.

Being there again, Thutmos felt the comfort of Aeon's presence and Chasm hadn't stopped smiling, happy that he'd come. She remembered their first time being there, feeling how much Thutmos would have liked to stay, even though she knew he could not. The war between them had forced her to change her opinion of making Earth her home. Her duty as a member of Our Union no longer felt the same. Where once she felt she had no choice to choose what her purpose was, that feeling was replaced by a desire to do as she willed. Her will begged her for peace, and she believed that she should do nothing but oblige it.

"Will you not consider terms of peace with Carnok?" asked Chasm, always willing to beg the question of Thutmos.

"We stand on opposite ends of the spectrum it is true," said Thutmos alluding to something Primsec had said earlier. "Yet, where I would not look to meddle in the lives of the lower beings, Carnok would be their ruler," said Thutmos touching a hand to his chin in thought. "How can I not stand in opposition to such tyrannical behavior by one such as us?"

"You are still not thinking of the consequences of engaging in battle with Carnok," said Primsec. His face held the expression of someone pained by another's failure to see the silver lining of their assertions.

"All the worlds will suffer," said Chasm.

"Will they not suffer the same by me doing nothing?" replied Thutmos opening his hands, palms turned up.

"Do not be blinded by your emotions," said Primsec almost angry.

"I cannot watch the worlds suffer because Carnok is too greedy to still his hand. Hasn't he taken enough?" said Thutmos stopping for a moment.

Primsec and Chasm turned to him, watching his face, studying him as Thutmos looked into the sky, his left ear twitching, and then suddenly his right.

Thutmos felt a dark presence in his mind, one he'd felt before but one that he hadn't felt for a long time. "Dark Angel," said Thutmos aloud. Primsec and Chasm reacted, frowns dressing their faces as they asked *where* together. "Wait," said Thutmos closing his eyes, feeling a stronger presence brimming around his mind. Chasm's eyes went wide with shock and hope, as she began to press her mind out toward it. "Are you mad," said Thutmos to Chasm as he heard Carnok's voice in his mind for the first time in a long time.

Will you end this and return to your quadrant so that we may be as we once were, thought Chasm to Carnok. Thutmos's face wrinkled with anger at Chasm's request, but he did not interrupt, he listened as Carnok replied.

I have dug a hole too deep to climb out of; therefore I must continue to dig until I find the other side, said Carnok metaphorically.

Everdon and Luminar materialized from nowhere, Everdon wearing a mask of excitement while Luminar's face was even angrier than Thutmos's was growing. The sands of the desert swirled aside as Luminar touched to the ground, her rage radiating off her being. She could taste revenge on her tongue for Trurow's death, and she clenched her fingers to keep from bursting.

Besides, I doubt that our dear big brother would be willing to cast aside his emotions in order to reach a truce, said Carnok with great sarcasm.

I've heard you. You will see this treachery to its end, thus, I shall come to stand in your way, thought Thutmos pressing his mind out towards Carnok. Kinozl and Forecon's presence drifted into the collective of Our Union as Thutmos finished speaking.

There is a more reasonable way to end this feud, thought Primsec to all the remaining members of Our Union.

No, there is no other course, no return to the collective mind that we were for so many millennia. War is imminent and it must be waged for the benefit of all the lower beings that live upon the worlds we've had a hand in making, thought Everdon to them all, but pressed his mind furthest toward Carnok. *You have loosed the splintered piece of yourself called Dark Angel on the first planet.*

Thutmos's eyes burst open with furious anger as Everdon spoke of Merridia. His heart pounded in his chest and the Earth began to shake as his rage boiled over. A tornado swept up the sands of the deserts as Thutmos gnashed his teeth together. *Feel my rage brother, know its power before you face its wrath,* thought Thutmos to Carnok.

Those who follow you will fall before my might. I pray that my dear Primsec remain a neutral party for I shall have no mercy on those who pursue me, thought Carnok as his mind departed from the collective.

"He's unshielded, I can still feel his presence," said Luminar still jittery, ready to leave.

"We know that he has set his foot upon Merridia and un-leashed Dark Angel. He will not retreat, there is no way we can avoid this war," said Thutmos.

"Indeed," said Everdon solidifying his notion with a smile and shaking of his head *yes.*

"This is your last chance to allow this to play out as it shall. Merridia is but one planet," said Primsec almost begging.

"Carnok would see that my words long ago hold no meaning. He knows that my heart is still with my old friend Corvus," said Thutmos quieting his anger as he spoke to Primsec.

"Will you risk the universe for one planet?" said Chasm.

"Each living thing is significant, no matter how old," said Primsec, sounding as if he were in agreement of Thutmos's course of action.

"Come with me brother, you see all that I see," said Thutmos offering his hand.

"I cannot. There are things that you have chosen to ignore," said Primsec taking a step back.

"Chasm," said Thutmos looking her way.

"I have made my choice," she said balling her fists.

"Then I take my leave and bid you farewell. We must go now if we are to save Merridia from Carnok's ambition," said Thutmos saddened by their dismissal of his offer.

Thutmos, Everdon, and Luminar vanished from Primsec and Chasm's sight.

"What will come of this war?" said Chasm.

"Nothing good," replied Primsec, "nothing good at all."

Line Of Defense

Darkness surrounded her everywhere as she sat up straight on the altar and swung her legs over one side. All of the fires in the room were gone, no longer flickering and reflecting their light off the walls. Scicremeon could see the wall in the distance, her blue eyes glowing in the darkness. Looking at herself she felt no different, but she could see a blue aura cast around her body. At first she thought it was the glow from her eyes, but realized the aura was vibrating and humming around her.

She narrowed her eyes as she looked down and jumped to the floor of the Chamber of Fires. With her eyes she searched around until she found the door and began walking toward it. As she began to move she felt heavier than she had before, and her stomach felt full as if she'd eaten too much.

Her steps echoed in the room as she traveled toward the door, noticing for the first time how long the walk was. It had seemed shorter when she'd come in, her mind focused on saving Aton. Presently, she wondered on everyone who'd been in the room with her. Her last memory was watching Pearl and Mastadon run from the room as the fires consumed the space. She'd lost consciousness a few moments after, and didn't know exactly how long she'd been out.

Scicremeon opened the door and immediately felt like the world had just come on, as the presence of eight beings rushed at her. She recognized Pearl, Mastadon, and Van Taven, but three were mysterious to her, though three were directly connected to her. The other seemed to be a spiraling mass of ambivalence that she couldn't read. And then as she thought of the boy she'd come to love, she felt the presence of Dark Angel and a small glimmer of Aton somewhere behind him.

The sunlight hit her face after she rounded a dozen or so corridors and began to push open the door in front of her, not entirely sure of where she was within the palace. She was following the feelings in her chest and the presence of the beings whose minds she could feel. As the door swung out, she found herself walking up a short flight of stone steps. As she scaled the short staircase, she saw the back of The Ragnon. *I wonder how different a fight would be now,* she thought finding some amusement in the memory and hope for another round with the beast.

She marched toward the edge of the mountain and looked over the precipice below and saw Pearl and Mastadon flanked by two women and another man. Slowly as she focused her eyes on them, she could recognize them from the stories she had read. In his sprawling white robes was Black Dawn's uncle, Gorgon-Ray. Standing a few feet to his right was Phray, the one she'd known as the Beautiful Huntress; seeking the hand of Black Dawn, the one thing that she could never have. And far off on the opposite side, standing next to Mastadon, was Maji, the queen of the Merridian gods.

Behind them stood Mysticgo, seemingly unafraid with his eyes pressed upward, watching a floating Dark Angel still possessing Aton's body. To his right stood Van Taven, who looked spent, tired from all of the ordeals he had been through. If it were up to her, he wouldn't have been there on the field. It looked like a battle was getting ready to rage and he seemed more like a wounded deer than a soldier ready for combat.

Opposite the gods and the magicians, standing still below a hovering Dark Angel was a red faced being that made the gods seem small in comparison. His face was cool, comfortable, and he seemed to be calculating, his eyes darting from one and then another in swift succession. She knew the gaze, Lance had taught her. He'd always say, *make them think you didn't fear them, even if you did. And if you didn't, spend even less time looking at them. It'll make them nervous, they'll be afraid of you, even if you think you'll lose. Any man who's afraid is usually a man who can't win.*

Worked for me, she thought, thinking of the many times she'd faced a horde of opponents and succeeded when the odds were far too unfavorable. Sometimes she didn't know how she managed to make it out alive with the few bruises she got. *I used to think it was luck,* she thought as she looked at her gauntleted hand and felt the suffocating feeling of the energy inside of her, and watched the energy swirling around her.

He seems too relaxed, Scicremeon thought to herself as she watched the man with the red face and black lips. He seemed too cool, content with being outnumbered. He had no weapon in his hand or on his person, but then she figured Dark Angel was weapon enough. He had been strong enough to floor three gods and two magicians with very little effort.

Then she noticed that he wasn't there, leading the charge, standing at the forefront of the line of defense the gods and magicians had made. He wasn't hovering like Dark Angel was above the head of anyone. She couldn't feel his presence or that of his father. She pushed her mind out to reach for them, and couldn't find them. Looking a few strides ahead of the line of gods she saw it. Reality struck her as she saw the black breastplate with the red phoenix. The gauntlets he wore were there tossed to either side of the breastplate. The black blade of his sword rested a foot or two beyond the armor that she'd grown to love as a girl. *Where is Black Dawn,* she thought to herself as if pleading. Her heart sank as she thought of him beaten and there was no one else there who could have been responsible. It could have been no one else, just the red faced being standing in opposition to the gods and Dark Angel in Aton's body, who appeared to be his servant.

"You'll have to kill us take the city," said Maji in defiance to Carnok as he stared at her smiling.

"That end would be regrettable, but it may be my only course if you choose not to kneel and follow my commands," said Carnok coolly.

"This is our home old one, your place is in the far reaches," said Gorgon Ray casting his watchful eyes on Carnok's.

"I have removed from this world the strongest two among you. That wretched black eyed fool you called king, and his meddlesome son, who the histories have praised," said Carnok disgusted. "They have both watched me coming and have seen the future I have planned, though the details were kept secret from them. But those gifts are gone now, and all you can do is either become a part of my plans, or die in opposition," said Carnok, his expression changing from calm to a serious scowl.

"Guess we'll all be dying today," said Mastadon. He wore a big smile and laughed hard.

"It is your order to give Maji," said Carnok, "would you allow a child to make such a decision."

Maji looked down at the ground and balled up her right fist, pulling it to her lips and breathing a long breath on top of her hand.

She thought for a long a moment, whispering something to herself. When she looked up, her face was hard, her eyes focused, but nothing of fear or anger rested there. Her tone was slow and measured as she began to speak. "For you who seems to know much of us, and we knowing little of you, must have forgotten the words of our mortals." Maji turned and looked at Mastadon and winked her right eye so Carnok could not see. "He who harms my king shall suffer in pain."

As her sentence drifted into the air, Mastadon brought his hands behind his head, hammer in hand, and flung it at Carnok. The top of the hammer smashed into his chest, sending him sprawling five feet into the ground.

"How do you like that for a decision," said Mastadon hopping up and down readying himself for a fight as his hammer zoomed back to his hand.

"Kill them all!" screamed Carnok as he stood up.

Dark Angel spun fast, moving inside of a raging tornado toward the line of gods. Dirt and blades of grass kicked up into the vortex swirling around him. Van Taven's hands alit with fire and sent a flaming ball toward Dark Angel. The ball of fire was sent flying back toward his position and he dived sideways to avoid it.

"Amateur," said Mysticgo as he watched Van Taven heave himself to the ground.

Dark Angel kept coming, Aton's arms folded across his chest, as he began to spew burning balls of flames from his eyes in every direction. Pearl raised her arms and brought up a shield of ice to protect herself, while Gorgon Ray rolled to his side. Maji took flight towards the spinning vortex and began opening her arms. She yelled out to Mysticgo, and he looked up as he was racing away from the center where the fight was.

"Join with me," said Maji as she watched Dark Angel coming toward her, just a few feet away.

"A rain of hail and ice," said Mysticgo loudly, still running away.

"My thoughts exactly," said Maji raising her gauntleted hand as her eyes began to glow. A bolt of lightning ripped across the sky as dark clouds began moving over the sky rapidly.

A rush of rain and frozen rain dropped down upon Dark Angel, as the weather continued to shift abruptly. Sharp pieces of ice caused numerous lacerations upon Aton's body that knocked Dark Angel off balance. The tornado spiraling around him began to dissipate into nothingness and Maji quickly shot toward him and kicked him out of the air, knocking him hard onto his back.

Pearl pushed her shield of ice toward him, but Dark Angel raised his hand quick enough to catch it. A hot flame swept around it, melting it as he stood up into the mud that the rain and ice had made below him. The lacerations on his arms began to heal and he laughed hideously.

Carnok was walking slowly toward Dark Angel, and Gorgon Ray began to trudge in his direction. Their eyes met and Carnok smiled as the distance between them closed. Dark Angel took flight into the air again throwing fireballs at the others. Mastadon marched toward Carnok as his uncle did and Carnok quickly took notice.

"This is hardly fair, two against one," said Carnok turning up his palms as if to say come on.

"We'll go easy on you," said Mastadon twirling his hammer around once.

"I meant not fair for you of course," said Carnok laughing softly.

Mastadon charged forward, hammer above his head and jumped ten yards, heading toward Carnok. He swung his hammer, the fat head of his hammer singing in the air. Carnok side stepped the blow and caught the hammer just below the head with his foot and kicked it down. Mastadon's legs went flapping into the air as the hammer landed a foot deep into the ground. Mastadon's eyes darted to the side as he felt himself lose control over his attack. He saw Carnok's head moving slowly up and down as if saying *yes*.

Smack!

The instep of Carnok's foot found Mastadon's chin. He passed out cold the moment the blow landed and went flying head first into the mountain. His body ripped through the hard rock a hundred feet.

By now Gorgon Ray had settled in front of Carnok and rested against his staff.

"Will you please allow me to pass, I have business to attend," said Carnok politely to Gorgon Ray.

"I wish that I could," said Gorgon Ray kicking up his trident and lunging toward Carnok. The sharp end of his trident collided with Carnok's hand and he used it like a blade, warding off Gorgon Ray's attacks. Gorgon Ray moved with blinding speed, increasing the speed and power of each attack, as he marched Carnok backward.

Gorgon Ray began to smile as his effort appeared to trouble Carnok, his face twisting into rage as the blows came faster and faster. Gorgon Ray's staff pushed against Carnok's chest driving him back, his feet pattering hard against the ground as he back pedaled fast, appearing to be ready to stumble. Gorgon Ray wheeled around swinging his staff at Carnok's stomach with howling fury. Carnok smiled and phased away. Gorgon Ray turned with all his might swinging and hit only air.

"Too slow old god," said Carnok, as he phased ten feet behind Gorgon Ray. Gorgon Ray spun around quickly and Carnok clapped his hands together hard. Gorgon Ray felt all the bones in his back shatter and he collapsed to the ground, falling on his face. His staff clanked twice before falling a few feet from him.

Van Taven saw Gorgon Ray fall and struggled to his feet. He raised his hands and began chanting a spell, focusing on Carnok. Blocks of iron sprang up from under the ground and folded into chains, with manacles at the end of them. They clamped around Carnok's arms, legs, and neck, squeezing tight around his limbs.

"Child's play," murmured Carnok as the chains broke upon the sound of his voice. Reaching his hands out as if interlocking fingers with a lover, Carnok closed his hands hard and the bones in Van Taven's hands cracked and broke in several places. Pounding the ends of his hands together, Carnok watched Van Taven's knees snap as he crumbled to the ground in excruciating pain. Van Taven went to reach for his knees, but found his hands in more pain.

"They are slowing us down," said Carnok to Dark Angel who was embroiled with Pearl, Maji, and Mysticgo.

Phray stood a few yards from Carnok, having not moved since Dark Angel roared toward them inside the vortex of the tornado. Her eyes were wide with wonder, seeing Mastadon and Gorgon Ray taken down by Carnok. Van Taven's defeat only proved how truly powerful Carnok was. Everything inside of her told her to run, but she was frozen with fear.

"I can smell your fear," said Carnok as he paraded toward her.

Phray was shaking her head *no*, her hands out in front of her in submission. As her fear rose, her feet pressed into the ground, and a wave of golden energy sprung up around her. The ground began to rumble and the great voice of a woman opened out into the air. "In place of the sovereign you must rule," said The Mother Merridia as golden energy began to bathe Phray. Her eyes turned black as The Black Moon and the golden wave of energy folded into Phray. "Bring down the Dark Angel," said The Mother Merridia, and the ground folded back to normal.

Carnok shot a black mass of energy at Phray. Phray reacted quickly, faster than her usual speed, bringing up a wall of golden energy. Carnok's blast rocked her shield and sent her sailing in the air. As she tumbled midflight, she pushed her hands down and righted herself.

"More delays," said Carnok. He raised his hand in Mysticgo's direction and swatted across his body. Crack. Mysticgo's left cheekbone snapped in two places as he pitched sideways, falling to the ground unconscious. "I must get to the flames Dark Angel. See that these creatures do not delay me further," said Carnok vanishing from the field below the mountain.

Scicremeon watched in horror as each of them fell, gods and magicians alike. Hardly any of them had been in close proximity to the red-faced being who struck them down like flies. *Who is he?* She wondered trying to remember the name Dark Angel spoke. His calm before the gods was no act of false courage. It was no ruse to throw his enemies off balance to make them think he didn't have fear. The red-faced hulk of a figure was too much for all the gods she had read about to deal with, and he knew it. *What could I do?* She thought to herself as she watched him vanish from the field of battle.

As Carnok disappeared, Phray launched herself toward Dark Angel to aid Maji and Pearl in their fight against him. Though Scicremeon knew Dark Angel possessed Aton, all that she could see was him. She could see past the fiery eyes and menacing voice.

He was still her student, her friend. *He's the only family I have,* thought Scicremeon as a single tear fell from her eye.

When Phray joined the battle, the tide began to turn against Dark Angel. She watched, and the gods seemed to be able to mount a successful offense against him. He struggled to gain the upper hand, as he seemed to have had against them, even when Van Taven and Mysticgo were involved.

Scicremeon could still feel the presence of the magicians and she was comforted to know that they were still alive. Behind her she heard something moving in the palace. *The flames he said,* she thought to herself as she looked at her glowing aura. Then, her memory began to come to her eyes as she remembered using the Strings of Fate to absorb The Blue Ember to free herself. But unknowing, she drew in all the fires inside the chamber and it overwhelmed her.

Dark Angel was reeling against Phray's new strength and Maji and Pearl kept pressing him, with energy blasts and gusts of freezing rain. The gods were relentless in their assault, and Dark Angel kept growing weaker and weaker. Scicremeon could feel Aton's consciousness trying to rise up from under the pressure of Dark Angel's consciousness. He felt her too, calling out to her, begging for her to save him.

"I will," yelled Scicremeon aloud to Aton. "Pearl, remember that it is Aton," said Scicremeon.

Pearl nodded in recognition of Scicremeon's words.

Scicremeon turned and ran quickly, rushing past The Ragnon, down the small staircase and back into the palace. As she rushed through the palace, she kept repeating the words that Lance had always said. "Do anything, do anything, do anything," as she rushed down each corridor.

The doors were familiar, big and imposing as they had been before. What lie behind those doors now she was aware of; for all of its contents were inside her, and there was nothing there but blackness? As she moved to open the door, she could hear voices behind it, tense, and angry.

"Forecon, you said this was where it was," said the red-faced being she'd seen make sport of the gods.

"I told you Carnok, that this is the Chamber of Fires," said Forecon.

"Kinozl," said Carnok.

"Yes brother, he speaks the truth," said Kinozl.

"Without the power of the flames I...," said Carnok stopping.

Scicremeon hadn't noticed but she'd brushed up against the door, causing the sound to echo inside of the chamber. *Do anything*, she thought to herself and pushed the door open hard. The door slammed into the wall of the chamber with a resounding boom. As she entered the room she knew that Carnok was the red faced being and Forecon was the one who appeared to be the skeleton of a dead man. Kinozl was unlike Carnok and Forecon, appearing to be saddened, her beautiful face filled with the pain of loss. Scicremeon knew the look, and she was sure that is the way she would look if something were to happen to Aton.

"Madam Scicremeon," said Carnok bowing to her.

Her face turned into an awful scowl of anger and annoyance. His feats of power no longer alarmed her or scared her, and he'd become like everyone else. She hated those words, miss, mam, and most of all madam. Madam screamed woman of refinement. A woman who ought to be respected for her title and looks. She knew she was beautiful but she didn't wear paint on her face and nails, and she didn't mind going a few extra days without shaving. Her business was war and blood and in that moment she remembered it. The faces of her victims flooded into her consciousness and washed away the sorrowful obligation that she felt for Aton. "Do I look like your grandmother," said Scicremeon, steel in her voice, rolling her eyes in exasperation.

Scicremeon saw Kinozl smile softly before her lips became a straight line. Forecon chuckled a bit and Carnok laughed his sarcasm without speaking.

"Of course not, seeing as I never had one," said Carnok tapping the altar with his knuckles. "But it seems that you are in possession of something far older than any grandmother," said Carnok looking at the blue aura swirling around Scicremeon's body.

"See something you like," said Scicremeon as she watched Carnok studying her body, his head tilting in every direction taking in her presence. She watched him sniff and take in whatever he smelled in the air, obviously savoring the aroma.

"Very much my dear," said Carnok rubbing his hands together looking at Kinozl and Forecon.

The man and woman who stood as tall as Carnok began stalking toward Scicremeon and she pulled her sword by reflex. Standing at the ready, Scicremeon watched as Forecon and Kinozl fanned out to try and take her flanks. As the two following Carnok's orders walked slowly in her direction, Carnok walked toward her, looking at her.

"Do they still refer to The Blue Ember, as the Fires of Aygron," said Carnok raising an eyebrow to Scicremeon.

"What do you know of my father?" said Scicremeon.

"Far more than you do my dear Scicremeon, daughter of the Stormblade," said Carnok with a smile. "I should, since I am the one who killed him." Carnok began laughing devilishly as anger tore at Scicremeon's face.

Her hand gripped her sword tighter and she stood waiting for him to come.

"To think, I compelled good King Chale to send his armies to Merridia again, after so many one sided defeats at the hands of your father. But your brothers were nothing like your father. They lacked his thirst for blood. Your father took sheer pleasure in watching a man's back hit the ground. Funny, history always seems to favor the warlords, and not those who make peace. I still wonder how I missed your mother's pregnancy," said Carnok rubbing his chin.

Scicremeon wanted to call him a liar, say that his words were untrue, but she believed him. He relished in taking the blame for her father's death. It's what she would have done; rubbed it in as he was doing.

"I knew your father had no heart to tend to the fields and be a good husband. And Marside in all its barbarism demands revenge. Thus I split myself in two, one trickster and one swordsman. They were two very different opponents, but neither could your father best. The black-eyed king did not offer his hand that day either, and thus it was easy. The Blue Ember was supposed to leave him, return to the Chamber of Fires, where I could seize it. But it went to you and I had to wait until it manifested itself," said Carnok standing two feet from Scicremeon, a smile still painted on his face as he told the story.

Tears were streaming down her face and she forgot that she was a god and had no need for air. She was panting, her chest heaving up and down, the painful feelings of a fatherless child rising up inside of her. *Better to die, sword in hand, than wrinkled old, cold in bed.* The words hung in her mind for a moment as she thought of her favorite line from her father's journal. His wisdom extended outside of fighting, but when he wrote about war, he seemed most alive to her. And she knew the things she had been told by Lance, were things her father believed in. He'd written it many times early on in his journal when his prowess was not yet established. It was in those days where he felt fear and wanted nothing more than to live in the face of death, when he wrote, *do anything.*

Scicremeon sprang forward, her sword swinging wildly in a circle as Forecon and Kinozl tried to press toward her. On the back swing, she aimed at Carnok's neck, The Blue Ember covering her sword as it did her body. He laughed as she missed and it only served to anger her further. She moved with more speed than Gorgon Ray had, and felt more powerful than ever before. The second blow nearly struck and Carnok let out a short gasp of air. Forecon and Kinozl stalked her from behind, but each time they got within five feet, The Blue Ember would burst out toward them, growling like an angry beast.

"Die you coward," said Scicremeon pushing faster toward Carnok. She slammed the point of her sword into Carnok's chest and watched sparks fly between her sword and his chest. He began to stumble and Scicremeon loosed the Strings of Fate, the golden bands gripping him by the throat. "Uh," said Scicremeon as she began to pull at his life force. "Die!" she screamed aloud, her anger echoing through the chamber as Carnok reached for his neck.

Scicremeon felt his life force pour into her, filling her up, and then she felt it expanding inside of her. She felt like she was ready to burst but as she drew in more, she felt herself becoming intoxicated, her body growing weaker.

A viscous frown took over Carnok's face as he righted himself and stood over Scicremeon as she fell to her knees. Her energy was spent and she knew it had been a mistake to try and take his life with the Strings of Fate.

Carnok pulled the strings from his neck and they recoiled back into the Hand of Destruction. He grabbed her by the throat and raised her up over his head, looking into her eyes. She let her sword fall to the floor as she grabbed at his wrist with both hands.

She tried clawing at his red flesh, but it was too hard, and screeched loud like stone being dragged across metal.

"Valiant effort my dear, I am truly impressed. You would have made a fine servant of my cause. But you have the flames, and I cannot allow you to keep them," said Carnok.

A small comet the size of a pebble floated from Carnok's right eye and struck Scicremeon across the chin. Her eyes closed, seeing nothing but black.

Sacrifice

The suns of Merridia blazed hot upon the surface as the three of them decreased their size and crossed into the planet's atmosphere. Merridia was turning fast in its orbit as it always had, a great portion of the planet covered in darkness. Thutmos could see the firelight flickering in the villages and cities across the planet aiding the great light of The Black Moon. The mortals of the old planet didn't know that up in the heavens, a great battle was raging between a malevolent spirit hell-bent on their destruction, and the gods who ruled them.

Thutmos could feel the energies colliding between them, three gods facing the splintered presence of his brother Carnok. He knew Dark Angel well, an old nemesis of all the worlds. This wasn't the first time Carnok planned on the destruction of a planet through Dark Angel's hand. At times he'd succeeded, but whenever Dark Angel crossed paths with Corvus, he'd fallen. The spell he'd casted on the day Corvus was born didn't allow for anyone to overpower him while on Merridia. Dark Angel's separation from Carnok's true self made him susceptible to that power.

"I cannot sense Corvus," said Everdon curiously.

"I've noticed he is not there on Merridia. But I cannot find his consciousness anywhere else either," said Thutmos, his brow falling over his eyes.

"Black Dawn is not there either," said Everdon.

"Then the situation is as bad as we've imagined," said Thutmos beginning to push his mind out to Everdon and Luminar.

Their pace quickened and in a matter of seconds they could see Algar, the palace rising up on top of a mountain. The presence of their siblings was strong inside the palace and they knew their presence was felt as well. Luminar and Everdon looked at one another, as they felt another presence within the palace. Suddenly they both looked toward the fight between the gods and Dark Angel and their eyes expanded in surprise at the same time.

"Yes, he's taken the body of a child this time," said Thutmos, a frown wrinkling his face. "The boy is special, he's chosen wisely," said Thutmos as if impressed.

"What does it mean?" said Luminar hungry for information.

"The boy allowed Dark Angel to thwart Corvus's power on Merridia," said Thutmos.

"Indeed," said Everdon anger painting his face.

"It is almost the perfect combination of power," said Thutmos moving faster. "But like everything it has its weakness. The Mother Merridia has placed another of her children in the role of sovereign in Corvus's absence. Dark Angel's strength is waning, but...," said Thutmos with a slight smile. Then his face turned to a mask of contemplation as he stopped speaking midsentence.

"I see now," said Luminar. "How can we reverse the effect?" she begged of Thutmos.

"We must break the bond," said Thutmos looking bemused, "but the consequences could be great if their minds become one." Thutmos finished and felt a surge of power rise up in Dark Angel and he watched him swat Pearl to the ground, sending her sliding thirty feet.

"Intervene," said Thutmos to Everdon and Luminar, the two of them turning toward the fight that Pearl was knocked out of.

Two beams of light shot from the palace as Forecon and Kinozl made a beeline for Everdon and Luminar. Only a few seconds elapsed as a magnificent sonic boom erupted, cracking the ground several miles.

"Take Carnok, we'll break these two," said Everdon excited as Forecon collided with him.

Thutmos pressed his mind out to them, *take care*, and then vanished from the field outside of the palace.

Scicremeon had regained consciousness, her back pressed again against the stone altar that had seemed like her prison before she absorbed The Blue Ember. The fullness that she'd felt before had gone away, and she could see that many of the fires she'd absorbed were back where they had been when she entered the chamber. The kaleidoscope began to reform around her, and the Chamber of Fires was becoming the bright hot place it had been before. She could feel Carnok's cold breath on her face as he stood over her, his hands gliding from side to side, drawing the fires out of her.

A hot ball of green flame rose from out of her stomach and whiffed its heat back in its old place. The great strength she felt when she'd struck Carnok with her sword seemed to run away from her. She gasped as another ball of fire left her body.

"What are you doing?" said Scicremeon to get him to talk, wanting him to stop so she could think of a way to free herself again.

"Taking what you stole," said Carnok with a smile, still waving his hands.

He can read my mind, thought Scicremeon trying to shield her thoughts from him.

"Even with these primordial life giving energies, you cannot hope to keep your mind closed to me," said Carnok looking at her quizzically. "It is a shame I'll have to kill you," he said as if pained by the prospect of her death.

"Will you really?" said Scicremeon somewhat sardonically.

"Yes child. But at least you have some humor about it, which makes the prospect of that end far more regrettable for me," said Carnok, in his most endearing voice. His eyes glistened as if he was going to shed a tear.

"You should do it now, because if it were me your neck would already be broken," said Scicremeon trying to sit up, unable to push against the force that kept her back pressed to the altar. Her teeth were grinding together, her lips stretching across her face, as the veins in her neck bulged. Her anger poured out and a rush of The Fires of Aygron spewed from her mouth.

"In due time my dear, in due time," said Carnok leaning over her, his hands pressed against the altar, his face directly over her own.

"Do it now," she said trying to push her head up so he could feel her warm breath on his face.

"Once I have The Blue Ember, I will put you out of your misery," said Carnok as he stood back up and began waving his hands over Scicremeon again.

"Why do you need it if you're so powerful," said Scicremeon trying to bide her time again. She wanted nothing more for him to stop waving his hands again.

"There are others like me. Watchers of the universe we were, The Twelve, all of us, titans, children of Aeon, Maker of All Things," said Carnok, his hands no longer waving, clasped behind his back.

"Ages ago, long before any of the mortals of Merridia breathed in life, we were of one mind in Our Union. Though we were a collective, I soon found that I was the weakest among us in power. There was a pecking order, even among this sacred bond of minds that were to watch and keep the balance. My brother, the oldest of us was the first, the strongest, called by our Father, The Most Favored. With his voice he could force his will upon us, though seldom did he. He was too busy contemplating, bored, seemingly tired of the way things were. And when I found what his wants were I decided that I wanted the same thing. I spread fire and discord across the universe and when I did, I finally knew my purpose," said Carnok looking up, the dancing flames shedding light on his face.

Scicremeon's scowl changed; her face relaxing as Carnok spoke, moved by his voice, the presence of truth apparent. She couldn't read any lie in his telling and deep interest rose up inside of her.

"I made the Dark Angel to be the negative, to be the force that was counter to the expectation of righteousness. It was always there with us, the other side of the balance, but we were made to think that we should all serve the same purpose. But how can there be good without evil, happiness without sorrow? Nature is unkind, and unyielding to the whims of those who do not have power. I having the least of my brethren decided that I should be as powerful as The Most Favored. That is where your father came in. He was my first sacrifice to this end," said Carnok woefully.

"How could my father serve the purpose of someone who even the gods cannot challenge?" she said remembering how easily he had beaten Mastadon and Gorgon Ray.

"At every turn my brother foiled my plots, but with each defeat I grew more determined. He knew I sought the life giving energies of the Spring of Creation. And so he gave them away to his beloved Corvus," said Carnok.

The image of the king of the gods of Merridia quickly registered in Scicremeon's mind. Carnok told her of the spell that Thutmos had cast at Corvus's birth and how his power was too great to be challenged on Merridia. He told of her of how Dark Angel, being a piece of himself could not stand up to Corvus's power, and that he'd always overcome him.

"Over time, Corvus's power became so great that even one such as I would be hard pressed to supplant him upon the soils of this sphere. His removal would have to happen quickly, within a small window of time when an opposing force was strong enough to overcome him. For on Merridia, everyone is at the mercy of Corvus. But that power could not be detected, it had to be suppressed as it made its way here," said Carnok shaking his head *yes* as the realization crept into Scicremeon's expression.

Aton, she thought floored, unable to think of him as an instrument of the destruction of the mightiest god on Merridia. Dark Angel had him, pressing his consciousness away from the world. Keeping him veiled in the darkest reaches of his own mind, so he could supplant the order of things upon Merridia.

"So you destroy a boy in order to see your plans through," said Scicremeon disgusted.

"Destroy?" said Carnok curiously. "No, the boy is the perfect vessel."

"Vessel?" said Scicremeon confused.

"For Dark Angel," said Carnok smiling wide. "He was born at the perfect time. Every one hundred million years it happens, all of the planets in the universe align. But each time it happened, no one was ever born, not until twelve years ago." Carnok giggled happily, great joy painting his face. "When my brother stole these flames of life and placed them here under the protection of Corvus, that black eyed fool gave the most precious one of them all to your father."

"Why didn't he take it for himself?" asked Scicremeon, the anger she had kept bottled up for so many years spilling out again. Here she was in the presence of her father's killer and she had no way to stop him, no means to defeat him. *Wouldn't the fire be better protected by a god*, she thought to herself. The question *why*, wracked her mind.

"Because it could only be given to a mortal," said Carnok rolling his eyes. "And for so long as that mortal bore children, The Blue Ember would pass down the line, keeping me from its power. When the flame did not come to me after Dark Angel's departure from Merridia, I knew there was another child. Thus I had to wait." Carnok finished and moved his arms from behind his back.

"Why?" said Scicremeon, not wanting him to begin again. She had never feared death, but knowing when it would come was unsettling.

"There are rules to everything. The Law of Power does not lend itself to chance. Had you not possessed The Blue Ember, the very gauntlet you wear would have incinerated your flesh. Black Dawn meant to protect you from your father's fate and keep the flame from the hands of his father's enemies."

"But-,' said Scicremeon cut off.

"Falling in love with you only made the prospect of your godhood more appealing," said Carnok with a sly smile as he watched Scicremeon's cheeks flush red. "Since you had no children, you going to Chalendor a mortal was too risky. There would be no barrier between me and the flame. But if you were a god, the flame could only be taken while you were in the Chamber of Fires. He knew Dark Angel could not win a battle against his father, but the good thing was he had no knowledge of me." Carnok smiled wide and then waved his hands above Scicremeon and the flames in the room whooshed and flapped harder as if caught in a powerful gust of wind.

A yellow flame shot from her gut; then red, then white, then orange, each setting itself down amongst the others. Scicremeon shook her head no, the flames leaving her faster than before. She tried to speak, but Carnok shushed her, a screeching wind cutting between his teeth, and her mouth closed. She was unable to move it, and her mind raced. *Please answer me*, she thought, pressing her mind toward Carnok.

"You've delayed me long enough and my brother will breech my defenses, soon. I'll need you to die before then," said Carnok with a sad expression that reeked of sarcasm and indifference.

Scicremeon closed her eyes as she felt the flames inside her leaving, her former godlike strength feeling weak compared to the power she'd held. *If only I'd acted earlier,* she thought wondering what the outcome would have been had she sprang into action while she stood upon the mountain. But her gut told her that Carnok would have only had to drag her further by the throat to the Chamber of Fires. He'd been clear that even with the strength of the flames she'd be no match for him. That much he proved after she touched him with her sword.

The Blue Ember rose up around her as the last flame found its resting place. Slowly, the blue flame rose up into the air, leaving her, gathering a few feet above her. The flame began to build, pushing itself out toward the other flames, connecting to them, creating a vortex within the Chamber of Fires. Scicremeon could feel the flame being pulled up, and pieces of her life force being swept up with it. Her eyes glowed, two beams of blue light connecting to The Blue Ember above her. She screamed and a beam of blue light erupted from her mouth. Her knuckles slapped against the altar, beams shooting out of her palms into the ember.

Weaker and weaker she grew, her life force being dragged out, all of the flame that sprung up around the altar drifting toward the dark blue fire above. Fatigue began to set in and the jewels on her gauntleted hand stopped glowing, and the Strings of Fate drifted upward toward the flame connecting to the ball of blue fire. The golden strings began to glow and then the reverberating gold light swept down the string and rushed into her chest and then back out, dragging her life force upward to the fire.

Her eyes rolled around in her head, her life flashed before her eyes, a thousand images seemed to sprint across her eyes all at once in vivid detail. Her head slid from side to side as she felt intoxication drifting into her veins, but she hadn't had a drink in weeks. None of her bodily functions seemed to work, but her hearing was acute as her mind began to drift, her body weakening by the second.

"Goodbye my dear," said Carnok and she saw his hand go up.

Scicremeon had always thought she wanted to see her death, watch her killer swing the final blow, while she looked into his eyes with defiance. She imagined herself cursing and spitting, pushing them to get on with the deed. Her anger and her rage, her careless nature even in her defeat, would break their spirit, their resolve, and haunt them for all of their days. She knew with Carnok this would not be the case. There was nothing she could say or do that would still his hand. She was a barrier to his power, nothing more than an obstacle to be traversed.

She forced her eyes closed and sucked in air that she didn't need. She heard his arm swing fast and felt the inevitability of the moment creep into her mind. But a weighty voice, full of power and wrath changed her mood. She released the breath when she heard him saying.

"I have always been there to make sure that you fail, brother," said a voice more powerful, more regal than she had ever heard. And in his words she found comfort. A smile painted her face when she heard Carnok speak.

"Now we end this brother."

In their minds they could hear Carnok and Thutmos doing battle. Even Maji and Phray could hear that something was amiss within the palace. The entire structure shook violently and the heavens of Merridia changed through a hundred different weather patterns. The planet was sprinting in its orbit and The Black Moon had passed them a hundred times in a matter of seconds. Phray and Maji could feel the presence of beings, strong like Carnok though their power wasn't nearly as potent. They were warring above them, moving too fast for even gods to see. They appeared as blurs in the changing weather conditions as the planet sped through its orbit, years seeming to pass them by as if they had never happened.

Below them, on the surface of Merridia, they could feel children dying, the oldest of the mortals growing weary, falling sick, dying, and young people aging more rapidly than they should.

Maji and Phray looked at one another with fear, their eyes telling one another that they didn't know what they should do. The palace continued to shake and the outer walls began to crack as they heard loud booms echoing from inside. Above them the same was happening as the blurs continued to race across the heaven sky, sending shockwaves rippling across the heavens.

Out of nowhere they heard a voice in their minds, its power heavy and full of malice. They'd felt it before from the red faced being who fell their fellow gods. His voice begged those above.

I need your power now, it said in pain, the echoing booms still erupting within the palace walls. The western-most tower that rose up high into the clouds cracked off and fell to the ground below the mountain. Sheets of magnificent gold broke away and fell to the ground as the entire planet began to shake. Death was all around them, more of their mortal children falling dead below. More of the young had become old, and sickness and weariness took them.

The gods could taste the fear as the mortals fell down dead under the weight of the war around them. The war that they had been engaged in set off a chain reaction of destruction.

"This must have been the great calamity Dorrin had spoken of," said Maji to Phray who was still standing there shocked.

"What can we do?" asked Phray.

Crack!

A resounding echo of the impact reverberated through the air as Dark Angel had swept down and batted Maji down, her eyes rolling into the back of her head. Dark Angel's eyes were blazing orange in Aton's face, the boy's small body wrapped in fiery energy, his small lips squeezed together in a ferocious grimace.

"Now it's just you and me," said Dark Angel, the vicious tenor of his voice scraping through the air.

Above them they heard four loud cracks, four simultaneous gasps of surprise and shock. The violent shaking of the planet ceased, and the death below stopped. The rapid orbit slowed to its normal crawl and four beings high above them fell down black against the ground where they stood. Phray was shocked at what had occurred, seeing the beings twice her size fall to their deaths, the war between them that was ripping Merridia apart, seemingly over.

As Dark Angel whirled around after having swatted Maji down, Phray wondered what she could do. Who could win against the red-faced one now that he had the power of four like him? She knew that their sacrifice would make him stronger.

In horror she watched as the top of the palace ripped open, the red-faced being and another being even larger, his face as black as space; rising up from out the palace. The walls of the palace began to shake and then they faltered, the entire structure cracking under intense pressure. The red-faced being and the black-faced being rocketed toward space, growing at an alarming rate, ten times, and then twenty times the size they are already were. Quickly they broke out of Merridia's atmosphere and she could no longer see them.

Still looking at her, Dark Angel was smiling, Aton's hands balled into fists.

"I'm going to break you in half," said Phray, her face a mass of anger.

Phray and Dark Angel rushed toward each other and thunder and lightning erupted across the heavens again as the palace of the Merridian gods tumbled to rubble.

Child Of Providence

Chasm and Primsec broke into Merridia's atmosphere a few moments after Forecon, Everdon, Luminar, and Kinozl fell to their deaths. They'd felt all of the death on Merridia, the disastrous power of the battle echoing across the cosmos. Primsec and Chasm felt each death and it gnawed at them. The demise of Merridia seemed imminent, an inevitable effect of the fight between the members of Our Union. The sudden end of the catastrophic effects gave them a measure of comfort, but they could feel another battle, far more disastrous echoing in the blackness of space.

On their way to Merridia they saw stars devoid of light, suns cracked and cold. Dozens of planets had shattered and drifted from their orbits. Entire galaxies between Earth and Merridia had faded from existence. The effects of the war between The Twelve had spread far from the center of the universe. A chain reaction of destruction had begun that had to be stopped.

They believed that taking sides would cause more harm than good, and thus they had stayed away. Yet, as they sat there feeling, knowing what would happen, they were spurred into action by intense sorrow. If they didn't do something, then they would be accepting the outcome of the winner. One of them would win, Thutmos or Carnok, but the universe would suffer regardless.

Chasm convinced Primsec to come and he flew by her side, unhappy, not even the glimmer of a smile permeating his being. He was melancholy, almost broken by the loss of more of his brethren. His feelings poured from him, slipping into the universe, hoping to repair the things that were broken. There were some things he could save, but others had already entered the Void of No Return, where not even one of Our Union could return dead things to life.

"Can you feel that?" said Chasm, feeling as if something were pulling at her essence.

"Yes, the intensity has been increasing as we came nearer to Merridia," said Primsec as they got closer to Phray and Dark Angel. "Their bond is not yet complete."

"Then I can help the boy to severe their bond," said Chasm staring intensely at Aton, possessed by Dark Angel.

"Are you willing to make such a sacrifice?" said Primsec looking at her, his eyes full of the pain in his heart.

"I am not as strong outside of Thutmos's company and you are our best hope in seeing an end to their quarrel. There is hope that he may listen to you," said Chasm closing her eyes hard, forcing back her own sorrow.

Aton was still pressed hard against a wall in a dark room, still reeling from his encounter with Carnok. Dark Angel's presence was growing, meshing with his consciousness. He could feel it happening, like a tip toeing walk up his essence. Who and what he was, was changing. Aton felt the anger and hatred that consumed Dark Angel's mind. Any time he tried he'd failed; failed to keep himself away from the want to cause pain, to seek out vengeance, and to kill. He felt the pleasure that Dark Angel felt each time one of the gods fell. There was an intense love of the deed when he struck Maji down. He had reveled in the destruction of the palace of the gods as Carnok warred with another of his brethren.

The enjoyment that rushed over Dark Angel when the four titans above them fell was intoxicating, even to Aton. When it happened he felt horrible, as his heart and mind craved for more. As he remained folded in a ball, stuck beneath the force of Dark Angel's mind, he no longer tried to fight the impulses. He often lost his nerve and offered pieces of himself. Only when he gave himself unto Dark Angel did he feel in any ease from the overwhelming torment. Only then did the voices stop. For all of the destruction that Dark Angel craved, there was comfort in it. It was easy not to feel, to let go of himself and yield to the dark side.

Each time he questioned his heart, and sought the calm and quiet of his own mind, Dark Angel's voice would seep into his ear. Carnok's presence would enter his mind and walk toward him begging for his hand. It implored him to forget his own life, to be made anew. *I'll take you home,* the voice kept saying. *Don't you want to go home?* That's what they'd ask, as it was all that Aton wanted.

He wanted to go back to Marside and see his mother, sit with her by the fire as she made him a blanket. He craved the barrels of ale that he'd spend the day making and rolling to the market. Scicremeon would be there leaning against a beam, chewing on straw or the meat of some unlucky beast she'd taken down in the woods. The way he had known was hard, but it was all that appealed to him. It was the only thing he could hang onto now. Any time he let go, he lost himself.

Aton could feel his fist crashing into Phray's gut and then her face, driving her backwards. He felt the hot balls of fire spewing from his eyes, assaulting the ground as Phray slipped out of the way.

Her strength was greater than his own and Dark Angel's. But he could feel a sea of fire and vengeance building up inside of his gut.

Phray was strong, but he knew once the sea inside him had filled, then a ferocious wave would spill over and the strength he'd felt when his hands threw Corvus from the planet would return. It was only a matter of time. All the confidence that the new sovereign was feeling would melt away.

Don't hurt them anymore, thought Aton to Dark Angel.

They would kill us, thought Dark Angel to Aton as he spun to avoid a projectile from Phray.

Please, thought Aton again.

Give in and become who you were born to be, thought Dark Angel, offering Aton to give of his entire self. *Your hand is not enough, give of your essence,* thought Dark Angel with more force.

Aton retreated again, trying not to yield his essence to Dark Angel. He knew if he did, there'd be no return. He wouldn't be able to go back.

Unexpectedly, he felt a benevolent spirit behind his body, and Dark Angel turned, his eyes going wide, astonished at who he saw. Her body cast a shadow over Aton's small frame and Dark Angel tried to retreat, but she caught Aton by his neck. The black mist began to creep from him, covering the woman's body, still connected to Aton.

He felt her fold into his consciousness, while Dark Angel tried to fight her. Aton heard Phray's feet pattering as she sprinted up behind him, and jumped into the air. The blow nearly landed but the black mist of Dark Angel's presence reached out. Aton felt the sea inside him explode outward, smashing into Phray, assaulting her with rapid bursts of booming attacks.

Phray's back crashed into the ground ten feet as she fell down unconscious.

Suddenly, the woman who had Aton by the neck was inside of his mind. He could see her, a blue light glowing all around her. She looked magnificent, calm, walking slowly toward him, a smile painted across her face. She stretched out her hand, palm facing up, and Aton's eyes met her own. Her eyes were warm and welcoming, glistening in the darkness of his mind.

Behind her he could see Dark Angel hovering, creeping along slowly behind her, his fiery eyes on Aton. Dark Angel's head shook side to side, his face pleading, the frown on his face a threat. On his left and right he saw two images of Carnok; hand outstretched making his way toward him.

"Keep your eyes on me child," said the woman walking toward him, a smile still on her face.

Aton's knees were pressed into his chest, his arms wrapped around them. He kept his eyes glued to the woman who had drawn closer to him, her voice enchanting, though nothing of it scared him. He could sense the honesty in her voice and pushed himself up against the wall. He stood flattened to the wall, his arms touching the hard surface of his mind.

"Who are you?" begged Aton, his voice cracking, still afraid of Dark Angel and the presence of Carnok there in his mind still approaching.

"I am Chasm," said Chasm standing before Aton, looking down upon him.

Aton tilted his head back to look up at Chasm, amazed at her beauty. Her presence comforted him and he no longer felt afraid.

"Are you going to save me?" said Aton bedazzled by Chasm, no longer thinking of or feeling the horrors that Dark Angel pressed upon him.

"No, you must save yourself," said Chasm.

"How?" begged Aton confused at her remark.

"I will break the bond between you and I will tell you your real name, Child of Providence," said Chasm whispering in Aton's ear.

Chasm's face began to glow a brilliant gold, Aton was unable to see, blinded by the magnificent light. He saw her hand reach upward, disappearing into her face and then coming back out slowly. In her hand was a ring of gold, the magnificent light that had lit up her face gone, her normal color returning. Chasm held the golden ring together with her palms and placed it upon Aton's head.

Aton's eyes blinked rapidly, changing every color in the color spectrum and then stopped suddenly. His eyes shined a brilliant gold as the ring began to seep into his head. As the ring disappeared he watched Chasm's eyes roll into the back of her head, her lovely face turning the darkest black he'd ever seen. He watched her fall straight back, nothing to stop her fall, and as she hit the ground her entire body shattered. A wave of energy burst up from the place where she fell and shot through him. The ring that had slipped into his head burst outward, colliding with the two Carnoks and Dark Angel in his mind sending them flying from his sight.

Aton saw the cracked ground below him, blades of dead grass and broken rock surrounding him. His eyes tingled, and he blinked slowly, his head feeling light as he looked at his hands. They were upon earth, moving at the behest of his mind. He wiggled his fingers quickly and smiled, happy to be in control himself.

Picking up his head he looked in front of him and saw the black dust of Chasm floating away into the air. Dark Angel was standing already, his pale face angry, his eyes burning, full of rage.

"You betrayed me," said Dark Angel menacingly.

"You lied to me," said Aton.

"Never," said Dark Angel emphatically walking toward Aton. "I am going to take you home now."

"I don't need you to," said Aton, his voice growing deeper, sounding like a man fully grown.

"Why not?" said Dark Angel, his eyes erupting with flame, his hands glowing with hot orange fire.

"Because I know who I am now," said Aton.

"Just who is that, hmmm," said Dark Angel drawing up his hands together over his head. "A dead boy," said Dark Angel whipping his hand down, a ball of fire heading toward Aton.

"No," said Aton looking at the ball of fire blazing toward him. Dark Angel gasped in shock as Aton reached out in front of him, catching the ball of flame on his palm. "I am Syaxis," said Aton as his eyes glowed a brilliant gold. Golden energy wrapped itself around the fireball, consuming it, the energy in Aton's hand radiating like the sun.

Shifting his weight, Aton pushed his hand forward and a beam of energy rushed forward too fast for Dark Angel to react, slamming into him. Instead of knocking him backward, the golden beam of energy enveloped him compressing Dark Angel. Dark Angel screamed with fear, the energy folding him inside of a ball the size of a man's fist. Aton could hear him screaming, promising him that he'd come back to take his revenge as the ball bobbed there.

For a few more seconds the ball of energy floated in circular motions and then shot toward space, out of Merridia's atmosphere.

"Ugh," Aton gasped and began falling down weak, his eyes returning to their normal brown hue. His lids closed over his eyes and he fell asleep, falling.

"Aton!" screamed Scicremeon as she caught him, just before he hit the ground, falling on her butt, the boy cradled in her arms. "Uh," she said relived. "You're going to be in trouble when you wake up boy, big trouble," said Scicremeon, tears falling on her cheeks as she kissed Aton on the forehead.

Around them was nothing but carnage. The heavens were in turmoil and the planet began to shake violently again. Scicremeon sat there with Aton rocking back and forth, feeling the battle being waged between the two titans who had destroyed the palace of the gods. Merridia had begun to spin rapidly again and she could feel the people below her aging and dying again.

The war wasn't over, and she could feel that her life force and all the gods fallen about the broken ground not yet dead, beginning to feel the effects. Lightning and thunder filled the heavens and she saw two of the suns of Merridia shatter and disappear from their orbit. Scicremeon was horror struck as she sat there rocking back and forth with Aton in her arms. *Lance, old friend, I don't know if doing anything now will matter*, thought Scicremeon. She knew at that moment that her own fate, no longer rested in her hands.

The Law Of Power

The cosmos were in disarray and Primsec could feel the universe unraveling around him. The turmoil in Merridia had begun again and with Thutmos and Carnok fighting, the ripple effect happened faster. He'd seen Carnok throw two of the suns of Merridia at Thutmos before the two disappeared from the solar system.

He'd chased them through a myriad of galaxies as they fought, spreading their destruction everywhere. Each time they changed locations, it set off a chain reaction that spread out across the cosmos. And every time the calamity of one galaxy reached out and touched another, the destruction sped up, binding together to create a single event. Primsec guessed it wouldn't take long before all of the destruction the two were causing would become woven together.

Primsec pressed his mind out to them dozens of times, but neither responded, though he knew they could hear him.

Through another galaxy he went behind his two brothers. The galaxy seemed untouched by their fight, even as they drew closer. And then Primsec felt what he'd always felt when he'd entered there. The presence of Aeon stirred from the third planet in a barred spiral galaxy. He saw them racing toward it, growing smaller as they shot through the atmosphere, a huge sonic boom erupting upon impact.

Faster Primsec went following them, decreasing his own mass as he zipped through Earth's atmosphere, landing where he believed Thutmos and Carnok had fallen.

Thutmos's hand rung Carnok's neck, keeping him pressed down upon his knees. Thutmos's mouth was twisted in anger, his eyes set on Carnok's as the two stared at one another. Carnok's arms dangled by his sides and he made no attempt to free himself from Thutmos's grip. He only stared at Thutmos with his fiery eyes, a smirk lining his face.

"I have always been there to stop you," said Thutmos angry.

"That you have been brother."

"Did you think that this time would be any different?"

"Oh yes, this time I had allies. This time I was able to make the others see."

"See what?"

"That we want the same thing. Only you still don't know it."

"Your riddles bore me. They have always bored me," said Thutmos emphatically, pushing Carnok as he released his grip and took a step back.

"My riddles are truth. You are still unwilling to believe what you know and thus you do not act," said Carnok walking toward Thutmos who had turned from him.

"What? That our lord has given of his essence to these creatures," said Thutmos fuming.

"Yes, it was promised to us," said Carnok, "The Law of Power states-."

"The Law of Power states that I am first among the children of Aeon. That none shall have my place in all the days of life before or after The Bringer of All," said Thutmos raging, as he cut Carnok off. "This is the place from which you have stolen your power. Where you have spread your poison and discord; and it shall be the place of your fall. You've tried to take from Our Union to suit your goals, but our essence did not lie in our shells. But in these," said Thutmos raising his hand to his forehead.

Four of the golden rings he'd take from the fallen members of Our Union drifted from his head and floated around above him. Their humming intensified as they moved and Carnok could hear the voices of his brethren. He gasped at feeling their presence.

"The Law of Power cannot be undone," said Thutmos. "You could never have become first among us, for I am first among us until the ending of time and beyond."

Carnok fell to his knees and bowed to Thutmos, his head pressed to the ground. He smelled the jasmine flowers around him in the field of grass that stretched out for miles. The soil was wet from rain and he watched the insects crawling below him. He could feel Aeon's presence even in them. A man walked through the field and Aeon's presence enveloped him and he wept.

"Are you ready to do your duty?" said Thutmos standing over Carnok.

"Yes my lord," said Carnok touching Thutmos's boot, groveling to him like a servant. "I shall serve your will."

"Then join your brethren so that you might," said Thutmos. "This fight has long been over," his voice rolling like a billion raging storms, pressing down upon Carnok, willing him, forcing him to comply.

"My power wanes, it flees me," said Carnok.

"The fires of the Spring of Creation, the essence of these creatures does not belong to you, but to all the worlds," said Thutmos.

"You have broken our sacred bond and the Chain of Balance has been remade anew."

Carnok stood and opened his arms, watching as Thutmos raised his hand to him. Thutmos's palm was just a foot from Carnok's chest. They stood there for a long moment like that, Thutmos doing nothing, Carnok waiting, his eyes facing the heavens of the Earth. He felt comforted there as Chasm and Primsec had. He felt Aeon's presence emanating from everything there.

"Have you understood the new balance brother," said Primsec walking toward them, four golden rings rotating above his head as he drew closer to them.

"Brother," said Thutmos thrilled to see Primsec there.

"Have you?" said Primsec, his voice earnest as he looked for Thutmos to answer.

"Brethren," said Thutmos as he heard the rings humming above Primsec's head as they circled around. He could hear their voices. Hearing them caused him a simultaneous joy and pain all at once.

"Answer me this thing which I ask," said Primsec.

"I will not stop. No! I will not give him my forgiveness until he is but a memory of Our Union," said Thutmos screaming at Primsec.

Suddenly an intense humming came from the sky, where the sun shined down upon the Earth. There was a trail of brilliant gold light behind it as it came. A whooshing sound occurred as another golden ring came and bobbed between Carnok and Thutmos.

"Chasm," said Thutmos woefully.

"Yes, she sacrificed herself for the child of the Syaxis alignment," said Primsec almost harshly.

"He would have succeeded had she not," said Thutmos. The realization setting in and he blinked his eyes in pain.

"But our brother has been stopped because of her sacrifice. The enchantments he placed upon Forecon and Kinozl destroyed all of our brethren at once, giving him more power. The Blue Ember was nearly his as well, but he has been stopped. There is no longer any need for this. The universe weeps for you to end this now," said Primsec begging with Thutmos.

"He must be punished," said Thutmos shaking his head *no* and casting a hateful grimace toward Carnok.

"You really have not seen," said Primsec shocked, his mouth hanging open as he watched Thutmos's face still stuck in a grimace. He felt the anger radiating from within him and it was greater than Carnok's had ever been in all the millennia that they had kept the balance.

"Or he has not wanted to," said Carnok turning and looking at Primsec with a devious smile.

"Can you not see that he wants you to do this, he's understood the new chain," said Primsec walking forward and standing at Thutmos's side, his lips nearly touching his ear. "Will you not listen to your heart, look for the guidance of Our Father?" he begged. His tears were running hot now, falling from his eyes in every color, his face changing colors rapidly, his entire body shimmering in all the colors of the cosmos.

"No," said Thutmos emphatically, the air coming from his mouth slow and hard.

The Earth went dark, the sun no longer shining on where they stood as Thutmos's power rose up inside him. The Earth shook violently as Merridia had, but the things there did not die. No mountains erupted, no waves rose, the sky did not fall, and the people did not die. Time ceased, nothing moved at all any longer on the Earth. The insects below them were frozen, unable to go about their daily lives pillaging whatever they could find. The rodents didn't dig through the ground looking for warmth or to hide from their predators. Men and women stood still, arms locked in the motion of their swinging as they were walking upon the Earth, spears held in their hands, focused on their targets, but unable to be loosed.

"Then I shall leave you to it all," said Primsec smiling as he backed away from Thutmos. Reaching into his face, he pulled the golden ring from his head and released it, his body exploded in dazzling color and dissipated out of existence.

"Do it," said Carnok stepping forward toward Thutmos, "now that you have no one in your ear, give me my punishment my lord."

Thutmos obliged Carnok, a wave of blue energy sweeping from his palm enveloping Carnok, creating a crater around them as the energy swept up in a ball, radiating tremendously. Nothing but Carnok was affected and his red body began to break apart, dissipating into air. The blackness from his lips spread over his face as he turned to dust scattering out of existence.

Carnok's ring bobbed there as the speckles of his physical shell continued to leave the Earth. Carnok's golden ring joined the others and they all drifted over Thutmos's head, their voices humming, as they circled above him. Reaching his hands up, the golden rings zipped into Thutmos's head, filling him with their power.

"I shall make the world anew, in my image," said Thutmos his eyes narrowing as he smiled deviously.

Punishment

Time folded back upon the Earth and the darkness faded, the great yellow sun, shedding its light upon the Earth, warming it and the inhabitants upon her soil. Thutmos felt the energy of Aeon again permeating life there and he smiled. Earth was as it had been made by Aeon, untouched and untarnished by the fires of Carnok's ambition and Thutmos was pleased.

He walked upon the waters of a calm sea and kneeled down placing his hand inside. A school of fish swam around his hand. Many of them jumped from the water and back in, over and over. They were happy, carefree creatures, enjoying the pleasures and comfort of life. Thutmos could feel that they lived life according to what they were, and how they were made. Impulse drove them as they had not great minds to change the nature of anything.

"I have protected you all from the discord of my brother," said Thutmos to the school of fish and they quickly swam away at the rumbling of his awesome voice. He smiled at their misplaced fear for he would not harm them.

Looking to his left he saw a group of people playing in the water, small children with their parents. They ran and jumped, wrestling with one another in the cool water. Thutmos smiled, pleased at their happiness.

He started toward them and then they all stopped suddenly, frozen in time again. This time no darkness flooded the Earth and the sun still shined brightly from its orbit.

"Ugh," said Thutmos as he felt the one power greater than his own awaken again to the physical world. The weight pressed down upon him and he fell to his knee involuntarily. "Lord," he said feeling Aeon's presence blazing toward him, hot and full of wrath.

The sun's brilliance was magnificent, casting a near blinding light on any man upon the Earth who'd dare look upon it. But the light in front of him was far more radiant, standing above him in wondrous magnificence. Those perfect eyes pressed down upon Thutmos and he felt them burning hot on his flesh. He looked up and those eyes flashed, causing his own eyes pain, forcing him to put his head back down.

"Do not speak child," said Aeon's voice, thundering like a trillion raging storms and the fires of a billion suns. His voice cast pain upon Thutmos, something that he'd never felt before. Thutmos's hands hit the ground hard as the pain pushed him down further, his forehead nearly touching the ground. "You have done well in protecting this abode from your brother's treachery and the punishment you cast upon him in destroying his corporal form. That much I can smile about," said Aeon with a smile that Thutmos could feel, though the might of Aeon still pressed down upon him. "But you have closed your mind to your true duties-," began Aeon.

"My Lord I-," said Thutmos trying to cut in.

"Silence," said Aeon.

Thutmos gasped as the word became reality, cutting off his ability to speak. He felt a knot form in his throat, choking him, filling him with fear.

"You have not watched the universe properly, refusing to understand things when you should have. What purpose did you have for questioning your place as the Chieftain of The Ripples of Time and Space? Even in dismissing Carnok's fears of Earth's purpose and my supposed betrayal of Our Union, you questioned my motives when it was not your place to question, only to do. You knew Carnok well, and you knew him to serve his purpose, almost too well. The balance must be maintained and the way of nature is cyclical. It was for him to seek power and to never obtain it. True," said Aeon perceiving the thoughts of Thutmos's mind before he finished developing them; "he did destroy the corporal bodies of the others, but you knew well that their essence lied in the Angel's Halo Force; the golden rings that you now possess as your own. And with them you would make the world anew," said Aeon, his disappointment touching Thutmos's mind.

The choking feeling left Thutmos's throat and he twisted his neck to one side, feeling the remnants of the effects. The sensations he felt were usually reserved for mortals. They were born to break, to age, wither and die. Their lives were short, every moment precious and valuable, for it could never be had again. Unlike him, they had not the luxury of years too long to count.

"I would become one with my brethren again, take me from this corporal realm," said Thutmos pleading with Aeon.

"My dear Thutmos, you are The Most Favored of all my children. The very one I shared more secrets with any other. Who unto, I gave the power of authority over his brethren. By the sheer power of your voice you could have commanded them," said Aeon, his voice rising in power and then quickly falling back down to its normal tone. Thutmos ached for the moment that Aeon's voice surged, feeling pain again. "It was good that you did not exercise this power and cast your will upon them at every turn. You were all truly one in Our Union. However, you did not do it enough. You could have brought Carnok to heel long ago. You have always contemplated what it would have been like to rule. The honey in Carnok's words was sweet. Yet, once past that sweetness the bitter taste of poison ruptured your mind and his wants were the same as yours; long suppressed by your feelings of duty. He was the instrument through which you would obtain the ultimate power of The Twelve," said Aeon as he turned his back to Thutmos who reached up to touch Aeon. "You allowed his treachery to go unchecked for too long once Asteron fell. "Yes," said Aeon again perceiving Thutmos's thoughts before they fully formed, "he had grown stronger, but the power of your voice could have splintered the shield he and those who followed his will had formed against you."

"Forgive me my Lord," said Thutmos waling.

"I already have, but you shall have your punishment my child," said Aeon turning back around swiftly.

"I shall do my duty," said Thutmos, placing his hand upon the warm ground again, turning his eyes to the ground.

"There will take another great sacrifice to undue the injury that has been caused by this great feud. While you have kept the Earth unscathed, much of the universe is in near disrepair. There are others who have fallen that even I shall not bring back from the void, for it will go opposite to the nature of things set forth by the Spring of Creation," said Aeon, as the brilliant golden light that was his projection shot toward Thutmos. "See what you have ignored."

Thutmos saw it, having ignored it while he warred with Carnok. He felt the sufferings of the lower beings, the death of many great stars, and planets. Entire galaxies were fallen, others fractured, and entire dimensions were displaced. Thutmos's weeping grew in intensity when he saw the world that he loved most above all suffering. Many had fallen dead on Merridia due to the war of Our

Union. He knew now the error of his judgment and knew that even making the world anew would have caused many to suffer still.

"For your punishment, you shall be resigned to the planet you so love. There you shall serve the child that you have loved above all others, for your enchantments were able to keep him safe in the wake of Carnok's treachery. For the many that have fallen to their deaths through the destruction caused by this war; you shall be the keeper of Merridia's dead. You shall feel their pain and sorrow. You shall hear their weeping and moaning, and the grinding of their teeth. Feel the lust of their hatred and the wonders of their hearts unfulfilled. All of their sufferings shall be yours for a period of time equal to the injury that remains after I have repaired the damage done," said Aeon raising his right hand.

One by one the eleven golden rings flew from Thutmos's head and he felt his power dramatically decrease. He heard the murmurings of his brethren and closed his eyes, afraid to bring his eyes to meet their halos.

"The Angel's Halo Force shall replace the assembly of Our Union to keep the Chain of Balance, for you destroyed the second chain when you destroyed Carnok. It is the thing Primsec tried to make you understand, but your thirst would not be quenched by reason. In time a new assembly shall rise to replace the watchers of old. But your power shall not be a part of this force. Not while you still have form. It cannot be of this physical plain, for the control which could be exercised through its power could be far more injurious than the calamity that has touched this universe already," said Aeon binding the golden rings together as one.

An intense song reverberated across the Earth and then Aeon tossed the single ring of the Angel's Halo Force into the air. The ring shot up into the wide expanse of space and exploded out, touching and covering all the parts of the universe. That which Aeon decided he would save was repaired to the degree with which he'd allow.

Placing his hand forward toward Thutmos, he uttered the words *Charm of the Sacred,* and a red ring came out of Thutmos's head and fell into Aeon's waiting hand. Aeon uttered the words *Spring of Creation* and a brilliant blue ring of fire burning like The Blue Ember, swept from Thutmos's head into Aeon's other hand. And then he uttered the word *Authority* and a black ring radiating the same golden energy of the other halo's floated from Thutmos's head.

When the last ring left Thutmos's head he felt the power he'd long had diminish almost entirely. He stood up, nine feet tall, having diminished in size and knew his powers were now like those of the gods of Merridia. Potent in their own right, but the whole of the universe would no longer move to the sound of his voice or the thoughts in his mind.

"In time I shall come to commune with you, but until that time you shall be feel much trepidation as the God of Death of the Merridian underworld," said Aeon. There was a flash of light and then he was gone.

Thutmos found himself immediately standing at the center of the Merridian underworld. Millions upon millions of the dead surrounded him. He heard their cries, their stories, the lies that they still told. He felt their anguish as his own at every moment, and tears fell from his eyes, creating a sea of hell fire and brimstone.

Behind him a throne rose up, black, and ragged, no beauty in it and Thutmos sat down, his mouth wrinkling into a sorrowful scowl. He placed his elbow on the arm rest and leaned his face into his hand as he heard the dead ones around him begging. They were pleading with him to give them comfort and to ease their hunger. They wanted him to keep their families safe, to take revenge on their enemies, and grant them a second chance at life. None of it could be done. He knew it, yet still wished that he could. But he could only take in their pain and their suffering as his own. And when it seemed like he had taken it all and they had a measure of peace, it would come again with more fervor. That would be his reality, his unyielding punishment.

Rule well the dead and you may again find yourself in favor of your Lord. He heard Aeon's voice in his mind, for as long as the words were said, and then it was gone. That was the last comfort he would be afforded until he'd paid his debt for the injuries caused.

Ten Thousand Years Later

The ship was far larger than The Runner that had taken her to Chalendor on her quest for revenge many years ago. Men walked around her listening to orders as she sat there brooding, her cheek resting on her balled fist. Her dark blue eyes panned the bridge of the ship, hoping that someone wasn't doing their duty so she could punish them to relieve some of her frustration. None of them were foolish enough and she smiled displeased, rolling her eyes.

"Too boring for you is it, Scicremeon" said Van Taven, with a smile standing off to her left, looking at a scroll.

"You've made them steady in their duties. They no longer make the mistakes of the past," said Scicremeon with a smile.

"None of them would survive your wrath," said Van Taven laughing.

"Neither would you," said Scicremeon turning her head to look at Van Taven.

"True, but at the very least there'd be a little resistance," said Van Taven smiling and bouncing his eyebrows up and down.

"You're a tad better than your former years," said Scicremeon standing and stretching as if her muscles ached.

Both Van Taven and Scicremeon's face wrinkled into puzzled expressions as they looked at one another and then turned around.

When they turned they saw a tall man with brown hair, and big brown eyes with a golden ring around them, standing with his arms clasped behind his back. He wore a long black coat, rising just above his ankles, a golden three-headed dragon stitched from the collar that rose up to his chin, down to the bottom of the coat. Looking around, he curled his lips down, nodding his head slowly up and down and then smiled wide.

Van Taven began to rush over and Scicremeon rolled her eyes and jutted out her tongue like a girl annoyed at boy who had gotten too much praise.

"Syaxis, it has been too long," said Van Taven giving him a big hug.

"How I hate that name," said Scicremeon as Syaxis walked over and hugged her, looking at her up and down.

"Scicremeon," said Syaxis as they drew back staring at one another.

She couldn't keep the scowl on her face that she'd tried to hold. She loved him still, and even more now. "Aton," said Scicremeon, a bit giddy as her hard façade melted way.

"I'm surprised Corvus has not punished you yet," said Syaxis as they turned and faced the window of the ship, watching the men around the bridge working.

"He knows there's nothing I won't do to find him," said Scicremeon.

"Do you still believe he is out there," said Syaxis somewhat depressed, "it has been a long while."

"I cannot give up hope," said Scicremeon turning her head away as she breathed in deeply.

"Imagine that," said Van Taven smiling. "She now cares for two people and tolerates me enough to only threaten me every two centuries or so," said Van Taven.

"There was a time when I was only tolerated," said Syaxis to Van Taven.

"I guess there is hope for me too," said Van Taven.

"Why have you come, Corvus would not have allowed you out of his sight for long?" said Scicremeon to Syaxis.

"He wants you to find Kelvin. He's up to something, stirring the pot again. The boy still can't fly, so he's taken a ship of his own," said Syaxis.

"That's punishment enough," said Scicremeon rolling her eyes.

"Have fun," said Syaxis with a big smile, full of the sarcasm she could read in his mind.

"Mam, something just went by," said one of the men, sitting near the window of the ship, tapping on a console.

"By Corvus," said Van Taven as the man turned, raising his hand, his face young.

"We have something on radar, it's gone past us quite fast," he said as Scicremeon stalked over to him, her face unbearably wrinkled, her teeth grinding against one another.

"Here it comes," said Syaxis leaning forward slapping his leg laughing.

"Chart a course for that dot," said Van Taven, as he started to chuckle hard as he marched toward his own seat next to Scicremeon's.

She stood over the man, breathing hard in and out, and the focused expression on his face turned to fear as he saw the blue of Scicremeon's uniform, and every eye on the bridge of the ship was on him. His eyes went wide as he turned to see Scicremeon leaning directly in his face, her teeth audible as if ready to snap and eat him.

His lips began to shake as she opened her mouth, still frowning. He leaned back, his chair touching the console as she asked him.

"Do I look like your grandmother?"

Meet The Authors

De'Quan Foster was born on the 16th day of August in 1994. He began writing the Danger Kids series when he was eleven, on May 19, 2006. As a child, Foster was bullied and made fun of for his appearance and some of the interests he had. Some of those interests included the *Star Wars* films, *Marvel* and *DC* comics—their movie adaptations, and the *Harry Potter* book series. He drew inspiration from these interests and soon began developing the Danger Kids. *The Twelve is* his first published work.

A.S. Washington was born on the 19th day of September in 1983. He graduated from Temple University with a degree in Economics, and lives in New Jersey where he works with at-risk teenagers. As a boy he fell in love with books and began writing his own stories. In December of 2011, his debut novel, *The Virgin Surgeon* was published. In the summer of 2012, his first collection of poetry, *The Musings of My Epic Mind* was published. *The Twelve* is his third published work.

For more on these authors and the Danger Kids Universe go to:

TWITTER.COM/MRDEFOSTER

MRDEFOSTER.WORDPRESS.COM

TWITTER.COM/ASWASHINGTON

FICTIONANDFOLLY.COM

www.ingramcontent.com/pod-product-compliance
Lightning Source LLC
Chambersburg PA
CBHW050545260626
47157CB00002B/452